Frank M. Robinson

Co-author with Thomas Scortia of such bestselling thrillers as *The Glass Inferno, The Prometheus Crisis* and *The Gold Crew*, Frank M. Robinson is also an accomplished master of short fiction. A LIFE IN THE DAY OF ... AND OTHER SHORT STORIES is Robinson's own selection of landmark tales from a career that spans nearly three decades from the height of the cold war to the aftermath of the summer of love.

Linking them are Robinson's reminiscences of his love affair with writing, editing, and especially with science fiction, that infinite playground of the imagination in which he learned his craft. Included are not only the eerie and moving title story and the hard-edged novelette "The Hunting Season," but seven other journeys into the unknown by one of the field's most skilled storytellers.

A Life In The Day Of...
And Other Short Stories

A LIFE IN THE DAY OF... AND OTHER SHORT STORIES

Frank M. Robinson

BANTAM BOOKS
TORONTO · NEW YORK · LONDON · SYDNEY

A LIFE IN THE DAY OF . . .
AND OTHER SHORT STORIES
A Bantam Book / November 1981

Illustrations by David Perry.

"The Maze," copyright © 1950 by Street & Smith Publications, Inc. Originally appeared in *Astounding Science-Fiction*, June, 1950.

"The Reluctant Heroes," copyright © 1951 by World Editions, Inc. Originally appeared in *Galaxy Science Fiction*, January, 1951.

"The Fire and the Sword," copyright © 1951 by World Editions, Inc. Originally appeared in *Galaxy Science Fiction*, August, 1951.

"The Hunting Season," copyright © 1951 by Street & Smith Publications, Inc. Originally appeared in *Astounding Science-Fiction*, November, 1951.

"The Santa Claus Planet," copyright © 1951 by Everett F. Bleiler & T. E. Dikty. Originally appeared in *The Best Science Fiction Stories, 1951.*

"The Wreck of the Ship John B.," copyright © 1967 by the HMH Publishing Co. Originally appeared in *Playboy* Magazine, June, 1967.

"East Wind, West Wind," copyright © 1972 by Harry Harrison. Originally appeared in *Nova 2.*

"A Life in the Day Of," copyright © 1969 by the HMH Publishing Co. Originally appeared in *Playboy* Magazine, June, 1969.

"Downhill All the Way," copyright © 1974 by Touch, Ltd. Originally appeared in *In Touch*, June, 1974.

ISBN 0-553-13455-8

Published simultaneously in the United States and Canada

Bantam Books are published by Bantam Books, Inc. Its trademark, consisting of the words "Bantam Books" and the portrayal of a rooster, is Registered in U.S. Patent and Trademark Office and in other countries. Marca Registrada. Bantam Books, Inc., 666 Fifth Avenue, New York, New York 10103.

PRINTED IN THE UNITED STATES OF AMERICA

0 9 8 7 6 5 4 3 2 1

For my brother, Mark

Contents

As I write this, Voyager II is sending back photographs of Jupiter and one of its major satellites, Io. The photographs are stunning, though I can't help thinking—and feeling guilty when I do—that Jupiter looks a little like a gigantic spinning top and Io resembles an overripe tangerine. I watch the black and white photographs assemble line-by-line on the television screen and I'm awed by the relatively few years that have passed since I first started reading about spaceships and other planets, and the reality of the fly-by itself. I'm also somewhat saddened that we seem to have added more lifeless worlds to the collection already whirling through the Solar System. With each passing year, John Carter of Mars, the intrepid meteor miners of the asteroid belt, and those Heinlein types farming the Jovian moons become more and more the stuff of dreams and less and less the meat of prophecy.

Somewhere between a crater and a suspected Ionian cliff a mile high and a hundred miles wide, we cut to interviews with the Project scientists. I've listened to such interviews before and I smile to myself, knowing the lead question before it's ever asked. How did they get into this business in the first place?

There is no hesitation. "I guess it all began when I started reading science fiction as a kid . . ."

I suspect that if you grilled the scientists who work for NASA, you'd find that almost all of them read science fiction when they were young and probably went into the sciences as a result. In one sense, the publication of the first issue of *Amazing Stories* in 1926 led inevitably to the Jupiter probes of 1979.

Hugo Gernsback, F. Orlin Tremaine, and John W. Campbell, Jr.—those editors most important in the history of science fiction magazines—have a lot to answer for.

Not all of the readers became scientists, of course. Some of us became writers instead.

For myself, it began in 1939 when my brother Mark sent me to the second-hand magazine store to pick up some light reading for him. He had entrusted me with a quarter and further proved his faith by saying I could use my own judgment on what I brought home.

Mark was 16 years old and devoted to sports story magazines. I was thirteen and cared for sport stories not at all. Even before arriving at the store—"Bob Thorne's Back Number Magazines" and don't ask me why I remember the name after all these years—I had decided to by some copies of *Argosy* or *Blue Book*. Both magazines occasionally ran stories by Edgar Rice Burroughs and Mark and I were still in the Tarzan phase.

A quick glance verified that Mark had read all the jockstrap publications on hand and I drifted over to the stacks of *Argosy* and *Blue Book*. For whatever reason, there were none that looked interesting. I was painfully aware that the quarter that burned in my pocket wasn't my own and furthermore, since the sports story pulps were all half price, I was expected to return home with some four or five magazines. Nevertheless, the two-for-a-quarter bin beckoned irresistibly.

That afternoon, I went home clutching two copies of *Astounding Science-Fiction*. (The cover price of *Astounding* was 20¢ but genial Bob charged a premium for science fiction). My brother was furious but I was hooked. Between them, those two issues contained the first and third installments of Clifford Simak's "Cosmic Engineers," Jack Williamson's "Crucible of Power," L. Sprague de Camp's "Living Fossil" and the first installment of Williamson's "One Against the Legion." John W. Campbell, Jr., had not only nailed me down as a faithful reader but later that year, he also nailed down Isaac Asimov, A. E. van Vogt, Bob Heinlein, and Ted Sturgeon as contributors and started using Hubert Rogers regularly on his covers.

I'm boring you with this much detail only to prove that dyed-in-the-wool science fiction fans never forget their first issues and that 1939 was an exceptional year for a thirteen-year-old to be introduced to science fiction. It's only partly true that the Golden Age of science fiction is when *you* start to read it. By any standards, 1939 was unusual . . .

The Campbell *Astounding* was the first science fiction magazine I started buying regularly but the others soon followed. I read them in the morning, I read them in the afternoon, and I ruined my eyes reading them after dark and

under the covers. What's more, I never threw them away—
I collected them like other boys collected postage stamps.
I was the archetypical science fiction reader later described by Joanna Russ as ". . . nervous, shy, pleasant boys,
sensitive, intelligent and very awkward with people. They
also talk too much."

My mother would have considered Joanna Russ very
perceptive.

Long-time science fiction fans know the rest of the
evolution by heart. I soon discovered the letter columns and
wrote regularly. *Comet Stories* deciphered one—my handwriting was no better then than it is now—and printed it. And
sometime during that period, Ray Palmer, the editor of
Amazing Stories, paid me five dollars for a cartoon idea. I
think Ray either felt sorry for me or identified with the
skinny kid who had dropped up to the offices to see him
(*Amazing* was published in Chicago then). No matter. It
was a sale. The very first.

There were no science fiction fans in Forest Park, where
my family lived, but Chicago was close by and in 1941 I
became a member of a local science fiction club. I'll be
damned if I remember what we did aside from discussing
the current magazines. One member, Ronald Clyne, an exceptional young artist, was later to do book jackets for
Arkham House. Another, Charles McNutt, became a popular
contributor to *Playboy* and TV's "Twilight Zone" as Charles
Beaumont. (Chuck read *Amazing* but I was an *Astounding*
fan and by virtue thereof, something of an intellectual snob).
Still another, Walt Liescher, who worked in a beanery
beneath the Howard Street "el," introduced me to the rest
of fandom.

Life was never to be the same. My family had moved
around quite a bit in the Chicago area and I had never
really put down roots or made friends. On the other hand,
either through the mail or in person, fellow science fiction
fans became immediate buddies. Unlike my neighborhood
peer group, they didn't think me strange for reading about
rocket ships or six-armed, green-skinned Tharks on Mars.
I started attending small, local conventions in Bloomington
and Joliet. Like every other fan I met, I took it for granted
that when you visited somebody, they put you up—even if
you had never seen each other before. Mothers took to it
rather well but then, most science fiction fans were young,
white and middle-class. There were few surprises among the

kids who came calling; the number of black, Oriental, or Latin science fiction fans was amazingly small. (Regretfully, it still is.)

In the early forties, I started hanging out at "Slan Shack," a communal living arrangement of six—the number varied—in Jackson, Michigan. Slan Shack regularly threw mini-conventions and at one of them, I met my first author—Dr. Edward Elmer Smith, Ph.D. Doc was a cereal chemist, specifically for a firm that made doughnut mixes. As the creator of the popular "Lensman" series, he was one of my literary heroes. Doc had been writing science fiction since the twenties and was popularly accorded the role of Grand Old Man. He played it well and I can't remember a convention where he wasn't surrounded by a group of youngsters much like myself. Eventually I graduated from Doc's universe of Arisians and Eddorians and the offspring of Kimball Kinnison and grew to admire Doc for his other attributes, his kindness and his humanity.

Early on, I was bitten by the publishing bug and one Christmas season made $50 delivering Christmas baskets for "Stop and Shop," an upper-class downtown grocery store. I invested it in an Underwood Model No. 5 and taught myself to touch-type. Publishing an amateur magazine was, obviously, next. Bob Tucker, the first fan I knew to become a professional writer (oddly, he broke into print with detective novels and only later turned to science fiction), had started a postcard-sized fanzine devoted to news about the professional magazines, the comings and goings of fans, conventions, etc. He passed it on to me. I built a homemade mimeograph and, along with fellow fan Ed Connor, ran the card for almost a year on a weekly basis. Toward the end, we multigraphed it, added photographs—for a buck you could buy a sheet of 100 stamp-sized prints of any photo you sent in—and called the result "Fanewscard Weekly—Illustrated."

I didn't realize it then but a pattern was being set that I would follow all my professional life. Being a editor was a lot of fun—but I also liked being a creative writer. Unlike Fred Pohl, I never succeeded in being both at once.

After graduation from high school, I landed my first professional job in publishing. A friend of the family was a sports reporter for the old *Chicago Herald and Examiner* and offered to use his influence in getting me a job as copy boy. He didn't have to use much. We were two years into

World War II and warm bodies were welcome almost any place. The *Examiner* didn't hire me but another Hearst affiliate, the local bureau of International News Service, did.

It was exciting work. I was a member of an elite: I knew what was happening in the world a good three hours before anybody else did. In addition to being general go-for, I picked up the livestock reports every morning at the stock-yards, kept the teletypes supplied with paper, and listened to the head copy boy philosophize on how, for a nickel, the daily paper was society's biggest bargain (it was and still is, even at twenty cents). I was also present when orders came through from Hearst headquarters at San Simeon not to mention certain elements, among them uranium, in news stories.

I didn't think anything of it.

In the spring of 1944, I left INS for what was, to me, an even more glamorous job: Office boy for Ziff-Davis, pub-lishers of *Amazing Stories* and *Fantastic Adventures*, as well as *Flying*, *Radio News*, and *Popular Photography*. It also paid better. Trucking mail around to the different editorial of-fices at Ziff-Davis was less exciting than spiking stories hot off the wire at INS but it had its compensations. Most im-portant was the chance to meet flesh-and-blood writers, as well as to hang out with editor Ray Palmer and managing editor Howard Browne. I was also in charge of the stock-room where they kept the back issues; within a week I had filled out my own files at home. Magazine collectors are greedy and without principle and I was no exception.

(One of my duties, incidentally, was to *count* the monthly returns on the various magazines. It was the middle of World War II and publishers sold as many copies as they could print—the returns on *Amazing* and *Fantastic* were less than one percent. Realizing this, the production manager showed true genius. Instead of reducing the size of the magazines to keep them monthly, he cut back to a quarterly basis and actually upped the number of copies printed. Editorial overhead was slashed, as were per-copy production costs, and *Amazing* sold 185,000 copies an issue, more than any science fiction magazine before or since.)

Working at Ziff-Davis was a primer on how to put a magazine together, something I was to find valuable later on. There was an art department where I could watch covers being painted and a production department where I could see the huge flats of cover proofs from the printers. And since Palmer and Browne, between them, edited only one magazine a month (*Amazing* and *Fantastic*, plus *Mammoth Detective*, which was Browne's particular baby), lunchtime and most afternoons were one long pinochle game. They even had time to BS their eager, if naive, office boy.

Meeting Ray Palmer for the first time had been something of a shock. He was severely hunch-backed, the result of a childhood accident. Even though my step-father had suffered a similar accident early in life, I wasn't sure how to react to him. Palmer was matter-of-fact about it and it certainly appeared to be no handicap in either his personal or professional life. He had married a beautiful woman, fathered a family, and settled down in a more-than-comfortable house in Evanston, a northside suburb. He did tell stories of supporting himself during the early days of the Depression by copper-sheathing steep church roofs—something nobody else would do because of the danger. That may have been apocryphal but less so was his claim that Ziff-Davis had hired him on a commission basis tied to the sales of *Amazing*. Reportedly, they put him on a straight salary when he started to earn more than B. G. Davis within a year of hiring.

If there was any bitterness in Palmer, it was directed at science fiction fandom. He himself had been a fan in the early '30s, plugged the various conventions in his magazines, and contributed enormous quantities of artwork to convention auctions. But the fans loved *Astounding* and were more or less contemptuous of *Amazing*, regarding the majority of its stories as hack and juvenile. (They were about to become even more contemptuous: Palmer had discovered a writer who "remembered" Lemuria and was going to print his reminiscences.)

Howard Browne, unlike Palmer, had no previous connection with science fiction. As a matter of fact, Browne didn't care for it. He was a detective story fan, his heroes being Hammett and especially Raymond Chandler. In addition to editing *Mammoth Detective*—a huge publication of 320 pages in its early issues—and *Mammoth Mystery*, he wrote 'tecs under the name of "John Evans," creating his own character of Paul Pine in the image of Phillip Marlowe. One of Howard's proudest moments was his discovery of Roy Huggins, who later made a name for himself in television, producing "77 Sunset Strip" and "Maverick" among other shows.

A large, bluff, balding man, Browne had an infectious love for the hardboiled detective story that I soon shared. Browne also taught me that a writer actually researches things, he doesn't just make them up. (Ray's advice had been somewhat less scholarly: "When the action slows down, drop another body through the skylight.") I had wandered into his office one lunch period and he showed me a book of morgue photos. I thumbed through it, lost my lunch, but learned that people didn't die by clutching their side and crumpling slowly to the floor, saying "You got me, man." An enlightening bit of knowledge for a seventeen-year-old . . .

The Mutt and Jeff of the editorial world, Palmer's and Browne's views of the world at large reflected their personalities: Palmer tended to react with a cynical if detached amusement, Browne with a delighted disbelief and frank amazement, blinking wide-eyed behind his thick glasses. I vastly admired them both.

The Ziff-Davis stable of writers at the time included David Wright O'Brien (killed in the war), Don Wilcox, Leroy William P. McGivern (at this writing, McGivern has just published his twenty-second novel, a Book-of-the-Month Club selection), and Bob Bloch, specialist in both humor ("Lefty Feep") and stomach-turning horror (he later wrote "Psycho"). Most I met briefly at the offices; the others I met at the weekend poker parties at Palmer's house where I was fleeced with great regularity. Mingling with the great and near-great carries a price . . .

In December of 1944, I was drafted. I had tried to enlist before, at seventeen, and been rejected. At eighteen, my "compound myopic astigmatism" was reclassified as "simple myopia" and I went into the Navy. I did my boot at Great Lakes and three months of "pre-radio" at Chicago's Navy Pier. There wasn't much time for science fiction or fandom. Occasionally I'd go into the city to sell my cigarette rations to Bill Hamling and Chester Geier, two more members of the Ziff-Davis stable. Hamling, a handsome, enormously energetic man, had once published a professionally-printed fan magazine, Stardust. (He had, incidentally, enlisted early in the war but lost part of his hearing in an obstacle-course accident.) Like a number of fans, he had wanted desperately to break into writing. Palmer gave him that break and during most of the war years, he delivered 30,000 words a month to Ziff-Davis—science fiction, detective, and later, western.

Hamling's life-style struck me as idyllic (by this time, of course, I wanted to be a writer). He and Geier, who was completely deaf, maintained offices on the north side, complete with tiny anteroom and battered couch. Hamling was glad to see me, not only for the cigarettes but because I served as a captive audience. Enthused by his own prose, he would rip a page out of the typewriter, read it aloud, and wait for my reaction. I thought it egocentric; it never occurred to me that in a few years I'd be doing the same.

My service saga was dull. I finished training as an electronics technician and finally went to sea, only to discover that I suffered from chronic seasickness. Two years after I was drafted, I was out, my memories of the Navy confined pretty much to sitting on a lower bunk with a bucket between my knees.

"V-E" and "V-J" days had been memorable, of course. So had the day they dropped the Bomb on Hiroshima. (That Hiroshima was a tragedy didn't occur to me at the time—nor to many other people. It was War and the dropping of the Bomb had been rationalized as necessary to bring the war to an end. The casualty figures didn't translate into real human beings; they were just another "body count.") As far as my fellow swabbies were concerned, I was the immediate expert: The Bomb meant the end of War. Since nobody else had it, it was going to be Pax Americana. And, of course, it meant that there would now be unlimited power, power too cheap to meter. I may have been one step ahead of the power companies in promoting that one . . .

As my past experience at INS and Ziff-Davis had marked me, so did the experience in the Navy. I applied for the GI Bill and went to college (a small liberal arts college in Wisconsin, Beloit) to major in physics. It turned out to be a major mistake. When it came to physics, I didn't have rhythm nor much of anything else. The moment of truth came when I went up to a graduate colloquim at the University of Wisconsin. In the lecture room, the blackboards were arranged one behind the other and operated much like window shades. When the instructor finished writing on one of them, he yanked on a cord to send it to the ceiling and immediately started writing on the one behind it. By the third blackboard, I was hopelessly lost and for the first time questioned my ability to become another Oppenheimer. I had been planning on going to graduate school in Virginia and now had second thoughts. I would never, I realized, be more than a second banana in physics. I didn't have the mind for it.

My alternative ambition now crept back. I carried two minors in addition to my physics major: anthropology and English, specifically creative writing. (Creative writing courses, if they do nothing else, give you the opportunity and the incentive to write. But they don't give you much more. Almost all of them are set up the same way: You write a story and then it's read in front of the class, its authorship a secret. Your fellow students are asked for their opinion and, nursing their own bruised egos, they leap to the fray. Few of them are specific as to the story's faults and nobody knows what to do about them. Comments such as: "It doesn't quite make it," "I don't think the ending is right," or "It didn't convince me" aren't very helpful. Don't look to the instructor for help; he probably hasn't written fiction either. If you want to take a writing course, go to a night school where the instructor may be a practicing writer or an editor with wit enough to teach writing as a craft and not as an esoteric art.)

Lest I be accused of biting the hand that first blue-penciled me, I hasten to state that Chad Walsh, my English professor at Beloit, was both writer and editor and while his field wasn't fiction per se, he made up for it with enthusiasm and encouragement. The high point for me was one day when the assignment had been to write a horror story. Mine was read aloud to hushed silence. It took me a few minutes to realize that this time, though I didn't know exactly how I had done it, somehow I had done everything right. The hushed silence was actually applause.

I took my "graduate" course in fiction writing that summer. I had applied too late for my usual summer job in the Gary steel mills so I had a lot of time on my hands. Oliver Saari, a friend and science fiction fan who had sold some stories to John Campbell in the late thirties and early forties, offered to teach me all he knew. It was considerable. Saari was an engineer and had an analytical mind; he hadn't written a large number of stories but he knew the *whys* of fiction writing as well as anybody I ever met. (Saari came from Minneapolis and was a good friend of Gordon Dickson and Poul Anderson; he was of immense help to them, too.) I showed him my early stories. One, in particular, had promise. I rewrote it and asked for further suggestions. What he suggested was that I rewrite it once again; he also made some astute criticisms. I rewrote it again. And again.

The story was 8,000 words long and that summer I must have rewritten it eight times. But by the end of the summer, I was a professional writer.

I do not know exactly when I crossed the line but I do know that the line of demarcation between amateur and professional is a very sharp one. It is so sharp that I am convinced it can occur in the middle of a paragraph. All of the things that you have been trying to do, the balance between action and exposition, between dialogue and description, the sense of pacing, the ability to portray character so the reader can at least tell one from another, suddenly come together in just the right mix.

You may not sell the next story you write but from then on, you will be a *professional* writer.

The first story I ever sold was written in 1949 and published in 1950. Harry Truman was President, the minimum wage had been jumped from 40 to 75 cents an hour, and Alger Hiss was on trial for allegedly passing secrets to the Soviets. People were reading Nelson Algren's "The Man with the Golden Arm" and John O'Hara's "A Rage to Live"— as well as "The Waters of Siloe" by Merton, "Peace of Soul" by Bishop Sheen, "The Greatest Story Ever Told" by Oursler, and "A Guide to Confident Living" by Norman Vincent Peale. Religion was very big then. (The major names in science fiction were Robert Heinlein, Isaac Asimov, Ted Sturgeon, and Ray Bradbury so things weren't as different as you might think.)

The "Wac Corporal" hit an altitude record of 250 miles, leading me to believe that space travel might really be possible in another 50 years, and the XB-47 jet bomber had crossed the continent in 3 hours and 46 minutes for an average speed of 607.2 mph. Technologically speaking, it was an interesting time to be alive.

I was then in my junior year at Beloit and anxious to try my hand at another story. (Saari had visited the college, bringing along Poul Anderson. Poul was not only encouraging, he gave me one of the simplest and most practical tips an experienced author could give a beginner: write in "scenes" of approximately a thousand words each—it's invaluable when it comes to plotting and "pacing" your story.) In anthropology, I had become fascinated with intelligence and intelligence tests and the story sprang from that. What would constitute a good intelligence test for a human being, if given by an alien? What sort of maze would they have *us* run? Sheer survival is, of course, a test of one kind of intelligence and for purposes of story, it seemed the most dramatic one.

In May of '49, I sent "The Maze" off to John Campbell at *Astounding*. He liked it but was overstocked; did I have any shorter lengths? I agonized over the rejection, then took a gamble and cut the story from 9,000 words to 7,000 and tried again. Campbell replied that he wanted to buy it but was suddenly overstocked on shorter lengths as well. He would hold it for purchase later or return it if I wanted to submit it elsewhere (fat chance).

He bought it in August and I got a check for $140. (It's not exactly small change now—it was an enormous amount to me back then, when the average weekly pay was something like $60). As any writer will tell you, there is nothing that equals the euphoria of your first sale. I had sold the second time out—Campbell had rejected the story written under Ollie's tutelage—to the market that I respected most. What more could I ask?

That John actually publish it, that's what more I could ask. He held the story for almost a year and finally printed it in the June, 1950 issue, on the stands the middle of May— a week before I graduated.

I bought a dozen copies and distributed them to friends around the campus, just to prove I hadn't lied when I said I had actually sold a short story the year before.

The Maze

"Civil Service will be looking for you—in fifteen days," he said.

"We'll be lucky if we're still alive in fifteen days," I said grimly.

"That's what I like about you, Bob—always the optimist."

I shrugged. "You know how it will turn out in the end. The pity of it is we have to keep trying. To give up would classify us as being stupid. And we can't afford to look stupid, can we?"

He started cracking his knuckles until my nerves felt like they do when you scratch a blackboard with your fingernails.

"You've been through the maze three times now," he said.

"I know." It was hot in the cube but right then I felt cold as ice.

Camden and I sat on the ground, leaning back against the glassite walls of the cube. The light filtering through made us look like seasick sailors. I felt tired.

Suddenly there was a plucking at my mind, an insistent urge to remember—to remember back to the first day of my vacation. Another trip through the maze was due. I knew how it would start—but how would it end this time?

It would start out like days usually do on Venus—terrible.

I yawned and brushed the sweat off my forehead. Morning on Venus is always the same. Wake up with a thick head and a short temper and a damp feeling in the hollows of the bed where little puddles of sweat had collected. I yawned again, rolled over on the soggy sheet, and tried to catch a few more minutes of sleep.

The insistent buzzing of the visor wouldn't let me. I switched on "voice" and buried my head under the pillow.

"Robert Germaine? This is the Bureau of Assassination Information. Acknowledge, please."

My heart did a sudden thump and I was wide awake.

"This is Germaine," I said.

The caller continued. "Notification of Intent to Assassinate victim Robert Germaine. Marcus Kennedy III registered with the Bureau his intent to assassinate the above named person

12

beginning at noon on the 23rd day of May. Cause: the attentions of the secretary Janet Chandler." He faded from the screen and the set went dead.

It was perfectly legal—if I could kill Kennedy before he got me, they'd never convict me of murder. And vice versa for Kennedy. There was only one slight catch. I was practically fresh from Earth, with no more friends than I could count on the fingers of one hand. Kennedy was rich, influential, and powerful. He could afford a bodyguard. And if I did knock him off, one of his friends would register their intent with the Bureau. I couldn't win.

Abruptly, I tried to minimize Kennedy and the notice. I couldn't afford to let myself get scared—a mind paralyzed by fear would be nothing but a handicap in trying to outwit Kennedy.

Funny, I thought, wake up the first morning of my vacation and have an assassination notice staring me in the face. It was almost as if I hadn't awakened at all and the whole thing was just part of a nightmare I was having.

I took a cold shower, toweled myself, and put on my shorts. That was the only good thing about the planet—just put on your undies and you were dressed for the day. Guys like me who did publicity work for the Venus Colonial Office played up the informality of daily dress for all that it was worth, but it never did counterbalance the planet's many failings.

I looked at my watch. I had three hours before noon—and there *was* an obvious step I could take before then.

I went back to the visor and dialed a number. A portly looking businessman came on the screen.

"Acme Protection Service at *your* service, sir."

"What would be the charge for the assassination of Marcus Kennedy III?"

"One moment please." He came back with a thick ledger and began flipping through it. "One million dollars would be our charge for Kennedy. One half down, which would be nonreturnable, and the other half upon successful completion of the murder."

"What are the statistical chances of success?"

He clucked sympathetically. "Nine point three percent. His bodyguard is well trained."

"How about straight protection for me?"

"Protection for the legal thirty-day assassination period would be a thousand dollars a day. You understand that this includes food tasters and the immediate services of a reputable physician in case of trouble."

"Chances?"

"Considerably better. Our chances of successfully protecting you are forty-three percent."

I couldn't afford either one and told him so. He frowned. "We can offer you advisory service for a flat fee of fifty dollars, payable on your visor bill."

"I'll take it. What do you advise?"

He waited a moment until the visor had registered the contract.

"Disappear."

At more than fifteen bucks a syllable, advice was coming high nowadays.

I snapped the off-switch angrily and then thought better of it and dialed again. This time I switched the selector over to "color."

The girl on the screen smiled a warm greeting. "Oh, it's you, Bob. I—"

"Marcus Kennedy III has just declared open season on Germaines and I'm to be the prize trophy of the season," I interrupted. "The reason he gave was you." She didn't say what I expected her to so I said it myself.

"You could go back to him," I suggested. "After all, which would you like the most? To be married to a wealthy old man and live in luxury the rest of your life or have a little urn of my ashes on your mantelshelf?" The way I phrased it, it didn't even seem like a contest.

"Don't be silly, Bob, neither," she said, escaping the horns of the dilemma with a woman's logic.

"Fine," I said sarcastically. "What do you propose I do?"

"Disappear," she said calmly. "Hide out for thirty days. At the end of it, Kennedy can't touch you. In fact, he'd be obliged to protect you. If anything happened to you then, he'd be the first to be suspected. Once the legal thirty-day period is up, it'd be his neck if you were killed.

"To say nothing of mine. Thanks for the tip—though I'm not crazy about spending my vacation behind dark glasses and whiskers. Doesn't exactly sound heroic, either."

She made an annoyed sound. "Heroism and its emotional connotations went out in the twentieth century. Besides," she added, her eyes softening, "I'd much rather have you alive, Bob."

It was two minutes before I realized the set was off.

Jan's suggestion was a good one but where on Venus could I go? I didn't know many people—certainly nobody influential enough to intercede with Kennedy. The policy of VCO—like any other business on Venus—was strictly hands off. All Terra men are warned when they come to Venus to watch their step in local affairs.

I was still thinking about it and getting no place when the noon mail arrived. I heard it drop from the mail chute onto the kitchen table but I let it sit. I had more important things on my mind than the latest printer's proofs on pamphlets for the VCO. Besides, I was on vacation.

The "mail" exploded five minutes later.

I clawed my way out of the plaster and splintered furniture into a room filled with smoke—I could hear the crackle of flames in the kitchen. I wasn't bleeding much—mostly bruised and shaken up with a king-sized headache.

The crackling of the flames sounded louder and I opened the door leading to the hallway. A bleak expanse of fire steel stood just outside, effectively sealing off my apartment. Fire precaution, I remembered, to keep the fire from spreading. One of the strong points the apartment building offered when I rented there.

The smoke made me choke and I staggered to the fire escape on the outside. As soon as I opened the screen, the beam of a needle gun seared the plastic door frame beside my head.

I dropped to my knees and rolled against the wall. A portion of it gave to my touch and half a second later I was plummeting down the clothes chute. I landed in the basement of the building with a jar that knocked the wind out of me. Things to file and forget, I thought—a small pile of dirty shorts doesn't do much good in breaking a four-story slide.

Outside, a detachment of the Security patrol had arrived along with the usual crowd of curious onlookers, the eager spectators who would patiently wait for the Security boys to bring out my charred body. I came out of a side entrance and slowly worked my way through the mob, hoping nobody was noticing me.

It wouldn't take Kennedy long to figure out that I had escaped. I had, at the most, an hour's start before he organized a search that would probably prove to be fatally successful.

I don't know what brought Oliver Camden and his experimental farms to my mind—I suppose by logical elimination.

Try to think of the most remote, the least populated, the least likely place on Venus where a guy would want to go and you automatically think of Camden's Extraterrestrial Biological Research Farms.

It had its points. Venus is a difficult planet on which to get "lost." The towns are few and the only link between is the tubeways, or in most cases, the swamp buses that paddle over the marshy surface. It would be simple for Kennedy to station a man at the tubeways and the bus station to watch for my departure. Or else, alert men in other towns to await my arrival. I still had half an hour's lead, though. If I left now and got off at some spot between towns, I stood a good chance of ditching Kennedy's bloodhounds.

To try and remain in the city itself under an assumed name and a disguise was impossible. The endless questioning and red tape of the Venusian bureaucracy made the first impractical—and to try and disguise yourself when all you wear is a pair of shorts was equally out of the question.

I had to leave town and get off at some halfway point. The only halfway point I knew of was Camden's Farms.

I paid the fare at the bus station and idly watched the people getting on. An old lady was the first after myself. Then a sailor from the Venusian Navy and his girlfriend hopped aboard for a sight-seeing ride and a dark seat in the rear. A tourist from Terra got on next—you could tell he was from Terra by the fancy shorts and halter he wore. He waddled down the aisle, spotted me by one of the windows, and eased down next to me.

The swamp bus pulled out of the station, its huge wheels starting their monotonous sucking sound, and I turned on the seat visor to take my mind off the bleak scenery.

"Been on Venus long?"

"Two years."

"Practically a native, eh? Quite a country. Great for rheumatism and asthma. Where you going to now?"

"Two towns up," I lied.

Suddenly the seat visor lit up with what I knew was going to be a familiar face before the thirty days was over. It was the lard-white, slightly-bloated face of Marcus Kennedy III. I went to turn off the scope but my fat friend from Terra stopped me.

"Gotta hear this," he wheezed.

Kennedy started to speak. "Ladies and gentlemen, Kennedy Enterprises is starting a great new contest for our visor audiences. All you have to do is identify the person whose photograph we show to you on the screen and notify Kennedy Enterprises immediately. The photos may be of your town mayor or they may even be of the person sitting next to you as you watch this. To the first person who notifies us of the identity and whereabouts of the person in the photograph, we will award one thousand dollars in cash. Here is the first photo."

I had to admit it was a good likeness.

"Kennedy doesn't miss a trick, does he?" my fat friend said in a low voice, pressing a needle gun against my side. "That was just in case I didn't catch up with you. Now suppose you and I get off at the next stop and wait for Mr. Kennedy, eh?"

Fat boy must have trailed me from the fire—but since I was still alive, that meant he had orders to treat me kindly. I shoved against him so that the needle gun was clamped between his body and mine.

"If you pull the trigger now, your gun will backfire," I said quietly. "The gases can't escape from the muzzle." Fatty blinked hesitantly and I brought up my hand from the rear and caught him at the base of the neck. I let him slide a little, propped him up in the seat so it looked like he was sleeping, and fed him some stimo-capsules from the vending machine on board. When Kennedy caught up with Fatty, out cold and stinking of stimo, there'd be hell to pay.

I got off at the Farms—or what I thought was the Farms.

"You go down the road about a mile," the driver said. "Just be careful you stay on it. You'll have a tough time if you ever get off." The paddles started up again and a second later the bus had disappeared into the fog.

I started out sloshing through the mud, still thinking of my departure from the city. So far my plans had developed more flaws than a piece of cracked china—and one of the worst was the walk to the farms along the semisolid strip of mud laughingly called a road.

It was two hours later when I staggered up the wooden walk leading to the administration building for the Farms.

"Have a drink," Ollie offered. I took the glass, swallowed, and then had sense enough to start sipping it like it was nectar—it wasn't every day you get a good grade of Earth-import bourbon.

Ollie hadn't changed much in the two years since I had

seen him last. A little more on the tubby side, a little whiter—he had been neglecting his sunlamp—and a lot balder. But still the same old, sharp-minded Ollie.

"What have you been doing lately?" he asked, settling himself in a chair.

"Working for VCO—sold my soul as a publicity man. How about you?" I asked innocently.

"Still testing and getting no place."

"Testing? Testing what?"

Ollie sighed. "I thought everybody knew why I came to this fungus-ridden fever spot. Research on the Squanchies, Bob."

"But—"

He held up a hand. "Tell you more after supper. I'll be better fortified to answer any and all stupid questions then."

The meal wasn't bad—he had an indentured cook who seemed to be fairly happy with his lot and was quite skillful in hot-weather cookery. Usually, it takes time to wean most new cooks away from the starches-and-fried-foods routine.

After the ice cream and menthol mints, Ollie opened up with what it was all about.

"How intelligent are you, Bob?" he asked, filling up my glass with bourbon.

"Bright enough to recognize good liquor when I taste it." I caught the look on his face. "Oh. You mean seriously? I had a fairly high GCT on my Terra Transfer examination—about an IQ of 140. Nothing exceptional. Why?"

"How intelligent is your dog?"

"Why, I don't know," I floundered. "Fairly bright for a hairless, I guess."

"What if you wanted to find out for sure?"

"Uh . . . I suppose I'd have to conduct tests, something like that. Oh, I get it! You're—"

". . . Trying to figure out how intelligent the Squanchies are."

I pushed my empty glass forward for a refill. "Just between you and me, who cares—outside of the realm of knowledge for the sake of knowledge?"

Camden chuckled. "In a way, it's funny. Two powerful groups are pouring money into the project for two entirely different reasons. One group, here on Venus, is interested in a large supply of cheap labor. But any labor, to be useful beyond the extent of a beast of burden, has to have a certain minimum intelligence. There's another group on Terra who were instrumental in getting the Extraterrestrial Protection bill passed a decade ago. You remember the bill? It calls for the protection of all extraterrestrial forms of life that can be described as intelligent, according to qualifications set forth in the bill itself. That's the picture—one group wants to know how intelligent the Squanchies are so they can exploit them; the other wants to know so they can protect them. Comic, in a way."

"I suppose it's harder than it looks, eh?"

"Have some bourbon—it improves that mind of yours. You're right. It's tough. You can't go up to the beasties, draw a picture of the solar system, point to yourself and say 'one-two, one-two, me intelligent, how about you?' "

"O.K.," I laughed. "So you foiled the fancies of the fic-tioneers. What do you do—give 'em a Stanford-Binet?"

"Very funny. There are several preliminary things we have to go through. First, you have to establish a means of com-munication—which is, incidentally, very difficult to do. Since we and the Squanchies are about on a par with you and your dog as far as communication goes, only tests in which the beastie goes through some sort of activity are eligible.

"Then you have to figure out what you mean by intelli-gence. The dictionary says 'the ability to reason'—which leaves a lot to be desired. And once you figure out what you mean by 'intelligence' you have to figure out a way to 'grade' that intelligence. And don't forget that all intelligence is com-parative. Are we interested in how intelligent a Squanchy is compared to another Squanchy—or to a human being? And if you're going to compare them to Homo sap, there's a mil-lion more things that have to be taken into consideration.

"In the first place, you couldn't expect it to do things that it isn't physically capable of doing. A Squanchy could never brachiate like a great ape, no matter how vital it was that it do so. And we can't set up tests for them using the same standards as we do on Terra. There are measuring sticks we use on Terra that are darned reliable. Sex and the rule of self-preservation, for example. We can make the *assumption* that they apply to living things on Venus—but can we be sure? We're dealing with things that have no connection with Terra; they're not beings like us, neither are they of our envi-ronment."

"You must have learned something in two years," I said cautiously.

Camden shrugged. "More physical progress than anything

else. We've built up the station, got a staff together, built
warehouses, built the 'cube' for the Squanchies, found out
what they eat and information like that. They're peculiar in
their diet, by the way—fresh shrubs and muck-reeds doesn't
suit them, it has to be rotten. Half of our first group wouldn't
respond at all until we found that out."

"How are you going to figure out whether the Squanchies
you test are bright—for Squanchies . . . or are they idiot
members of the species?"

"Don't know for sure. Test what we think is a representative sample and hope for the best."

"I suppose there's a reward if you succeed and a bit of un-
pleasantness if you don't?"

"You're so right. The cheap labor group will run me off
Venus—or at least make it unhealthy for me. The humane
group would probably forget about being humane, accuse me
of being in league with the first bunch, and try to do me in if
I went back to Terra.

"One thing for certain—I'd never hold another job on either planet."

For a guy who loved his work like Camden did, the future
looked none too inviting.

I went on a tour of the Farms with Camden the next
morning. The first stop was the "cube"—a huge, glass-sided
affair looking like a gigantic, plastic building block. A cleared
space extended all around it and inside was a jumble of vegetation, muck, and water—it looked like the cube had been
open on one side and just inverted over a typical section of
Venus.

"It's closed at the bottom, too," Camden said, "so they
can't burrow out. Makes a pretty good cage for the beasts.
Easy to observe but it still keeps them, as nearly as possible,
in the same environment that they're used to."

We walked along it and I began to appreciate the immen-
sity of the cube; it was over two hundred yards on an edge.
We went to an observer's platform and looked in. I didn't see
much at first besides the towering trees, the unhealthy looking
vegetation, and the stretches of muck and mud that cradled
stagnant pools of water. Then I watched for movement and
spotted a Squanchy. It wasn't too pleasant to look at. It stood
about four and one half feet high—a slit-faced, toothless,
green-scaled travesty of a human being. Small gills that

opened in the neck dilated in synchronism with the thing's breathing.

"I've seen them before," I said, "only then I wasn't sober. It looks more vicious than bright, too savage to be intelligent. I should think they would be quite a menace."

"They were considered to be when humans first landed— any alien being would probably be considered a menace by the first landing parties. Since the first days of colonization, though, they've been hard to find. They avoid the cities and towns. Their hides were never worth much, which probably saved them from organized extermination. The dozen or so in the cube represent a lot of sweat and ingenuity on our part. If elusiveness was a symbol of intelligence, then here are the brains of the solar system."

We walked over to another vantage point.

"What have you done so far?" I asked, gazing curiously into the murky depths of the cube.

Camden frowned. "Oh, we've done some of the basic work. We've dissected a few, traced the pattern of their motor receptors and effectors, found out which part of their brains—we think it's their brains—control which part of their bodies. We've studied growth in the young of the species and established that development is from the general to the specific in matters of movement and feeling. That is, they learn to perform general movements and actions before they go on to specific things, like grasping, or throwing, or pushing buttons—that sort of thing. We know as much about them that way as we do about any mud puppy back on Terra. But do they think? Are they reasoning creatures? I'm no nearer to knowing the answer to that than I was two years ago. If you're interested, I'll take you to the test lab. Martin is running off some tests today."

I nodded and we started over. The test lab was a big shed-like building located on the northern side of the cube.

"What's the general system you're using?" I asked. "I had some psych in secondary, but I've forgotten most of it by now."

"The system is fairly simple. The precise method by which a Squanchy thinks actually is not important to us, so long as the end result is the same. That is, given a problem, can they solve it? That's all there is to it. Of course, the problems we set up for them are more directly related to their environment."

Martin—one of the biologists at the station—met us at the door of the shed and motioned us in.

"How do the Squanchies do? Stupid, bright, or just plain dumb?" I asked.

"I don't know," Camden said sourly. "We haven't had a response that could be classed as either one."

At the other end of the building, Martin was fussing around a large cage that seemed subdivided into corridors. A Squanchy huddled in a cage that was much smaller. Apparently it was to be released into the larger cage when Martin was through with his adjustments.

"What do you mean, you can't classify them? That seems like admitting defeat at a rather low level. If you can't classify their responses, it seems to me that your two years here haven't paid off at all."

He looked at the Squanchy's cage thoughtfully. "On the surface, I suppose it looks as if you're right. Actually, as I suggested before, we've got a good deal of information. Don't forget that no information at all, biologically or otherwise, existed about the Squanchies before we came here. So far we've failed in what we directly set out to do. Sometimes I'm inclined to think that our difficulty is a very simple one that escapes us because of its simplicity. Other times, I'm just . . . well . . . confused. Regardless of everything else, a Squanchy is still an animal with a central nervous system that has to eat to exist and follows a standard pattern of reproduction. You'd expect that there'd be *some* similarity between it and animal species on Terra."

He grinned crookedly. "Only there isn't. You can set up a very simple test that a moronic white rat could run and they'll fail it completely—but still not fail it in a standard way. We had one where three different paths led from the Squanchy cage to another containing a choice bit of rotting muck-reed. One of the paths was easily accessible, the others were rigged so that it got a whiff of chlorine gas if it tried to use them. Squanchies react to chlorine, incidentally, as we would to a gigantic dose of hydrogen sulphide or ammonia. It took the right path the second time out; it never repeated after that, neither did it try the chlorine paths. It didn't do anything—it just sat."

He wiped his glasses and continued in a low voice. "Ten million dollars worth of research just sat on its haunches and got hungry. Practically any animal on Earth could have learned the maze and after the first three trials, they could have repeated it correctly every time. But a Squanchy? Uh-huh.

"You'd think," he continued, "that a Squanchy would have to have a certain minimum intelligence to exist in an environment like this. It must have to solve problems concerning its existence every day—unless it has the great grandaddy of all fairy godfathers watching over it."

He lowered a view-through glass sheet that enabled us to watch the test but hid us from the Squanchy, then pressed a button releasing the Squanchy into the maze. It blinked sleepily at first, scratched a part of its scaly arm, and then apparently caught scent of the muck-reed. It lumbered along the main corridor of the maze and turned right. A whiff of chlorine drove it back. Without hesitation, it turned left and gobbled the muck-reed. The second time through it seemed quite hesitant, came to the turning point, and after five minutes of due deliberation, turned left. The third time was even worse. It didn't seem to want to attempt it at all.

"Maybe he's had all the muck-reed he wants," I suggested.

"They eat it by the bushel," Camden said, "and this particular specimen has been starved for three days to make sure he'd be interested."

Back in the cage, the Squanchy, after much deliberation and false starts, had again arrived at the turning point. Once there, its hesitancy vanished. It promptly turned left again. This time, it was met with the chlorine gas. The Squanchy backed away warily, then turned and ambled back to its own cage, seemingly devoid of any more interest in the affair.

Camden shook his head sadly. "See what I mean, Bob? There you see two years of research sitting on its haunches and searching for water fleas. Maybe you can dope it out—I can't." He started back to the shack and I followed.

I sprawled out on the couch and let the sweat run off me onto the floor. It was hot and muggy, one of those days when newsprint would be so damp it would fall apart in your hands. The obsolete air-fan Camden had turned on did nothing but warm up the air still more. For the hundredth time I forced myself to forget about the ski slopes at Rainier and concentrate on something else. More than one climate man will tell you there's been colonists on Venus who have gone insane because they let their dislike of the weather grow into a mania.

Camden slouched behind his desk and idly tapped the top

of it with a pencil. He was thinking hard but no new ideas were developing—he had got to the point where you do nothing but go around in circles.

"All of your tests turn out like that?" I asked.

He snapped the pencil and tossed the pieces into the disposal chute.

"Just about. Same sort of reaction. Complete the test once, perhaps, and then stall on the rest of it. No rules in the book that cover that. Given a simple test, any living organism improves his performance of the test as the number of practice periods increase. Apparently our Squanchies are the exceptions. The more repetitions, the less response. Maybe they operate on the law of diminishing returns or something."

"No logical reasons why?"

"None that I know of."

It was hard to keep from surrendering to the idea that it was all Camden's worry and none of my own. I felt the sweat run down my back and balanced the clammy discomfort against the energy required to get off the couch and take a shower.

Camden guessed what I was thinking.

"Bob, it's none of your affair. Let's shower for dinner."

At the table, he seemed lost in thought. If I asked a question, he wouldn't answer; and if I repeated it, he'd look up and ask me what I had said.

"You know, Ollie," I said, "you and I have somewhat similar problems. You try to solve the riddle of the Squanchy's intelligence—or lack of it—and I deal with the stupidity of an animal that by all rights should turn in a lot better performance than he does."

Camden looked puzzled. "Which one's that?"

"Man," I said, feeling somewhat smug over my little simile.

"To illustrate," I continued, "did you ever stop to wonder how they get people to come to Venus in the first place?

"You know I work for the Venus Colonial Office—publicity work and that sort of thing. Find out a lot of interesting items, soom good, some bad, depending on how you look at it. VCO twists them so they all sound good. You remember the ads in the papers back on Terra and the colorful posters around the Rocket Fields and take-off ports? Come to Venus, the Planet of the Tropics! The heat and humidity are good for everything from asthma to yaws. Or you consider that not much of the planet is explored and you bill it glamorously as the Planet of Mystery, which not only sounds intriguing but sexy. You gloss over the fact that any Colonial has the right to homicide by presenting it as Adventure at Every Step! You stress the fact that Every Settlement is a Model of Sanitation and Every City a Masterpiece of Cleanliness, forgetting to state that they better be or fungus and disease would decimate the planet in a week.

"Well, that's my job—take a king-sized Turkish bath and present it as a Paradise in the Rough!"

I took my fork and stabbed savagely at the piece of tropical butter on my plate.

"People are stupid, Ollie. If they were bright, they wouldn't fall for the stuff I put out. Venus is a foreign culture, Ollie. If people had any brains at all, they'd use them in observing the culture and looking over exactly what they were getting into. They'd find out about the weather and the customs before rushing in to spend two years trying to find a sure cure for prickly heat. Either that or get into an argument with some Colonial and find out—too late—that if he doesn't like you, he has a right to homicide."

Camden yawned. "Very interesting, Bob. I'll sleep on it."

"Have nightmares about your ignorant Squanchies, more than likely," I muttered.

It felt like an earthquake. I clutched the sheet frantically and jerked my eyes open. Camden was shaking me up and down by the shoulders. He stopped when he saw me open my eyes.

"You're a hard man to wake up! What ignorant idiots we've been, Bob! The answer's been in front of our eyes all the time and we never realized it!"

"O.K.," I grumbled, "the sun is shining and the birds are singing and I'm to be Queen of the May. What's the big idea of waking me up?"

"Tell you at the cube, come on!"

I hadn't seen anybody dance around on two legs so excitedly in a long time. He threw my shorts and halter at me and we ran out to the cube. The entranceways were open, the glassite doors standing wide. The silence was almost tangible; there were no sounds from any of the other buildings in the living quarters compound. The huts that housed the laborers seemed empty.

I yelled at the top of my lungs, partly to see if anybody was around and partly to break the tension.

There was no reply.

Camden and I headed for one of the glassite doors and ran inside. We slowed down then, both of us realizing the difficulty of searching forty thousand square yards of Venusian muckland right then.

"I suppose we ought to search the compound first," Camden said slowly.

There was the quiet *whoosh* of hydraulics behind us. We whirled—and faced a blank expanse of glassite wall, unmarred by any opening.

"Martin or one of the others playing a joke?" I suggested, knowing perfectly well that they wouldn't.

"Poor joke," Camden said grimly. We walked to the walls and looked out at the compound and surrounding muckland, made green by the glassite. Figures were moving in the distance and I pounded on the glassite, trying to hail them.

The figures came closer. I felt sick. The figures were Squanchies, slouching purposefully to the cube.

"How come?" I asked, pointing to the figures outside.

"Turnabout," Camden said quietly.

I watched them for a minute.

"They're not stupid, are they?"

"That's a masterpiece of understatement. No, they're not."

"When did you figure it out? Last night?"

"Yes. I told you I'd sleep on what you said. I didn't. I stayed awake and thought about it. It seemed to me that someplace in that tirade of yours was an idea." He paused. "It's too bad that it didn't occur to me sooner.

"In your confessional last night you said that anybody with brains would use them in observing our 'culture' before jumping in. It occurred to me that that's what the Squanchies have been doing, maybe one of the reasons why they're so hard to find."

"How about the ones you did catch?"

He shrugged.

"Maybe some of them let themselves be caught—sacrificed themselves in the interests of Squanchy science. What better way of evaluating the intelligence of a race than to let them try and test *your* intelligence?"

"How about the test failures? How do you explain them—if they're so bright!"

Camden almost smiled. "It's relatively easy to make up intelligence tests for animals lower on the scale than us, but how would you go about making up ones for those that were higher! If a lower animal made up an intelligence test for us—by their lights—how do you think we would fare? Do you think you could figure out the factor of repetition, for example? That's one of the things that really stumped our beasties. Invariably they would perform a test correctly the first or second time but how about after that? Having performed it correctly—and knowing they performed it correctly—could they figure out the reason why we wanted them to do it again and again? If you were in their position, could you do it? You'd probably do what they did—sit on your haunches and wait for our next move."

"Why do they have us locked in now?" I asked, feeling that I already knew the answer.

"Turnabout, Bob. We're to be the subjects and they the experimenters. They found out all they could one way; now they're going to try it our way."

Late that afternoon we found out what had happened to the others. We saw it when we rounded a small hill in the cube, simply walking around for the exercise. It wasn't very pleasant. Both Ollie and I got sick. I couldn't help thinking of his phrase: *We know as much about them that way as we do about any mud puppy back on Terra.*

"You made a lot of mistakes when you were conducting tests, didn't you?" I asked.

Camden nodded. "I know—there's nothing to prevent them from making mistakes either. Maybe fatal ones."

"Nice thought," I said.

I wondered what they would do. It would probably be clever, and it wouldn't be—nice.

I sat and waited.

My head ached. *"What happened?"* I asked.

"You've been in the maze," Camden said.

"What maze? I thought the Squanchies were going to do something to us?"

"They did." He laughed dryly. *"I have to go through this each time you come out of it. Tell me everything that happened to you from the first morning of your vacation."*

I did.

"Looking back over your memory of events, do you notice anything peculiar about them?" he asked.

I thought for a while. "One small thing," I said. *"I came out here to get away from Kennedy; but once I got here, apparently I never thought of him again. That seems odd."*

"Anything else?"

"Well—for a guy like me, I seem to have led a pretty exciting life for a while."

"You never knew Kennedy," Camden said quietly. "It never happened. You woke up the first morning of your vacation, showered, had breakfast, and read a novel. Late that afternoon you came out to the Farms. Nothing happened on the way. From there on, your memories are real. But you never knew Kennedy. You never were trapped in a burning building, you never were held up on the swamp bus. Your memories from the moment you woke up to when you arrived here are false. It never happened."

My head was spinning. "What did they do?" I asked dully.

"The ten-hour period from the time you awoke the first morning of your vacation to when you got off the bus has been made into a mental maze. The Squanchies blanked out your memories for that length of time, put in a few 'key' memories of things that could happen, and let you fill in the gaps. The visor call from the Bureau was one of these; so was the explosive letter and the burning apartment, so was the fat man on the bus. You filled in the gaps in your memories so they'd be coherent. You figured out how to get out of the burning building on your own, you figured out how to dodge the fat man.

"It's a good intelligence test; they put you, mentally speaking, in a certain jam and you figure your way out of it, mentally speaking. Simple—they pose a problem and you solve it. They posed the problem of the burning apartment—you solved it by thinking of using the laundry chute as an exit. There's always a solution—provided you can think of it. The beauty of it is, it actually never happens. No apparatus, no physical preparation. It's all in your mind."

"I think I see," I said. "How would I fail to pass the test, though? If it's all in my mind, what would be the sign of failure?"

"What would be the mental state of a person who thought he had died—knew that he had died?"

"Oh." After a while I said: "What about you?"

"They haven't done anything to me," he said slowly. "I think I'm the control for you."

"How many times have I been through?" I asked.

"Four."

"I've been lucky. I wonder if it can keep up?"

Camden looked away. "You're pretty bright," he said.

But I knew what he meant.

I sat down on the ground and leaned back against the glassite wall. I felt tired.

Suddenly I stiffened. There was a plucking at my mind, an insistent urge to remember—to remember back to the first day of my vacation. Another trip through the maze was due. I knew how it would start—but how would it end this time?

It would start out like days usually do on Venus—terrible.

Seeing your name in print for the first time can do strange things to a man. What it did to me was make me scrap any further thoughts of graduate school in physics. I had been reluctantly making up my mind not to go and now I had an excuse. Not only had I made a hundred and forty bucks the easy way ("easy" would become a debatable adjective rather quickly) but "The Maze" had been well-liked, coming in second in "The Analytical Lab"—high marks for a new author. Campbell even called me a "strong new contender."

That did it. I would become a free-lance writer. I would have my own office, complete with anteroom and battered couch. First, of course, I'd have to live at home (my family was now living in Long Beach, Indiana) and pile up a few sales.

The life of a free-lance is not one I lightly recommend. The science fiction writer who lived in New York could pay personal calls on the editors. He could leave off manuscripts, pick them up, and personally pressure editors or agents for monies owing.

If you lived in the Midwest, it was a different cup of tea. You lived according to the whims of the man who dropped off your mail in the mornings. And unless you were extremely disciplined, you found yourself unable to work until after he paid his call. Free-lancing is hard not only on the budget, it plays hell with the nerves. . . .

Still, it was the perfect time to be breaking in. New magazines were springing up all over. Palmer had left Ziff-Davis to start *Other Worlds* in late '49. A detective story writer and critic, Tony Boucher (along with J. Francis Mc-Comas) had started *The Magazine of Fantasy and Science Fiction*. In late 1950, Bill Hamling also left Ziff-Davis to publish *Imagination*. Most significantly, Horace Gold started *Galaxy*, a magazine designed to challenge *Astounding*. Horace and *Galaxy* were to become a big market for me.

I acquired an agent (Fred Pohl), bought half-a-dozen typewriter ribbons, and went into business. At first, things went smoothly. I followed "The Maze" with another "circle" story (nothing succeeds like success). Campbell returned it with the notation that if I solved the central problem—rather than leaving it to the reader's imagination—he'd buy it. I did and he did.

The next story Fred submitted to *Galaxy* and Horace bought it. There was a lot that I liked about it and a few things that, in retrospect, I don't. Horace's editorial requirements were much broader than John Campbell's, resulting in a string of off-beat classics. In rapid succession, Horace published Bradbury's "The Fireman" (the predecessor to "Fahrenheit 451"), Heinlein's "The Puppet Masters" and Bester's "The Demolished Man." Horace also published a number of stories where the "idea" or concept was subordinated to character. At its best, you got a quality of human portrayal that had been sadly lacking in science fiction (see Ted Sturgeon's "Baby Is Three," in this case a fine blend of *both* concept and character). At its worst, you got kaffee-klatsch science fiction in which the "idea" that should be at the core of good SF has been replaced by sentimentality and an embarrassing case of over-write. (I once wrote a story that qualified in terms of the above. I wrote it in one sitting in a sudden burst of misplaced inspiration. I mailed it that night and the next morning dashed down to the post office to see if I could get the manuscript back. I couldn't. Unfortunately, I also couldn't retire the story after the first submission. It sold the first time out.)

"The Reluctant Heroes" had an idea that I liked very much. It was strictly a problem in human management: For safety's sake, a member of the first research team on the moon should stay behind to break in the replacements. Reason dictates it should be the Best Man Possible. So much for the basic idea. I wrote it as a story-within-a-story, essentially using a "frame" technique. But the "frame" really isn't necessary and is predicated on a not-very-valid premise.

For the record: Under similar circumstances, I'm sure there would be women on the moon. Do I think, in actuality, the Commission—pardon me, NASA—might treat the hero the same way? Of course I do.

As to the italicized "frame": I'll let it stand for historical accuracy. But still. . . .

The Reluctant Heroes

THE VERY young man sat on the edge of the sofa and looked nervous. He carefully studied his fingernails and ran his hands through his hair and picked imaginary lint off the upholstery.

"I have a chance to go with the first research expedition to Venus," he said.

The older man studied the very young man thoughtfully and then leaned over to his humidor and offered him a cigarette. "It's nice to have the new air units now. There was a time when we had to be very careful about things like smoking."

The very young man was annoyed.

"I don't think I want to go," he blurted. "I don't think I would care to spend two years there."

The older man blew a smoke ring and watched it drift toward the air exhaust vent.

"You mean you would miss it here, the people you've known and grown up with, the little familiar things that have made up your life here. You're afraid the glamour would wear off and you would get to hate it on Venus."

The very young man nodded miserably. "I guess that's it."

"Anything else?"

The very young man found his fingernails extremely fascinating again and finally said, in a low voice, "Yes, there is."

"A girl?"

A nod confirmed this.

It was the older man's turn to look thoughtful. "You know, I'm sure, that psychologists and research men agree that research stations should be staffed by couples. That is, of course, as soon as it's practical."

"But that might be a long time!" the very young man protested.

"It might be—but sometimes it's sooner than you think. And the goal is worth it."

"I suppose so, but—"

The older man smiled. "Still the reluctant heroes," he said, somewhat to himself.

Chapman stared at the radio key.

Three years on the Moon and they didn't want him to come back.

Three years on the Moon and they thought he'd be glad to stay for more. Just raise his salary or give him a bonus, the every-man-has-his-price idea. They probably thought he liked it there.

Oh, sure, he loved it. Canned coffee, canned beans, canned pills, and canned air until your insides felt as though they were plated with tin. Life in a cramped, smelly little hut where you could take only ten steps in any one direction. Their little scientific home of tomorrow with none of the modern conveniences, a charming place where you couldn't take a shower, couldn't brush your teeth, and your kidneys didn't work right.

And for double his salary they thought he'd be glad to stay for another year and a half. Or maybe three. He should probably be glad he had the opportunity.

The key started to stutter again, demanding an answer.

He tapped out his reply: *"No!"*

There was a silence and then the key stammered once more in a sudden fit of bureaucratic rage. Chapman stuffed a rag under it and ignored it. He turned to the hammocks, strung against the bulkhead on the other side of the room.

The chattering of the key hadn't awakened anybody; they were still asleep, making the animal noises that people usually make in slumber. Dowden, half in the bottom hammock and half on the floor, was snoring peacefully. Dahl, the poor kid who was due for stopover, was mumbling to himself. Julius Klein, with that look of ineffable happiness on his face, looked as if he had just squirmed under the tent to his personal idea of heaven. Donley and Bening were lying perfectly still, their covers not mussed, sleeping very lightly.

Lord, Chapman thought, I'll be happy when I can see some other faces.

"What'd they want?" Klein had one eyelid open and a questioning look on his face.

"They wanted me to stay until the next relief ship lands," Chapman whispered back.

"What did you say?"

He shrugged. "No."

"You kept it short," somebody else whispered. It was Donley, up and sitting on the side of the hammock. "If it had been me, I would have told them just what they could do about it."

The others were awake now, with the exception of Dahl, who had his face to the bulkhead and a pillow over his head.

Dowden rubbed his eyes sleepily. "Sore, aren't you?"

"Kind of. Who wouldn't be?"

"Well, don't let it throw you. They've never been here on the Moon. They don't know what it's like. All they're trying to do is get a good man to stay on the job a while longer."

"*All* they're trying to do," Chapman said sarcastically. "They've got a fat chance."

"They think you've found a home here," Donley said.

"Why the hell don't you guys shut up until morning?" Dahl was awake, looking bitter. "Some of us still have to stay here, you know. Some of us aren't going back today."

No, Chapman thought, some of us aren't going back. You aren't. And Dixon's staying, too. Only Dixon isn't ever going back.

Klein jerked his thumb toward Dahl's bunk, held a finger to his lips, and walked noiselessly over to the small electric stove. It was his day for breakfast duty.

The others started lacing up their bunks, getting ready for their last day of work on the Moon. In a few hours they'd be relieved by members of the Third research group and they'd be on their way back to Earth.

And that includes me, Chapman thought. I'm going home. I'm finally going home.

He walked silently to the one small, quartz window in the room. It was morning—the Moon's "morning"—and he shivered slightly. The rays of the Sun were just striking the far rim of the crater and long shadows shot across the crater floor. The rest of it was still blanketed in a dark jumble of powdery pumice and jagged peaks that would make the Black Hills of Dakota look like paradise.

A hundred yards from the research bunker he could make out the small mound of stones and the forlorn homemade cross, jury-rigged out of small condensed-milk tins slid over crossed iron bars. You could still see the footprints in the powdery soil where the group had gathered about the grave. It had been more than eighteen months ago, but there was no wind to wear those tracks away. They'd be there forever.

That's what happened to guys like Dixon, Chapman

thought. On the Moon, one mistake could use up your whole quota of chances.

Klein came back with the coffee. Chapman took a cup, gagged, and forced himself to swallow the rest of it. It had been in the can for so long you could almost taste the glue on the label.

Donley was warming himself over his cup, looking thoughtful. Dowden and Bening were struggling into their suits, getting ready to go outside. Dahl was still sitting on his hammock, trying to ignore them.

"Think we ought to radio the space station and see if they've left there yet?" Klein asked.

"I talked to them on the last call," Chapman said. "The relief ship left there twelve hours ago. They should get here"—he looked at his watch—"in about six and a half hours."

"Chap, you know, I've been thinking," Donley said quietly. "You've been here just twice as long as the rest of us. What's the first thing you're going to do once you get back?"

It hit them, then. Dowden and Bening looked blank for a minute and blindly found packing cases to sit on. The top halves of their suits were still hanging on the bulkhead. Klein lowered his coffee cup and looked grave. Even Dahl glanced up expectantly.

"I don't know," Chapman said slowly. "I guess I was trying not to think of that. I suppose none of us have. We've been like little kids who have waited so long for Christmas that they just can't believe it when it's finally Christmas Eve."

Klein nodded in agreement. "I haven't been here three years like you have, but I think I know what you mean." He warmed up to it as the idea sank in. "Just what the hell *are* you going to do?"

"Nothing very spectacular," Chapman said, smiling. "I'm going to rent a room over Times Square, get a recording of a rikky-tik piano, and drink and listen to the music and watch the people on the street below. Then I think I'll see somebody."

"Who's the somebody?" Donley asked.

Chapman grinned. "Oh, just somebody. What are you going to do, Dick?"

"Well, I'm going to do something practical. First of all, I want to turn over all my geological samples to the government. Then I'm going to sell my life story to the movies and then—why, then, I think I'll get drunk!"

Everybody laughed and Chapman turned to Klein.

"How about you, Julius?"

Klein looked solemn. "Like Dick, I'll first get rid of my obligations to the expedition. Then I think I'll go home and see my wife."

They were quiet. "I thought all members of the groups were supposed to be single," Donley said.

"They are. And I can see their reasons for it. But who could pass up the money the Commission was paying?"

"If I had to do it all over again? Me," said Donley promptly.

They laughed. Somebody said: "Go play your record, Chap. Today's the day for it."

The phonograph was a small, wind-up model that Chapman had smuggled in when he had landed with the First group. The record was old and the shellac was nearly worn off, but the music was good.

> *The roads are the dustiest,*
> *The winds are the gustiest*
> *The gates are the rustiest,*
> *The pies are the crustiest,*
> *The songs are the lustiest,*
> *The friends the trustiest,*
>   *Way back home.* *

They ran through it twice. . . .

They were beginning to feel it now, Chapman thought. They were going to go home in a little while and the idea was just starting to sink in.

"You know, Chap," Donley said, "it won't seem like the same old Moon without you on it. Why, we'll look at it when we're out spooning or something, and it just won't have the same old appeal."

"Like they say in the army," Bening said, "you never had it so good. You found a home here."

The others chimed in and Chapman grinned. Yesterday or a week ago they couldn't have done it. He had been there too long and he had hated it too much.

The party quieted down after a while and Dowden and

* Copyright by Bregman, Vocco & Conn, Inc.

Bening finished getting into their suits. They still had a section of the sky to map before they left. Donley was right after them. There was an outcropping of rock that he wanted a sample of and some strata he wished to investigate.

And the time went faster when you kept busy.

Chapman stopped them at the lock. "Remember to check your suits for leaks," he warned. "And check the valves of your oxygen tanks."

Donley looked sour. "I've gone out at least five hundred times," he said, "and you check me each time."

"And I'd check you five hundred more," Chapman said. "It takes only one mistake. And watch out for blisters under the pumice crust. You go through one of those and that's it, brother."

Donley sighed. "Chap, you watch us like an old mother hen. You see we check our suits, you settle our arguments, you see that we're not bored and that we stay healthy and happy. I think you'd blow our noses for us if we caught cold. But some day, Chap old man, you're gonna find out that your little boys can watch out for themselves!"

But he checked his suit for leaks and tested the valve of his tank before he left.

Only Klein and Chapman were left in the bunker. Klein was at the work table, carefully labeling some lichen specimens.

"I never knew you were married," Chapman said.

Klein didn't look up. "There wasn't much sense in talking about it. You just get to thinking and wanting—and there's nothing you can do about it. You talk about it and it just makes it worse."

"She let you go without any fuss, huh?"

"No, she didn't make any fuss. But I don't think she liked to see me go, either." He laughed a little. "At least I hope she didn't."

They were silent for a while. "What do you miss most, Chap?" Klein asked. "Oh, I know what we said a little while ago, but I mean seriously."

Chapman thought a minute. "I think I miss the sky," he said quietly. "The blue sky and the green grass and trees with leaves on them that turn color in the fall. I think, when I go back, that I'd like to go out in a rain storm and strip and feel the rain on my skin."

He stopped, feeling embarrassed. Klein's expression was

encouraging. "And then I think I'd like to go downtown and just watch the shoppers on the sidewalks. Or maybe go to a burlesque house and smell the cheap perfume and the popcorn and the people sweating in the dark."

He studied his hands. "I think what I miss most is people—all kinds of people. Bad people and good people and fat people and thin people and people I can't understand. People who wouldn't know an atom from an artichoke. And people who wouldn't give a damn. We're a quarter of a million miles from nowhere, Julius, and to make it literary, I think I miss my fellow man more than anything."

"Got a girl back home?" Klein asked almost casually.

"Yes."

"You're not like Dahl. You've never mentioned it."

"Same reason you didn't mention your wife. You get to thinking about it."

Klein flipped the lid on the specimen box. "Going to get married when you get back?"

Chapman was at the port again, staring out at the bleak landscape. "We hope to."

"Settle down in a small cottage and raise lots of little Chapmans, eh?"

Chapman nodded.

"That's the only future," Klein said.

He put away the box and came over to the port. Chapman moved over so they both could look out.

"Chap." Klein hesitated a moment. "What happened to Dixon?"

"He died," Chapman said. "He was a good kid, all wrapped up in science. Being on the Moon was the opportunity of a lifetime. He thought so much about it that he forgot a lot of little things—like how to stay alive. The day before the Second group came, he went out to finish some work he was interested in. He forgot to check for leaks and whether or not the valve on his tank was all the way closed. We couldn't get to him in time."

"He had his walkie-talkie with him?"

"Yes. It worked fine, too. We heard everything that went through his mind at the end."

Klein's face was blank. "What's your real job here, Chap? Why does somebody have to stay for stopover?"

"Hell, lots of reasons, Julius. You can't get a whole relief crew and let them take over cold. They have to know where things are, how things work, what to watch out for. And then, because you've been here a year and a half and know the ropes, you have to watch them to see that they stay alive in spite of themselves. The Moon's a new environment and you have to learn how to live in it. There's a lot of things to learn—and some people just never learn."

"You're nursemaid, then."

"I suppose you could call it that."

Klein said, "You're not a scientist, are you?"

"No, you should know that. I came as the pilot of the first ship. We made the bunker out of parts of the ship so there wasn't anything to go back on. I'm a good mechanic and I made myself useful with the machinery. When it occurred to us that somebody was going to have to stay over, I volunteered. I thought the others were so important that it was better they should take their samples and data back to Earth when the first relief ship came."

"You wouldn't do it again, though, would you?"

"No, I wouldn't."

"Do you think Dahl will do as good a job as you've done here?"

Chapman frowned. "Frankly, I hadn't thought of that. I don't believe I care. I've put in my time; it's somebody else's turn now. He volunteered for it. I think I was fair in explaining all about the job when you talked it over among yourselves."

"You did, but I don't think Dahl's the man for it. He's too young, too much of a kid. He volunteered because he thought it made him look like a hero. He doesn't have the judgment that an older man would have. That you have."

Chapman turned slowly around and faced Klein.

"I'm not the indispensable man," he said slowly, "and even if I was, it wouldn't make any difference to me. I'm sorry if Dahl is young. So was I. I've lost three years up here. And I don't intend to lose any more."

Klein held up his hands. "Look, Chap, I didn't mean you should stay. I know how much you hate it and the time you put in up here. It's just—" His voice trailed away. "It's just that I think it's such a damn important job."

Klein had gone out in a last search for rock lichens and Chapman enjoyed one of his relatively few moments of privacy. He wandered over to his bunk and opened his barracks bag. He checked the underwear and his toothbrush and shaving kit for maybe the hundredth time and pushed the clothing down farther in the canvas. It was foolish because the bag was already packed and had been for a week. He remembered stalling it off for as long as he could and then the quiet satisfaction about a week before, when he had opened his small gear locker and transferred its meager belongings to the bag.

He hadn't actually needed to pack, of course. In less than twenty-four hours he'd be back on earth where he could drown himself in toothpaste and buy more tee shirts than he could wear in a lifetime. He could leave behind his shorts and socks and the outsize shirts he had inherited from—who was it? Driesbach?—of the First group. Dahl could probably use them or maybe one of the boys in the Third.

But it wasn't like going home unless you packed. It was part of the ritual, like marking off the last three weeks in pencil on the gray steel of the bulkhead beside his hammock. Just a few hours ago, when he woke up he had made the last check mark and signed his name and the date. His signature was right beneath Dixon's.

He frowned when he thought of Dixon and slid back the catch on the top of the bag and locked it. They should never have sent a kid like Dixon to the Moon.

He had just locked the bag when he heard the rumble of the airlock and the soft hiss of air. Somebody had come back earlier than expected. He watched the inner door swing open and the spacesuited figure clump in and unscrew its helmet.

Dahl. He had gone out to help Dowden on the Schmidt telescope. Maybe Dowden hadn't needed any help, with Bening along. Or more likely, considering the circumstances, Dahl wasn't much good at helping anybody today.

Dahl stripped off his suit. His face was covered with light beads of sweat and his eyes were frightened.

He moistened his lips slightly. "Do—do you think they'll ever have relief ships up here more often than every eighteen months, Chap? I mean, considering the advance of—"

"No," Chapman interrupted bluntly. "I don't. Not at least for ten years. The fuel's too expensive and the trip's too hazardous. On freight charges alone you're worth your weight in platinum when they send you here. Even if it becomes cheaper, Bob, it won't come about so it will shorten stopover right away." He stopped, feeling a little sorry for Dahl. "It won't be too bad. There'll be new men up here and you'll pass a lot of time getting to know them."

"Well, you see," Dahl started, "that's why I came back early. I wanted to see you about stopover. It's that—well, I'll put it this way." He seemed to be groping for an easy way to say what he wanted to. "I'm engaged back home. Really nice girl, Chap, you'd like her if you knew her." He fumbled in his pocket and found a photograph and put it on the desk. "That's a picture of Alice, taken at a picnic we were on together." Chapman didn't look. "She—we—expected to be married when I got back. I never told her about stopover, Chap. She thinks I'll be home tomorrow. I kept thinking, hoping, that maybe somehow—"

He was fumbling it badly, Chapman thought.

"You wanted to trade places with me, didn't you, Bob? You thought I might stay for stopover again, in your place?"

It hurt to look in Dahl's eyes. They were the eyes of a man who was trying desperately to stop what he was about to do, but just couldn't help himself.

"Well, yes, more or less. Oh, God, Chap, I know you want to go home! But I couldn't ask any of the others; you were the only one who could, the only one who was qualified!"

Dahl looked as though he was going to be sick. Chapman tried to recall all he knew about him. Dahl, Robert. Good mathematician. Graduate from one of the Ivy League schools. Father was a manufacturer of stoves or something.

It still didn't add, not quite. "You know I don't like it here any more than you do," Chapman said slowly. "I may have commitments at home, too. What made you think I would change my mind?"

Dahl took the plunge. "Well, you see," he started eagerly, too far gone to remember such a thing as pride, "you know my father's pretty well fixed. We would make it worth your while, Chap." He was feverish. "It would mean eighteen more months, Chap, but they'd be well-paid months!"

Chapman felt tired. The good feeling he had about going home was slowly evaporating.

"If you have any report to make, I think you had better get at it," he cut in, keeping all the harshness he felt out of his voice. "It'll be too late after the relief ship leaves. It'll be easier to give the captain your report than try to radio it back to Earth from here."

He felt sorrier for Dahl than he could ever remember having felt for anybody. Long after going home, Dahl would remember this. It would eat at him like a cancer.

Cowardice is one thing for which no man ever forgives himself.

Donley was eating a sandwich and looking out the port, so, naturally, he saw the ship first. "Well, whaddya know!" he shouted. "We got company!" He dashed for his suit. Dowden and Bening piled after him and all three started for the lock.

Chapman was standing in front of it. "Check your suits," he said softly. "Just be sure to check."

"Oh, what the hell, Chap!" Donley started angrily. Then he shut up and went over his suit. He got to his tank and turned white. Empty. It was only half a mile to the relief rocket, so somebody would probably have got to him in time, but. . . . He bit his lips and got a full tank.

Chapman and Klein watched them dash across the pumice, making the tremendous leaps they used to read about in the Sunday supplements. The port of the rocket had opened and tiny figures were climbing down the ladder. The small figures from the bunker reached them and did a short jig of welcome. Then the figures linked arms and started back. Chapman noticed one—it was probably Donley—pat the ship affectionately before he started back.

They were in the lock and the air pumped in and then they were in the bunker, taking off their suits. The newcomers were impressed and solemn, very much aware of the tremendous responsibility that rested on their shoulders. Like Donley and Klein and the members of the Second group had been when they had landed. Like Chapman had been in the First.

Donley and the others were all over them.

How was it back on Earth? Who had won the series? Was so-and-so still teaching at the university? What was the international situation?

Was the sky still blue, was the grass still green, did the leaves still turn color in the autumn, did people still love and cry and were there still people who didn't know what an atom was and didn't give a damn?

Chapman had gone through it all before. But was Ginny still Ginny?

Some of the men in the Third had their luggage with them. One of them—a husky, red-faced kid named Williams—was opening a box about a foot square and six inches deep. Chapman watched him curiously.

"Well, I'll be damned!" Klein said. "Hey, guys, look what we've got here!"

Chapman and the others crowded around and suddenly Donley leaned over and took a deep breath. In the box, covering a thick layer of ordinary dirt, was a plot of grass. They looked at it, awed. Klein put out his hand and laid it on top of the grass.

"I like the feel of it," he said simply.

Chapman cut off a single blade with his fingernail and put it between his lips. It had been years since he had seen grass and had the luxury of walking on it and lying on its cool thickness during those sultry summer nights when it was too hot to sleep indoors.

Williams blushed. "I thought we could spare a little water for it and maybe use the ultraviolet lamp on it some of the time. Couldn't help but bring it along; it seemed sort of like a symbol . . ." He looked embarrassed.

Chapman sympathized. If he had had any sense, he'd have tried to smuggle something like that up to the Moon instead of his phonograph.

"That's valuable grass," Dahl said sharply. "Do you realize that at current freight rates up here, it's worth about ten dollars a blade?"

Williams looked stricken and somebody said, "Oh, shut up, Dahl."

One of the men separated from the group and came over to Chapman. He held out his hand and said, "My name's Eberlein. Captain of the relief ship. I understand you're in charge here?"

Chapman nodded and shook hands. They hadn't had a captain on the First ship. Just a pilot and crew. Eberlein looked every inch a captain, too. Craggy face, gray hair, the firm chin of a man who was sure of himself.

"You might say I'm in charge here," Chapman said.

"Well, look, Mr. Chapman, is there any place where we can talk together privately?"

They walked over to one corner of the bunker. "This is about as private as we can get, Captain," Chapman said. "What's on your mind?"

Eberlein found a packing crate and made himself comfortable. He looked at Chapman.

"I've always wanted to meet the man who's spent more time here than anybody else," he began.

"I'm sure you wanted to see me for more reasons than just curiosity."

Eberlein took out a pack of cigarettes. "Mind if I smoke?"

Chapman jerked a thumb toward Dahl. "Ask him. He's in charge now."

The captain didn't bother. He put the pack away. "You know we have big plans for the station," he said.

"I hadn't heard of them."

"Oh, yes, *big plans*. They're working on unmanned, open-side rockets now that could carry cargo and sheet steel for more bunkers like this. Enable us to enlarge the unit, have a series of bunkers all linked together. Make good laboratories and living quarters for you people." His eyes swept the room. "Have a little privacy for a change."

Chapman nodded. "They could use a little privacy up here."

The captain noticed the pronoun. "Well, that's one of the reasons why I wanted to talk to you, Chapman. The Commission talked it over and they'd like to see you stay. They feel if they're going to enlarge it, add more bunkers and have more men up here, that a man of practical experience should be running things. They figure that you're the only man who's capable and who's had the experience."

The captain vaguely felt the approach was all wrong.

"Is that all?"

Eberlein was ill at ease. "Naturally you'd be paid well. I don't imagine any man would like being here all the time. They're prepared to double your salary—maybe even a bonus in addition—and let you have full charge. You'd be Director of the Luna Laboratories."

All this and a title too, Chapman thought.

"That's it?" Chapman asked.

Eberlein frowned. "Well, the Commission said they'd be willing to consider anything else you had in mind, if it was more money or . . ."

"The answer is no," Chapman said. "I'm not interested in more money for staying because I'm not interested in staying. Money can't buy it, Captain. I'm sorry, but I'm afraid that you'd have to stay up here to appreciate that.

"Bob Dahl is staying for stopover. If there's something important about the project or impending changes, perhaps you'd better tell him before you go."

He walked away.

Chapman held the letter in both hands, but the paper still shook. The others had left the bunker, the men of the Second taking those of the Third in hand to show them the machinery and apparatus that was outside, point out the deadly blisters underneath the pumice covering, and show them how to keep out of the Sun and how to watch their air supply.

He was glad he was alone. He felt something trickle down his face and tasted salt on his lips.

The mail had been distributed and he had saved his latest letter until the others had left so he could read it in privacy. It was a short letter, very short.

It started: "Dear Joel: This isn't going to be a nice letter, but I thought it best that you should know before you came home."

There was more to it, but he hadn't even needed to read it to know what it said. It wasn't original, of course. Women who change their minds weren't exactly an innovation, either.

He crumpled the paper and held a match to it and watched it burn on the steel floor.

Three years had been a long time. It was too long a time to keep loving a man who was a quarter of a million miles away. She could look up in the night sky when she was out with somebody else now and tell him how she had once been engaged to the Man in the Moon.

It would make good conversation. It would be funny. A joke.

He got up and walked over to his phonograph and put the record on. The somewhat scratchy voice sang as if nothing had happened.

> *The home food's the spreadiest,*
> *The old wine's the headiest,*
> *The old pals the readiest,*
> *The home gal's the steadiest,*
> *The love the liveliest,*
> *The life the loveliest,*
>   *Way back home.**

The record caught and started repeating the last line.

He hadn't actually wanted to play it. It had been an auto-

matic response. He had played it lots of times before when h
had thought of Earth. Of going home.

He crossed over and threw the record across the bunker
and watched it shatter on the steel wall and the pieces fall to
the floor.

The others came back in the bunker and the men of the
Second started grabbing their bags and few belongings an
getting ready to leave. Dahl sat in a corner, a peculiar expression on his face. He looked as if he wanted to cry and
yet still felt that the occasion was one for rejoicing.

Chapman walked over to him. "Get your stuff and leave
with the others, Dahl." His voice was quiet and hard.

Dahl looked up, opened his mouth to say something, and
then shut up. Donley and Bening and Dowden were already
in the airlock, ready to leave. Klein caught the conversation
and came over. He gripped Chapman's arm.

"What the hell's going on, Chap? Get your bag and let's
go. I know just the bistro to throw a whing-ding when we
get—"

"I'm not going back," Chapman said.

Klein looked annoyed, not believing him. "Come on,
what's the matter with you? You suddenly decide you
don't like the blue sky and trees and stuff? Let's go!"

The men in the lock were looking at them questioningly.
Some members of the Third looked embarrassed, like out-
siders caught in a family argument.

"Look, Julius, I'm not going back," Chapman repeated
dully. "I haven't anything to go back for."

"You're doing a much braver thing than you may think," a
voice cut in. It belonged to Eberlein.

Chapman looked at him. Eberlein flushed, then turned and
walked stiffly to the lock to join the others.

Just before the inner door of the lock shut, they could hear
Chapman, his hands on his hips, breaking in the Third on
how to be happy and stay healthy on the Moon. His voice
was ragged and strained and sounded like a top-sergeant's.

Dahl and Eberlein stood in the outer port of the relief ship,
staring back at the research bunker. It was half hidden in the
shadows of a rocky overhang that protected it from
meteorites.

"They kidded him a lot this morning," Dahl said. "They
said he had found a home on the Moon."

"If we had stayed an hour or so more, he might have changed his mind and left, after all," Eberlein mused, his face a thoughtful mask behind his air helmet.

"I offered him money," Dahl said painfully. "I was a coward and I offered him money to stay in my place." His face was bitter and full of disgust for himself.

Eberlein turned to him quickly and automatically told him the right thing.

"We're all cowards once in a while," he said earnestly. "But your offer of money had nothing to do with his staying. He stayed because he had to stay, because we made him stay."

"I don't understand," Dahl said.

"Chapman had a lot to go home for. He was engaged to be married." Dahl winced. "We got her to write him a letter breaking it off. We knew it meant that he lost one of his main reasons for wanting to go back. I think, perhaps, that he still would have left if we had stayed and argued him into going. But we left before he could change his mind."

"That—was a lousy thing to do!"

"We had no choice. We didn't use it except as a last resort."

"I don't know of any girl who would have done such a thing, no matter what your reasons, if she was in love with a guy like Chapman," Dahl said.

"There was only one who would have," Eberlein agreed. "Ginny Dixon. She understood what we were trying to tell her. She had to; her brother had died up here."

"Why was Chapman so important?" Dahl burst out. "What could he have done that I couldn't have done—would have done if I had had any guts?"

"Perhaps you could have," Eberlein said. "But I doubt it. I don't think there were many men who could have. And we couldn't take the chance. Chapman knows how to live on the Moon. He's like a trapper who's spent all his time in the forests and knows it like the palm of his hand. He never makes mistakes, he never fails to check things. And he isn't a scientist. He would never become so preoccupied with research that he'd fail to make checks. And he can watch out for those who do make mistakes. Ginny understood that all too well."

"How did you know all this about Chapman?" Dahl asked.

"The men in the First told us some of it. And we had our

own observer with you here. Bening kept us pretty well informed."

Eberlein stared at the bunker thoughtfully.

"It costs a lot of money to send ships up here and establish a colony. It will cost a lot to expand it. And with that kind of investment, you don't take chances. You have to have the best men for the job. You get them even if they don't want to do it."

He gestured at the small, blotchy globe of blue and green that was the Earth, riding high in the black sky.

"You remember what it was like five years ago, Dahl? Nations at each other's throats, re-arming to the teeth? It isn't that way now. We've got the one lead that nobody can duplicate or catch up on. Nobody has our technical background. I know, this isn't a military base. But it could become one."

He paused.

"But these aren't even the most important reasons, Dahl. We're at the beginnings of space travel, the first bare, feeble start. If this base on the Moon succeeds, the whole human race will be Outward Bound." He waved at the stars. "You have your choice—a frontier that lies in the stars, or a psychotic little world that tries and fails and spends its time and talents trying to find better methods of suicide.

"With a choice like that, Dahl, you can't let it fail. And personal lives and viewpoints are expendable. But it's got to be that way. There's too much at stake."

Eberlein hestiated a moment and when he started again, it was on a different track. "You're an odd bunch of guys, you and the others in the groups, Dahl. Damn few of you come up for the glamour, I know. None of you like it and none of you are really enthusiastic about it. You were all reluctant to come in the first place, for the most part. You're a bunch of pretty reluctant heroes, Dahl."

The captain nodded soberly at the bunker. "I, personally, don't feel happy about that. I don't like having to mess up other people's lives. I hope I won't have to again. Maybe somehow, some way, this one can be patched up. We'll try to."

He started the mechanism that closed the port of the rocket. His face was a study of regret and helplessness. He was thinking of a future that, despite what he had told Dahl, wasn't quite real to him.

"I feel like a cheap son of a bitch," Eberlein said.

The very young man said, "Do they actually care where they send us? Do they actually care what we think?"

The older man got up and walked to the window. The bunkers and towers and squat buildings of the research colony glinted in the sunlight. The colony had come a long way; it housed several thousands now.

The Sun was just rising for the long morning and farther down shadows stabbed across the crater floor. Tycho was by far the most beautiful of the craters, he thought.

It was nice to know that the very young man was going to miss it. It had taken the older man quite a long time to get to like it. But that was to be expected—he hadn't been on the Moon.

"I would say so," he said. "They were cruel, that way, at the start. But then they had to be. The goal was too important. And they made up for it as soon as they could. It didn't take them too long to remember the men who had traded their future for the stars."

The very young man said, "Did you actually think of it that way when you first came up here?"

The older man thought for a minute. "No," he admitted. "No, we didn't. Most of us were strictly play-for-pay men. The Commission wanted men who wouldn't fall apart when the glamour wore off and there was nothing left but privation and hard work and loneliness. The men who fell for the glamour were all right for quick trips, but not for an eighteen-month stay in a research bunker. So the Commission offered high salaries and we reluctantly took the jobs.

"Oh, there was the idea behind the project, the vision the Commission had in mind. But it took a while for that to grow."

A woman came in the room just then, bearing a tray with glasses on it. The older man took one and said, "Your mother and I were notified yesterday that you had been chosen to go. We would like to see you go, but of course the final decision is up to you."

He sipped his drink and turned to his wife: "It has its privations, but in the long run we've never regretted it, have we Ginny?"

One of the easiest ways of developing an "idea" for a science fiction story is to use the method of transposition. That is, take a historical situation or a current problem and transpose it into some far tomorrow. Isaac Asimov was tremendously successful in transposing the Roman empire into a galactic one for his "Foundation" series. And Frank Herbert did much the same thing by shifting a familiar nomadic civilization on Earth to a far planet and a distant future. (A toast to science fiction's fascinating worlds of water, ice, and desert rather than the desolate lumps of rock we're finding!)

Transposition also works with psychological problems and situations. For example, take suicide. . . . Suicide and its attendant problems of alienation are both fascinating and abhorrent, particularly to the young. We've all had friends who had everything to live for and yet chose not to. Why? What made them pull the trigger or slash their wrists or take an overdose or jump? In cases of poor health or business reversals, the reasons may be deplored but at least they're understandable. In other cases, they remain . . . elusive.

Elementary research on the subject led to the dictionary. Alienation: ". . . the condition of being an outsider, the state of estrangement between the self and the objective world, or between different parts of the personality."

The topic was big in the early '50s and ready-made for a science fiction story. With a different plot, it could just as well have been done as a "mainstream" story, though marketing might have been difficult. The "slicks" wouldn't have touched it and I ran the risks of "exceeding my grasp" if I tried the "quality" magazines (The New Yorker, Harper's, etc.) or the "little" magazines. I decided to cast the theme in a science fiction format and stumbled across one of the more endearing traits of the genre: In science fiction it's possible to tackle ideas and concepts that otherwise might be forbidding, and do so without the gnawing fear that you're outrunning your skills or trespassing in an area where you're not an authority. You can play with a concept and develop a thoroughly satisfying story without fearing that the critics will crucify you for tackling a Hemingway-esque theme without Hemingway's talent. (I took the risks later, however. And as a grace note, I'd like to add that the skills of many of the current crop of science fiction writers are such that they need have little fear of "exceeding their grasp.")

"The Fire and the Sword" first appeared in *Galaxy*. A few years back, Harry Harrison included it in a collection titled *Author's Choice*. I wrote a somewhat emotional introduction for it, remarking that a person can be either alienated from society or alienated because of society—and pointing out the obvious, that in its extreme form alienation kills. In retrospect, the Tunpeshans of the story aren't the good guys at all, they're the villains. I just didn't realize it at the time I wrote it.

It was now 1951 and I was riding fairly high, selling almost everything I wrote. But there were several clouds on the horizon, all of them far bigger than a man's hand. . . .

The Fire and the Sword

Why do people commit suicide?

Templine tightened his safety belt and lay back on the acceleration bunk. The lights in the cabin dimmed to a dull, red glow that meant the time for takeoff was nearing. He could hear noises from deep within the ship and the tiny whir of the ventilator fan, filling the air with the sweetish smell of sleeping gas. To sleep the trip away was better than to face the dull monotony of the stars for days on end.

Oh, they kill themselves for lots of reasons. Maybe ill health or financial messes or family difficulties. An unhappy love affair. Or more complex ones, if you went into it deeper. The failure to achieve an ambition, failure to live up to one's own ideals. Weltschmerz, perhaps.

He could smell the bitter fragrance of tobacco smoke mingling with the gas. Eckert had lit a cigarette and was calmly blowing the smoke at the neon "No Smoking" sign, which winked on and off in mechanical disapproval.

He turned his head slightly so he could just see Eckert in the bank facing him. Eckert, one of the good gray men in the Service. The old reliables, the ones who could take almost anything in their stride because, at one time or another, they had had to.

It was Eckert who had come into his office several days ago and told him that Don Pendleton had killed himself.

Only Pendleton wasn't the type. He was the kind who have everything to live for, the kind you instinctively know will amount to something someday. And that was a lousy way to remember him. The cliches always come first. Your memory plays traitor and boils friendship down to the status of a breakfast food testimonial.

The soft red lights seemed to be dancing in the darkness of the cabin. Eckert was just a dull, formless blur opposite him. His cigarette was out.

Eckert had come into his office without saying a word and had watched his scenery-window. It had been snowing in the window, the white flakes making a simple pattern drifting past the glass. Eckert had fiddled with the controls and changed it to sunshine, then to a weird mixture of hail amid the brassy, golden sunlight.

And then Eckert had told him that Pendleton had taken the short way out.

He shouldn't get sentimental. But how the hell else should he remember Pendleton? Try to forget it and drink a toast to him at the next class reunion? And never, never be so crude as to speculate why Pendleton should have done it? If, of course, he had . . .

The cabin was hazy in the reddish glow, the sleeping gas a heavy perfume.

Eckert and he had talked it out and gone over the records. Pendleton had come of good stock. There had been no mental instability in his family for as far back as the genetic records went. He had been raised in a middle-class neighborhood and attended a local grammar school where he had achieved average grades and had given his instructors the normal amount of trouble. Later, when he had made up his mind to enter the Diplomatic Service, his grades had improved. He had worked hard at it, though he wasn't what you would call a grind. In high school and later in college, he was the well-balanced type, athletic, popular, hard-working.

How long would it be before memories faded and all there was left of Pendleton was a page of statistics? He had been on this team, he had been elected president of that, he had graduated with such and such honors. But try getting a picture of him by reading the records, resurrect him from a page of black print. Would he be human? Would he be flesh and blood? Hell, no! In the statistics Pendleton was the All-Around Boy, the cold marble statue with the finely chiseled muscles and the smooth, blank sockets where the eyes should be. Maybe someday fate would play a trick on a hero-worshiping public and there would actually be kids like that. But they wouldn't be human; they wouldn't be born. Parents would get them by sending in so many box tops.

He was drowsy; the room was filled with the gas now. It would be only a matter of minutes before he would be asleep.

Pendleton had been in his second year as attache on Tunpesh, a small planet with a G-type sun. The Service had stumbled across it recently and decided the system was worth diplomatic recognition of some kind, so Pendleton had been sent there. He had been the first attache to be sent and naturally he had gone alone.

There was no need to send more. Tunpesh had been in-

spected and certified and approved. The natives were primitive
and friendly. Or maybe the Service had slipped up, as it
sometimes did, and Tunpesh had received something less than
a thorough survey.

And then an unscheduled freighter had put in for repairs,
one of the very few ships that ever came by Tunpesh. The
captain had tried to pay his respects to Pendleton. Only Pendleton wasn't there. The natives said he had killed himself
and showed the captain the little flower-covered plot where
they had buried him.

Tunpesh had been Pendleton's second assignment.

*The natives were oh-so-friendly. So friendly that he had
made sure that a certain box was on board, filled with shiny
atomic rifles, needle pistols, and the fat little gas guns. They
might be needed. People like Pendleton didn't kill themselves,
did they? No, they didn't. But sometimes they were
murdered.*

It was almost black inside the cabin now; only a thin red
line around the ceiling told how close they were to takeoff.
His head was thick with drowsiness, his eyelids a heavy
weight that he knew he couldn't keep open much longer.

Eckert and he had been chosen to go to Tunpesh and investigate. The two of them, working together, should be able
to find out why Pendleton had killed himself.

*But that wasn't the real reason. Maybe Eckert thought so,
but he knew better. The real reason they were going there
was to find out why Pendleton had been killed and who had
killed him. That was it.*

Who had killed Cock Robin?

The thin red line was practically microscopic now and
Templin could feel his lashes lying gently on his cheeks. But
he wasn't asleep—not quite. There was something buzzing
about in the dim recesses of his mind.

Their information on Tunpesh was limited. They knew that
it had no trading concessions or armed forces and that nobody from neighboring systems seemed to know much about
it or even visited it. But a staff anthropologist must have been
routinely assigned to Tunpesh to furnish data and reports.

"Ted?" he murmured sleepily.

A faint stirring in the black bulk opposite him. "Yes?"

"How come our anthropologist on Tunpesh didn't come
across with more information?"

A drowsy mumble from the other cot: "He wasn't there
long enough. He committed suicide not long after landing."

The room was a whirling pool of blackness into which his mind was slowly slipping. Takeoff was only seconds away.

Why do people commit suicide?

"It's a nice day, isn't it, Ted?"

Eckert took a deep and pleasurable breath. "It's the type of day that makes you feel good just to be alive."

Warm breezes rustled through Eckert's graying hair and tugged gently at his tunic. The air smelled as if it had been washed and faintly perfumed with the balsamy scent of something very much like pine. A few hundred yards away, a forest towered straight and slim and coolly inviting, and brilliantly colored birds whirled and fluttered in the foliage.

The rocketport, where they were standing surrounded by their luggage, was a grassy valley where the all too infrequent ships could land and discharge cargo or make repairs. There was a blackened patch on it now, with little blast-ignited flames dying out around the edges. *It won't be long before it will be green again*, he thought. The grass looked as though it grew fast—it would certainly have plenty of time to grow before the next ship landed.

He looked at the slim, dwindling shape that was the rocket, and was suddenly, acutely aware that he and Templin would be stranded for six months on a foreign and very possibly dangerous planet. And there would be no way of calling for help or of leaving before the six months were up.

He stood there for a moment, drinking in the fresh air and feeling the warmth of the sun against his face. It might be a pleasant six months at that, away from the din and the hustle and confusion, spending the time in a place where the sun was warm and inviting.

I must be getting old, he thought, *thinking about the warmth and comfort. Like old dogs and octogenarians.*

Templin was looking at the scenery with a disappointed expression on his face. Eckert stole a side glance at him and for a fleeting moment felt vaguely concerned. "Don't be disappointed if it doesn't look like cloak-and-dagger right off, Ray. What seems innocent enough on the surface can prove to be quite dangerous underneath."

"It's rather hard to think of danger in a setting like this."

Eckert nodded agreement. "It wouldn't fit, would it? It would be like a famous singer suddenly doing a jazz number in an opera, or having the princess in a fairy tale turn out to be ugly." He gestured toward the village. "You could hardly class that as dangerous from its outward appearance, could you?"

The rocketport was in a small valley, surrounded by low, wooded hills. The village started where the port left off and crawled and wound over the wooded ridges. Small houses of sunbaked, whitewashed mud crouched in the shadow of huge trees and hugged the banks of a small stream.

It looked fairly primitive, Eckert thought, and yet it didn't have the earmarks, the characteristics of most primitive villages. It didn't seem cluttered or dirty and you didn't feel like beating a hasty retreat when the wind was blowing toward you.

A few adults were watching them curiously and the usual bunch of kids that always congregated around rocketports quickly gathered. Eckert stared at them for a moment, wondering what it was that seemed odd about them, and they stared back with all the alert dignity of childhood. They finally came out on the field and clustered around him and Templin.

Templin studied them warily. "Better watch them, Ted. Even kids can be dangerous."

It's because you never suspect kids, Eckert thought, *you never think they'll do any harm. But they can be taught. They could do as much damage with a knife as a man could, for instance. And they might have other weapons.*

But the idea still didn't go with the warm sun and the blue sky and the piny scent of the trees.

One of the adults of the village started to walk toward them.

"The reception committee," Templin said tightly. His hand went inside his tunic.

He couldn't be blamed for being jumpy, Eckert realized. This was his first time out, his first mission like this. And, of course, Pendleton had been a pretty good friend of his.

"I'd be very careful what I did," Eckert said softly. "I would hate to start something merely because I misunderstood their intentions."

The committee of one was a middle-aged man dressed in a simple strip of white cloth twisted about his waist and allowed to hang freely to his knees. When he got closer, Eckert became less sure of his age. He had the firm, tanned musculature of a much younger man, though a slightly seamed face and white hair aged him somewhat. Eckert still had the feeling that if you wanted to know his exact age, you'd have to look at his teeth or know something about his epiphyseal closures.

"You are *menshars* from Earth?" The voice was husky and pleasant and the pronunciation was very clear. Eckert regarded him thoughtfully and made a few mental notes. He wasn't bowing and scraping like most natives who weren't too familiar with visitors from the sky, and yet he was hardly either friendly or hostile.

"You learned our language from Pendleton and Reynolds?" Reynolds had been the anthropologist.

"We have had visitors from Earth before." He hesitated a moment and then offered his hand, somewhat shyly, Eckert thought, in the Terrestrial sign of greeting. "You may call me *Jathong* if you wish." He paused a moment to say something in his native tongue to the kids who were around. They promptly scattered and picked up the luggage. "While you are here, you will need a place to stay. There is one ready, if you will follow me."

He was polite, Eckert thought. He didn't ask what they were there for or how long they were going to stay. But then again, perhaps the natives were a better judge of that than he and Templin.

The town was larger than he had thought at first, stretching over a wide expanse of the countryside. There wasn't, so far as he could see, much manufacturing above the level of handicrafts and simple weaving. Colored patches on far hillsides indicated the presence of farms, and practically every house in the village had its small garden.

What manufacturing there was seemed to be carried on in the central square of the town, where a few adults and children squatted in the warm afternoon sun and worked industriously at potter's wheels and weaver's looms. The other part of the square was given over to the native bazaar where pots and bolts of cloth were for sale, and where numerous stalls were loaded with dried fruits and vegetables and the cleaned and plucked carcasses of the local variety of fowl.

It was late afternoon when they followed Jathong into a small, whitewashed house midway up a hill.

"You are free to use this while you are here," he said.

Eckert and Templin took a quick tour of the few rooms. They were well furnished, in a rustic sort of way, and what modern conveniences they didn't have they could easily do without. The youngsters who had carried their luggage left it outside and quietly faded away. It was getting dark; Eckert opened one of the boxes they had brought along, took out an electric lantern and lighted it. He turned to Jathong.

"You've been very kind to us and we would like to repay you. You may take what you wish of anything within this box." He opened another of the boxes and displayed the usual trade goods—brightly colored cloth and finely worked jewelry and a few mechanical contrivances that Eckert knew usually appealed to the primitive imagination.

Jathong ran his hand over the cloth and held some of the jewelry up to the light. Eckert knew by the way he looked at it that he wasn't at all impressed. "I am grateful," he said finally, "but there is nothing I want." He turned and walked away into the gathering darkness.

"The incorruptible native." Templin laughed sarcastically.

Eckert shrugged. "That's one of the things you do out of habit, try and buy some of the natives so you'll have friends in case you need them." He stopped for a moment, thinking. "Did you notice the context? He didn't say he didn't want what we showed him. He said there was *nothing* that he wanted. Implying that everything he wanted, he already had."

"That's not very typical of a primitive society, is it?"

"No, I'm afraid it's not." Eckert started unpacking some of the boxes. "You know, Ray, I got a kick out of the kids. They're a healthy-looking lot, aren't they?"

"Too healthy," Templin said. "There didn't seem to be any sick ones or ones with runny noses or cuts or black eyes or bruises. It doesn't seem natural."

"They're probably just well brought-up kids," Eckert said sharply. "Maybe they've been taught not to get in fights or play around in the mud on the way home from school." He felt faintly irritated, annoyed at the way Templin had put it, as if any deviation from an Earth norm was potentially dangerous.

"Ted." Templin's voice was strained. "This could be a trap, you know."

"In what way?"

The words came out slowly. "The people are too casual, as though they're playing a rehearsed part. Here we are, from an entirely different solar system, landed in what must be to them an unusual manner. They couldn't have seen rockets more than three or four times before. It should still be a novelty to them. And yet how much curiosity did they show? Hardly any. Was there any fear? No. And the cute, harmless little kids." He looked at Eckert. "Maybe that's what we're

supposed to think—just an idyllic, harmless society. Maybe
that's what Pendleton thought, right to the very end."

He was keyed up, jumpy, Eckert realized. He would probably be seeing things in every shadow and imagining danger to
be lurking around every corner.

"It hasn't been established yet that Pendleton was killed,
Ray. Let's keep an open mind until we know for certain."

He flicked out the light and lay back on the cool bed, letting his body relax completely. The cool night wind blew lazily through the wood slat blinds, carrying the fragrance of
the trees and the grass, and he inhaled deeply and let his
thoughts wander for a moment. It was going to be pleasant to
live on Tunpesh for six months—even if the six months were
all they had to live. The climate was superb and the people
seemed a cut above the usual primitive culture. If he ever retired some day, he thought suddenly, he would have to
remember Tunpesh. It would be pleasant to spend his old age
here. And the fishing was probably excellent . . .

He turned his head a little to watch Templin get ready for
bed. There were advantages in taking him along that Templin
probably didn't even realize. He wondered what Templin
would do if he ever found out that the actual reason he had
been chosen to go was that his own psychological chart was
very close to Pendleton's. Pendleton's own feelings and emotions would almost exactly be duplicated in Templin's.

A few stray wisps of starlight pierced through the blinds
and sparkled for an instant on a small metal box strapped to
Templin's waist. A power pack, Eckert saw grimly, probably
leading to the buttons on his tunic. A very convenient, portable, and hard to detect weapon.

There were disadvantages in taking Templin, too.

"Just how primitive do you think the society is, Ted?"

Eckert put down the chain he had been whittling and
reached for his pipe and tobacco.

"I don't think it's primitive at all. There are too many
disparities. Their knowledge of a lot of things is a little more
than empirical knowledge; they associate the growth of crops
with fertilizer and nitrogen in the soil as well as sunlight,
rather than the blessings of some native god. And they differ
a lot in other respects. Their art and their music are advanced. Free art exists along with purely decorative art, and
their techniques are finely developed."

"I'm glad you agree, then. Take a look at this." Templin

threw a shiny bit of metal on the rough-hewn table. Eckert picked it up and inspected it. It was heavy and one side of it was extremely sharp.

"What's it for?"

"They've got a hospital set up here. Not a hospital like any we know, of course, but a hospital nonetheless. It's not used very much; apparently the natives don't get sick here. But occasionally there are hunting accidents and injuries that require surgery. The strip of metal there is a scalpel." He laughed shortly. "Primitive little gadget, but it works well—as well as any of ours."

Eckert hefted it in his palm. "The most important thing is that they have the knowledge to use it. Surgery isn't a simple science."

"Well, what do you think about it?"

"The obvious. They evidently have as much technology as they want, at least in fields where they have to have it."

"How come they haven't gone any further?"

"Why should they? You can live without skycars and rocket ships, you know."

"Did you ever wonder what kind of weapons they might have?"

"The important thing," Eckert mused, "is not if they have them, but if they'd use them. And I rather doubt that they would. We've been here for two weeks now and they've been very kind to us, seeing that we've had food and water and what fuel we need."

"It's known in the livestock trade as being fattened up for the slaughter," Templin said.

Eckert sighed and watched a fat bug waddle across a small patch of sunlight on the wooden floor. It was bad enough drawing an assignment in a totally foreign culture, even if the natives were humanoid. It complicated things beyond all measure when your partner in the project seemed likely to turn into a vendettist. It meant that Eckert would have to split his energies. He'd have to do what investigating he could among the Tunpeshans, and he'd have to watch Templin to see that he didn't go off half-cocked and spoil everything.

"You're convinced that Pendleton was murdered, aren't you?"

Templin nodded. "Sure."

"Why?"

"The Tunpeshans know why we're here. We've dropped enough hints along those lines. But nobody has mentioned

Pendleton; nobody has volunteered any information about him. And he was an attache here for three years. Didn't anybody know him during that time? We've let slip a few discreet statements that we would like to talk to Pendleton's friends, yet nobody's come around. Apparently, in all the three years he was here, Pendleton didn't make any friends. And that's a little hard to believe. It's more likely that his friends have been silenced and any information about him is being withheld for a reason."

"What reason?"

Templin shrugged. "Murder. What other reason could there be?"

Eckert rolled up the thin, slatted blinds and stared out at the scenery. A hundred feet down the road, a native woman was going to market, leading a species of food animal by the halter.

"They grow their women nice, don't they?"

"Physically perfect, like the men," Templin grumbled. "You could get an inferiority complex just from watching the people here. Everybody's so damn perfect. Nobody's sick, nobody's unhealthy, nobody is too fat or too thin, nobody's unhappy. The only variation is that they don't all look alike. Perfection. It gets boring after a while."

"Does it? I hadn't noticed." Eckert turned away from the blinds. His voice was crisp. "I knew Don Pendleton quite well, too," he said. "But it isn't blinding me to what I'm here for. We came to find out what happened to him, not to substantiate any preconceived notions. What we find out may be vitally important to anybody serving here in the future. I would hate to see our efforts spoiled because you've already made up your mind."

"You knew Pendleton," Templin repeated grimly. "Do you think it was suicide?"

"I don't think there's such a thing as a suicide type, when you come down to it. I'm not ruling out the possibility of murder, either. I'm trying to keep an open mind."

"What have we accomplished so far? What have we found out?"

"We've got six months," Eckert said quietly. "Six months in which we'll try to live here inconspicuously and study the people and try to cultivate informants. We would get nowhere if we came barging in asking all sorts of questions. And don't forget, Ray, we'll all alone on Tunpesh. If it is a

case of murder, what happens when the natives find out that
we know it is?"

Templin's eyes dueled for a moment. Then he turned his
back and walked to the window. "I suppose you're right," he
said at last. "It's nice living here, Ted. Maybe I've been
fighting it. But I can't help thinking that Don must have liked
it here, too."

One of the hardest things to learn in a foreign culture, Eckert
thought, is when to enjoy yourself, when to work and when
to worry.

"*Pelache, menshar?*"

"*Sharra!*" He took the small bowl of *pelache* nuts, helped
himself to a few, and passed the bowl on. This was definitely
the time to enjoy himself, not to work or worry. He had
heard about the *halera* a few days ago, and, by judicious hint-
ing to the proper authorities, he and Templin had been invited. It was a good chance to observe native customs. A
little anthropology—with refreshments.

The main courses started making the rounds and he took
generous helpings of the roasted *ulami* and the broiled
halunch and numerous dabs from the side dishes of steaming
vegetables. Between every course, they passed around a small
flagon of the hot, spiced native wine, but he noticed that nobody drank to excess.

The old Greek ideal, he thought: *moderation in everything.*

He looked at Templin, sitting across from him in the huge
circle and shrugged mentally. Templin looked as if he was
about to break down and enjoy himself, but there was still a
slight bulge under his tunic, where he had strapped his power
pack. Any fool should have known that nothing would happen at a banquet like this. The only actual danger lay in
Templin's getting excited and doing something he was bound
to regret later on. And even that danger was not quite as
likely now.

There will be hell to pay, Eckert thought, *if Templin ever
finds out that I sabotaged his power pack.*

"You look thoughtful, *menshar* Eckert."

Eckert took another sip of the wine and turned to the Tunpeshan on his left. He was a tall, muscular man with sharp
eyes, a firm chin and a certain aura of authority.

"I was wondering if my countryman Pendleton had offended your people in any way, Nayova." Now was as good

a time as any to pump him for what he knew about Pendleton's death.

"So far as I know, *menshar* Pendleton offended no one. I do not know what duties he had to perform here, but he was a generous and courteous man."

Eckert gnawed the dainty meat off a slender *ulami* bone and tried to appear casual in his questioning.

"I am sure he was, Nayova. I am sure, too, that you were as kind to him as you have been to Templin and myself. My Government is grateful to you for that."

Nayova seemed pleased. "We tried to do as well for *menshar* Pendleton as we could. While he was here, he had the house that you have now and we saw that he was supplied with food and all other necessities."

Eckert had a sudden clammy feeling which quickly passed away. What Nayova had said was something he'd make sure Templin never heard about. He wiped his mouth on a broad, flat leaf that had been provided and took another sip of wine.

"We were shocked to find out that *menshar* Pendleton had killed himself. We knew him quite well and we could not bring ourselves to believe he had done such a thing."

Nayova's gaze slid away from him. "Perhaps it was the will of the Great One," he said vaguely. He didn't seem anxious to talk about it.

Eckert stared bleakly at his wine glass and tried to put the pieces of information together. They probably had a taboo about self-destruction which would make it difficult to talk about. That would make it even harder for him to find out by direct questioning.

A native fife trilled shrilly and a group of young men and women walked into the room. The circle broke to let them through and they came and knelt before Nayova. When he clapped his hands sharply, they retreated to the center of the circle and began the slow motions of a native dance.

The sound of the fife softened and died and the slow monotonous beat of drums took its place. The beat slowly increased and so did the rhythm of the dancers. The small fires at the corners of the hut were allowed to dwindle and the center of the circle became filled with the motions of shadows intermixed with the swift, sure movements of glistening limbs. Eckert felt his eyebrows crawl upward. Apparently the dance was the Tunpeshan version of the *rites de passage*. He glanced across the circle at Templin. Templin's face—what he could see of it by the flickering light—was brick red.

A voice spoke in his ear. "It is hard for us to imagine anybody doing what *menshar* Pendleton did. It is . . ." and he used a native word that Eckert translated as being roughly equivalent to "*obscene*."

The dancers at the center of the circle finally bowed out with small garlands of flowers on their heads that signified their reaching adulthood. Acrobats then took the stage and went through a dizzying routine, and they in turn were succeeded by a native singer.

They were all excellent, Eckert thought. If anything, they were too good.

The bowl of *pelache* nuts made its way around again and Nayova leaned over to speak to him. "If there is any possibility that I can help you while you are here, *menshar* Eckert, you have but to ask."

It would probably be a mistake to ask for a list of Pendleton's friends, but there was a way around that. "I would like to meet any of your people who had dealings with Pendleton, either in business or socially. I will do everything not to inconvenience them in any way."

"I think they would be glad to help you. I shall ask them to go to you this coming week."

It wasn't a driving rain, just a gentle drizzle that made the lanes muddy and plastered Eckert's tunic against him. He didn't mind it; the rain was warm and the trees and grass smelled good in the wet.

"How would you classify the culture after seeing the ceremony, Ted?" Templin asked.

"About what you would expect. An Apollonian culture, simple and dignified. Nothing in excess, no striving for great emotional release."

Templin nodded soberly. "It grows on you, doesn't it? You find yourself getting to like the place. And I suppose that's dangerous, too. You tend to let your guard down, the way Pendleton must have. You—what was that?"

Eckert tensed. There was a gentle padding in the mud, several hundred feet behind them. Templin flattened himself in the shadows alongside a house. His hand darted inside his tunic and came out with the slim deadliness of a needle gun.

"Don't use it!" Eckert whispered tersely.

Templin's eyes were thin, frightened slits in the darkness. "Why not?"

Eckert's mind raced. It might be nothing at all, and then

again it might be disaster. But there was still a chance that Templin might be wrong. And there were more immediate reasons.

"How many charges do you have for that?"

"Twelve."

"You think you can stand there and hold them off with only twelve charges for your needle gun?"

"There's my power pack."

"It's no good," Eckert said softly. "The batteries in it are dead. I was afraid you might do something foolish with it."

The footsteps were only yards away. He listened intently, but it was hard to tell how many there were by the sound.

"What do we do then?"

"See if they're following us first," Eckert said practically. "They might not be, you know."

They slid out from the shadows and ducked down another lane between the houses. The footsteps behind them speeded up and came down the same lane.

"We'll have to head back for our house," Eckert whispered.

They started running as quietly as they could, slipping and sliding in the mud. Another stretch past the shuttered, crouching houses and they found themselves in the square they had visited on the day they had landed. It was deserted, the looms and pottery wheels covered with cloth and reeds to keep off the rain. They darted across it, two thin shadows racing across the open plaza, and hurried down another path.

The last path led to the small river that cut through the city. Templin looked around, gestured to Eckert, waded into the water and crouched under the small bridge that spanned it. Eckert swore silently to himself, then followed Templin in.

The cold water swirled under his armpits and he bit his lips to keep himself from sneezing. Templin's emotions were contagious. Would he have worried about the footsteps? He frowned and tried to be honest with himself. Perhaps he would—and perhaps he wouldn't have. But he couldn't have let Templin stay there and face the unknown approachers. Not Templin.

Footsteps approached the bridge, hesitated a moment, then pattered on the wooden structure and faded off down the muddy path. Eckert let his breath out slowly. The footsteps were curiously light.

There was only one pair of them.

"I would like to know something," Templin said coldly. He stripped off his power pack and let it fall to the floor of their house. "Why did you decide to substitute dead batteries in the pack?"

"Because," Eckert said shortly, "I was afraid you would do something with it that you might regret later. You're inexperienced in situations like this. Your reactions aren't to be trusted. One false move here and we could follow Pendleton, however he died. You know that." He wriggled out of his tunic and slowly peeled off his wet trousers.

There was a timid knock at the door. He wrapped a blanket about himself and motioned to Templin to stand to one side. Templin grabbed a small stool, hefted it in one hand, and complied.

Eckert went to the door and casually threw it open.

A girl stood there, half in the outer darkness and half in the yellowish light from the room, covered with mud to the knees and drenched to the skin.

"The *menshar* forgot this at the *halera*," she said softly. She quickly handed him his pipe and a soggy bag of tobacco, and disappeared instantly into the rain. He listened for the sound of her footsteps in the soft mud and then closed the door.

Templin put down the stool and stared stupidly at the pipe and the tobacco sack. Eckert placed them carefully on the table and began to towel himself.

"We probably face as much danger from our own imaginations as from anything else," he said grimly. "Tell me, would you have fired first, or would you have waited until you found out for sure who she was and what she wanted when she first started to follow us?"

"I don't know," Templin said sullenly.

"Then I'll leave to your imagination the position we would be in now, if you had given in to your impulse."

"We haven't found out much, have we?" Templin demanded some days later.

"No," Eckert admitted. "We haven't."

He riffled through the thick stack of cards on the table. Statistically, the results were not only interesting but slightly phenomenal. During the three years or so that Pendleton had been on Tunpesh, he had met and known approximately seven hundred of the natives. By far the greater majority of these, of course, were purely casual and meant nothing. Almost a hundred, though, had had extended relations with Pendleton in business or social affairs. Of this hundred, none—not a single one—would admit that he had known Pendleton well or could be considered a friend of his. About all they had to say was that Pendleton had been healthy and easy to get along with, and one warm night he had shocked the community by going off and shooting himself.

"Like Richard Cory," Eckert said aloud.

"Like who?" Templin asked.

"Richard Cory. A character in a poem by a Twentieth Century poet, Edwin Arlington Robinson. Apparently he had everything to live for, but 'Richard Cory, one calm summer night, went home and put a bullet through his head.' "

"I'll have to look it up some day," Templin said. He pointed to the stack of cards. "That's so much waste paper, isn't it?"

"Yes, it is," Eckert said reluctantly. "To be frank, I had hoped we'd know a lot more by now. I still can't understand why we haven't dug up anybody who will admit having been his friend."

"How do you know they're telling the truth? Or, for that matter, how do you know that the ones we've seen so far are the ones who *actually* knew Pendleton?"

Eckert drummed his fingers on the table. *You handle different human cultures for twenty-five years and you get to the point where you can tell if people are lying or not. Or do you? Maybe just an old man's conceit. Age alone never lent wisdom. Regardless of the personal reasons that Templin might have for thinking the Tunpeshans are lying, the fact remains that they very easily could be. And what should you do if they are?*

There was a polite knock at the door.

"We've got another visitor," Templin said sarcastically. "He probably saw Pendleton at a *halera* four years ago and wants to be sure we know all about it."

The Tunpeshan looked faintly familiar to Eckert. There was something about the man's carriage . . .

"I met you the day you landed," the Tunpeshan began, and Eckert remembered. Jathong, the guide who had shown them to the house.

"You knew Pendleton?"

Jathong nodded. "I and a fellow weaver took over his small office after he had left it." Eckert recalled the small office in the square with the bolts of cloth on display, and the

small mud brick on the window ledge with the incised letter-
ing reading:

DONALD PENDLETON, SERVICE ATTACHE.

"Why you didn't tell us this before?"

"I didn't know what kind and how much information you
wanted."

We didn't ask him, Eckert thought, *so he didn't volunteer
any information. Polite, to say the least.*

"How long did you know him?"

"Since he landed. I was the one appointed to him."

"What do you mean—appointed to him?"

"To try to learn his language, and try to teach him ours."

Eckert felt his interest rising. Jathong, then, must have
known Pendleton fairly well.

"Did he have any enemies that you know of?"

"Enemies?" Jathong seemed ignorant of the meaning of the
word, so Eckert explained. "No, he had no enemies. He
would naturally have none such on Tunpesh."

Templin leaned forward, tense. "If he had no enemies, why
did he have no friends? You, for example, knew him longer
and better than most. Why is it that you weren't his friend?"

Jathong looked unhappy, as if being forced to say something he wanted not to say. "Pendleton was *kava*—I cannot
explain it. The concept is difficult. You would not understand."

He might be running the danger of throwing too many
questions at Jathong, Eckert realized, and having him freeze
up or turn vague. But it couldn't be helped. They had made
no progress at all by subtlety, and time would eventually run
out.

He tried to broach the next question delicately. "Did Pendleton know any of the women of your race?"

"He knew some of the women, as he knew the men."

The answer didn't tell Eckert what he wanted to know.
"Was he in love with any woman?" It sounded crude the way
he put it, but it was hard to think of any other way of asking
it.

Jathong looked at him incredulously, as if Eckert had asked
him if Pendleton had had two heads.

"That would have been impossible. None of our women
would have—could have—been in love with *menshar* Pendleton."

One line of inquiry just gone phht, Eckert thought. *But*

Pendleton wasn't one to let a broken heart get him down anyway.

"Why not?" Templin cut in harshly. "He wasn't hard to look at and he would have made a good husband."

Jathong diplomatically turned around to face Templin. "I have told you once—Pendleton was *kava*. It would have been quite impossible."

The answer to what had happened to Pendleton probably lay in Jathong's inability to explain his own terms, Eckert believed. One could get just so close, and then the definitions became vague and useless.

He asked a few more questions and finally dismissed Jathong. The interview, like all the others he and Templin had held during the last week, had been worthless. They knew nothing more than they had when they landed.

"I still think they're lying," Templin said almost savagely. "Or perhaps the ones who really know something haven't come around."

Eckert got his pipe and sat near the doorway, letting the sunlight streaming through the foliage of a nearby tree dapple his face with a checkerboard pattern of modulated lights and velvety shadows.

"If they're evading us or if they're lying, then the society is a dangerous one for us. But I still can't believe it. They're not warlike. They don't seem to have many weapons and definitely none of an advanced type."

"How could anybody know for sure?"

Eckert methodically knocked the cold ashes out of his pipe and added more tobacco. "Easy. Despite what you read in story books, no civilization lives simply, governs itself simply, and yet possesses 'super-blasters.' The sword-and-blaster combination just doesn't exist. Any weapon above the level of bows and arrows or knives is the product of a well advanced technology. Along with weapons, of course, you have to have good communications. Now take an ordinary radio and think of the degree of knowledge, technology, and industrialization that would have to exist to supply it. There's nothing like that here."

Templin came over to the warmth streaming in through the doorway. "It almost seems that they're acting in concert, though—as if there were some kind of plot, where, by prearrangement, everybody knows exactly what to say."

"You're wrong again. You can practically smell a dictatorship or a tyranny, which is the only situation in which almost one hundred per cent of the population will follow the same line through fear of the consequences if they don't. In a situation like that, the people are frightened, unhappy. You can hardly say that's the case on Tunpesh."

"No," Templin admitted, "you couldn't. But, still, you have to admit that the answers we've received so far are just too unanimous—and too sketchy. All agree that Pendleton was a fine fellow; all agree that he had no native friends."

Eckert nodded. "I'll go along with that. And I think it's time we did something about it. Tonight we'll have to start eliminating certain ideas."

He took a small case from their pile of luggage and opened it. Inside was a small, battery-powered box with various dials set on the front and the usual electrodes and nerve probes protruding from the sides and the top.

Templin looked at it with surprise.

"That will be dangerous to use, won't it?"

"It might be more dangerous not to. Time is getting to be a factor and we have to make some progress. We have a safety margin of a sort in that we can erase memories of its use, but the procedure is still risky."

"Who do we use it on?"

"As long as we're going to use it," Eckert said grimly, "we might as well start at the top."

When they had started out, the investigation had seemed fairly simple to Eckert. There were two possibilities—either Pendleton had committed suicide or he had been murdered. Knowing Pendleton's record, the first possibility had seemed remote. A few weeks on Tunpesh had convinced him that the second possibility was also remote. One or the other had to be eliminated. The second would be the easiest.

There were other reasons as well. Templin was still convinced that Pendleton had been killed, and Templin was an emotional man with access to powerful weapons. The question was not what he might eventually do, but when.

The night looked as if it would be another rainy one. It was cooler than usual and dark clouds were scudding across the starlit sky. Eckert and Templin stood in the shadows of the house, watching the dark lane for any casual strollers. Eckert looked at his watch. A few minutes more and Nayova would come out for his evening walk.

Eckert had just started to think longingly of his bed and

the warmth inside his house when the door opened and Nayova appeared in the opening. Eckert held his breath while the
chieftain stood uncertainly in the doorway, testing the night
air, and then let it out slowly when Nayova started down the
lane.

They closed in on him.

"The *menshars* from Earth," he said without alarm. "Is
there something you wish?"

"We would like you to come with us to our house for a
while," Eckert started in.

Nayova looked puzzled. "I do not understand. Would not
tomorrow do as well?"

"I'm afraid it'll have to be tonight."

Nayova was obviously not quite sure of their threat.

"No, I . . ."

Eckert caught him before he touched the ground. Templin
took the rag off the butt of the needle gun, lifted the ruler's
feet, and they disappeared into the brush along the lane.

They would have to sneak back to the house, Eckert knew,
and hope that nobody saw them lugging the unconscious native. He laughed a little grimly to himself. Templin had expected cloak-and-dagger. It looked as if he was going to get
more than his share of it, after all.

Once inside the house, Eckert arranged the electrodes and
the small nerve probes on Nayova, who had come to.

"I am sorry," Eckert said formally, "but we find this necessary. You understand that we have to find out all we can
about Pendleton. We have no choice."

He found it difficult to look the ruler in the face, even with
the realization that this was strictly in the line of duty and
that the chieftain would not be hurt.

"But I have cooperated with you in every way possible!"
Nayova protested. "I have told you everything we know!"

"That's right," Templin said bluntly. "And now we're going
to ask you the same questions."

Nayova looked blank for a moment and then reddened as
he understood.

Templin turned to the dials on the little square box.

"We would like to know," Eckert said politely, "where
you were two weeks ago at this time of night."

Nayova looked surprised. "You know that I was at the
halera, the coming-of-age ceremony. You were there with
me, as my guests. You should assuredly know I was there."

Eckert looked over at Templin, who nodded shortly. It had been a standard question, to test the apparatus.

"Did Pendleton have any enemies here on Tunpesh?"

Nayova emphatically shook his head. "To the best of my knowledge, *menshar* Pendleton had no enemies here. He would have none."

Templin's face showed its disappointment.

"Who were his friends?"

"He had no friends."

Templin glowered angrily, but he said nothing.

Eckert frowned. The same answer—Pendleton had had no enemies and yet he had had no friends.

"Would you say he was well liked here?"

"I would say no."

"Why not?"

A shrug. "It is hard to explain and you would not be able to understand."

"Did somebody here kill Pendleton?"

Eckert could hear Templin suck in his breath.

"No."

"Ask him that again," Templin cut in.

"Did somebody kill Pendleton?"

"No."

"Did Pendleton kill himself?"

A trace of disgust showed on Nayova's face.

"Yes."

"Why?"

"I do not know."

Templin gestured to Eckert to take the box. "Let me ask him." He came around and faced the native. "Why did your people kill Pendleton?"

"We did not kill him. We had no reason to wish him harm."

"Do you expect us to believe that Pendleton killed himself? We knew him better than that."

"You may believe whatever you wish. But men change and perhaps he did. We did not kill him. Such an act would have been repugnant to us."

"I think that's enough," Eckert said calmly.

Templin bit his lip as Eckert touched another dial on the machine. Nayova suddenly jerked, looked blank, and slumped in the chair.

Eckert took off the electrodes. "Help me take him back, will you, Ray?"

They carried Nayova to his house, stayed with him until he showed signs of recovering, and then left.

"Why didn't you use a drug?" Templin demanded.

"Possible allergy or serum reaction. We don't know enough about these people to take chances—they're humanoid, not human."

"They can fool machines, though, can't they?"

Eckert didn't reply.

"All right. I know they can't," Templin said grudgingly. "He was telling the truth all the time, wasn't he?"

Eckert nodded. "I never did think he was lying. They don't seem to be the type; their culture doesn't allow for it."

They were silent for a while, walking quietly in the lanes between the shuttered, seemingly untenanted houses.

"I'm glad," Templin said quietly. "It's off my mind. It's hard to believe that anybody here would . . . deliberately kill somebody else."

Templin's reactions would be worth something now for Eckert to study. They wouldn't be inhibited by his conviction that the natives had murdered his best friend. Just what reactions and emotions he would display, Eckert wasn't sure, nor how Templin's psychology, so similar to Pendleton's, would help solve the problem.

They had eliminated one possibility, but that still left them with the one they had started with.

Why had Pendleton taken the short way out?

A breeze scampered through the open door and played tag with the papers on the desk. Eckert swore without annoyance and calmly started chasing those that had been blown on the floor.

"What did Pendleton have to say in his reports?" Templin sat in the doorway, his eyes barely open. He had begun taking siestas in the early afternoon, after their usual light lunch. It was pleasant to sit on the worn wood and feel the warmth of sun and smell the crisp freshness of the outdoors, or maybe watch the kids playing in the lane, catching the butterflies that floated past in the afternoon air.

"About what you'd expect. Mostly reports on the industry, climate, system of government, and general anthropological information that he thought might prove interesting. As far as I can see, he didn't lack enthusiasm for making the reports. If anything, he grew more enthusiastic as time went on. He practically wrote us treatises on every phase of life on Tunpesh."

Templin's eyes closed all the way.

"Any indication in his reports that he didn't like it here?"

"Just the other way around. Everything points to the fact that he liked the climate, the people, the way they lived."

"I don't blame him," Templin murmured. "This is a lovely place to be. The climate is wonderful, the people are happy, hard-working. The society itself seems to be—perfect. Sometimes you can't help but compare it too damn favorably to Earth."

Eckert shoved the papers to one side and came over to where Templin sat. He felt rather lazy himself. The warmth and sunshine corroded ambition, as it did in most climates like this.

"You know, there isn't any crime here," Templin continued. He laughed to himself. "Except the minor crime wave we caused when we landed here five months ago. No criminals, no villains foreclosing mortgages, no gamblers bleeding the gullible white, and nobody trying to sell gold bricks. I can't get over it."

A butterfly flapped into the sunlight that glistened on his tunic, like a drop of water on a piece of black velvet. It hung there for a moment and then was off, its wings flashing.

Eckert watched it go in a sort of torpor. It was pleasant to relax and slip the leash off your thoughts quietly and see where they took you. Maybe it was a sort of letdown. They had expected six months of danger in a potentially criminal culture, and instead it had been paradise.

As Templin said, you couldn't help but compare it to Earth. No greed, no belligerency, no contempt for the rights of others. No cynicism, no sarcasm, and no trampling crowds in the stores. The little important things . . .

"Where did you go last night, Ray?"

Templin stirred. "A community meeting. Almost like a Quaker meeting. You get up and say what you think. The one last night was about some local government issues. They talked it over, decided what to do, and how much each person should contribute. The original democracy, Ted."

Eckert was wide awake. "I wonder why I wasn't invited." He felt slightly put out that Templin should have been asked to something like that and he hadn't been.

"I wasn't invited," Templin said. "I invited myself."

"Have you noticed," Eckert mused, "we haven't been invited to too many functions lately?"

"They know we're busy," Templin said lazily. "They're too polite to ask us to go some place if they thought we were busy doing something else."

"You like it here, don't you, Ray?"

Templin brushed idly at a marauding mosquito. "It took me pretty long to warm up to it, but I guess I do."

They only had a month left, Eckert knew—a month to do practically nothing but lie in the sun and watch the people. Oh, they could go through the motions of investigating and look over Pendleton's old records and reports, but there was nothing in them of any value.

He yawned and sat down and settled his back against the door frame. It began to look as if they'd never find out why Pendleton had done what he had. And it didn't seem to matter, somehow.

Eckert opened the door slowly. Templin was asleep on the bed, the sunlight lying in bands across his tanned, bare back. He had on a strip of white cloth, knotted at the waist in imitation of what the natives wore.

It was mussed now, and the knot had started to come loose.

He looked a lot healthier than he had when they had first landed. More peaceful, more content. He appeared to have gained ten pounds and shed five years in the last six months.

And now the vacation was over. It was time to go back.

"Ray," Eckert called out to him softly.

Templin didn't stir, but continued his soft and very regular breathing.

Eckert found a book and dropped it on the floor with a thud. Templin woke up, but didn't move.

"What do you want, Ted?"

"How did you know it was me?"

Templin chuckled, as if it were hugely funny. "Riddles yet. Who else would it be? No Tunpeshan would be rude enough to wake somebody up in the middle of a nap, so it had to be you."

"You know what you would have done if somebody had awakened you like that five months ago?"

Templin tried to nod, but was slightly handicapped by the bed underneath him. "I would have pulled my trusty atomgun and plugged him."

Eckert went over to where they kept their luggage and started pulling the boxes out from the wall. "Well, I've got good news for you. A liner just landed to pick us up. They were going through this sector and they got an order from the Service to stop by for us. Some cargo-wallopers will be here in a few minutes to help us with our gear."

"Ted."

Eckert paused.

"Yes?"

"I'm not going back."

"Why not?" Eckert's face had a look of almost clinical curiosity on it.

"Why should I? I like it here. I want to live here the rest of my life."

The pieces began to fall in place.

"I'm not so sure you'd like it, Ray. Not after a while. All your friends are back on Earth. Everybody you know is back there. It's just the novelty of something new and something different here. I've felt that way a lot of times in different cultures and different societies. You'd change your mind after a while."

"Those aren't reasons, Ted. Why should I go back to a world where most of the people are unhappy at some time and a few people all the time? As far as I'm concerned, Tunpesh is my home now, and I don't intend to leave it."

Eckert was fascinated. It was like a case history unfolding right before his eyes.

"Are you sure you would enjoy it here for the rest of your life? Have you made any friends to take the place of those back home?"

"It takes time to become acquainted, even more time to make friends," Templin said defensively.

"You can't desert the Service," Eckert pointed out. "You still have your duty."

Templin laughed in his pillow. "It won't work, Ted. Duty's just a catch word, a jingo phrase. They can get along without me and you know it."

"What about Pendleton, Ray? He died here, you know, in mysterious circumstances."

"Would going back help him any? He wasn't murdered; we know that. And why do people commit suicide? For which one of several thousand possible reasons did Pendleton? We don't know. We'll never know, and if we did know, what good would it do?"

He had changed a lot in six months, Eckert saw.

Too much.

"What if I told you I knew why Pendleton killed himself?" Eckert asked. "And that you would do the same if you stayed here?"

"Don't use it, Ted. It's poor psychology. It won't work."

The pieces made a perfect picture. But Templin was going back whether he wanted to or not. The only difficulty was that, deep underneath, Eckert sympathized with him. Perhaps if he had been younger, less experienced . . .

"Then you won't go back with us?"

Templin closed his eyes and rolled over on his back. "No."

There was dead silence. Templin could smell the piny scent of the woods and feel the warmth of soft sunlight that lanced through the blinds. Some place far away, there was the faint chatter of kids at play, but outside of that it was quiet.

Too quiet.

Templin opened his eyes in sudden alarm. "Ted! Don't!" He caught the gas full in the face and tumbled back on the bed, unconscious.

Eckert opened the hatch to the observation cabin as quietly as he could. Templin was seated on one of the pneumatic couches, staring soberly at a small yellow star in the black sky. He didn't look up.

"It's me, Ray," Eckert said.

Templin didn't move.

"I suppose I owe you an apology," Eckert began, "but I had to gas you to get you to leave. Otherwise you wouldn't have left. And the same thing would have happened to you that happened to Don Pendleton."

"You're sure of that?" Templin asked bitterly.

"Reasonably. You're a lot like Pendleton, you know. In fact, that's why you were selected to go—not so much because you knew him as the fact that psychologically you were a lot like him. We thought that by studying your response to situations there, we would have a picture of what Pendleton's must have been."

Templin didn't want to talk about it, Eckert realized, but it had to be explained to him.

"Do you want to know why Pendleton killed himself?"

Templin shrugged listlessly.

"I suppose we should have seen it right away," Eckert continued. "Any race that is so happy with their way of life that they show no curiosity about strangers, the way they live, or what possessions they have, must have something to be happy about. Tunpesh is something that might happen only once in a thousand civilizations, maybe less, Ray.

"The environment is perfection and so are the people, or at least as near to perfection as it's possible to get. An intelligent people who have as much technology as they desire, living simply with themselves and each other. A fluke of nature, perhaps. No criminals, no insane, no neurotics. A perfect cultural pattern. Tunpesh is a paradise. You didn't want to leave, neither did I, and neither did Pendleton."

Templin turned on him. "So it was paradise. Would it have been criminal if I had stayed there? Who would it have hurt?"

"It would have hurt you," Eckert said gravely. "Because the Tunpeshans would never have accepted you. We're too different, Ray. We're too aggressive, too pushy, too persistent. We're not—perfect. You see, no matter how long we stayed there, we would never have fit in. We lived in a harsh society and we bear the scars of it. Our own environment has conditioned us, and we can't change. Oh, we could try, but it would crop up in little ways. Because of that, the natives could never genuinely like us. We'd never belong. Their own cultural pattern wouldn't allow them to accept us.

"Their cultural pattern is like the Fire and the Sword that were placed outside the Garden of Eden, after Adam and Eve were driven out, to keep it sacrosanct. If you're an outsider, you stay outside. You can never come in."

He paused a moment, waiting for Templin to say something. Templin didn't.

"The natives have a word for it. *Kava*. It means, I suppose, *different*—not necessarily inferior, just different. We should have seen it as time went on. We weren't invited places; they seemed to avoid us. A natural reaction for them, I guess I have to admit."

Eckert cleared his throat huskily. "You see, what happened to Pendleton," he continued awkwardly, "is that he fell in love with paradise, but paradise would have nothing to do with him. By the time three years were up, he knew that he was an outcast in Eden. And he couldn't leave, to come back and try to forget. He was stranded in paradise and had to look forward to spending four more years there as a pariah. He couldn't do it. And neither could you."

He was quiet for a moment, thinking of the cool, scented air and the warm sunshine and the happy kids playing on the grassy lanes.

"I suppose it didn't affect you at all, did it?" Templin asked venomously.

A shadow crossed Eckert's face. "You should know better than that, Ray. Do you think I'll ever forget it? Do you think I'll ever be satisfied with my own culture again?"

"What are you going to do about it?"

"It's dangerous to human beings, Ray. Looking at it brutally, their culture has killed two of our people as surely as if Tunpesh were populated by murderous savages. We'll probably send a larger commission, throw it open to commerce, try to change it."

Templin gripped the sides of the couch, his face strained and tense with anxiety. "What happens to it depends on the report you make, doesn't it?"

"Yes, it does."

"Then make up something in your report. Say the climate is bad for Earthmen. Say anything, but don't let them change Tunpesh!"

Eckert looked at him for a long moment, remembering.

"Okay, Ray," he said slowly. "We'll leave paradise alone. Strictly alone. It'll be put on the quarantine list."

He turned and left.

Behind him, Templin swiveled around in his chair and gazed bleakly at the tiny mote of yellow fading in the blackness of space.

A moment for digression: Probably the most frequently-asked question of a science fiction writer is "where do you get your ideas?" The easiest answer, of course, is "everywhere and anywhere." It shuts off debate . . . but it also begs the question. And it's not very truthful. There *are* specific answers.

One is that, quite simply, editors will assign ideas, frequently their own, to authors to develop. John W. Campbell did this constantly. (One of the more fascinating examples is the background and some of the plot for Robert Heinlein's "Sixth Column." Campbell had at one time written a novella titled "All" under his pseudonym of "Don A. Stuart." When he became editor of *Astounding*, he retired the story since it was impolitic to sell to competing publications and, for whatever reason, he didn't choose to run it himself. Later, he turned the background over to Heinlein. Taken together, "All" and "Sixth Column" make a fascinating study of how the master and his star contributor handled the same theme.)

Other editors, notably those at Ziff-Davis, would have story conferences and assign story ideas that were essentially editor-author collaborations. And some editors copped out completely and let the cover art serve as inspiration. That is, the artist would bring in a cover he had dreamed up on his own and the editor would assign an author to "write a story around the cover." Some good stories have been written this way—notably Algis Burdy's "Who"— but I still think it's idiotic (though I confess I've written stories around covers myself).

Sometimes story conferences and assignments can backfire rather unexpectedly. I once developed a story idea with Bill Hamling when he was editing for Ziff-Davis, wrote it up, and sent it off to Fred Pohl, who was then my agent. Knowing that Bill would probably change whatever title I used, I simply slugged it "Untitled Story" and let it go at that. Unbeknownst to me, John Campbell urgently needed a story of the same length to fill an issue and Fred shipped it over to him. Because he was really pressed for time—or perhaps hated the story, John didn't bother with a title either and ran it as "Untitled Story." (Bill Hamling had every right to complain and I apologized. My apologies weren't very sincere: *Astounding* paid twice as much as Ziff-Davis would have and I needed the money. Besides, it wasn't me, it was my agent. . . . To my surprise, the story was voted second best in the issue.)

I've since written novels on assignment but I look upon the whole process with mixed feelings. If one of your own ideas goes sour, you can drop it. But it's difficult to drop an idea an editor has assigned (and for which he may have paid a hefty advance). Also, you can't avoid the feeling that the editor is looking over your shoulder. And finally, it's simply not *your* idea.

I have the sneaky feeling that little of this applied to Campbell. Other editors tended to assign *plots*. John assigned *ideas* that were conceptual and technical and intriguing in and of themselves. (Shortly before he died, when he was visiting in Chicago, we discussed a story about a black hole. I never did anything with it—somebody else did—but I remember John watching me like a hawk to see if I would take fire from it.)

Which still leaves: where *do* you get your ideas? The answer: from newspapers; from magazine articles, especially those in the semi-technical and technical journals; from doing simple research where you run across a serendipitous bit of information; and, frankly, from reading other people's stories (you may expand on another author's idea, use a different phase of it or develop a facet that he overlooked. In recent years, it's gone so far that some writers—with permission of the original author or his estate—have borrowed whole universes and concepts. Note the novels by the "successors" to both Robert E. Howard and Doc Smith.)

And, naturally, you mine your own experiences and background. "The Santa Claus Planet" was the direct result of my own college minor in anthropology. The story deals with an other-planet variation of the potlatch ritual of the very real Kwakiutl Indians of the Pacific Northwest. It was originally written as an assignment story (the plot and idea were mine, however) for a friend who was editing anthologies of the "best" science fiction stories of the year. He wanted an "original" story, rather than a reprint, to bolster the sales potential of the series. I was proclaimed the year's bright new star and paid a quarter-of-a-cent per word and all the prestige I could eat.

I was, regretfully, at a stage where that was considerable. . . .

The Santa Claus Planet

"I think the town is over this way, sir," Hawsworthy said, his words coming out in little puffs of steam.

Leftenant Harkins waited until there was a brief calm in the flurries of snow whirling about him, then shielded his eyes and stared in the direction that Hawsworthy had pointed. There was a small cluster of lights in the distance—a good two or three snowy miles away, he judged sourly—but it couldn't be anything but the twinkling lights of some primitive village.

He sighed and pulled the collar of his heavy tunic tighter around his neck, then turned for a last look at the *Churchill*, the sleek and shiny line-cruiser bulking huge in the valley a few hundred yards to the rear. Her ports were radiating a cozy, yellow warmth and he could catch glimpses of her officers and enlisted men standing around the brightly bedecked tree in the main lounge. He even fancied that he could hear the strains of *Cantique Noel* and smell the hot, spicy odor of the wassail drifting up on the cold, sharp air.

Christmas Eve . . .

He bit his thin lips in disappointment. Outside in the cold on a fool's errand while inside the *Churchill* the Christmas celebration was just getting started. He had done the best he could in making arrangements with Ensign Jarvis to save him some of the wassail, but knowing Jarvis's own enthusiasm for the monthly liquor ration, they were shaky arrangements at best.

A sudden gust of snow hid the ship and he and Hawsworthy wheeled and started trudging towards the faint glow on the horizon.

It was traditional in the service, Harkins thought, to set the ship down on some hospitable planet for Christmas. Christmas wasn't Christmas without the solid feeling of the good earth under you and the smell of pine and the soft mistiness of snow drifting gently down from the sky.

Naturally, there had been a lot of enthusiasm aboard ship. The commissary had been busy all week filling the ship with the appetizing odors of synthetic roast goose and plum pudding and the pleasant spiciness of fruit cakes. And the car-

83

pentry shop had spent many a hard afternoon building the tree out of fine dowels and daubing it with green paint, just in case they were unable to obtain the genuine article.

Then—only an hour ago, Harkins thought bitterly—the captain had asked to see him and his own personal enthusiasm had collapsed like a pricked balloon.

The captain had discovered that the planet supported a human culture, so it was naturally incumbent on the *Churchill* to send forth a deputation to invite members of the Terran speaking community—if any—aboard to celebrate Christmas with the crew, present the ship's credentials to the powers that might be, and try and arrange for possible planet leave.

And as he had once dabbled in anthropology, the deputation was to be made in the person of Leftenant Junior Grade Harkins. Which meant that he would miss most of the celebration. On top of that, he had drawn Hawsworthy for an assistant. (There was nothing wrong with Hawsworthy, of course, except that he had an amazing talent for making you feel ill at ease and unsure of yourself. He was a twenty-year man and you always suspected that his feelings towards the junior grades were composed more of toleration than respect.)

"It can't be much further, sir. I think I can make out some of the buildings." The lights of the town were considerably nearer now and the rough shapes of small houses had begun to separate themselves from the snow-filled blackness.

A fool's errand, Harkins thought for the twentieth time. The records showed that the people were nothing but primitives, but that hadn't prevented the captain from doing "the decent thing" and sending out a representative anyway. Tradition. The people were probably fish-eaters, and any authority to which he might present the ship's credentials undoubtedly resided in the painted and scarred body of the village witch doctor, probably hiding under his cooking pot right then.

Then they were on the summit of the last hill before the town, gazing down at the village below; a village where the streets were neatly laid out, the houses were a large cut above the usual thatched or skin affair, and primitive arc-lamps were strung across the snowy streets.

Harkins felt uneasy. It wasn't at all as primitive as it should be.

They walked into the seemingly deserted town and had

proceeded a few blocks when Hawsworthy suddenly stopped and pulled out his pistol. "Something's coming, Leftenant."

Harkins's heart rose into his mouth. There was a measured tread of feet down a side street, and a moment later a procession marched into view. Four natives dressed in rich furs were in the van and behind them came an opulently decorated sleigh, pulled by a large, splay-footed animal. The procession halted and four natives in front bowed low.

For the first time, Harkins noticed that they were carrying what were obviously meant to be gifts. Huge, circular sheets of beaten copper with crude designs hammered in them, and hampers containing what looked like carcasses of not-too-recently slaughtered alley cats. The natives straightened up and proffered the gifts, then backed away, obviously expectant.

Harkins accepted the gifts awkwardly, after which there was a long and increasingly heavy silence. Finally a voice within the sleigh spoke.

"Don't just stand there—destroy the gifts, then hand them your pistols."

Harkins gasped. The voice spoke his own tongue excellently.

Hawsworthy chewed his lower lip and looked belligerent. "If we do, sir, we'll be unarmed and at their mercy. I wouldn't advise it."

"Please show yourself," Harkins said to the curtained sleigh.

The curtains parted and a man stepped out. He was plump and betrayed the usual signs of easy living but his eyes were alive and his face showed a familiar ruddiness. The Terran type, Harkins thought, amazed; he showed it distinctly.

"Do as I tell you and nothing will happen to you," the man urged.

"We would like to see your ruler," Harkins said stiffly, thinking of an alternative.

The fat man put his hands on his hips and cocked his head at them. "You're looking at him. The name's Harry Reynolds and I run this planet—at least, this section of it."

Harkins digested this in silence, then awoke to his responsibilities as a representative of the *Churchill* and introduced himself and Hawsworthy.

"You're sure no harm will come of this?"

"My word," Reynolds said expansively.

Harkins pondered for a moment, then flamed the copper shields and the hampers and handed over his pistol.

Hawsworthy did the same. The natives smiled, stripped the cartridges from the pistols, broke the plastic barrels, and finally bowed low and withdrew.

It was then that it occurred to Harkins that things were looking up. The natives were friendly, a Terrestrial was running things, and chances for planet leave looked highly probable.

Then another thought hit him. He turned to Reynolds and saluted. "Sir, the officers and men of the *Churchill* would be highly complimented if you consented to celebrate Christmas with them on board ship."

Reynolds accepted with alacrity and Harkins gestured to the sleigh. "I'd suggest using your sleigh, sir; we'd save time."

Later, seated on the warm cushions of the sleigh and skimming over the countryside, Harkins reflected proudly that his commandeering of the sleigh was a master stroke. Not only was Hawsworthy duly impressed with his quick thinking, but it looked highly possible that they'd get back to the ship before Jarvis had had a chance to consume all the wassail.

It was going to be a pleasant evening at that, he thought, and not the least of its pleasantness was going to be when he pinned Reynolds down and found out just how he happened to be running things.

He looked at Reynolds's ruddy face out of the corner of his eye. There was probably quite a story to it.

Back in the *Churchill*, the junior grades soon had Reynolds surrounded.

"What do you call this planet, Mr. Reynolds?" Jarvis asked, glass in hand. "Something quite different than the numbers and letters the star maps give it, I imagine."

Reynolds ran a finger down the side of his nose and looked thoughtful. "The first few weeks I was here, I thought that I would call it the 'Santa Claus Planet.' "

Jarvis looked puzzled. "The Santa Claus Planet?"

"Yes. You see, the natives had made quite a ceremony out of giving gifts—but that's all part of the story."

Harkins seized the opening. "Tell us about it. Back in the town, you said you ran this section of the planet. I couldn't help but wonder just how you did it."

Reynolds filled his glass again. "You can chalk it up to imagination—and quite a dose of plain, dumb luck. It started about thirty years ago, when I was returning to Canopus from a business trip. My tubes blew and I had to make a forced landing on this planet. Naturally, I was stranded until I could make repairs . . ."

Reynolds groaned and slowly opened his eyes. The cabin seemed to be spinning tightly around him and he fought for control of his stomach, then gave up the struggle and turned on his side and let everything come up. After that, the feeling of nausea gradually passed and the cabin settled down, but it settled at a thirty-degree slant. He vaguely recalled the crash and rolled his eyes slightly to take in all of the cabin. What loose equipment and furnishings there were had been swept down the inclined deck to come to a rest in a broken, jumbled mass against the far bulkhead; he couldn't tell what other damage there might be but thin curls of blue smoke were drifting up from the engine room—the slightly acrid smoke of burning insulation.

But the ship was still whole, he thought grimly, and he was still alive, which was a wonder considering that he had been juggled around the inside of the rocket like a pair of dice in a shaker. He moved one arm experimentally and then the other. They were stiff and sore and blood had dried on a few nasty looking cuts, but no bones were broken.

The feeling of nausea hit him again and he retched, then gathered his courage and staggered to his rubbery legs. The port on the side of the cabin nearest the ground was shattered and fresh, cool air was blowing through the opening. It smelled good and helped clear more of the cobwebs from his head. Inspection of the hatch a moment later showed that it was hopelessly stuck so he found a broken handrail and laboriously battered out the fragments of quartz still in the port, then painfully crawled through and dropped to the grassy ground below.

He lay where he had fallen collecting his strength, then stumbled over to a stream not far from the ship. Half his shirt served as a washrag to help scrub off the grease and grime and clean his wounds; out of the other half he made crude bandages. He was gasping from weariness when he finished and slumped down on the bank to take stock of his situation.

The task of repairing the ship wasn't an impossible one— maybe two weeks, maybe less. In the meantime, he was stranded on the planet.

He found a self-lighter cigarette in his pants and drew in on it, watching the tip turn to a cherry red coal.

Stranded.

But he couldn't have been stranded in a better place, he reasoned. He had crashed in a low, broad valley with the stream running through the center of it. A carpet of grass dotted with the pink of some alien flower covered most of the ground, while surrounding the valley were low hills and forests of huge, fernlike trees. The weather seemed warm and temperate and the sky was a rich, tropical blue, with fleecy shreds of clouds drifting slowly by.

He brushed a lock of thinning black hair away from the bandage wrapped around his head and frowned. According to his star map, the natives were human—probably the degenerate remnants of those who had colonized the planet hundreds of years ago—but friendly.

At least they better be, he thought; there weren't any weapons on board ship to speak of.

The warm sun made him drowsy and he let his thoughts wander where they would. Two weeks here and then off to Canopus where a somewhat shrewish wife and his small, sickly daughter would undoubtedly demand a long and detailed explanation of what had kept him. They would probably refuse to believe a truthful story about blown tubes so he would have to devote a part of his next two weeks to fabricating a wildly implausible and slightly incriminating story that they *would* believe.

But until then, he had two weeks of hard work and solitude ahead of him. In a way, a very pleasant vacation.

He plucked a blade of green grass from the side of the bank and chewed on it for a while. The work could commence tomorrow; he'd have to rest and recuperate today.

He turned on his side and dozed the rest of the day.

The sun had barely risen the next morning when Reynolds was up and inspecting the damage done to the ship. The bottom jets were fused and crumpled, the generators would have to be rewound, and stanchions and handrails and brackets on the inside would have to be welded back in place.

He got a shovel from inside the ship and walked around to the tube assembly, the dew on the grass dampening his canvas work shoes. It might be wise, he thought, to dig a hole under the rear jets, leaving the rocket balanced on a ridge of earth, so he could get at them. That would be the biggest job and the most difficult, and next to the generators, the most important.

He shifted awkwardly in his overalls, then pushed the shovel into the ground, heaved, and threw the dirt over his shoulder. It was rich, fertile looking loam which looked as if it had never been farmed. The people were probably strictly a hunting society . . .

The sun was hot and he found he had to take frequent rests from the digging. He had never been the muscular type in the first place and with his arms as sore as they were, it was tough going. But by noon, he had worked himself into a pit about waist-level and by late afternoon, he was shoulder-deep. He had long since taken off his heavy, twill work shirt and the sweat had soaked into the undershirt and burned into some of the cuts that hadn't healed yet.

There were two feet to go before the tubes would be completely unearthed, but he had to rest. He ached in a million places and blisters had formed, broken, and reformed on his swollen hands. He put the shovel to one side and sank quietly down on the cool dirt.

Five minutes later there was the quiet pad of feet above him and a soft voice said: "We bring presents for the man from the rocket."

He looked up, startled, his hand clutching the shovel for a possible weapon.

There were three of them at the top of the pit. Two of them were alert-eyed, bronzed men, dressed in richly decorated animal hides. They were inspecting him curiously, but not with the curiosity of natives who had never seen strangers before. Reynolds guessed, and rightly, that there had been visitors to the planet in the past.

The third member of the party—the one who had spoken to him and apparently the only one who understood his language—was a rather pretty girl with the soft, rounded features that so many native girls seem to have. He looked at her with more than casual interest, noting that her skirt was of machine-made cloth, probably the bottom half of a *mother hubbard* that wandering missionaries among the stars liked to clothe their heathen charges in. She had cut off the upper half of the garment, apparently preferring the sunshine and freedom.

Reynolds climbed to the top of the pit and made a half bow, then showed that his hands were empty. (What the devil did you do in a case like this?) The men were carrying what he supposed were gifts: thin shields of beaten copper with crude native designs hammered on them, a few blankets made up of thick furs, and baskets full of freshly slaughtered meat that didn't look at all appetizing.

The men set the gifts on the ground in front of them, then stepped back with malicious smiles on their faces. They chattered for a moment to the girl in their native language.

"These are the challenge gifts of my people, the Mantanai," she intoned ritualistically, her face solemn. "We shall return tomorrow to accept what you give in return."

Reynolds had a feeling that he wasn't supposed to benefit by the gifts.

"What do you mean 'challenge gifts?' " he asked.

She looked like she was going to explain, then changed her mind and gave a short shake to her head.

Reynolds felt the tension build up in him. Her attitude confirmed his opinion that he was going to be in for a difficult time.

The girl turned to leave with the men.

"Wait a minute," Reynolds asked softly. "Is there a Father around?"

She shook her head again and Reynolds thought there was a trace of pity in her eyes.

"No," she said. "The good Father has returned to the skies."

He suspected that she didn't mean the Father had left the planet in the usual manner.

"What happened to him?"

She hesitated a moment and he could feel the slow ooze of sweat on his forehead. Behind her, the other two natives were frowning and shaking their heads with impatience.

"He—he didn't win the game of the Giving of Gifts."

Reynolds cooked his supper over a campfire beside the ship but he had lost most of his appetite and didn't eat much. The gifts from the natives were Greek gifts, he thought. There was something ominous about them, something far different than the friendliness that usually prompted gift giving.

He worried about it for a while, then turned into his crude bed of blankets and air mattress. There was a lot of work to be done the next day, natives or no, and he needed his sleep.

He had just started to doze off when he heard the stealthy footsteps of something moving just beyond the dim circle of light cast by the glowing coals of the fire. The sounds came nearer and he pointed his electric torch in the direction of the quiet rustling and flicked the switch.

The girl stood there, blinded by the glare of the light.

"What do you want?" he asked harshly.

She wet her lips nervously. "The good Father was kind to me," she said, almost in a whisper. "You reminded me of him."

Primitive tribes usually had little regard for their women, he thought, outside of the children they might bear or the work they could do in the fields or in making clothing for the men. The Father's kindnesses had apparently made quite an impression on her.

"What's that got to do with you coming here?"

"I thought that I would tell you about the Giving of Gifts," she said. "I thought that you would like to know."

That was damn sweet of her, he thought cynically—then softened a bit. She was probably running quite a risk in coming to him.

"Tell me about it," he said gently.

She sat down beside him, the light from the coals catching the highlights of her body.

"Father Williams used to say that my peole, the Mantanai, were the original capitalists," she started, pronouncing the word uncertainly. "That to us, coppers and furs and grain weren't the means to an end, but an end in itself. That we liked to accumulate wealth merely to play games with it and because it brought—prestige."

She was parroting Father William's words, he realized; they meant little to her but she was confident that they meant a lot to him.

"What kind of games?"

She thought for a minute, trying to find a way to phrase it. "We use our coppers and furs in duels," she said slowly. "Perhaps one chief will give a feast for another and present him with many coppers and blankets. Unless the other chief destroys the gifts and gives a feast in return, at which he presents the first chief with even greater gifts, he loses honor."

He was beginning to see, Reynolds thought. The custom of conspicuous waste, to show how wealthy the possessor was. Enemies dueled with property, instead of with pistols, and the duel would obviously go back and forth until one or the other of its participants was bankrupt—or unwilling to risk more goods. A rather appropriate custom for a planet as lush as this.

"What if one of the chiefs goes broke," he said, explaining the term.

"If the winning chief demands it, the other can be put to death. He is forced to drink the Last Cup, a poison which turns his bones to jelly. The days go by and he gets weaker and softer until finally he is nothing but a—ball." She described this with a good deal of hand waving and facial animation, which Reynolds found singularly attractive in spite of the gruesomeness of the topic.

"What if a stranger like myself is concerned?"

She looked at him sadly. "Then the pride of the tribe is at stake—and the penalty for losing is always death."

He digested this in silence. "Is that the only way they use their wealth?"

She shook her head. "No. They use it for buying a wife or a house or in paying for a grandson."

She started looking anxiously over her shoulder and he could sense her fear of discovery growing, overcoming her memories of the kindnesses of Father Williams. He quickly steered the conversation into other channels and found out, among other things, that Father Williams had given her the Christian name of Ruth. He idly wondered what it would have been if Father Williams had been a Buddhist or a Mohammedan. At length, she arose to go.

"You'll come back again some other night, won't you?" Reynolds asked wistfully, suddenly realizing how lonely it was to be in a dangerous situation and have nobody you could talk to.

She hesitated, then flashed him a quick smile and fled into the darkness.

After she had left, Reynolds mused about his position with a sinking heart. They'd be back tomorrow and he'd have to present them with gifts that they considered superior to what they had given him. But he had nothing extra, nothing that he could actually spare.

The only solution—and it was only a stop-gap solution, he realized somberly—was to gradually strip the ship and hope that he had her fixed and ready for flight before the deadly game had reached its climax.

The native representatives and Ruth were back the next day, along with a large crowd of curious onlookers. Reynolds waited inside the ship until they had begun to grow restless, then stepped out carrying his presents.

But there was a ritual to be followed first. He had built a bonfire earlier that morning and he now lighted it. Then he dragged forth the furs and the hampers of meat and the coppers that had been given to him the previous day. He faced the crowd and held up the meat contemptuously, then flung it on the fire. The representatives flushed, but there was an approving murmur from the crowd. The furs he looked at scornfully, then tore the stitches where they had been sewn together and tossed them into the flames. The sheets of beaten copper, which he had previously weakened with acid, he broke into small pieces over his knee and cast them after the furs. The crowd roared approval but Reynolds had no illusion as to their temper. They liked a good "game" but they had no doubt as to what its conclusion would be.

He gestured to Ruth to come over and translate for him to the two red-faced representatives. his voice was loud enough so the crowd could catch the scorn in it, though they didn't understand the words.

"Tell them that the Mantanai bring children's gifts, that they, are not fit to accept; that their tribe must indeed be poor if this is all they can afford. Tell them the gifts I shall give them will make theirs look like the castoffs of beggars."

Then he started enumerating his own gifts in turn. One air mattress, two wool blankets, a chair of stainless tubular steel. He hesitated. There wasn't a sound from the crowd, so he continued adding to the pile. A white twill space uniform, a chest of exquisite silver he had meant as a conciliatory gift for his wife, and a set of pale, translucent pottery he had picked up on Altair. The crowd was murmuring now, impressed. Finally, with a show of disdain, he threw on a sleek, black jacket of heavy, shiny leather.

Once again the crowd roared approval, then started to drift away. Ruth nodded slightly; for the moment he had won. But only for the moment.

He worked furiously all afternoon and long into the night, his welding torch a bright spot of white in the blackness. How much time he had left, he didn't know. But it wouldn't be much.

The next morning he was awakened by the clamor of the crowd outside the rocket. The natives and a sober-faced Ruth were waiting for him, along with a file of men carrying heavy bundles in their arms.

The challenge gifts for the day had arrived.

It was a week since he had crashed on the planet, Reynolds thought jitterily, and despite working practically every waking hour, the job of repairing the ship was still only half done.

And the deadly game had progressed apace.

Everything not absolutely essential to the operation of the ship had gone. Stanchions, railings, ladders—every bit of shiny, glittering metal that he had thought might appeal to the native eyes as being of value. And then all the dishes, the linens, his voco-writer, and most of his clothing had followed. All delivered to the property-crazy natives who had looked them over curiously, then destroyed them to show how worthless the items were in comparison with their own wealth.

And in return, what had he done? How many coppers and furs and blankets had he been forced to destroy? And it meant nothing to the natives because the planet was so lush that there was much, much more where that had come from.

It was the contents of his ship against the resources of a planet and there wasn't the slightest doubt as to how it would turn out.

"I've stripped the ship," he said quietly.

Ruth moved closer to the fire, the yellow light playing on her smooth, tan skin.

"I know," she said. "You've lost the game."

He couldn't have done much better, though, he thought grimly. He had played it out with what he had as well as he could, analyzing the native sense of values so he had some idea of what they attached worth to.

"When will they come for me?" he asked dryly.

She was staring into the fire, the leaping flames reflected in her green eyes.

"Tomorrow, maybe the next day. And then next week you will be nothing but . . ." She left the sentence unfinished and gave an expressive shudder instead.

Reynolds felt a little sick with fear. There was no way out. If he ran away, he would be running away from his ship and all chance of ever getting home. His chances of surviving alone on the planet would be slim anyway.

"My father will be here tomorrow to watch," Ruth said.

"Your father?"

She showed her teeth. "My father. The chief, the wealthiest man in the village."

They were all turning out, he thought, to watch Reynolds entertain at the big celebration.

Then he caught the look on her face and tried to forget his own troubles. She wasn't having an easy time of it, risking her life to give him information and do what little she could for him.

"How did Father Williams ever get into this mess?" he asked.

"When he first came here," she said, "there was a big sickness. Father Williams helped the Mantanai and my father let him clothe me and teach me your language. But after a few years they forgot and made Father Williams play the game of the Giving of Gifts." She paused, and then repeated: "He was very kind to me."

If he ever got out of it alive, Reynolds thought, he'd build a monument someplace to the memory of Father Williams.

The clearing around the ship was jammed the next morning, natives of all shapes and sizes jockeying for position to see Reynolds' final humbling and open admittance of the wealth of their tribe. As interested as brokers on the floor of the stock exchange watching the quotations on the board, Reynolds thought dryly. He wondered how some of the natives would do if they were suddenly transferred to his own society. With their lust for wealth and shrewdness at manipulating it, they would probably own the universe within a year.

As usual, he had a bonfire all ready to light. Then he made a great show of stacking the mounds of coppers and furs and tanned skins and the hampers of food; probably enough to feed and clothe the village for a month, he reflected.

"The people of the Mantanai are mighty," he intoned solemnly, Ruth translating, "and their feats at trapping the *arapai* are sung in hunting songs passed from father to son." He picked up several of the thick, luxurious furs lying on one of the piles. "But these cannot be the pelts of the *arapai*; rather, they are the thin and smelly hides of the wood rat." And he threw the pelts scornfully into the flames, following them up with the others in the stack. The crowd "oohed" and Reynolds knew the chief's face was burning.

He picked up one of the huge sheets of copper next.

"I have heard tales of the mighty value of the *Copper-of-Many-Suns,* and have heard its praises from many throats. But why then, did you not bring it to me? Why this ugly imitation that would not fool a child of six, this piece of hammered *hunswah*?" He broke it into pieces along the lines etched by acid, and consigned it to the flames. The *Copper-*

of-the-Autumn-Feast and the *Copper-of-the-Laughing-Waters* followed.

It was forty minutes later when he had finally thrown the last of the hampers of food into the oily flames, to the approval of the crowd.

Then the chief was striding towards him, magnificent in his richly decorated furs. Ruth trailed after him, her face calm but her eyes showing fright.

"You have destroyed the mighty coppers and the soft skins of the *arapai*," the chief said silkily, "but they were wealth of no great importance. You, perhaps, have gifts that would put these to shame, gifts that will show your might and your own great wealth."

He was faintly sarcastic, knowing full well that Reynolds had stripped his ship.

"I have," Reynolds said calmly, catching the startled look in Ruth's eyes. He pointed to a pile of goods just outside the port of the rocket that he had spent most of the night assembling. "Succulent and tasty foods, breads and meats that will last your tribe for many days, and a machine that will take the basest of materials and turn them into the choicest of delicacies."

The pile included all the provisions he had had on board, including his synthetic food machine.

As before, the crowd good-naturedly shouted their approval and left, knowing that the climax had merely been postponed another day or so.

After they had gone, Reynolds could feel the fingers of fear grip his heart once more. There was no way back now, except the slim chance that Ruth might be able to help him restock on the sly with native foods.

The day was a cloudy one, an excellent day for working on the rocket. The clouds cut the enervating heat of the sun and Reynolds felt filled with a new enthusiasm. Even the odor of burning grease, fired by the heat of his welding torch, smelled good to him. He was a day away from finishing his repairs; another twenty-four hours and he would be on his way to Canopus with an explanation for his delay that was so bizarre it was almost bound to be believed.

He had finished with one of the last strips on a firing tube and was just reaching for another clay-covered welding rod, when he spotted the procession coming down the valley. The chief and the two stern-faced representatives and Ruth. And, as always, the thrill-seeking crowd.

Only twenty-four more hours, he thought agonizedly, and that was to be denied to him! One more turn of the planet's axis and he would have been gone . . .

"You are to go to my father's house for the next feast," Ruth said heavily. "They are planning it to be the last one."

He dropped his welding torch and made ready to follow Ruth to the village. There was no chance of changing for dinner, he thought grimly, with only one pair of pants left to him. All his other clothing had gone the way of "gifts."

The chief's house was an elaborate, thatched affair with a large circular opening in the roof. Beneath this opening was the open fireplace, black with the ashes of many fires. Currently there was another fire in it, roasting the huge haunches of meat for the feast and broiling the tubers buried in the coals around its periphery.

The feast was an elaborate one to which, apparently, the entire village had deen invited. The enclosure was packed with hot, sweating natives whose eyes were glued on every mouthful of food that Reynolds took and every move he made.

The condemned ate a light meal, Reynolds thought, *and he didn't enjoy a single bite of it.*

The interminable meal and entertainment finally came to a halt and the chief raised his arms for silence. At his signal, a dozen of the young men in the hut disappeared and came back bearing the cartons of supplies and the food machine that had been Reynolds' "gift" a few days before.

"The stranger is mighty," the chief said solemnly, "and has shown that he possesses great wealth. But, alas, his wealth is as nothing to that of the Mantanai." One of the men threw a carton on the flames and Reynolds watched it puff up in smoke. "It is as the dew in the morning, compared to the waters in the ocean." Another carton. "The number of people in this village compare to the blades of grass in the valley."

It was insane, Reynolds thought; a cultural mania that apparently would go to any lengths. A fanatical, perverted capitalism run wild.

The last of the cartons had been consumed in the fire and the food machine reduced to twisted metal when the chief turned to Reynolds.

"It is now our turn to show the might of the Mantanai, the great springs of wealth of our people."

Again the twelve young men disappeared and came back hauling the usual variety of gifts, but this time in an incredible profusion. An exclamation went up from the crowd that quickly dwindled to awed silence as the chief enumerated the gifts.

"The furs of a hundred *arapai*, caught in the prime period of spring, switched and tanned with the gentlest of willow bough . . . the *Copper-of-the-Many-Winters* . . . the *Copper-of-the-Endless-Snows* . . . twenty-two hampers of the plumpest and most perfect of fowls . . . the *Copper-of-the-Wild-Crows* . . . three hampers of the reddest of wood-berries, noted for their succulence and flavor . . ."

The mere enumerating took half an hour and by the time he was finished, the center of the hut was packed with the hampers and furs and the reddish wheels of copper.

The chief finished and turned triumphantly to Reynolds.

"What have you to offer now, stranger? It is your turn for the Giving of Gifts!"

Ruth finished translating by his side and sat down on the floor beside him.

"I have nothing to offer," Reynolds told her in a low voice.

"We are finished then," she said softly.

Now that he had finally reached the climax, Reynolds felt too tired to feel fear. "Say a prayer for me and Father Williams," he said in a dull voice.

She shrugged faintly. "We will say one together."

The way she said it made him glance at her, startled. "What do you mean?"

She laughed softly. "Because we shall be together. They know that I have been helping you. While you have been playing the game, I have been safe. But now that you have lost, whatever happens to you will happen to me."

The crowd was ominously still, waiting for the climactic moment when Reynolds and Ruth would be seized and forced to drink of the Last Cup. The chief was even ready to motion to his aides to seize them, when Reynolds got to his feet and strode to the center of the room.

He stared bitterly at the surprised crowd for a moment, then spat on the nearest copper and hurled it into the fire.

"The gifts of the Mantanai are as the gifts of small children," he said loudly. "The wealth of old women."

He kicked through the assembled gifts like a small cyclone, pulling at the furs and edging the hampers towards the fire, until at last the huge fire had spread to twice its original circumference and the flames had begun to crisp the thatch around the hole in the roof and blister the natives closest to the fire.

When he finally stopped, the crowd was watching him in expectant stillness, waiting for his offer.

"I offer in turn," he said slowly, "a gift of the house of many fires, the arrow of shining metal that voyages among the heavens; my rocket."

There was a roar of astonishment and heads bobbed in eager approval.

He had won again, Reynolds thought weakly, but the comedy was in its last act.

Ruth came to see him early the next morning and they found a secluded spot on the bank of the stream, not far from the now guarded rocket.

"You were very brave," she said.

He resisted an urge to be modest.

"I know."

"My father was very much surprised."

"I rather suspected that he would be," Reynolds said indifferently.

She was quiet for a moment, staring intently into the waters of the stream.

"Will you be sorry not to go back?"

"Of course," he said automatically, then began to give it some thought. Would he be sorry about not going back? If he stayed away, he would be taken for dead and insurance would amply provide for his family. And being provided for was all that they had wanted of him anyway.

Besides, the people here weren't bad people, despite their twisted outlook on matters of property.

"Well, now, I don't know," he added thoughtfully. "Perhaps after a while I could learn to forget . . ."

She laughed and then asked: "Will you like being a chief?"

He hunched himself up on one elbow and stared at her questioningly. She wasn't smiling any more.

"You will be a chief soon," she said. "At least for several days."

"How do you mean?"

She gestured at the village and the surrounding land. "They will destroy the rocket this afternoon; then all this will be yours as their last gift."

He felt expansive. "That means I've won, then, doesn't it?"

She shook her head. "You will own the village and land, but only for a while."

It was a very clever idea he thought, suddenly no longer appreciating the beautiful day or Ruth's company. They would give him title to the village and all the lands of the tribe, and there the game would end. Since he was unable to return an even more worthy gift, the remaining portion of the custom would be carried out, during the performance of which he would automatically become an absentee landlord, so to speak, and the property would all revert back to the original owners.

The game was surely at an end. He couldn't very well destroy their "gift" or give them something in return; he was a bankrupt.

He was admiring their landscape and the beautiful stream and the fine tropical weather with a sort of sickly enjoyment, considering it was probably the last time he would be able to do so, when the idea struck him. Why not? What had he to lose?

"How much time have we left, Ruth?"

She looked up at the sun. "Not long, perhaps a few of your hours."

"That's time enough." He grabbed her wrist and then ran downstream, to a small cul-de-sac along the bank, not far from the ship.

The drums of lubricating oil—an even half dozen—were still where he had cached them, to prevent any possible fires when he had been welding on the ship. He found a rock and pounded the spout of one until it broke and the oil was free to gush out, then turned the drum on its side and started rolling it rapidly along the bank, the oil spilling out on the grass and spreading over the calm waters of the stream.

By the time the few hours were up, Reynolds had finished with the last of the drums of oil and was ready to receive the chief and the thrill-seekers from the village.

"The wealth of the Mantanai is great."

(There was a pounding from within the rocket as natives cheerfully hammered the generators and the coils and the delicate thrust machinery with rocks and crude metal bars.)

"The wealth of the Mantanai is as the sands on the beach."

(There was a shaking and rattling sound from the rocket as the delicate meters and instruments were pounded to fragments of glass and metal.)

"The wealth of the Mantanai is as boundless as the stars in the heaven."

(There was a hissing noise as the huge bonfire was lit in the control room.)

Reynolds watched the destruction of the rocket calmly; he had accepted its ultimate fate for what seemed a long time now. But his turn was coming.

After a long and elaborate ceremony, Reynolds was gifted with the village and the lands surrounding it and presumably the people in it. Then he stepped forward with a lighted torch in his hands.

"The lands of the Mantanai are as the egg of the vulture: worthless. A poor land, with a poor people. See, I think little of it!" and he cast the torch at a wet spot on the ground.

The wet spot flared into flame that became a rapidly twisting snake of fire, leading down to the stream. A moment later, the waters were thick with flames and oily, black smoke.

It looked like Reynolds was indeed bent upon the destruction of the land.

The chief's face was white. "The stranger really means this?"

Reynolds nodded grimly and the first of the drums that he had cached behind the village went up in a roar and a gush of flame. The assembled natives paled. Another drum went up.

"We shall be killed!" the chief cried, his eyes rolling white.

Reynolds smiled. "The property of the Mantanai and the Mantanai themselves are as nothing."

Another drum.

"But you, too, shall die!"

Reynolds shrugged. "My last gift. I knew you wouldn't want to ascend into the skies without taking me along."

The chief suddenly knelt and kissed Reynolds's calloused feet. "The wealth of the stranger is mighty; that of the Mantanai is small and insignificant." His face was terror stricken. "The stranger has won the game!"

The last of the drums went up with a loud explosion.

"Perhaps," the chief pleaded, "the wealth of the stranger is so great that he can overlook our own small lands and village?"

They were learning humility at a late date, Reynolds thought. But he nodded solemnly and extended his hands toward the flaming oil barriers around the village. There were no more sudden gushes of flame and gradually the oil on the stream burned out.

He had won, Reynolds thought shakily, won on a bluff with practically no time to spare. Another ten minutes and the flames would have died by themselves, exposing his deception.

But he was still stranded, and stranded now for the rest of his life. There were compensations, of course, chief among which was the fact that he would be spared his unhappy homecoming on Canopus.

And this planet was comfortable, the weather was nice. And he had always been the comfort-loving sort, anyway.

And then there was Ruth.

"About the girl Ruth," he said to the Chief.

The chief's face immediately grew stern. "She interfered with the game of the Giving of Gifts. She will have to take the Last Cup."

Reynolds was aghast.

"But look here, I own the village and all the lands surrounding it! I . . ."

The chief shook his head. "It is tradition." Then his face grew sly. "But perhaps if the stranger was willing to consider a gift, the girl could be spared."

There wasn't any doubt as to what he was driving at.

"What do you want?"

Firmly. "The village and lands to revert to their owners."

Later, on the bank of the stream, Ruth leaned her head in the crook of his arm and gazed dreamily at the sky.

"You know why you won, do you not?"

"Certainly. They were afraid they were going to lose all their property."

She shook her head. "Partly. But mostly because you were willing to lose your life, your last gift as you said. They could never have matched it."

He nodded vaguely, not too much interested, and told her his plans for the future and just where she fitted into them. He should have seen long ago, he thought, that her efforts to help him hinged on more than just the past kindnesses of Father Williams.

She didn't reply to his final question.

He flushed, thinking that possibly his conclusions had been all wrong.

"You forget," she said softly. "The bridal price."

He lay back on the bank, his head whirling. With the reversion of the village and lands back to the tribe to save Ruth's life, he was broke. He had no property of his own.

He had won his life—and hers—he thought, but he had finished as a bankrupt in the most brutally capitalistic society that nature had ever created, without even the bridal price for the woman he loved!

Reynolds finished the story, and sipped the last of the wassail in his cup.

"Then when we gave those natives our guns," Harkins said, "it was doing essentially what you had done. Short circuiting the ceremony of the Giving of Gifts by offering our lives, the ultimate gift, the one that couldn't be topped."

"Essentially," Reynolds agreed, "though that's a simplification."

"I don't understand," Jarvis cut in, puzzled. "Harkins here says that the town has been considerably modernized. How was that accomplished?"

Reynolds swirled the last few drops of liquor in his glass and watched the small whirlpool thoughtfully.

"I'm a comfort-loving man myself, and as I became more wealthy and consequently gained more power in the village council, I saw to it that my own ideas for civic improvement were carried out." He started looking around for the wassail bowl. "Quite simple, really."

There was a short silence, leaving an opening for the strains of *Good King Wenceslas* and *Silent Night* emanating from a small group of overly-merry carolers in another corner.

Harkins looked Reynolds slowly up and down and thought to himself that the man was lying like a rug. There were gaps in his story big enough to run the *Churchill* through.

"I was wondering, Mr. Reynolds," he said. "You had to give back the village and lands to save the girl's life." (The way Harkins phrased it, he obviously didn't approve of Reynolds taking up with the native girl, but that was neither here nor there.) "And that left you as poor as the proverbial churchmouse. Just how did you gain your wealth and influence?"

"I worked a full year," Reynolds said, "before I earned Ruth's bridal price. Even at that, her bridal price wasn't great, less than that of some of the other belles of the village.

(Their tastes in feminine beauty weren't the same as ours, you understand.")

"I don't quite see what bearing that has on it," Harkins said stiffly.

Reynolds felt around in the folds of his cloak, then passed over a simple drawing to Harkins. It was a crude line drawing of a plump, pleasant-faced woman surrounded by her family.

"I think I told you before, that the natives also used their wealth in paying for their grandsons. That is, a father-in-law would pay a hundred percent interest on the bridal price his daughter's husband had given him on the birth of his first grandson. Two hundred percent for the second child and four hundred percent for the third, doubling each time. Now most of the Mantanai don't care much for many children, but Ruth and I had always thought that we would like a large family. And Ruth's father, you remember, was the wealthiest man in the village."

Harkins was staring open-mouthed at the drawing, counting the number of children and frantically doubling as he went along.

"Of course, a good deal of luck was involved," Reynolds said expansively. "Fifteen children—all boys!"

As years go, 1951 had a lot to recommend it. Playing on broadway were Tennessee Williams's *The Rose Tattoo*, *I Am a Camera*, the dramatization of Christopher Isherwood's Berlin stories (it was eventually to become *Cabaret*), *The King and I*, and a dramatization of Arthur Koestler's *Darkness At Noon*. People were reading *The Caine Mutiny*, *Catcher in the Rye*, *From Here to Eternity*, and *The Sea Around Us*. In movies, it was *An American in Paris*, *The African Queen*, and *A Streetcar Named Desire*. (Just in case you think everything was quality, the hits in pop music were "Come On A My House," "Kisses Sweeter Than Wine," and Johnny Ray warbling "Cry" and "Little White Cloud that Cried." The more things change, etc.)

Japan signed a peace treaty, the state of war with Germany was declared at an end, CBS broadcast the first commercial color TV program, transcontinental dial telephone service began on an experimental basis, and a reactor testing station in Idaho generated the first electricity from atomic power.

I told you 1951 had a lot going for it . . .

Unfortunately, on a personal (and otherwise) basis, there was a lot *not* to recomend it. For one thing, I was discovering that I was not a prolific writer. Sometimes a short story took a day and a night; other times it took a month. I once did a novel—which didn't sell—in about three weeks. (I re-read it the other day; it was just about what you might expect of a novel written in three weeks.) In addition, my agent was having financial troubles and as a consequence, so was I. There was even a brief period when somebody could have bought my entire collection of science fiction incunabula for $500.

And then, suddenly, it didn't matter. We had become deeply involved in Korea. U.S. forces arrived at the Yalu river and Chinese volunteers responded by crossing it in droves. MacArthur was relieved by Truman ("Old soldiers never die; they just fade away . . . I now close my military career and just fade away"—well, almost, anyway) and a jittery Washington was suddenly uncertain whether or not this was the Big One.

One of the results was that reservists were abruptly called back into service. I had joined the "inactive" reserve—"we'll call you only after we call everybody else"—on being discharged after World War II. I was now to regret my patriotic folly. I received seventeen copies of "orders to report" and once again caught the train for Great Lakes. The physical consisted of a doctor who looked like a greengrocer, ichorstained smock and all, asking a group of us if we had any disabilities. We all raised our hand. Three days later, I was hanging over the rail of a rust-bucket sailing out of Norfolk. (Along with me were one poor soul who had had three weeks to go for an engineering degree, and an elderly radioman whose son was in the Air Force, whose daughter was in the WACS and whose wife was rolling bandages for the Red Cross. Washington had really panicked.)

I was to be gone for something like two years and though I took along a portable typewriter, there wasn't going to be much opportunity for writing.

One of the last stories written before leaving was "The Hunting Season," which ran as the lead story in the November *Astounding*. (I missed out on the cover; that was devoted to an article on the filming of George Pal's version of "When Worlds Collide.") I liked the story; it was much more of an action story than anything I had done in the past, and it was well-received.

Another digression here: An author may find himself most comfortable in writing stories of a particular length. Some writers may only write short stories, or concentrate their major efforts in that field (Ray Bradbury and Harlan Ellison, for two examples). Others discover they're more compatible with longer lengths. (Bob Heinlein, though he has done short stories that I envy, hasn't written one for years.) With "The Hunting Season," I started to try my hand at longer lengths and found them both easier and more fun to write. There was more room to develop plot and character, and certainly more room for a chase.

I'm fond of "The Hunting Season" for another reason beside its action content: To a degree, it allowed me to combine two genres in one—science fiction and the mystery story. I don't know if Howard Browne ever read it but if he did, I'll bet he liked it. . . .

The Hunting Season

The Warders strutted up and down,
And kept their herd of brutes,
Their uniforms were spick and span,
And they wore their Sunday suits,
But we knew the work they had
been at,
By the quicklime on their boots.

"The Ballad of Reading Gaol,"
Oscar Wilde

David Black was afraid.

He had tried to control it but he knew it showed in the glistening shine on his pale face, in the nervous jump of his cheek muscles, and in his restless pacing back and forth on the faded rug, alternating between the rumpled bed and the worn writing desk, with stops every few minutes at the soot-streaked window to note the position of the setting sun.

It was late afternoon. An hour or so more and the hunting season would begin.

He crossed over to the bed and sat down. He was afraid, he thought, like so many others must have been. Afraid with the fear that showed in the sudden palsy of your hands, the fear you could smell in the sweat that soaked your clothes.

But the State had promised to review his case, he thought. And when they did, there wasn't any doubt that he would get a reprieve. The State, in its benevolence, would call him back and restore his rights as a citizen. Perhaps they would reprimand him for having expressed his thoughts as he had, but it would go no further.

The thought cheered him somewhat. The State would rectify its error and that would be that. But they would have to hurry—

He forced it from his mind. The noises from the street drifted through the partially open window and he listened attentively, sorting them out and identifying them in his mind.

There was the honking wail of the conveyances-for-hire, the cries of the newsprint vendors, and the mumble of the early evening crowd, looking for a happy time in the hot and steaming heart of the city.

The noises and cries of the human jungle: the jungle that he was soon going to have to hide in.

He lay back on the bed, his head raised a little by the pillow, and stared at his room. It was neo-American, early Western Civilization period; a relatively shabby room, even by twentieth century standards, equipped with a primitive bed with protesting springs and gray linen worn to the thickness of tissue, a wooden writing desk with deep scratches on the top, and the usual floral patterned wallpaper that was peeling in spots. There was no ventilation and no breeze—the curtains hung stiffly by the open window—and the room was filled with the muggy heat of summer. Outside the window, the red neon sign of the candy shop just below winked on and off, first suffusing the room with a reddish glow and then fading off into blackness.

The room wasn't essentially different from a monk's cell of the middle ages, he thought. But for what he had been able to pay, he couldn't have expected anything better.

His hand automatically felt in the pocket of his pants and came out with a leather billfold. There were cards in it that gave him a synthetic identity, good for at least the three days of the hunting season, and a few green money bills of small denominations, barely enough to live on for that length of time. He moistened his thumb and started to count the few bills, then went through the pieces of silver.

He had just finished when there was a knock on the door.

He stiffened and shot a glance towards the window. It was dusk and the street illumination bulbs had been turned on, but a pale glow still lingered in the west. A half hour of grace remained. Reed must be paying him an early visit before the hunt, not an unusual thing to do. He had done it himself upon occasion.

He got up from the bed and brushed his damp black hair back from his forehead, then opened the door.

Reed stood smiling in the doorway, wearing the usual uniform of the hunt: an all-black, finely tailored suit of the particular time period the hunt was being held in, with a thin red thread woven in around the collar and the cuffs. The black of the suit represented the web of the huntsman, the

red the trail of the hunted. Reed himself was a tall, somewhat
thin man, with tightly compressed lips and a hungry looking
face.

"You still have half an hour, David," he said. "I didn't
think you'd object to seeing me before the hunt begins." His
voice was husky and well-modulated, studiously polite.

Black smiled somewhat hesitantly. "I don't believe I have
any choice," he said, standing to one side.

Reed came in and eased his light frame into the straight
backed chair by the writing desk. "That's right," he said,
"you don't." He settled back in the chair, making sure the
crease in his pants cut over his knees correctly, and looked
the room over casually, paying special attention to the
rumpled bed and the well-filled ash tray on the bed table.
"Afraid, David?" His voice was tinged with mock concern.

Black felt a growing sense of shock. He didn't know exactly what he had expected; perhaps a *you-and-I-know-this-
is-all-a-mistake* attitude, or an expressed hope of stringing the
hunt along until a reprieve arrived from the State. But Reed
was treating him like any other quarry, as if he had every in-
tention in the world of carrying the hunt through to its logical end.

"Just nervous," Black lied, his face fading to a chalky
white. "I've had too much experience with the hunts to be
frightened."

Reed smiled bleakly. "I like your spirit, the hunt promises
to be that much more entertaining. But don't forget that all
your experience happens to be on the other side." He paused
a moment for the effect, then asked casually: "Do you have
any idea how many citizens have signed up as huntsmen?"

Black resisted an impulse to ask; Reed would undoubtedly
answer his own question.

"Close to five hundred! Think of that, five hundred!" Reed
chuckled pleasurably. "You see, it was the lure of experienced game that brought them out."

Black stared blindly out of the window, not seeing anything beyond the pane of glass and not bothering to reply to
the voice at his back.

"Considering that you're a traitor to the State, you haven't
been treated too badly," Reed continued sharply. "You're
much better off than if we had held the hunt in sixteenth century Spain during the Inquisition or perhaps ancient Rome
during the reign of Caligula. You may even like it here dur-

ing the brief period of the hunt. It's a fairly civilized culture, at least in a material sense."

"Nothing has come of my petition to the State for another hearing and a reprieve, has there?" Black asked, trying to keep his avid interest from showing in his voice.

Reed shrugged. "I shouldn't expect one, if I were you. For myself, I think it rather brazen for a traitor to ask for one."

Another shock. "I don't consider myself a traitor, Reed."

"You questioned State theory, and you questioned it in public," Reed pointed out. He smiled. "You should learn to control your tongue."

It was becoming clearer by the moment, Black thought with despair. He had voiced objections to the hunts several times, but each time he had thought he had voiced them on a more or less personal basis, to a few private acquaintances. But there were cash rewards for those who denounced traitors to the State, and one of them had probably made capital of his utterances. And that one—though his accuser's name had never been mentioned at the trial—was probably Joseph Reed.

With sudden mental savagery he clung to his belief that the State would review his case and grant him a reprieve. They had to! In every other way, he had been an outstanding citizen—

There was a short silence and then he asked Reed suddenly: "You've studied up on this civilization, haven't you?"

"The mark of the experienced hunter, David."

Black stalked to the window and looked out into the neon-lit darkness. "I have only a few moments left," he said shortly. "I would like to spend them alone."

Reed stood up, ready to leave. "You know the rules?"

"You know I do."

Reed opened the door, then paused, his face thoughtful. "You have your choice of the way in which you want the hunt to end."

The quarry was always allowed that much of a choice, Black thought.

"From the front. One burn, right between the eyes."

. . Reed caught the implication and laughed. "Don't try to embarrass me, David." Then he was gone.

He still had twenty minutes to go before sundown.

Black locked the door of the room, then went into the not-too-clean bathroom, and stripped, stuffing his clothes into a paper bag. He nearly scalded himself before he found how the knobs for the shower worked, then he soaked himself thoroughly, sudsing every inch of his body with a cheap, deodorant soap.

There was a full length mirror on the inside of the closet door and he inspected himself briefly before going on to the next step. He was of medium height and fairly muscular, with the rugged, hard look that heavy physical exercise had given him. His face was broad and not too handsome, falling more into the trite classification of another time as "clean cut."

There was little he could do about his skeletal framework, he thought, or the little mannerisms of speech and action that were peculiarly individual, peculiarly his. But there were some things that could be changed. He hunched his shoulders together and let them slope forward a little, then practiced a slightly mincing gait in front of the mirror. It wasn't altogether satisfactory, and there would probably be lapses as he forgot himself, but at least it was different from his usual stride.

He turned from the mirror to one of the dresser drawers, took out a small jar, and applied a very thin coating of its contents to his body, working from his face down. A moment later he was one shade lighter. A few snips with the scissors gave his hair a shaggy but short look, and a little wax altered the lines of his face.

The dresser yielded a change of clothing complete from shorts to a carefully rumpled, cheap suit. He dressed and topped off the result with a pair of thick-lensed glasses. The results, when viewed in the mirror, weren't bad. The student type, a variety common to this particular age.

Then he began to feel a growing sense of hopelessness. The shower and the bath with the strong soap would throw off any mechanical sniffers that Reed might have—but only for a few hours. After that, the odor of the soap would wear off and the sweaty, telltale smell of his own body would replace it. And his change of clothing and facial disguise would fool only the most incompetent of huntsmen.

But even if he fooled only one, it would be worth it.

He placed the paper bag with his clothes in it in the metal wastepaper basket and flamed it with his Williams. There was a puff of smoke from the basket and the slight odor of scorched paint.

At least, he reflected, he had had sense enough to make

plans in case the State's reprive was delayed or late in coming.

Five minutes to go—

He could feel the moisture start to bead on his forehead again. Outside was the jungle of some four million people who would live their shallow lives and go their insignificant ways the next three days in total ignorance of the five hundred huntsmen among them. The five hundred eager citizens of his own time, all experts in the hunt, all carefully schooled in the culture of this century, all tensely waiting for the moment when they would start to comb the city for him.

And Reed himself was a relentless hunter, the kind who liked to toy with the quarry, who let the quarry think he had a chance up to the very last.

Black shivered, recalling the several hunts that he and Reed had been on together. But that was a long time back, when he had still enjoyed the favored rank of citizen; before he had been denounced to the State, convicted in the trial, and consequently made available as a quarry for the hunt.

It must be only a question of time before his reprieve was forthcoming!

He looked out at the dirty granite buildings, steaming in the summer heat, and felt a momentary touch of nostalgia, an intense longing for the neat and orderly existence he had recently led, for the youthfulness that had never questioned Authority, and the regimented thinking that had never allowed misfortune-breeding thought about the hunts.

Sixty seconds—

His chances were very slight. No quarry had ever survived the hunts. Reed would get him, if not the first day, probably the second, and definitely the third. And unlike Reed, he was at a disadvantage because he knew so little about the civilization he was stranded in. He was a stranger, he had never hunted here before.

But surely the State—

There was a mechanical *whirr* behind him.

He whirled. The noise was coming from a small machine attached beneath the bed. With slightly metallic overtones, it said in the suave tones of Joseph Reed: "It's sundown, David. We're waiting for you."

The hunting season had just opened.

II.

Silently we went round and round,
And through each hollow mind
The Memory of dreadful things
Rushed like a dreadful wind,
And Horror stalked before each
*   man,*
And Terror crept behind.

"The Ballad of Reading Gaol,"
Oscar Wilde

She was small and blonde and apparently lonely; she had settled at his table a few minutes before, unasked and unwanted.

"What's your opinion on the minorities question?" she asked.

He looked at her, puzzled. "Am I supposed to have an opinion?" he asked slowly.

She took in his cheap suit, pale face, and thick glasses with a practiced eye. "You look like the kind who should have an opinion," she said. "You look like you belong to one."

He said cautiously: "Maybe I do."

She nodded, faintly triumphant. "That's what I thought. I can spot them a mile away."

The words were unfamiliar, but the tone wasn't. The kind of tone that citizens used in referring to rankanfilers of his own time. His face flushed slightly.

His companion suddenly looked sorry. "Don't mind me," she said. "This is my night for being nasty. I was stood up and I guess I'm taking it out on you. Have a drink?"

He nodded and transferred his attention to the crowd, studying the faces of the people in the tiny room. Somewhere close by a hoarse voice whispered lyrics into a microphone, trying to drown out the yammering piano that accompanied it.

The girl gestured to a nearby waiter and turned back to her too-sober friend. "What made you pick out this particular spot? It's my own favorite."

She couldn't be a huntsman, he thought alertly. She was too soft, physically and mentally. And she didn't have the hard fire in her eyes that a citizen did; she was safe.

"I thought this would be just the place to get away from it all," he said dryly.

But he still had a long way to go, he thought. He had left his shabby hotel room at sundown, plunging into the neon-lighted wilderness, alive with a multitude of sights and sounds utterly unfamiliar to him. The swirling crowds and the blinking lights and shrieking noises had confused him for a moment, and then he had headed for the busiest section of the city, looking for the crowds where he would be inconspicuous. Inconspicuous—and safe from Reed's sniffers or any one of the five hundred anxious citizens searching for him.

He found just the section he wanted in the entertainment district of the city: the section snarled with traffic and throngs of people, red-faced from the reflection of the signs advertising the cheap wine houses and the theaters. He had chosen one of the wine shops at random and found a miraculously empty booth at the rear, where he could watch the people as they drifted in and out.

The waiter was back with two glasses, one for him and one for the girl. Black caught the green of a small roll of bills in her purse when she paid for them and he watched her carefully when she put the purse down on the leatherette seat beside her. It was on the outside, the strap hanging over the edge.

"Here's mud in your eye," she said, raising her glass. She hesitated when she had it up to her mouth and gave him a coy look. "If I'm going to drink a toast, I'll have to know your name."

"David," he said absently.

"I like plain names," she said. "They tell you so little about people."

He felt ill at ease. Women had always acted more circumspect in his own time, more along the lines of what the State had deemed worthy for the citizen class.

But he forgot. That class didn't exist here.

"You're a little on the shy side, aren't you?" the girl asked, her eyes laughing at him.

He wasn't listening. Two tables away a middle-aged couple were watching him intently. He stared back and then let his eyes slide away, but not before he had seen their look of intense interest change to one of half-concealed amusement.

His palms felt sticky. Maybe it was just his imagination, maybe he was mistaken.

The three-piece band broke into a ragged harmony and the minute dance floor was soon crowded with bumping couples.

"The best way to overcome shyness is to dance," the girl suggested, "if you feel up to it."

"I'm not very good," he said, and proved it in a torturous turn or two of the floor. The middle-aged couple were close behind him, watching every move.

He was right, he thought, panicky. He was caught in the huntsmen's web. They had spotted him already and it probably hadn't been too hard. The entertainment district had been the logical place for him to try and hide in, and a few hundred huntsmen could cover it without too much difficulty. They had probably been spotted around in the different establishments, just waiting for him to show up.

Back at the table, the girl said: "What's eating you? You look like you've seen a ghost."

"It's nothing," he said quickly. "Just warm in here."

"Maybe we ought to leave," she suggested. "I know just—"

"No thanks."

"I've been wasting my time, haven't I?" Her face was frozen in a tight smile.

He smiled. "You said it, I didn't."

Two tables down, the middle-aged man and his wife caught his eye and nodded slightly. They had spoke to the waiter a moment before and were now holding the same type of glass to their lips that he had. Black understood—a cat and mouse play. You have wine, we'll have wine. You have something else, we'll have something else. Just to let you know we know who you are, my boy.

There wasn't any doubt about it. They had the lean and hard look that rugged physical training gave to all citizens. And they were enjoying this. They wouldn't notify Reed or call for outside help until he went to leave. They wanted to see him sweat and struggle for a while.

He ran his finger down the list of drinks on the menu but the names were confusing and didn't tell him what he wanted to know, so he turned to the girl and asked her a carefully phrased question.

She looked at him curiously. "You meet the oddest whacks in this town," she said, half to herself. Then: "Try beer."

He switched to beer. The middle-aged couple did likewise. Several bottles later the middle-aged man got up and headed for the rear of the room. Black smiled grimly to himself and stood up to follow.

"Don't be long, David," his companion giggled, then turned back to look at the floor show where a tired M.C. was mouthing a tired comedy routine.

"Don't worry," Black said soothingly. "I'll be right back."

After he had left, the girl's slightly fuzzy expression quickly faded to one of beady-eyed sobriety. She looked down and noted with satisfaction that Black had stolen her money-filled purse, then turned her attention to the woman two tables down. The middle-aged man's wife was staring worriedly in the direction her husband and Black had taken, obviously debating whether or not to call the manager. Her fingers were playing idly with the catch of her handbag.

She would have to risk it but it had to be done, the girl thought. She got to her feet and weaved unsteadily toward the entrance. Halfway there, she lurched against one of the tables and accidentally knocked a handbag to the floor. Before she could stop herself, she stepped on it, then apologized drunkenly and retrieved it for the furiously angry woman it belonged to.

Outside, in the muggy night heat, she took a brief moment for self-congratulations. She had started Black's education and she had managed to furnish him with money that would undoubtedly come in handy. And when she had stepped on the handbag, she had felt the satisfying crunch and pop of the tiny tubes on a transceiver communication set.

Which meant that Black was, for the moment, in the clear.

He dropped from the window into a refuse laden alley smelling of garbage and stale beer and started running. Once on the open street he slowed down and headed east, toward the park bordering the lake.

His head was throbbing and he felt sick. There had been the two of them in the small, dirty washroom. He hadn't meant to do more than bind and gag the middle-aged man, but the man had struggled and tried to scream, to attract attention. So he had to . . . to—

To kill him. The expedient thing to do; the only thing that he could have done under the circumstances. But the middle-aged man had, in a sense, only himself to blame. He had forgotten one of the basics of the hunts—that cornered quarry are desperate and therefore dangerous.

He swore violently to himself. *He hadn't meant to kill the man! And conceivably it could prejudice the State against him.*

The changing lights on a traffic signal caught him halfway across the street and he found himself in the middle of a rushing stream of traffic, dodging the wildly honking cars and clanging trolleys and swearing at the shrill whistle of the traffic policeman that called attention to himself. Then the shadowed safety of the park swallowed him up.

He found a bench and sat down, relaxing in the blackness. Reed would be along, but not for ten or twenty minutes yet. Time enough to consider his situation and then be up and—running again. His position had improved but only slightly. He had successfully evaded the first huntsman and had stolen a large supply of the green paper money. In this culture, as in all others, it would be more than useful.

But the death of the first huntsman would make all the others that much more vigilant, that much more anxious to be known as the first to find him, the first—so to speak—to nail his pelt to the wall.

His thoughts broke off and he tensed. Somebody was coming up the walk.

He sank farther back into the darkness that hid the bench and held his breath; his hand curled tightly around the Williams in his pocket. The footsteps approached, paused at the bench, and then passed on.

"Sorry," a voice trailed back, "I thought it was vacant."

Just a young couple, strolling in the park in summer. A practice, he remembered, that the State frowned upon, but one not unknown.

He let his breath out in a slow sigh and picked up his thoughts where he had left them. The hunt itself was divided into three sections. The first from sundown to sundown. Then an hour break, and the hunt was on to the next sundown. Another hour break, and a hunt to the finish. If Reed was able to, he could end it during any one of those periods.

He probably wouldn't choose to do so, however. Reed would let him run until exhaustion and lack of sleep and the frustrating feeling of being cornered had begun to weigh on him and distort his common sense. It seemed likely that Reed would play with him until the very last part of the hunt.

But he didn't dare depend on it. Reed might consider that he would think along those exact lines—and plan accordingly.

He yawned. It was past midnight now. Most of the theaters and wine shops would be letting out and the merry-makers would be going home. The city would revert back to a desert, populated only by night watchmen.

And once the city became even partially deserted, he'd be that much easier to track.

He got up and started walking down the sidewalk, keeping within the shadow of the trees. Somewhere a few blocks behind him, he could hear the low purr of a car traveling slowly down the street. He turned and made it out, two blocks down. Its headlights were off. One block over was another car, motor idling, just creeping down the pavement. And under a street lamp, a block away, a man was lighting a cigarette and staring calmly in his direction.

They were waiting for him to do something.

Waiting.

He cut through one of the grassy stretches of the park and ran south, the only avenue of escape that didn't seem to be covered by his pursuers. His frantic stride took him through a few blocks of soft shrubbery and grass, and then the park was at an end. There was nothing beyond but a large, open court in front of a railroad station. The court was lit by a string of street lamps, so he couldn't cross it without being seen.

There was no escape that way.

A car, one of those that had been idling in the park before, drove up to the court. Nobody got out.

Sweat started to creep down Black's spine. This could be the final showdown as well as not. They knew he was dangerous, that he had killed one of the citizens in the hunt. They could very well have decided not to let him go farther. Even now they were probably just waiting for Reed to show up. And the cars had spotlights; they had only to light up his particular patch of shrubbery—

He glanced desperately about. In front of him was the court, and behind—and not too far behind—the soft pad of other footsteps on the springy grass. On his right was another well lighted and undoubtedly well patrolled street while on his left—

On his left was the edge of the park and the court, an iron railing and sheer drop to the freight yards of the train station—a maze of tracks, box cars and empty commuter trains sitting on their sidings.

He tensed his legs under him and made a sudden dash for the railings. There was an eerie silence broken only by the slap of his feet on the cement of the court and then he was at the railing. He extended his arms in front of him and dove over, doing a flip in the air so he would land on all fours. There was a split second of breathless falling and then he thudded into the cinders along the tracks, the sharp coals chewing into the palms of his hands. He scrambled to his feet and dodged behind some freight cars, then decided to follow the tracks still farther south, until he hit a residential section where perhaps he could lose himself again.

He paused only long enough to glance back and see the gentle bobbing of lanterns as a few men gathered at the railing where he had gone over. Then the lanterns dipped and he knew they were climbing down after him.

They still hadn't made a sound.

The houses were crowded close together along both sides of the narrow street. Some were small, clapboard affairs, the wood black and rotting from wet winters and rainy springs, sandwiched in between the frowning tenements of brick where the rooms were rationed one to a family. On some of the buildings, Black could see people sleeping on mattresses placed on the rusting fire escapes. Sometimes he even thought he could hear their snoring and other noises of slumber.

The alleys and the backyards were as quiet as the streets, but smelled worse. He doubled through several of them, through yards that were nothing but clay and cinders, and up alleys alive with little furry things that blinked their beady eyes suspiciously at him and then went back to rooting in the garbage.

It was a district that reminded him of the sections where the rankanfilers of his own time lived. A hundred thousand people burried alive in crumbling brick and mortar flats. He stopped under the street lamp at one intersection and cocked his ear, listening. There was no one in sight but he could *feel* the people in the buildings, tossing and muttering on stinking mattresses in bedroom cells or else pacing the floor, their eyes burning for the sleep that wouldn't come.

Or maybe couples had sprawled out on blankets in the backyards, snatching the oxygen from the dry clumps of faded green grass, waiting for a cooling breeze to work its solitary way down the thin canyons that separated the buildings.

It wasn't long before he sensed that the huntsmen had found him again.

A huntsman's car, prowling through the dimly lit streets,

smelling him out from a hundred thousand others. A gradual sense of activity in the neighborhood, foreign to the sleeping people in the buildings. Somebody he could hear walking a few blocks away, the slamming of a car door to let somebody out just around the corner.

The baying of the five hundred hounds.

He quit using the open street and clung close to the shadowy buildings, silently feeling his way through the alleys and the back yards. Near one of the buildings, a foot away from where he was walking, a small spot on the sidewalk hissed and grew red, then crumbled into powder.

A burn from a Williams, from somebody hiding across the street—still playing with him, still toying. He caught his breath and ran, leaping a wire fence and padding silently through the yards. The moon helped him for a minute and then it disappeared behind a cloud and he was in pitch blackness.

Something felt soft beneath his foot, and he stumbled to the ground. There was a flash of light as somebody lit a match a few feet away and he found himself staring into a startled face, whose expression quickly smoothed out to one of dangerous blankness.

The face said: "You don't belong here. You better move." There was a *click* from a piece of plastic the man held in his hand and the plastic sprouted a six-inch length of steel blade. "Now."

Black felt like the blood was going to ooze out his shoes and then he was up and away, running.

Running.

"What'll you have?"

"Something to drink."

"We don't serve drinks here—only coffee."

Black had the feeling that the counterman would be just as happy if he got up and left.

"Coffee, then. That's what I meant."

"Anything else?"

Black stared at the menu through bloodshot eyes and picked something else to go with the dark, bitter tasting brew that was called coffee. It was getting near morning and the small lunch counter was filling up with people on their way to work. They took fleeting notice of his dirty and torn clothing and the stubble on his tired face, and then turned back to their morning coffee and eggs with an outward show of disinterest that masked the curiosity within.

Early morning felt good, Black thought—the sun and the cool air, rolling up the night like a window shade. It felt even better to be in the lunch counter, with the sunlight streaming through the windows and highlighting the red-checked tablecloths, and the pleasant clatter of spoons clanking against cups and the sleepy mumble of early morning conversation.

He downed the last of the coffee and finished off the eggs, using a gray piece of bread to sponge up the yolk. Not so long ago, he thought with a sudden longing, mornings had been different. You were awakened along with a few hundred others, at the crack of dawn. You showered and dressed with military precision and left the barracks a half hour later for the antiseptic dining hall, where the food was plain but prepared under sanitary conditions and scientifically calculated to contain the minimum for the day in protein and carbohydrates and vitamins.

For a brief second he worried about the caloric and mineral content of what he was eating at the moment, then laughed grimly to himself and dismissed it.

He had another cup of the bitter coffee and casually inspected the people around him. They seemed to come in all shapes and sizes and wore a wide variety of garments, as wide a variety as the people in the wine shops the other night. Some had briefcases and were rather formally dressed; others had on old and patched clothing and were obviously going to work in factories.

No standardization, he thought somewhat distastefully, a simple sort of anarchy. Something like the rankanfilers in his own time.

He swallowed the last dregs of his coffee and got to his feet to pay the counterman. Enough people were on the streets to cover his movements: it would be safe to leave.

At the cash register, the counterman ticked off the items on his breakfast check, then punched the register and handed him a few coins in change.

Just before he turned away, the counterman lowered his voice and said with a sly smile: "You're too easy a mark, Black. Hunter Reed's going to be disappointed. Maybe you ought to start running again, hm-m-m?"

III.

He does not sit with silent men
* Who watch him night and day;*
Who watch him when he tries to
*   weep*
* And when he tries to pray,*
Who watch him lest himself should
*   rob*
* The prison of its prey.*

"The Ballad of Reading Gaol,"
                    Oscar Wilde

He had been herded, he thought grimly. Herded to the south side where Reed's men had kept contact with him every minute of the time, playing with him, playing the bitter game of wearing him down, tiring him out. They wouldn't close in for the kill until the last period, most likely, when he was fatigued from lack of sleep and jittery with the knowledge that his enemies were invincible. Then they would sit back and watch him blunder and stumble in the web.

The streets were alive with people, all of them too sleepy or too busy among themselves to notice him. For the moment, he had achieved the blessed sanctuary of anonymity. He caught one of the rumbling streetcars and rode a few blocks to a crowded intersection, then transferred to a bus and rode a few more. Inside of an hour he had left behind him a bewildering maze of transfers and cut backs and parallel riding. He felt reasonably certain that he had lost himself in the crowds, that nobody had been able to follow him.

There was a residential section not far from the heart of the city and he walked through it rather slowly, feeling momentarily safe from the perils of the hunt. It was a well kept up neighborhood, with neat looking, brightly painted bungalows and thick, green lawns. He looked at the homes with a touch of envy. They weren't highly standardized and were hardly what you would call functional, but there was still something bright and appealing about them—a something, he decided, that his own time lacked.

It was after breakfast and housewives were hanging out the wash while husbands of the executive stripe were just heading to work. After them came the sharp-eyed children on roller skates, roaring down the sidewalk to school—little girls with bright, print dresses and boys with worn corduroys and battered schoolbooks.

Black watched them curiously. There didn't seem to be any order to it. No marching, no uniforms, no squeaky voiced squad leader shrilling commands.

That was it, that's what made it seem so strange. There was no order to the society, no purpose, no goal. The people were too—individualistic.

The crisp newness of the neighborhood gradually faded to a sooty, run-down district of old houses and that gave way to a manufacturing belt around the center of the city.

With a start, he recognized where he was. Just beyond lay the park and the court and the railroad station. A different station, now, than the deserted one of the previous night. It was humming with activity, disgorging steady streams of people on their way to work or to a day's shopping. It was the time of day when the commuters come to town.

The station, he decided, would be his hiding place for the next few hours.

The voices of the twentieth century.

A harsh voice. *"Gitcher morning paper, allabout the war! Paper, mister?"*

"No thanks. I—"

A briskly professional voice: *This is a special for commuters only, this morning. A box of Mrs. Borrowman's chocolates to take to the girls at the office or to the wife at home. What about you, sir?"*

It took him a moment to understand that a brusque nod was sufficient—or you could ignore them altogether.

A hoarse, blind voice with a mechanical throat: *"The Ashland Limited for Woodstock, Crystal Lake, Beloit, Minneapolis and St. Paul now ready on Track 6. All aboard!"*

He bought a paper and settled on one of the hard wooden benches. It would be a good idea to buy a ticket to some city—any city—and leave Reed and his huntsmen far behind. But Reed would have the stations covered: that would be the first thing to occur to him. The train stations and the bus depots and the air terminals. They would all be watched by alert, eager huntsmen. Even now he was running something of a risk by being in the station, but the attention of any possible pursuers was most likely glued on the ticket windows, watching those who bought tickets out of the city.

His eyes left the paper for a moment and darted about the terminal. You could play a game and try and pick out Reed's men—

Like the solitary man at the lunch counter, watching the terminal in the big mirror behind the automatic coffee urns.

Or maybe not. He looked too tired, his eyes were too red. Probably a nightshift worker catching a bite before going home.

Or perhaps the woman waiting by a pillar, looking in her compact mirror and repairing her face.

A minute later she picked up her baggage and disappeared through one of the gates, when her train time was announced over a loudspeaker.

Black could feel the nervousness build up within him. It would take so little to walk up to the window, push some money through the wire wicket opening, and buy his freedom out of the city.

Perhaps—

The man in brown a few benches down!

Black could have sworn he was a huntsman, but the man suddenly got up and walked to the gate where people were streaming out. He cut into the crowd and took a suitcase from a rather plump, elderly woman, and the two of them left the station arm in arm.

Black was on his feet, clutching his wallet in sweating hands, walking towards the ticket window.

And then his heart started a frantic triple beat and his courage trickled out of him. Reed had followed his every move so far, there was no reason to imagine that he would have passed up the station. He couldn't afford to fool himself. To buy a ticket now would make for certain detection.

He walked into the men's washroom instead.

One of the washbowls was free and he sloshed his face with cold water, then inspected himself in the mirror. His eyes were red-rimmed from lack of sleep and a light, black stubble had sprouted on his face. There was a drugstore in the station proper and he went out and bought himself a shaving kit, then erased the beard.

He felt a little cleaner after that, but the facilities of the washroom were limited and he couldn't take a shower. And he smelled. His clothes were full of his own body odor, a sure clue to his identity for any sniffer.

He fumbled around his pockets and came out with a bottle that had been in the handbag he had stolen in the wine shop.

He uncorked the top and smelled it. The oily liquid inside had a rather pleasing odor, one that was strong and would probably be lasting. He spilled some on his hands and rubbed it on his face, and ran some through his hair. It was bound to baffle any of the mechanical aids that Reed might have.

He had just finished drying his hands when a man in a blue uniform—he had learned that such uniforms designated men of the local police department—came into the washroom and stopped short, then turned a leering face towards him.

"Hey, Joe, c'mere," he said over his shoulder. In a moment he was joined by another blue uniform. One of them came over and slapped Black sharply in the face.

"Just like spring, isn't it? But don't you think it's kinda strong?"

Black reddened. He could handle the both of them, but the uniform denoted authority and it was best not to antagonize it. He had enough difficulties as it was.

The other blue uniform suddenly stepped behind him, caught his arm, and twisted it sharply.

"You'll start no trouble here. On your way!"

It occurred to Black that in some way he had violated a taboo of the civilization.

"But I didn't—"

A sharper twist and a shoving motion towards the outside. "Yeah, we know. Beat it, bum!"

Once outside, Black's mind felt twisted with a curious, helpless anger. He had been a citizen once, with all the rights and prerogatives of one.

It was a new experience to be treated as . . . as—

Sundown.

An eternity of walking the streets, dodging trackers, and hiding in theaters and libraries—any place where a crowd would serve as a cover.

Sundown. An hour's rest before the fear would be on him again and he would be the hare at the head of the chase, dodging through the warrens of the city, desperately trying to find a hole to hide in.

Sundown. The end of the first period of the hunt. And in a small way, even if only by virtue of Reed's leniency, it was a triumph for him because he was still alive.

He opened the door of the hotel room and locked it carefully behind him.

"Five minutes sooner, David, and you would have been a fraction of a second too early."

Reed was sitting on the bed, holding a Williams in his hand. He looked disappointed.

Black tried to look as calm as he could. "But I got here too late, didn't I?"

Reed cocked the Williams and pointed it at his chest. "I'm not so sure—" He was tired, but not too tired to whirl to the window and breathe an involuntary sigh of relief at the steady blackness outside.

Reed laughed and put the pistol away. "A little jumpy, aren't you? But that will wear off sooner or later. Exhaustion will conquer your nerves." He looked amused. "You've had quite a time of it, haven't you?"

Black wanted to remain silent but he had to ask the question that was hammering at the back of his mind.

"Did the State—" he began stiffly.

"Grant you a reprieve?" Reed finished. He leaned back and roared. "Don't worry, David, if they do, I'll be the first one to let you know."

Black fell silent.

"I frankly didn't think you would jump the railing at the station," Reed continued, "but I already had men planted along that escape route, in case you did. Nasty section of the city you had to go through there. As a former citizen, you have my sympathy. It isn't easy to mingle with people like that."

Silence. The muted noises from outside the window, the drip of water in the bathroom.

"You looked quite haggard at the lunch counter, and I don't think you enjoyed your coffee and eggs too well." A slow smile. "I was in a business suit then, three stools down. We lost you on the street cars and buses and picked you up at the railroad station. You did the wise thing in not trying to leave the city; we couldn't have afforded that."

The slow crawl of a fly on the night table was fascinating. Black let it absorb his interest and Reed's words seemed to come from far away.

"I'm a little sorry about the incident in the station, too. It would have worked out quite well, by the way, in fooling the sniffers but you would have drawn considerably attention to yourself in another sense. It's always best to learn the customs and taboos of a civilization as soon as possible, David; they save you an endless amount of trouble."

The bed looked soft and inviting. He felt like he wanted to drown in sleep.

Reed was watching closely. "You drew first blood today, David, but you'll have to do better than that. I had frankly expected more of you. You used to enjoy quite a reputation as a hunter yourself, you know." He was lost in thought for a moment. "If you had come back early tonight, I think I would have ended the game then."

Reed waited for a reaction but didn't seem too disappointed that there wasn't one.

"As tired as you are," he mused, "it must have been a great temptation to come back here just . . . a . . . few . . . seconds . . . early."

Elizabeth Smith wondered when the time would come that she had had enough. When she no longer would be able to sit there calmly and teach rows of insufferable little children, all sitting stiffly in their chairs, all dressed in identical little uniforms, and all with the same intent expression on their faces. Rapacious little sponges, sopping up knowledge because the State expected every school child to do its duty.

Some day the endless parade of faces that shone with a military immaculateness, the careful restrained play, and the adult manner of the children-who-weren't-children would become too much, and she would simply stand up and walk out, never to come back. Not even to her part in the revolution.

But she didn't mean that, she thought hastily. The only chance that the children would become children again some day lay with her and John and the others.

She sighed and finished her lecture. "There will be exactly three minutes for a question period," she said briskly. "Any questions?"

A hand shot up in the second row.

"What are the fundamental differences between the citizens and the rankanfilers?" a childish treble asked solemnly.

The boy would be needling her, she thought, or it could be a planted question. Or it might even be a perfectly serious one.

"You were taught those differences in elementary," she said tartly. "It will pay you not to forget. A citizen, by reason of birth and breeding, is superior to a rankanfiler in both blood lines and native mental ability."

The boy then asked reluctantly: "What is the explanation for honorary citizens, then, who were not born to it?"

She must remember his name, she thought. In a few years he would be excellent material. He seemed capable of original thought, instead of the mere parroting that so often passed for thought.

She hesitated just long enough, to plant the seed of doubt in his mind, before she answered. "The State is perfectly capable of granting its own mark of superiority," she answered coldly. The answer sounded authoritative but meant exactly nothing. "That ends the questioning period, class is dismissed."

They filed out of the room with military precision. She got her books together and hustled down the corridor to the automatic lift. She had to hurry, to make good use of the fifteen minutes between classes.

She got out on the 110th floor and hurried down the corridor to a plainly marked door. She hesitated a moment, then pressed her palm to a resilient surface of the door for recognition purposes.

"Name, please," a mechanical voice sounded.

"Elizabeth Smith," she answered, "to see John Doe."

The door swung silently open and she entered. The man behind the desk in the room greeted her warmly. He was a tall man, on the gangly side, with a thin, ascetic face and the heavy-lensed glasses of a scholar.

"Is the room screened?" she asked.

The man nodded. "Of course." They made themselves comfortable on the small, utilitarian couch by the open window.

"How's the revolution going, John?" she began.

He grimaced. "Slowly, as to be expected. It's almost more of an evolution, than a revolution. Don't mistake me, though, I'm not advocating open revolt."

She laughed grimly. "You don't revolt that way against a culture as militaristic as this one. Sometimes I almost think we ought to let everything go and let the citizens die out in a thousand years from lack of breeding."

"Like the Spartans of ancient Greece, I suppose?"

"Well, why not?" she asked defensively.

"There's nothing basically wrong with the citizens as a class, Beth, you know that. It's the system that's all wrong, it's the system that has to be destroyed."

"Oh, I know that," she said moodily. "Sometimes, though, well . . . it all seems so futile."

He stood up and looked out of the window, his hands clasped behind him. "We make haste slowly, Beth. It's the best way." He changed the subject. "What about Black?"

"I took the time car back to the barbarian period he was stranded in and made contact with him in a small wine shop. He wasn't, of course, aware of my identity. I planted a statement about minority groups and then tempted him with the money in my handbag. Later that evening, he stole the handbag. There were two citizens in the shop observing Black, and he lured one of them away. Husband and wife team. I kept the wife from following Black or notifying Hunter Reed."

He nodded, pleased. "How do you think he'll come out?"

"I don't know," she said reluctantly. "It is true that he objected to the hunts, which made him worth our attention in the first place. But I'm not at all sure that he disagrees with the State itself as a governing body or with its other policies. At present, I think he's living in hopes of a government reprieve."

"A rather foolish hope."

"Perhaps, with contact with all classes in the civilization that he's in, he'll change."

Her companion seemed absorbed in the coming and going of the 'copters and rockets over the city and kept silent.

"Do you have any more news on Black, John?" she asked finally.

He turned to face her, smiling somewhat wanly. "He cuts quite a handsome figure, doesn't he, Beth? Broad shoulders, athletic. Not the pale, scholarly sort like myself."

"I am interested in neither his broad shoulders nor his engaging smile, but rather in what ways he could help us," she said coldly.

He smiled more naturally. "The State has labored so long to build up its superiority-inferiority myth that it sometimes crops out even on me—the stress they lay on the physical side."

"What about Black?" she persisted.

"We managed to keep a man on Black all during the night and most of the day. But it wasn't easy and it was highly dangerous. Our own men and the huntsmen were rubbing elbows all the time, though fortunately without discovery on *their* part. Our past experience gave us an edge in that respect."

"What did Black do after I left him?"

"What they all do, at first. Fled through all the sections of the city, devoting most of his energy to changing his locale once he suspected that he had been spotted. And as you know, that's a tiring and essentially useless procedure. Reed could have had him at any point during the hunt, though he apparently didn't prefer to do so. From our own psychological analysis of Reed, it appears statistically probable that Black will be spared until the last period." He shook his head doubtfully. "Whether Black survives or not depends primarily on himself."

"What do you think of his value to us?"

"Black, is, of course, the first citizen to be condemned to the hunts as a quarry—a sure sign of the State's inward decay, by the way—and would be quite valuable if he threw in his lot with us. But bear in mind that he would be valuable only if he recanted the theories of the State and was sincere in his recanting. And considering that the State has molded his mind in every line from sex to social structure since birth, I doubt very much that Black will suddenly discard those teachings now."

"I still think he's worth our surveillance," she said. "The situation that he's in, no reprieve from the State, and what we know is Reed's own suppressed brutality may shatter his illusions. And a study of the civilization he's now in may help, too. He'll *have* to make a forced study of it if he hopes to survive."

He shrugged. "We'll keep men on him and see what we can do to help. You can make contact with him again and certify his opinion on the State and if there's any hope for him." He paused. "I trust you remember," he said thinly, "that one traitor could betray the lot of us."

"I could hardly forget that. My own life would be forfeit as much as yours." Her face softened a bit and she came over and stood by the window with him, looking out at the gray countryside dotted with the military barracks of the citizens and the hovels of the rankanfilers.

"There's a student in one of my classes," she said, "who might bear watching. If we started indoctrination now, I think he would be quite useful later on."

"What's his name?"

"Richard Roe," she said.

"It's a good citizen name," he said, smiling. "But which Richard Roe is it?"

"The one with the fat face and the cowlick that won't stay down."

He sobered. "If he's got a curious mind, he'll pay heavily for it before everything is said and done."

She turned from the window, bitter. "How did the State ever become father and mother and lover and jailer?"

"It's a long story," he answered slowly, gently erasing the wrinkles in her forehead with the ball of his thumb. "Some day I'll tell you, Beth."

IV.

But they were in their first youth.
It is not the same.
You, who are young; remember that youth dies.

"Short Ode,"
Stephén Vincent Benet

The night was cool and a fine misty rain was falling, giving the street lamps a half-halo effect. Most of the evening crowd had been driven indoors and those who hadn't were huddled under awnings and overhangs, impassively waiting for the drizzle to end.

Black threaded his way from group to group, dodging as much of the rain as he could, well aware that the thinned out crowds made it that much more dangerous for himself; the veldt was always more dangerous to hide in than the jungle itself.

His muscles were aching and his head felt heavy, his eyelids a weight pressing down toward his chin. He was sleepy— and yet he didn't dare think about it. The more he longed for sleep, the more tired he became which meant the more he longed for sleep. He had purchased some caffeine tablets at a drugstore but they didn't help much. The best insomnia-producing agent, he reflected, was to concentrate on his own immediate danger.

He hadn't given Reed much difficulty, he thought wryly. And if he had shown up at the hotel early, that would have been the end of the game. It would have been too good a story for Reed to tell—how he had merely waited for the quarry to come to him. As easy as the proverbial shooting of ducks in a pond.

The rain was coming down harder now, in big drops that

sounded like hail on the wet awnings. The streets and the sidewalks were running with streams of water that gushed over the walks and gurgled into the gutters at the corners. It was a drenching night, the pavement a glistening, reflecting river.

Except for the little dry spots about the size of a small coin that appeared on the walk in front of him like spots before his eyes. Small dry spots that kept pace with him and emitted little puffs of powdered cement when they appeared. Tiny little dry spots on the soaked pavement that told him the game had started all over again.

He wouldn't be stampeded this time, he thought grimly. They wanted to see him run, to see him dodge and twist through the city. He'd be a moving target then, one that might be hard to hit but one they wouldn't lose track of either.

He gave a sideward glance to one of the store windows and caught a glimpse of his tracker half a block behind. From what he could see, his tracker was a young man with a rubberized overcoat pulled up around his ears and a gray felt hat shadowing his face.

The young, foolhardy kind, Black thought. The type he had been once, the type you could always count on to do something foolish.

He crossed over a block and stopped in front of a theater, his actions obvious. He paid for a ticket and found a pair of seats in the middle of an aisle, halfway down. He settled in one and waited patiently for the youthful huntsman to take the other. Despite the advertised air-conditioning, the moist odor of the people jammed into the auditorium lay like a light fog around him, sufficiently confusing for the sniffers. And there were no aisle seats available from which anybody could watch and be sure of getting out immediately if Black should start to leave.

The huntsman had no choice but to take the seat next to him or risk losing his quarry.

Black allowed his mind to wander for a fraction of a second, watching the antics of the shadows on the lighted screen, and then snapped back to an alertness as seats were pushed back along the aisle to let a newcomer in.

He waited until the newcomer had shed his raincoat and hat and had them on his lap, momentarily encumbering his hands. Then Black jammed his elbow sharply outward and down. It was all very silently done; there was no noise except for the tiny pop of vacuum tubes in the miniature transceiver strapped to the huntsman's side.

The youth hesitated for the barest fraction of a second, inhibited against violence by the presence of the crowd, and Black's hand snaked inside his raincoat and relieved him of his Williams.

"You're a fool," Black whispered softly in the darkness.

The young huntsman seemed about to say something, then clamped his mouth tightly shut. Black knew what his thoughts were: At first, an initial agonizing dismay to realize that he had failed in his detail. And then—

"You won't get away," the young man whispered back.

That was the secondary reaction. Even when you had lost faith in yourself, you still retained it in the large rorganization of the hunt, believing that you and your mission would be avenged by others.

"We're leaving here," Black said quietly. "You first, I'll follow. And I won't hesitate to kill you if I think it necessary."

How long had it been, he wondered, *since he had been the same type of overeager kid? Forty-eight hours, perhaps?*

He felt that he had aged quite a bit since then.

The rain had stopped except for a slight misting and people were out on the walks once again. The air smelled cool and sweet and the light from the neon signs seemed warm and friendly.

He glanced thoughtfully at his captive. He was young, with a stern face and a stiff upper lip that betrayed only a slight tremble.

"Why did you let me know you were following me?" Black asked. He already knew the answer. *To see you run, of course!*

"Rules forbid the disclosing of information to quarry," the young man recited stiffly, staring straight ahead.

"I see you remember your hunting lessons," Black commented dryly. "Very commendable." He added, in a half friendly fashion: "It wasn't too long ago that I was a hunter myself."

No answer to that, except possibly the slightest motion of the lip, curling in contempt. Black reddened slightly. It was probably best to ask it baldly.

"I understand the State was going to review my case," he said stiffly. "I am interested in the outcome." The huntsman would probably bargain with him but he had to risk it.

His captive smiled, enjoying a vast secret amusement at Black's expense. He said nothing. From his reaction, Black could guess what had happened but there was still a tiny shred of doubt. He had to hear it from the man's own lips.

"You will tell me what you know about it immediately, or you'll die right now," Black said quietly, the slightest tremble in his voice. He meant what he said and his captive's smile quickly faded.

"Your case was reviewed by the State and the decision was given that, in view of the facts, your request for review and reprieve was insolent presumption coming from a convicted traitor. The sentence stands."

Black felt like he wanted to go away some place and become quietly sick. The carpet had just been pulled out from under him, his last hope had vanished. He was strictly on his own, like any other quarry, and his probable end, as he saw it, would be the same.

"It was a stupid thing to do, to let me know you were following me," he said, changing the subject. "The State should have briefed you beforehand. But then, the State makes mistakes, doesn't it?"

Even as he said it, he knew it was a childish thing to do. A sudden desire to discredit the State because it had failed to act as he had wanted it to.

"The State is incapable of error," his captive said dogmatically.

And if he believed that implicitly, Black thought frantically, he would have to believe in his own guilt of having been a traitor to it.

"Is the State the only agency that can decide what is right and what is wrong?"

"The State knows best."

Black could feel the despair growing in him.

"Do you approve of the hunts?"

"It is the method approved by the State for the punishment of criminals; a fair method decided upon by a benevolent State."

Black took another sideward glance. The handsome face of the true believer, he thought, glorying in his own confidence in the State.

By now they had walked several blocks in an aimless direction, and the crowds had again thinned out. They were walking by the mouth of an alley when Black's captive suddenly turned and lashed out with his foot. As Black tripped and fell

the kid chopped down with the side of his hand, catching
Black on the back of the head. Things blurred for a moment,
and then the youth was dashing up the alley.

He couldn't let him get away, Black thought dimly, or
Reed would be down on him in no time. He cocked his Williams and pressed the silent trigger. Far down the alley there
was a sudden scream and a dull sound as something stumbled
and hit the cement.

There was no end to it, Black thought sickly. No end to
the hunts, no end to the killing, no end to the fear, carefully
sponsored and nurtured by the State.

He suddenly felt horribly in need of somebody to convince
him that the State was wrong and he was right, that the State
was corrupt and he was pure, that the State had betrayed his
trust and he had merely kept faith with himself.

Another night of hide and seek in the slums and back alleys of the city, he thought. A more successful night as huntsmen had been able to locate him only once—and that to their
sorrow. He had drawn blood twice again and with it a slight
measure of confidence in his own ability to outwit his pursuers.

Now he had another day to face. The days weren't so bad,
of course, far better than the terror-filled nights when every
noise was a menace and every shadow a threat. And there
was something cleaner, less frightening, about the possibility
of dying during the day.

He caught a glimpse of himself in a puddle on the walk
and winced. The neat, chiseled look that citizens usually had
was gone. His face was puffy and strained looking and there
was an untidy morning stubble fringing his jaw. What was
worse, though it didn't show directly, was sheer exhaustion and weariness that was slowly sapping his will to resist.

He would be fortunate, he realized indifferently, if he
could last the entire three days.

It was near noon when he tired of mingling with the
crowds on the walks and turned into a museum. He found an
empty bench halfway down a marble hall and eased himself
into it, letting the crowd swirl past him. It was quiet, except
for the slight murmuring of the crowd, and he gradually let
his surroundings absorb the greater part of his interest, leaving only a picket guard in his mind to watch out for huntsmen.

He looked around, slightly puzzled. There didn't seem to

be any exhibits of any kind. The people apparently, were only interested in the decorations on the wall. But of scientific exhibits, the usual dazzlingly smooth motions of shining machines and the soft oiled sounds of mechanical monsters, there was none.

He shouldn't linger too long, he thought cautiously, but the people in the museum intrigued him. He watched them, trying to figure out why it was they came here, and reluctantly came to the conclusion that it was indeed the decorations on the wall that had drawn them.

He stood up and walked over to inspect one. It was a painting showing two men in trunks, apparently fighting in some kind of armory, with a huge crowd eagerly looking on. Degenerate art, of course, something the State inveighed against but which he had never seen. Rather crudely done, too—though the coloring was striking—and not nearly so true to life as a photograph would be.

But still, perhaps it wasn't supposed to be. Despite the crude workmanship, the painting conveyed a certain feeling, a certain atmosphere.

He walked down the hall inspecting the paintings with a mounting feeling of excitement. At the end of the hall was a court, filled with somber statuary. The one nearest to him was a larger-than-life portrayal of a man with sandals and what looked like a sheet draped over his body. A small card near the base of the statue identified it as being of one "Sophocles—Greek Tragic Poet."

"It's quite good, isn't it?" a voice said. "It sort of gives you a feeling of . . . of majesty."

He almost forgot himself and let his hand dart for his Williams, then he backed cautiously away. She didn't, however, have the citizen stamp about her and he relaxed. Her hair was swept back into a severe bun while a pair of unadorned, horn-rimmed glasses kept guard on the bridge of her nose. A spinster type. Black thought, who spent her free time in the libraries and museums of the city.

"I've never seen anything like it," he said huskily. "I had thought at first that he must have been a statesman or a general."

The eyes behind the glasses looked at him in frosty amusement. "Don't you think that a poet should be immortalized in stone?"

"But they're . . . they're so unimportant."

She laughed. "The poets will live longer than the politicians, Son." They walked over to another one, which Black gaped at in open admiration.

"Haven't you been to an art museum before?" she asked finally, as Black lingered by the sculpture.

"We don't have them in my country," he explained. He could, he thought waste an hour or so. And there were many avenues of escape from the building.

"I see," she said, drawing the wrong conclusions from his trace of an accent. "You're a D.P., aren't you?"

"D.P.?"

"Displaced Person—a refugee from one of the nations over *there*."

He smiled slightly. "I suppose you could say so."

She hesitated a moment, thinking of the appropriate thing to do. "I wouldn't mind showing you around, if you would care to see more. I think you get more out of it if you have somebody to act as a guide."

He was running a risk, Black thought calculatingly. But this was too fascinating a phase of culture, something he had never seen before. And he was probably as safe playing the part of a spectator in a museum as he would be on the walks outside.

Two hours later his guide had to leave.

"You see," she said, pulling on a pair of light cotton gloves, "art isn't so much a pictorial representation of an event or people, as a photograph is, but more of the capture of emotion in oils or marble." She paused and looked at him shrewdly. "I'll bet you're not very familiar with poetry or literature, either, are you? No matter, you'll have to dig that out on your own, I don't have the time to take you through a library." She held out her hand to him in her brisk, schoolteacherish fashion. "Good luck."

At the entrance to the museum, Elizabeth Smith glanced back at him for a moment. Black was still standing where she had left him, studying his hands with a curious and detached interest.

V.

*"We are all good citizens,
We believe in the Perfect State."*

"Litany for Dictatorships,"
Stephen Vincent Benet

The department store had been an inspiration.

It was crowded with milling people—which made it an excellent hiding place—and it was very possibly the best place to study the civilization he was in. You could learn an enormous amount from the products a culture used and the range and variety of them. And this particular culture provided a fantastic number of products, enough to stagger the imagination.

He had worked his way from a main floor that dealt primarily with men's clothing and stationery to a second floor that displayed feminine undergarments—mildly shocking to him—and from there to floors that specialized in books and home furnishings and kitchen supplies. The very top floor featured radios and rugs and a department for small children. The latter carried such unusual items as dolls and "cowboy suits" along with the more traditional, at least in his own time, tin soldiers and toy tanks.

It was near closing time and the floors had gradually emptied of people. It was time to leave, he thought wearily, time to leave and face the last night of fear and horror.

He pressed the button on the elevator shaft, as he had seen others do, and frowned slightly when the dial above the door showed no sign of moving, to indicate the elevator was on its way up.

He swore softly, pressing the button again. No results. It came to him with a numbed surprise that it wasn't closing time, it was *past* closing time, that somehow the clerks had missed him when they had left and that his own absorbed interest in the toy section had made him forget the time.

He was locked in, alone.

The lights dimmed and went out and it became a semidusk on the floor. There wasn't any sense waiting for an elevator that wouldn't come, so he turned away and wandered back to the main display space. It was just as he had left it, except for the silence. You could almost hear the dust settle on the displays. The tin soldiers and the toy tanks were still keeping watch over the fuzzy haired dolls, and the button-eyed toy bears were still gazing owlishly off into space.

Black stared at them in the graying light, their lack of animation emphasizing his loneliness.

"You won't leave here alive, David," one of the fuzzy haired dolls said.

"You're a traitor against the State and you'll die for it," another lisped.

"One burn, right between the eyes," one of the bears shrilled.

Black could feel his scalp draw taut and his heart rise in his throat. His hand darted towards his Williams and he sprayed the entire counter, leaving it a smoking mass of blackened wood and charred toys.

"You shouldn't have done that, David." A huge peppermint stick man at the entrance of the toy department a few feet away had his say in a sticky tone of voice.

"Yes, indeed, you certainly shouldn't have, it will go hard on you now," an erector set robot said.

"You won't leave here alive, David," one of the charred lumps on the blackened counter repeated.

"You're a traitor against the State and you'll die for it," another lump gurgled.

"One burn, right between the eyes," a singed bear said, still looking owlishly at him with little tears of melted plastic for eyes.

"Yes indeed," the erector set robot began, and ground into action, heading towards him in creaking little steps.

Black left it a burned and twisted mass of miniature girders and fled, his heart pumping pure fear. Three floors lower he stopped and glanced frantically around. This particular floor featured home furnishings and kitchen supplies and there were trussed up rolls of linoleum at one end. He ducked low and made it down to that end, then slid behind the rolls.

He crouched there for what seemed hours, hardly daring to breathe, just listening for any noises and letting the clammy sweat gather under his arms and trickle down his back. His aching muscles had just begun to relax when the expected noise came.

"I can burn those rolls down little by little, David, until I flush you into the open." The voice came from behind a lounge chair arrangement. Black burned the chairs and dodged over behind a refrigerator display.

Reed's voice laughed back at him. "You'll have to give me more credit than that, David. My voice is no indication of where I am."

Black didn't bother to reply but cautiously crept a little farther from the linoleum.

"Do you want me to end it now, David, or shall we prolong it a bit longer?"

No answer.

There was a blinding light in front of him and the linoleum rolls started to smoke and burn. Reed was using a wide angle aperture on his Williams, fanning it in a blinding flare of light that acted as an effective cover for the source.

Black crept farther along the side of the room, then lay on his stomach and started to burn the legs of a table load of china several rows down. He worked cautiously, charring the bottom half of the legs without causing any suspicious smoke. The table suddenly sagged and spilled its load of china on the floor.

As expected, Reed automatically burned the spot, but the shot was a side shot from Black's angle and he could see the source of the beam. He took careful aim and fired at Reed's expected position. There was a sudden cry of anguish, though not—disappointingly enough—in Reed's voice, and Black took advantage of the opportunity to make a dash for the escalators and thunder down them again. Behind him came the crackle of fire as the inflammables on the floor he had just left caught fire.

He paused on the ground floor and strained his ears. There was a soft creaking on the escalator a floor or two above him as somebody silently made their way down. Reed had undoubtedly not been alone; there were huntsmen with him. And its was a huntsman he had hit in the home furnishings department—Reed would never have made a blunder like that.

It was getting darker inside the store, more filled with shadows. Black drew himself up against a far wall and waited. The hunt wouldn't last much longer, he thought painfully, but he would still try his best to escape, more from force of habit than anything else. He felt sick and his sides and head were aching with pain.

The bottom of the escalator was practically hidden from sight in the shadowy darkness and it would be difficult to tell when somebody came down it, except by listening as carefully as he could and firing at anything that moved.

Sweat from his forehead crept into the corner of his eyes and stung them. He blinked and cocked his ears again but heard only the beating of his heart, loud enough, he would have sworn, to give him away.

There was a slight movement at the escalator stairs and he fired. An answering beam smoked past his shoulder and ignited some bolts of fabric on a counter just behind him, and he moved hurriedly away, seeking cover behind some displays.

From somewhere in the store came the sound of the click of a knob turning in a door. Reinforcements were arriving for Reed's side, Black thought; the hounds were coming to tree him.

He moved closer to an alley exit of doubled glass doors. Closing time had been an hour ago and there wasn't any doubt that now was the last chance he'd have to leave. He turned his body sideways and hunched his shoulders, then hurled himself against the glass.

He was through in a shower of splinters and racing down the alley to temporary freedom.

But only temporary, he thought, for behind him he could hear the padding of other feet in the alley as the hounds came in full but silent cry.

Back on the streets again, in the neon-lighted wilderness. The glare and burn of the winking signs staring down at him, advising him to buy a hundred and one products from automobiles to mouthwash; the displays of brazen women tempting him to try a certain brand of tobacco; the people, smug and fat, wandering lazily arm in arm, down the street, from one wine shop to another; the shrill music, piped out to the loud-speakers hanging over the sidewalks, the jazzy jungle background noise.

And which of the people on the walk were genuine and which were a clever imitation?

Reed's men had finally succeeded in doing what they set out to do, he thought; to wear him down until he blundered and stumbled in their web. He was too tired to think logically about escape and his efforts were probably in vain anyway.

He headed towards the south side of the business district again, the section of the honkatonks and the flesh shows, the pawnshops and the little stores that sold good-luck charms and magic tricks. Then some inner sense warned him that he couldn't hope to evade them in that district, that it would be, instead, an ideal spot to kill him. One more murder in a district where they weren't at all uncommon. He headed out towards the lake.

A few blocks from the business district he knew it was no use.

Cars drove up to each end of the block he was on and small groups of men who had just turned the corner drifted up the walk after him. Black caught a ragged breath and turned into the building he was walking by, some sort of hotel by the looks of it.

The lobby, dark and musty smelling, was furnished with worn rugs and leather-covered furniture with cigarette holes in the leather. The floor was rubber-tiled with wood showing through some of the worn tiles, and there were little notices and posters on the lobby walls, some advertising dances and others listing the various churches throughout the city. A man's hotel, Black thought, you couldn't mistake it.

The clerk at the desk paid no attention to him and he turned down a flight of stairs that led to the basement. There were exercise rooms and athletic courts in the basement but these had been emptied for the evening. Black looked them over quickly, then fumbled for the light switch in another darkened room. He couldn't find it, hesitated a moment, and then advanced in the darkness when he heard feet on the stairs outside.

He had taken but three steps on a cold, tiled floor when he felt nothing beneath one foot, teetered for the moment on the edge of something, and then plunged into water that quickly closed over his gasping head.

A rhythmic pressure on his sides forced water out and made him choke for air on the intake. He was sick for a bit and then they had him on his feet, one holding him on each side while the third lightly slapped his face.

He blinked his eyes and opened them, to stare full into Reed's thin, smiling face. There was a light somewhere in front of him so all he could see was Reed and nobody else; the others fuzzed into blackness around the edges of his vision.

It must have been only a few seconds that he was in the pool, Black thought. They had fished him out pretty quick.

"You almost cheated the State of its quarry," Reed said pleasantly.

"Nobody ever succeeds in cheating the State of anything," Black said dully.

A hand came out of nowhere and slapped across his mouth, drawing blood.

"You have no faith in the State, David. I'm surprised."

"Yes, I have," Black denied, forcing the words out between thick lips.

"No, David, you have no faith in the State. You never did have, or you wouldn't have failed it, you wouldn't have rebelled against its dictates."

It seemed like he and Reed were alone in a huge dark space; he couldn't even hear the breathing of the others. There was only himself and Reed's calm, cold face with the half-friendly, half-reserved eyes.

"Perhaps the State made a mistake, perhaps some of those dictates were wrong—"

A balled fist caught him on the side of the head, jarring him and making him sick again. One of his ears suddenly developed a buzzing within it.

"The State is never wrong, David. You know that."

Weakly. "If you say so."

Something caught him just above the kidneys and made him double up, clutching his aching sides.

"Not if *I* say so, David. It's a self-evident truth, it's something that you've been taught from childhood and which you should know by now."

"Perhaps it's because I was taught it from childhood that I believed it, but that doesn't make it true!" The pain had torn it from him before he could stop, knowing full well the treatment that would follow.

Reed's eyes glittered with a sudden fury and his face twisted. "You shouldn't have said that, David."

Another jab to the kidneys and they started working on him in earnest, cutting him with silent blows from their belts. He opened his mouth to scream with pain and somebody jammed their hand across it.

"Repeat after me, David: The State is a Perfect State."

Somebody bent his arm behind him and forced it up.

"The State is a Perfect State." Without feeling.

"You don't sound as if you mean it, David." A shooting pain as his arm was forced higher. "The State is a Righteous State."

"The State is a Righteous State!" He repeated almost prayerfully.

"It is the duty of the State to decide what is best for its citizens." A tearing pain and he babbled it eagerly.

"And with the State as perfect and righteous as it is, you know you committed a great wrong in defying it, don't you, David?"

"Yes, oh yes!" he cried.

"And that in your defiance, the State is within its rights to regretfully deprive you of the greatest boon of the State, that of life itself."

"Yes," he whispered.

In the little circle of light, he could see that Reed had his Williams aimed at his head. The others were crowding in behind Reed now. The handsome, healthy faces of the State waiting with glistening eyes and bated breath for the flash of light and the tiny, telltale odor of scorched flesh.

"It then becomes my duty, as a Hunter of the State, to carry out its sentence. In defying the State you became politically unfit, and one politically unfit is one criminally unfit and must be eliminated. It will be as you requested, David. One burn, right between the eyes."

Black lowered his head and waited for the end of his pain.

Suddenly there was whispering in the background, and Reed turned to him with disappointment heavy in his voice.

"It took too long to make you see your errors, David; it's after sundown." His voice became filled with disappointed rage. "Remember me by this until an hour from now, then!"

Another heavy blow and the lights blinked out; he could hear them leaving.

He sagged limply down on the wet tile. He had lost something, something that had played a major part in his life. And now it was gone. The State itself had finally forced his admiration and respect for it to wither and die.

But even that had its compensations. It had taken a long time but he was no longer blind and he needed nobody else to convince him. The State was wrong and he was right, the State was corrupt and he was pure, the State had long ago betrayed its trust and he had kept faith not so much with himself as with something that was higher than the State.

He slowly lifted his body from the tile. He had another hour of freedom.

The grass was soft and green and smelled strongly of

clover. Elizabeth Smith plucked a blade of the clover and stuck it between her teeth, then hunched up on her side and stared at the far horizon. The heavy lines of the buildings of the city, some distance away, offered a strange contrast to the delicate tracery of the exhaust trails left overhead by the military rockets.

People are born and people die, she thought grimly, *but the institutions go on forever.*

She plucked another blade and continued staring moodily at the city, the gleam of the military barracks and the administration buildings standing out against the background of the rusting shacks of the rankanfilers. A neat, standardized world mobilized forever against a threat that had long since vanished.

John Doe stirred next to her. "Did you ever hear of anybody named Machacek?" he asked irrelevantly.

"People don't have names like that."

"Or Maccabbees or Butney or Glinka or Rosenberg or Fanti?"

She looked at him thoughtfully. "What's your point, John?"

"The world," he said bitterly. "That's what's wrong with it. Everybody is named something *safe* like Smith or Jones or Black or Johnson. Standardization is even extended to names. Move out of the norm even in that and you're subject to suspicion."

"How did it start?" she asked casually.

"It was a long time ago," he said, suddenly enthused. "Everybody had to have the same goal, everybody had to think the same if the State was to survive. Individual security had to give way to collective security and thus individuality had to die—even in names. People with unusual names were automatically suspected of treason against the State, so they changed their names to something different—something safer." He paused. "I looked it up in the records the other day. My family name used to be Steininger."

She laughed. "What about Black?" she asked. "We've analyzed before the only way to win against the State, and for that we need him—badly. And we can use his strength."

"I'm still the pale scholar, aren't I, Beth?"

She shushed his lips with hers. "What a revolution," she whispered a little later. "A schoolteacher and a jealous scholar, trying to pull down the whole facade of a strictly military government!"

He smiled down at her. "We had our own private revolt against the State a long time ago, didn't we, Beth?"

She nodded. "And now what do we do with Black?"

He frowned. "I'm not sure. He's been given a difficult time by Reed and the other huntsmen, and he reacted favorably on his first view of something diametrically opposed to his education of scientific militarism. So what? He had a few of those tendencies to begin with, but that doesn't mean he's turned against everything he's been taught is natural and right. I won't jeopardize the revolution merely because Black was fascinated by his first taste of art."

"What about what he went through in the hotel basement?"

"I can imagine what his reactions must have been. Sheer hate, once they left him. But would he retain that hate if the State offered to take him back, unlikely as it may seem? Or would he rationalize what had happened to him, admit that his guilt may have deserved such punishment, and be interested in recovering the good graces of the State? It's been his religion, Beth, and I would hate to chance it."

"You may have to."

He looked at her, puzzled, and tried to figure out the meaning behind her remark.

"What do you mean?"

"No revolution ever succeeds by standing still, John. You either go forward—or you fail. The longer eventual success is postponed, the greater the chance that somebody will discover the plot. And if this one is discovered, the State will draw enough strength from the fright of having discovered a plot in its midst, that its creaking existence will be perpetuated for another several hundred years. You know we need Black. We need him bad enough to take a chance on him."

"We need somebody with a different type of courage than the kind we have," he mused. "We'll try to save Black, then. You can go after him if you wish, Beth."

"What's his location now?"

He looked at her, somewhat worried. "I don't know. We trailed him all through the second part of the hunt and shortly after that, we lost contact with him."

She sucked in her breath sharply. "That means he's learned how to hide, doesn't it?"

He nodded, "And this is the last period of the hunt, Beth. It's up to us to find Black before Reed does."

VI.

Each narrow cell in which we dwell
  Is a foul and dark latrine.
And the fetid breath of living Death
  Chokes up each grated screen,
And all but Lust, is turned to dust
  In Humanity's machine.

"The Ballad of Reading Gaol,"
Oscar Wilde

It was a dirty street, lined with dirty shops and alive with dirty people; stubble-faced men with dull eyes and ragged clothes, who wandered aimlessly down the walk or sat on the curb and stared out at nothing at all. Those few well-dressed individuals on the walk carefully inched their way, avoiding the human wreckage that littered the scene.

Black sat on a curb with two other bits of flotsam. His clothes were dirty and ragged, and his face was stubbled and laced with dried blood along one cheek where Reed had cut him.

High above him, the sun burned down from the brazen bowl of the sky and Black fished a filthy strip of cloth out of one pocket to sponge his forehead with, then used it to bat lazily at the flies. They were thick along the gutters and in front of the stores, attracted by the smells.

"It's a hot day," one of the men next to him mumbled.

Black didn't bother answering.

"We need a bottle of wine," the man whined. "Only fifteen cents, split it three ways."

Black felt in the pocket of his soiled pants and found a nickel and flipped it to the man. "Don't take long, Harry."

Harry turned a thin, angular face towards him. "You always get yours, don't'cha?"

He was back in a minute. Black casually wiped the top of the bottle when it came to him and gulped his third, then passed it on to the old man on his right. When he got the bottle back, he glanced at the label and read it idly, then dropped the bottle in the gutter at his feet.

"You shouldn't a done that," Harry complained. "We get two cents back on the bottle."

"Add it to my share next time."

"Ya sure ya got the dough?"

"Stuff it, willya?" He cut the petty argument short and went back to staring dully at the street.

It was all in the attitude, a dim portion of his mind thought. The secret of successful hiding was not to imitate your background but to become a part of it. He would be safe where he was and doing what he was until after sundown. And then, according to the rules of the hunt, he would be entitled to all his property rights and rights as a citizen of the state.

But that wasn't what he wanted, he thought slowly and painfully. He had been hurt too badly. Not so much physically, as that the State had shattered its own illusions, betrayed his faith, and left him groping for something to take its place. And what he had finally found as a substitute to fill the vacuum was a desire for revenge.

He felt his elbow nudged. "How long you been on the Street, Mac?" The old man on his right asked the question dully, merely looking for conversation.

"Long enough," Black grunted. "Who keeps a record of how long they're on the Street?" Who indeed would keep a record of how long they had been marooned in his hell?"

"I don't suppose nobody does," the old man ruminated. "Not anybody. Myself least of all." He hawked and spit in the gutter. "You won't believe it but there was a time when I had a pretty good job—pretty good job and a good home. And then I lost it all. Never gone back, never gone back to the job or the wife or the kids. Grown up by now, I suppose, probably got married and got families of their own. But I've never gone back." He seemed oddly proud of the fact, and ashamed at the same time. "Wouldn't want an old man like me around anyway," he mumbled. He looked up at Black. " 'Nother bottle?"

Black found another nickel.

"Some of the old guys, they talk a lot, don't they," Harry said.

"Yeah, they sure do."

They split the bottle again and Black found a backrest against a lamp post and relaxed against it. The legion of lost men, he thought, haunted by their own memories.

He shook his head and tried to clear it, then gave it up. The best way of hiding, he reflected fuzzily, don't try at all. Just let yourself drift in a human boneyard—Harry and the old man and himself, all members of a degenerate humanity.

At least they proved the State's contention that there were such things, though he had never seen any before now.

Harry pointed to a few of the better dressed souls keeping a careful distance from the bums and drunks on the street. "Well dressed slobs," he sneered, "coming down here to show us how much better off they are! Luckier than we are, that's all."

"I don't know," the old man said. "Maybe they worked for what they got. There's a difference in men—some of 'em got backbone and guts, and others are made of sand." He shrugged and laughed a little wheezily. "We don't live like they do and we don't deserve to. We don't even live from day to day—we live from bottle to bottle."

Black's mind agreed alcoholically with the old man. A good brand of street corner philosophy at that.

Suddenly his mind snapped alert and he could feel the fear growing on him again. The old man was dull and lifeless, the hopeless type you could normally expect to find on the Street. His clothes were dirty and ragged and all he lived for was a bottle of wine and a listless conversation with anybody who happened to be sharing the curb with him.

The old man belonged there. But Harry didn't.

Harry was a little too aggressive, a little too pushy, and a little too bitter. Harry was trying too hard—he was a little too *professionally* ragged and dirty and down and out.

Black's mind worked desperately. It was possible that Harry had tracked him, but not too possible. It was more likely that Harry and other huntsmen had been stationed on the Street as a logical precaution in case he should have tried to hide there. What had probably happened was that he had run into Harry by accident.

He thought back to that morning when he and the old man and Harry had first run into each other. Harry had watched both he and the old man quite closely, and as the morning wore on Black remembered that Harry seemed to pick up some of their mannerisms and phrases. Like any good, competent huntsman Harry was trying to improve his masquerade.

Harry, Black thought with a vast sense of relief, was studying him.

He stood up and kicked the bottle off into the gutter. "I think I'll drag outa here. You get cramped sitting in one spot all day." He looked down at the old man a minute. "Take it easy, pop."

The old man numbled and fished the bottle out of the gutter; he didn't bother looking up. You met too many people on the Street during the day; people you'd probably never meet again.

Black strolled away, wondering tensely if "Harry" would follow. It seemed logical that he would. He had made a good contact and wouldn't want to throw it away.

Harry caught up with him just outside the Atlantic Garden Mission. "I'll tag along," he whined. "I ain't been on the Street too long; maybe you can give me pointers."

Black looked at him sourly, inwardly feeling elated. "The first pointer I can give you is to keep your nose outa other people's business. I didn't ask for company and I'm not looking for it."

"It's a free world! I can do as I please."

Black shrugged. "Suit yourself." He turned up an alley at the back of the mission. Harry remained at the mouth of the alley, a slight, stoop-shouldered figure almost lost in his ragged clothes. His deception, Black thought, was letter perfect with only one flaw. It was, in Harry's own eyes, just a deception. He wasn't "living" his part.

"Where you going?"

Black seemed to relent a little. "Bread and soup at the back door, then inside for some singing in payment." It sounded logical. Through the front windows they had seen some tattered specimens standing up and dutifully caroling. Harry hesitated, then followed him.

At the back he said: "I don't see no bread line."

"You can't expect them to be as efficient as the State," Black said softly.

Harry's face went carefully blank. "What's the State got to do with it? I don't get'cha."

Black smiled tightly. "I think you do," he said as he drove two stiff fingers deep into Harry's abdomen. Harry doubled up violently and the edge of Black's hand caught him on the small bone at the bridge of the nose, between the eyes. There was a soft snap and Harry slumped limply to the ground.

Black shook a little with the reaction. It had taken a lot of effort, more than he was actually able to expend. And there was always the chance that he might be mistaken—

He felt inside Harry's shirt, his hand trembling. He felt thin straps and followed them to a miniature transceiver strapped to Harry's back. He took it off and fitted it beneath his own shirt, and fastened the tiny flesh-colored earphone into his ear.

There was an even better way of lasting through the hunts than sinking passively into the background, he thought coldly. And that was to turn the tables and hunt Reed.

The ultimate winner would be whoever found the other first.

He spent the next two hours listening on his transceiver set to the reports that flowed into Reed from his huntsmen stationed throughout the city. Reed had, he was forced to admit, organized the hunt very efficiently.

The outskirts of the city and the lightly inhabited residential areas were those that were most lightly covered, as expected. A few men equipped with sniffers were stationed there, and had a given cross sectional area to cover. And there were huntsmen covering the main highway exits out of the city.

The majority of the huntsmen, however, were stationed in the more crowded sections of the city. Some were in the city's bureau of detectives, where they could keep track of reported murders, accidental deaths, and other crimes that he might unwittingly be involved in. There were a few in the fire department for the same purpose; all these precautions predicated on the theory that a man from another century might very well stumble into serious trouble in the civilization in which he was stranded, and thus twitch the web that would send the notice to Reed.

Every transportation station in the city was covered, from the air and railroad terminals to the bus depots. And then there were the several hundred huntsmen who had nothing to do except mingle with the crowds on the street, as Harry had done. How all of them had scattered throughout the city and slipped into places of importance had probably been ingenious, though not too difficult. They had been trained for their jobs, as he himself had once been trained for the hunts. And the people in a culture like this were notoriously easy to fool: faked credentials satisfied the need for Authority and a little loose money could solve any of the other problems that might arise.

The whole intricate hunting system was based on the quarry's moving around in its efforts to escape, Black thought. Once you panicked, the first urge was to flee, to flee, to run, and once you did that, the living web had no difficulty keeping track of you. You left a trail like any other beast in any other jungle.

He listened to a few more of the conversations and felt increasingly uneasy. There had been—unknown to him—a steady attrition among the huntsmen, unexplained by the statistical possibility that a few of them might be the victims of accidents. He had settled for a few himself, he knew, but that wasn't the answer either.

The point was that some other agency than either he or Reed was involved, and that this agency, whoever or whatever it might be, was eliminating huntsmen as casually as you would pluck flowers in a park.

But Reed, of course, would think it was his doing.

His earpiece buzzed. "Harold Jones, time to report." Black paid no attention and the earpiece buzzed again, somewhat impatiently. "Harold Jones, report please!"

He tensed. Harold Jones—"Harry." Reed was calling for a report but that report wouldn't be forthcoming. Harry was in no condition to report to anybody, ever. Which meant that Reed would investigate and then they'd have another lead on him, once they found Jones' body.

But if he answered in place of Jones and got away with it, it might be another three or four hours before Jones' body was found, a three or four hours that he could use looking for Reed. And then again, if Reed suspected—

He wondered if his nerve would hold out. It would be so easy to drift back to the Street—

"Nothing to report," he said flatly into his throat microphone.

"Check." And Reed switched over to another huntsman.

Black mentally congratulated himself for taking the chance, though he realized it hadn't been too much of one. Metal and tubes had a curious way of extracting personality and individual enunciation on a simple hookup like this. But he still had the task of locating Reed.

He went back to the Mission and became just enough of a repentant sinner to gain access to the Mission washroom. He washed and shaved and then dumped some dye into the bowl for a quick change of the color of his hair to a natural looking blond. His glasses were discarded and wax once again altered the shape of his face. It was a poor job. he thought, but he was too tired to do a good one. Maybe its very imperfection would be an aid to him.

Most of the huntsmen were stationed in the business dis-

trict and Black drifted that way, hoping to catch one who
would lead him to Reed. He was running a dangerous risk,
for there was always the possibility that he would be spotted
by one of the huntsmen before he could spot one of them.
But that was a declining possibility and he ignored it, letting
himself become as absorbed as possible in the people and the
shops around him. There would be no panicky movements
this time, no white-faced searching of everybody in the
crowds that would show his fear and mark him for easy spot-
ting.

And in half an hour he had found himself a huntsman.

Black located him by listening to the reports on the transceiver, and traced him to his station—the clothing store
where he "worked." Once inside it became a problem which
of the clerks was the huntsman. Black drifted through the
various departments and finally found him selling shirts and
ties behind the counter. He was a little too husky to be the
professional clerk type, and he was far too interested in the
people who came into the store.

And his taste in clothes, Black thought grimly, was a little
too conservative for this century.

He went up to the counter and started pawing through the
display of ties.

"Can I help you, sir?"

"I think you can, citizen," Black said in a low voice.

The clerk's hand darted towards his waist.

"I wouldn't, citizen."

The man's face grayed and Black realized he had a reputation. "What do you want?"

In a tired voice. "Where's Reed?"

Resolutely. "It's against the rules of the hunt to give information to a quarry."

"I'm too tired," Black said, "to play games. And I don't
have the time. Answers like that will lose you your life."

The young clerk recovered some of his poise. "What makes
you think I'm afraid of losing my life?"

"It all depends on how you lose it. I have a Williams
trained on you and adjusted so it won't char your clothing—
it will just cook you rather slowly."

"If I told you, I would be betraying the State, Black."

Black started fumbling with the ties again. "That's so, isn't
it?" His voice had a heavy, flat quality to it.

A light mist of sweat appeared on the clerk's face. "It will do you no good, Black. I would rather die for the State than betray it."

Ringing words, Black thought. He would have said the same at one time. "These are nice ties," he said casually. "I don't care much for the conservative ones, though. I like the bright colors and the large figures best."

The clerk's face was red and sweat had soaked through his shirt. Black turned his Williams up one notch higher. The clerk gasped.

Black found himself wishing the clerk would give in. By now, the skin beneath his clothes must be an angry red, prelude to blistering. He wondered, if he was in the clerk's place under the same circumstances, how much pain he would take before he cracked.

"You're killing me, Black!"

He looked at the clerk coldly. "That's the only time when a citizen becomes concerned about the taking of a life, isn't it? When it happens to be his own."

The clerk stood it for a minute more and then wilted. "Reed's at the same hotel you started out from."

"What room?"

"The one next to yours."

He could have expected that. "Thanks. Now hand over your Williams and your communications set."

The clerk did something behind the counter and a moment later handed over a paper bag with the articles inside. Black took them, then turned his Williams up another notch.

The clerk collapsed.

"What happened?" Another clerk hurried across from the suit racks, bleating the question.

"Heat prostration; you'll have to get him to a hospital immediately."

The clerk dialed a number, then turned a white face to Black. "It . . . it isn't fatal, is it?"

Black shook his head. "No, no it's not fatal," he said in a tired voice. He paused a moment, then added almost to himself: "But it will be a few hours before he regains consciousness."

And that was time enough.

VII.

I never saw a man who looked
  With such a wistful eye
Upon that little tent of blue
  Which prisoners call the sky.
And at every wandering cloud that
    trailed
  Its raveled fleeces by.

> "The Ballad of Reading Gaol,"
>   Oscar Wilde

He loitered across the street from the hotel for half an hour, careful to see what went on but not be seen in return, fighting to keep his eyes open and husband his strength for the final effort. He had to be wide-awake and alert, he told himself desperately. He couldn't afford a mistake.

The hotel entrance was flanked by a cigar store and a candy shop, while a drugstore occupied the main floor corner. During the time that he watched, a man brought a paper from the corner newsstand and sauntered slowly down the block, a few moments after he passed the entrance, another man left the hotel to go to the drugstore, apparently to get coffee. When he came back, the clerk in the candy shop took to the outside for a brief sunning until she, in turn, was relieved.

It was a complex, seemingly natural movement of people that managed to keep the entrance to the hotel under watch at all times. And inside the hotel lobby there were probably other watchers.

The front entrance, then, was out of the question so he worked his way around to the alley in the rear of the hotel. The back entrance was guarded, too, but not nearly as well. Black waited until the single guard had turned his back, then slipped off his shoes, followed him, and struck him from behind.

His time was running out, he thought. You could work your way so far through a guard system, but the farther you worked the greater the chance of discovery. At any moment the game could deal him his last hand; from now on he would have to depend on speed.

The floor that Reed was on was—miraculously enough—

clear. Reed very obviously thought he had taken enough precautions against a highly unlikely event.

Black approached the door very quietly, then threw it
open.

He found himself staring into the muzzle of a Williams,
aimed at the pit of his stomach. Reed was standing by the
window, facing him. A little to his left was the small trans-
mitter setup and a map of the city, dotted with small red
lights—the locations of the various huntsmen.

"Close the door behind you."

Black did as he was told, feeling a vast sense of failure. He
had come so far—

Reed waved him over from the door. "In all fairness, I
must admit that you almost took me by surprise. If it hadn't
been for an automatic trip signal in the hall, I think you
might have had me."

Black felt on the verge of collapse. He had come to the
end of the line and nature was demanding its payment for
three days and nights of tension and fear and lack of sleep. It
didn't particularly matter what happened now. He had lost
the game but there was compensation even in that. At least it
was over with, at least he was no longer the rat trapped in
the maze of the city.

"You'll have to have witnesses to verify that the quarry
met its requested end," he said dully.

Reed nodded. "I've already sent for some of the citizens
whom you may have seen downstairs. They'll be here in a
moment."

Black settled back in his lethargy, waiting. From where he
sat, he could just see a small corner of the sky through the
window. There were small white clouds in the sky, floating
slowly across his line of vision. Floating in utter freedom and
in complete indifference to the tragedies playing out their last
acts beneath it. Black had a sudden intense and childish longing—

"You know, you had escaped the web altogether this time,"
Reed continued affably. "I had no indication at all of where
you were until you had walked into this room just now." His
smile grew somewhat bleak. "You've proved to be a very
dangerous quarry; David. You've eliminated some of my best
huntsmen."

"There were bound to be casualties," Black said indifferently.

"That's quite true, but the number exceeded my expectations."

Black said nothing, though again he felt puzzled. Most of the time he had been too frightened, too worried about his own ability to hide, to give attention to eliminating the huntsmen after him.

Reed seemed faintly worried beneath his urbane exterior and Black wondered for a moment why, then had the answer in a flash.

The huntsmen that Reed had asked to come up hadn't appeared yet, though they had had more than enough time. The logical deduction to make was that they wouldn't appear, that whatever agency had engineered the death of so many huntsmen before was once again acting in his favor, granting him—if nothing else—time.

And with that thought he launched himself at Reed giving the hunter no warning whatsoever.

Reed grunted at the impact and tried to bring his Williams to bear, but the surprise had taken him off guard. It was over in a minute and a disheveled Black had him covered with his own burn pistol.

"You have, at best, only a few moments," Reed said coldly. "When the other huntsmen find you here, it won't be pleasant."

"No, it won't be pleasant then," Black answered, feeling an insane giggle wanting to well up within him. "But it's very pleasant now. Enough to outweigh the possibility of pain later on." He strode to one side of the room and kicked in the communication apparatus that Reed had set up.

Then he turned back to Reed. The memories of the days and nights of hiding in the alleys and slums, afraid of every shadow and every sound, crowded in on him. He suddenly lashed out and caught Reed across the face. The man staggered and blood trickled slowly down the side of his mouth.

"Tell me that the State is corrupt and a tyranny, Joseph," he pleaded.

"I won't betray the State," Reed said stiffly.

Another blow across his mouth, splintering the teeth.

"Say it!"

"I can't!"

"*Try!*"

"The State is corrupt!"

"*Again!*"

Reed's face was a reddened mask. *"The State is corrupt!"*

A small portion of Black's mind felt sick but he couldn't stop himself. He had paid too much for this moment in agony and fear, and this was the punishment that the State had taught him to extract of others.

He remembered with vivid clarity the punishment he had taken on the tile of the swimming pool. "The State is an imperfect state, Joseph!"

Reed fell silent, licking the blood away from his mouth, terror full in his eyes.

"Go ahead, tell me, Joseph! Tell me what I want to hear! That the State is a monstrous thing with the power of life and death over its charges! Tell me that the State is wrong and has broken its trust!"

He was on the brink of hysteria, he realized dimly, yielding to the exhaustion that had piled up. It would be but a moment until he broke down completely. And Reed was waiting for him to do so.

He had so little time, he thought blindly, to punish Reed, to make him feel as he had felt. He raised his hand again.

"All those things are quite true," a voice said calmly behind him, "but this has gone far enough. Let him alone, Black."

He hadn't heard the door open behind him. A woman and a man were there, and a few others crowding in behind them. The woman was the schoolteacher type, severe face and plainly dressed. He had the feeling that he had seen her once before, but he couldn't remember where. She came over and took the Williams from his limp hand.

Black sagged back into a chair, dully aware that the newcomers weren't huntsmen. And with that realization, he laced his fingers in front of his face and let the tears of exhaustion stream down his cheeks.

When he awoke, the feeling of utter exhaustion was gone and the feeling of deadly danger had passed with it. He felt cool and clean and knew that somebody had washed and shaved him, and then put him to bed between soft, white sheets.

"You feel better now?"

He turned his head to one side and looked at her. He had met her twice before, he realized, under wholly different circumstances. Once in a wine shop and once in the art museum. And she was now dressed, he noted with some dismay, in a rankanfiler's simple smock type dress. Her companion, a thin, scholarly looking man with a feeling of steel about him nonetheless, stood by the window.

Through the clear plastic of the window, Black recognized the gray hills and drab towers of his own century. He was home, he thought, but with none of the feeling of homecoming that was usually present. He was, at best, a hunted outcast, even though his present surroundings were anything but dangerous.

"You'll only get into trouble helping me," he said slowly. "The State is pretty thorough in searching for escaped criminals."

Elizabeth Smith laughed. "We're not exactly new at this, you know. Your name has been erased from all State records and your property has become State property. As far as the State is concerned, you were killed back in the twentieth century by hunter Joseph Reed. And there is an adequate number of witnesses to verify that. The hunt is over for you, Black, though you'll have to live under an assumed name and occupation now. No danger is connected with it, though since nobody's looking for you."

Black absorbed this in silence. "Where do you fit in all of this?" he asked hesitantly.

The man turned from the window and came over to the bedside. "Has it ever occurred to you that some of the quarry, at one time or another, might have got away?"

"No quarry's ever escaped!" Black denied.

The girl's voice was crisp. "You did."

"Do you think that escaped quarry are reported, Black?" John Doe asked.

Black's first impulse was to affirm that they were, and then he paused and gave it some thought. There was a chance that some incompetent hunters would risk the chance of being discovered in a lie rather than admit their failure and be subject to the laughter of the community.

"You were quarry at one time, weren't you?" he guessed.

They nodded.

Black was curious. They didn't strike him as being particularly resourceful or capable in the hunts, they didn't look like they would have the strength or the stamina to last—though neither had done him much good.

"How did you get away?"

"We don't look like the type who would, do we?" the man asked dryly. "But looks aside, Beth and I and some of the others were adapted by past experience and training to be the most elusive of all quarry. As you know yourself, ability to *become* a part of the civilization in which you are hunted is the most important single item in hiding. Now considering that the hunts are held throughout all time, who do you think would be the best equipped to hide?"

"I see," Black said. "The two of you are historians then."

"Close enough," the girl said. "Actually, historical librarians, and that's speaking in the past tense; we hold other jobs now. But as quarries, we were in a position to know more about the background and culture of each civilization than any citizen or hunter."

"You were the third party concerned, weren't you?" Black asked.

The man nodded. "To use an old sports phrase, we ran interference for you—we and the others."

"The others?"

"We aren't the only ones who have managed to win through the hunts. And we got together." He paused. "You may as well know sooner or later, Black, that we—and you, like it or not—are in a revolutionary movement against the State, that we hope to overthrow it."

The idea sank home rather slowly to Black and when he had fully grasped it, he was appalled. "And you want my help, don't you?"

"Would you?"

"Of course," Black said slowly. "Certainly."

The way in which he said it made it obvious what he was thinking. If he refused, he had a good idea of what would happen. But the revolution would never enjoy his full efforts.

"You've been raised under the State and indoctrinated in its theories very thoroughly," the scholarly man explained. "It's only natural that you would be reluctant to help. But the State hasn't always existed, Black. There have been other and better types of government."

Black looked interested and the man plunged on.

"Five hundred years ago, the State—it wasn't called the State then—existed in a pretty black world. There was a struggle for survival, and in order to win that struggle the State was forced to turn itself into a military nation. It succeeded, possibly beyond its wildest intentions. Art died, literature died, individual freedom died; and the nation itself divided into two classes—the military, and those who supported the military; what gradually became the citizens and the rankanfilers of our own time.

"The State, as a state, survived. And with its winning, the need for our type of State died. But history shows that even when the need for them disappears, institutions and customs still live on. The State has been mobilized against a nonexistent enemy for the last four hundred years, Black, and we think it's time it changed. We need your help."

"How could I help you?"

John Doe smiled. "How would you revolt against a state like this one, Black? By military means?"

"No," Black said reluctantly, "of course not. The best way would be to work from within, I suppose—to corrupt the State and the people who run it."

"That's right. That's why we need your help. You know the majority of citizens in high places better than we do. If you helped us, it would be to supply information about the personal habits and whims of those high in the government. And perhaps, you yourself would have to undertake highly important and dangerous missions." He paused. "To be perfectly frank, we need a renegade citizen—one we can trust."

"What type of government would you install?" he asked cautiously.

"A lot like the one you saw in the civilization you were stranded in." Elizabeth Smith cut in quietly. "Without its obvious faults. Individual freedom to do as you wished, freedom of expression in art and literature. There would be such a thing as family life instead of the sterile exhibition you now have where children are taken from their parents at birth and where procreation is carried out under State auspices. Not a very successful program, incidentally, for if you could see the birth rate figures, you would know that in another thousand years the citizen class will be extinct."

"I'm not so sure I liked everything I saw in that time," Black protested mildly.

"You saw both sides," she continued, somewhat bitterly. "Those people who lived in the slums may have lived there from economic necessity but it wasn't because the government forced them to. You saw the art museums and you saw the Street, you saw the slums and you saw the better residential district. A nation—one that is free—doesn't exist on a dead level, you know. Some people rise and some people sink, but they all can do as they wish."

They have saved his life, Black thought—he owed them

quite a bit. But still, he couldn't change exactly how he felt. He wet his lips nervously and tried to phrase his next question as delicately as he could. "I take it you contemplate a government where the rankanfilers would have an equal voice with the citizens?"

Elizabeth Smith looked startled, and then let her breath out in a small "Oh!" of dismay.

John Doe looked at Black with disgust and then spoke as if Black wasn't there, as if Black no longer concerned him. "It isn't worth the effort, Beth. We should've considered that his background would prejudice him."

She caught her breath and turned back to Black, her voice under obvious control. "We're not quite as *human* as the citizens, are we, Black?"

"I didn't say that," he defended.

"No, but that's what you meant." She wheeled a portable view-set up to the bed and stuck a roll of film in the viewcase, then held the earphones towards him. "Here," she offered. "You live the roles for a change."

The fear was back with him again, the fear of running and hiding and being caught. He was dashing down a cobbled street, with odd-looking, ancient houses bordering it. There were gutters along the sides of the street, swimming with garbage and filth. Every once in a while somebody leaned out of one of the windows along the way and poured fresh slops into the street below.

He was running, with dogs yapping at his heels and indignant housewives swatting at him as he sped by. He was finally cornered against a stone wall and the huntsmen eagerly gathered to see justice done. He felt a sudden burning in his chest and even as he fell, realized that he had never had a chance and wasn't supposed to have. That he had been condemned to death in a civilization he knew nothing of for a crime that he had never committed—

He was a young girl, staring wildeyed at the sudden hate written on people's faces as somebody shrieked "Witch!" and pointed an accusing finger at her. She didn't even know what the word meant, except that it was bad and capable of arousing hate in the crowd. She started to run and then the pack was after her, skimming stones and lumps of filth at her head.

It was only after she had half lost consciousness from the smoke of the faggots piled around her feet, that she got the ending she had requested—one burn from a Williams, right over her heart. But it came too late to save her from pain—

He was a boy, not more than twelve years old, in a vast and smoky city where the buildings seemed to tower for thousands of feet on either side. He was seeing the same city he had just left, Black realized, but through a child's eyes. He was running, running, running—with the frantic pumping of a twelve-year-old's short legs. In the split mind that he had, Black wondered how the end would come, for the boy had been too young to request a specific end. Then there was a sudden squeal of brakes and a shrill scream and he knew—

"The last one," somebody was saying, "was interesting because the huntsman decided it added such a novel touch to kill the quarry by a method not unusual to that particular culture."

He was holding his face in his hands, trembling. Elizabeth Smith leaned over and pointedly held her hand in front of his eyes. "It's just as human as yours, Black. It hurt me just as much when I cut it, and like you, I have to wash it to keep it clean. We're as human as you, Black. We live as long, we get just as sick, and we die with just as many regrets."

There was dead silence for a while. "Who were those people?" Black asked shakily.

"They were some of the ones we tried to save, Black, but got there too late. We only saw how it ended."

He took a sobbing breath and tried to control his trembling hands. There had been a time, he remembered, when he had been a hunter himself.

"How did the hunts ever start?"

"They began a long time ago," John Doe said softly. "They antedate even the State. They started out as manhunts for criminals and evolved into hunts for those who opposed the dictator states of the twentieth century. With the development of the State and time cars, the hunts were seized upon as a convenient means for utilizing the military setup of the State. They became a sort of game, but unfortunately bona fide political and criminal quarries became less and less plentiful. It gradually became the custom to falsely accuse rankanfilers of crimes to obtain them for quarries."

"I think I suspected as much," Black said painfully, "but it was hard to turn against the State." His voice sounded tragic.

"I was raised with the State as my religion. It was all I knew, it was my life."

"You'll have to make a new world, Black," Elizabeth Smith said. "You can't live in the ruins of the old one. Throw in with us."

He nodded and suddenly changed the subject. "What happened to Reed?"

"He's back as a small cog in the State machinery," she said. "He knows nothing about either John or myself or our organization, but he knows that you've escaped back *there*. But he's still claimed your death to the State."

"He should be killed," Black said harshly. "He did too much to me."

She frowned distastefully. "Is killing the best thing you can think of, Black?"

She and John Doe had the organization, Black thought slowly. They could manage what he had in mind, and even if the State discovered it, the State was an inflexible institution and would not admit its error. All they had to do was plant certain whispers, certain implications—

And for Reed there would then be the agony and the fear and the knowledge that the proverbial thirty pieces of silver for which he had once betrayed David Black carried a heavy interest with it.

And for Reed, there would be no reprieve.

Joseph Reed was afraid.

He had tried to control it but he knew it showed in the glistening shine on his pale face, in the nervous jump of his cheek muscles, and in his restless pacing back and forth on the faded rug, alternating between the rumpled bed and the worn writing desk, with stops every few minutes at the soot-streaked window to note the position of the setting sun.

It was late afternoon. An hour or so more and the hunting season would begin.

I was smarter when the Navy discharged me the second time. I had a degree in Physics and a background in freelance writing. Since more GI Bill was available, I decided to get a Master's in journalism and become a science writer. The best of all possible worlds . . .

I enrolled at Northwestern University in Evanston, a suburb just north of Chicago. Evanston was also the home of Ray Palmer's *Other Worlds* and Bill Hamling's *Imagination*. For the first time, it was possible to casually drop in on the editors, like my peers in New York. I did some work for Ray but more for Bill—*Other Worlds* had already started to fall on hard times. In addition, Bill's wife, Frances, set a great table. (Bea Mahaffey, Palmer's managing editor, made dandy fudge; Frances served a sumptuous meal.)

I graduated at precisely the time when the science fiction field was collapsing. Circulations had dropped and the demise of the American News Company, which distributed most of the magazines, hastened the process. Unfortunately, I had just completed a science fiction novel, written as a class project for a course at N. U. Despite the rapidly softening field, "The Power" sold to Lippincott (which published it as a "novel of menace"), was serialized in *Blue Book*, and shortly after publication was televised on the old "Studio One." (The book received a number of excellent notices and one devastatingly unfavorable review by Damon Knight, science fiction's critic-in-residence and an excellent writer and anthologist. It's a mark of how thin-skinned I was at the time that Damon's review is still fresh in my memory while the more complimentary ones have faded.)

165

The sale of a book was even more of a kick than the sale of my first short story. It was the Big Time, the Pay-Off. Presumably, the logical next step would have been a return to free-lancing, right? Wrong. I wasn't going to make the same mistake twice.

After graduation, I looked for a job as an editor. One opportunity opened up right under my nose. Bill Hamling's science fiction magazines were doing badly. The idea of starting a men's magazine made a lot of sense and Bill's good friend, Hugh Hefner, offered to set up a luncheon date for Bill with his own distributor. (Hefner and Hamling had once worked together at Publisher's Development Corporation on such titles as *Modern Man* and *Art Photography*.) Hefner had started *Playboy* two years before and it had become something of a publishing sensation. Like Bill, Hefner had worked out of his home, pasting up the first issue on the kitchen table. (I once served as bartender for a party Bill threw in his rec-room/basement. Hefner was one of the guests, a thin, quiet man who leaned against a wall most of the night, nursing a drink. I later interviewed him for my Master's thesis on pornography and the law. It never occurred to me to apply for a job, though *Playboy*, with its staff of a dozen or so at the time, was obviously a fascinating place to work.)

At lunch with the distributor, Bill extolled the virtues of his projected men's book. It was to be patterned after *True* and *Argosy* and had the perfectly respectable title of "Caravan." The distributor glowered. What was it going to be about, camels? Bill quickly switched to an alternate title, *Rogue*. The distributor relaxed; he could visualize the contents already.

I was managing editor of *Rogue* for the first three issues, then dropped out to look for a job that paid real money. (I was also somewhat rather prudish back then. Contrasting what we ran to what's currently published, I can't remember what I was prudish about.)

It turned out *Iron Age* had an opening for a midwest correspondent. With my degree in journalism and experience working for U.S. Steel in Gary, Indiana, I decided I was eminently qualified. What more did they want? The then midwest correspondent, an affable young man named Keith Bennett, was in charge of interviewing for his own successor. I trotted out my brand new degree in journalism and also mentioned that I had written a number of science fiction stories. Bennett brightened. So, he said, had he. The name suddenly clicked. "You wrote 'The Rocketeers Have Shaggy Ears' in the Spring, 1950 issue of *Planet Stories!*" I blurted. I don't know who was more amazed. It had been a catchy title, one that had stuck with me for years. It was the only science fiction story he had ever written . . .

The pay-off is . . . I didn't get the job. I was bright-eyed and bushy-tailed but also poverty-stricken. I wore tennis shoes and a one-dollar sportcoat that looked it. Hardly the right image for *Iron Age* . . .

The next publication wasn't so fussy. The editor of the Sunday supplement, *Family Weekly*, a case-hardened ex-newspaperman, asked me if I could write and when I said yes, asked if I could prove it. I showed him the contract for "The Power" and his next question was when could I start.

I worked for a year at *Family Weekly*, then slipped into Fritz Leiber's chair at *Science Digest* when Fritz left. A few years later, *Science Digest* (along with its companion, *Popular Mechanics*) was sold to the Hearst chain and moved to the East Coast. I stayed behind as managing editor of the new, slick *Rogue*. *Playboy*'s contract had come up for renewal and, afraid of losing it, the distributor urged Hamling to go "slick" with *Rogue* so he would still have a "class" men's magazine in the house. Bill enthusiastically agreed. Then *Playboy* elected to stay with the distributor after all and eventually that led to difficulties: Both Hamling and I were determined to make *Rogue* a competitor.

Since both Bill and I had been science fiction fans and writers, we seeded the magazine with science fiction stories and science fiction contributors. (*Playboy*'s editors were also fond of science fiction and published a lot of it; at the start, they even reprinted a few science fiction stories from Hamling's *Imagination*.) Harlan Ellison worked on the magazine for a year (and brought in Lenny Bruce as a columnist), Bob Bloch and Alfred Bester did columns, and we published both fiction and articles by Charles Beaumont (under the pseudonym of "C. B. Lovehill"), Mack Reynolds, Fritz Leiber, Tom Scortia, Bob Silverberg, George Clayton Johnson, William F. Nolan, Damon Knight, Wilson Tucker, Arthur C. Clarke, William Tenn, Fred Pohl, Ray Russell, Frederic Brown, etc. We also published Graham Greene, Ian Fleming, William Saroyan, Nelson Algren, and Philip Wylie among others. We even had an article on comedy by the man best equipped to write it—Gary Marshall, currently TV's multi-threat man with "Happy Days," "Laverne and Shirley," "Mork and Mindy," "The Odd Couple," etc., to his credit.

We should have made it.

But we didn't.

We finally had to shift to another distributor. (Annoyed by what he considered to be an imitation, Hefner demanded that *Rogue* drop its gatefold and its four-color cartoons. We refused and, since *Playboy*'s franchise was far more valuable to the distributor than *Rogue*'s, we had to leave.) Then the new distributor went broke, which left *Rogue* with just enough money in the corporate kitty to pay the salaries . . . plus 400,000 copies of the latest issue sitting on the loading docks with no place to ship them.

Bill scrambled desperately to save the magazine. He had once been unjustly characterized by a former associate as having "all that engine and no steering wheel" but his actions during this period couldn't be faulted. Within days, we had a new distributor and a new line of credit. (Bill Hamling had both courage and enormous energy. It was never what he *did* with *Rogue* that bothered Hefner; it was what he *might* do.)

Sadly, the handwriting was already on the wall. *Playboy* had come to dominate the field and Bill's claim that where there was a *Time*, there was also room for a *Newsweek* no longer held true. There was no way a 90-page *Rogue* could compete with a 200-page *Playboy* at the same cover price. . . .

(*Rogue* also suffered from some editorial decisions I made. The most glaring was when a prospective gatefold girl turned out to have been the original "topless bathing suit girl." We billed her that way on the cover but ran her nude on the inside, neglecting to include any of the bathing suit shots. Guess what photographs the disappointed readers *really* wanted to see. . . .)

By the end of 1965, after finally managing to put out the Christmas issue, I returned from the West Coast—the printer was in California—and told Bill that it was all over except for the memories. . . .

There were some great ones: Eating dinner with Charlie Beaumont in the Ambassador East (on Charlie's *Playboy* expense account) when the waiter brought over a plug-in telephone along with the message that "Hollywood was calling." George Pal was on the other end of the line, offering Charlie the script assignment for "The Brothers Grimm." It was my first taste of Hollywood glamour and I turned an appropriate green. . . . And there was the time when investigators from the State Attorney's office came around looking for the "Blake Pharmaceutical Company," a "cover" corporation for several racy paperback lines that Bill was publishing out of a back room. Patty O'Brien, our Irish secretary, brushed them off with a scornful: "Does this look like a drugstore to you?" It was also Patty who announced my own phone call from Hollywood: George Pal calling about the rights to "The Power." He offered me a chance to do the script but I was still trying to pump life into a failing *Rogue* and declined. . . .

And, of course, there was the Saturday afternoon when Bill and I debated what to do about cartoons for an issue already late at the printer's. Several years before, Bill had discovered a cartoonist named Interlandi who gradually became our staff cartoonist. He did almost all our full page cartoons, working under a dozen different names and with a variety of styles. Hugh Hefner liked Interlandi, too, and that week had signed him to an exclusive contract, purchasing all the cartoons in his studio, including those earmarked for our issue of *Rogue*. So we sat up in the offices and plotted dark revenge. . . .

Then Bill casually mentioned that he had once bought some cartoons from Hefner himself for *Imagination* but had never run them. (Hefner was an amateur cartoonist and had even published a book of his own cartoons titled "This Toddlin' Town." He was a skilled and shrewd publisher; a skilled cartoonist he was not.)

I promptly suggested that we run the Hefner cartoons along with a cover line announcing—in large type—"Cartoons by Hugh M. Hefner." (I'll confess to malice aforethought but it was a hot afternoon and we were both angry.) Bill thought it a capital idea and we wrote Hefner a letter requesting a photograph of him that we could run on our author's page. Mr. Hefner was not amused. The next week his secretary called to ask what the hell was going on. By this time I had second thoughts—it occurred to me that someday I might want to work for the man—and assured her that we couldn't find the cartoons. It was true, we couldn't. (But if we had. . . .)

So *Rogue* was sold. I paid off the staff, peddled the office furniture, and moved to Los Angeles to lick my wounded pride. And later that year, I once again started writing science fiction . . .

The first four pages of "The Wreck of the Ship John B." had actually been written ten years before. For some reason I had never finished it, put the pages in the file, and forgot about them. When I stumbled across them years later, they read with a freshness that surprised me. I completed the story and instructed my agent to send it to *Analog*, convinced it was right up John Campbell's alley. The agent ignored my instructions but I couldn't complain. The story sold the first time out.

To *Playboy*—which paid $3,000 and ran it as the lead-in issue.

The Wreck of the Ship John B.

I spotted the corpse the 1356th time period out. It was floating alone in the indifferent blackness of space ten billion miles from nowhere, the small jets attached to its space suit empty of fuel and the oxygen tank a depleted, echoing canister of aluminum. There was nothing else within immediate range, which meant that the body had drifted in the silent dark for thousands of time periods, the air in its suit gradually seeping out through a hundred microscopic pinholes and the cold seeping in, turning the man inside into a frozen, desiccated mummy.

It was sheer accident that I had picked it up at all. I had given up running the radar on automatic sweep hundreds of time periods before; but this particular period, for reasons I couldn't put a finger on, I had gotten tired of staring through my compartment ports, dreaming of home or trying to figure out what seemed so strange about the ship lately, and decided to run the gear through a routine check. It picked up the suit on the fourth sweep, right after I had fired it up. The sweep line in the viewing globe staggered to a halt, hunted for a moment, then narrowed to a bright thread of scarlet. The panic button flashed red and a split second later the "All Stations" alarm echoed throughout the *Cassiopeia* like the brassy trumpet call of doom—which, I suppose, it really was.

I must have stared at the globe for a full minute, idly scratching my tattooed captain's bars and wondering what the hell it could be, before I began working the magnifier to bring the hologram closer. When I could make out what it was, the sweat popped out between my shoulder blades and a chill grew in my stomach. I waited until the control console indicated all stations were manned—some 2.3 minutes behind optimum schedule, though I had really ceased to worry about optimum schedules long ago—then hollered into the squawk box for Coleman, our metalsmith, to suit up and drift out and get it.

Once the body was inside the air lock, other crew members acted as honorary pallbearers and bore it quietly into the communications compartment and laid it gently on the deck, using light magnetic clamps to secure it to the metal flooring.

It was quite an occasion and I guess we were all aware of it, or so I thought at the time—the first martyr to be recovered from space. A few minutes later, the rest of the crew had kicked silently into the compartment to cling to the brake rings and cold light tubes until the tiny cabin looked like a human aviary with ten nude and featherless birds clustered in it.

It must have been at least 500 time periods since we had all been in one compartment together and probably only slightly less than that since I had spoken to another member of the crew. During the long voyage, the humanity in you slowly evaporates, like a puddle of water in a hot sun, and you grow apart. It was probably different on military ships, but the *Cassiopeia* was a freighter and I was an elected captain and we weren't really a crew, we were future colonists—which meant young, brainy and noncooperative. The ship was completely automatic, of course, which made us strictly a group of passengers, like those in a crowded transit shuttle back on Earth. We had make-work, but eventually we grew bored and sick and tired of one another and then silent and hostile. The Colonization Board had expected that and made sure we had shadow screens and no weapons of any kind. For our part, we wore Privacy like an invisible suit of armor, and the day inevitably came when we didn't speak to one another at all.

Nobody said a word now, all stared expressionless at the thing on the deck. They were waiting for the captain to speak—and I didn't know what to say. I didn't look like a captain—I was short and skinny and cursed with a baby face and pale hair the color of ashes—and right then I didn't feel like a captain, either. I coughed, the noise sounding gross and vulgar in the humid cabin, and wondered how to begin, then realized I couldn't see the death mask behind the cracked faceplate of the space suit. The warm moisture in the cabin had condensed into an army of fine white crystals intent on burying the thing where it lay.

I kicked over to the suit, grabbed a floor ring to brake myself and hunkered down by the frosted metal. I brushed away the crystals from the plate, wiped my hands on my naked thighs and rocked back and forth on my heels, momentarily absorbed by the fragile face behind the plate. Then it was time to say something and I was suddenly acutely conscious of the soft whine of the central computer, the murmur of the ventilation machinery that never quite removed all the moisture and human stink from the air, and the shallow breathing of the naked crew in the cramped cabin. I could feel the temperature start to creep up even as I knelt there, and then the smell got to me and I almost gagged. We had no ship's laundry, no separate living quarters and no showers—cargo was too valuable, so space and weight were at a premium—which meant that living on board the *Cassiopeia* was like living in a crowded locker room just after the winning game, when you can taste the sweat in the steamy air.

I frowned, glanced up at Potter, the pimply-faced kid who was our life-systems man, and clicked my thumbnail against the faceplate with a great show of deliberation. "Not . . . pretty," I croaked. My voice sounded oddly loud and choked with rust.

Potter licked his lips, picked nervously at his scraggly beard, looked like he was going to say something, then merely nodded. Hulsman, our man in microcircuitry, the boyish blond type that fat old ladies love to mother, opened his mouth, noticed that nobody else was about to speak, closed it again and instead made fluttering motions with his hands. Reynolds, a pudgy medical tech, expert at splinters, boils, blisters, hives and shipboard circumcisions, fingered his nose and looked wise. Ball, the astronomer, tall, thin and professionally British, the man I had always thought should have been captain, was suddenly preoccupied with his loincloth. Skinny little Jimenez, our physicist, whom we had earlier dubbed Keeper of the Pile, hid behind his thick glasses and bushy red beard and tried to appear inscrutable, while Adams, Kentworthy and Herschel merely stared at the thing on the deck with varying degrees of distaste and—to my surprise—disinterest.

I made the mental note *crew all present and accounted for* and swore that this time period I would actually enter it in the log, then turned my attention back to the suit. The shrunken face and the dried eyeballs and the marble mouth. I shivered. If the suit's radio had been working, you could probably have heard him scream for hours. Then something caught my eye and I leaned closer, my own breath fogging the faceplate. The radio switch was off. *But that isn't done,* I thought. *Nobody leaves a ship with his radio off.*

I nodded to Coleman, now out of his suit, and asked: "Know age?"

He hooked a foot under a brake ring and squatted down, his badge of office, the screwdriver, tucked into his greasy loincloth, ringing slightly against the deck. He was a tiny, bandy-legged man with curly black body hair and heavy eyebrows and a broad nose that made his face look faintly anthropoidal. He wiped at the suit and grunted, "Old model, maybe two-three hundred years. Dark Ages stuff."

Which didn't tell me much, so I said, "Let's open him up."

We fumbled with the frozen fastenings, then dumped the body out of the suit like dice out of a cup; frost immediately silvered it with a thin rime. Potter and I inspected the body carefully while Coleman went over the suit. The corpse felt light and dry—papier-mâché. "Nothing," I finally muttered, baffled more by thoughts of what I ought to be looking for than by what I had found. "No wounds, he didn't bleed." I studied the faint expression, a human watermark barely discernible on the dried and frozen flesh. "Doesn't look unhappy, looks more . . . annoyed? Alive when he put the suit on, alive when he left the ship alone."

Alone?

I dove back to the viewing globe just as the alarm bell thundered throughout the ship once again.

I wrapped my legs around the control console, signaled the crew to remain in the cabin and let my fingers dance over the banked control boards. The ranges dwindled and the stars in the viewing globe exploded outward, touched the globe's surface and vanished in brief sparkles of light. A moment later, the globe held another hologram of a suit cartwheeling through space.

Same model, I thought. Another man from the same ship, another drifter dancing his solitary waltz. I ran my hands swiftly over the console again and the ranges grew, the stars shrinking in toward the center. The sweep line sprouted a dozen thin, red branches and a thick trunk—a dozen drifting men and the ship they came from.

"Want me to get them all?" Coleman asked, looking apprehensive. "There's time . . . fuel mass." He pointed to the corpse on the deck. "One isn't enough?"

I shook my head. "I want their ship," I said quietly.

I heard movement among the crew members behind me and Jimenez drifted around the console and grabbed a brake ring. He had that thin Latin skin and I could see the little veins pulsing at his temples. "Why?" It came out as a furious, muffled croak. "No business of ours—can't do anything anyway. Ship's dead, crew's dead, can't bring them back to life.

Not our business!" He was a scrawny little man and, with his dirty glasses and the cords standing out in his neck, he looked 30 years older than he really was; I had to remind myself that he and I both had an Earth year to go before we reached our majority.

I glanced at the others. They were looking at the viewing globe as if it held something that smelled bad. I was pushing it, I thought. But then, the derelict had been—what? Gutted by a meteorite, boarded by—something?

I shook my head and made slight corrections for the viewing globe. "Whatever happened to them could happen to us," I said logically. "Maybe we can find out what it was."

Jimenez hunched over the globe, the exploding stars disappearing into the reddish thatch that covered his thin chest. I was physically closer to him right then than I had been to anybody in hundreds of time periods, and the proximity made me nervous. His voice was carefully slow, the voice you use with an adolescent when you're underlining a warning. "It's not our business, Martin! And if there's danger, we have no weapons to protect ourselves or our ship. And since *that* crew is dead and floating Outside, there's obviously danger—and nothing we can use against it!"

"What's *it*?" I asked casually.

He got red in the face, glared at me for a moment longer, then shrugged his pipe-rack shoulders and said, "Have it your way." He let go of the brake ring and drifted a few feet over to the side of the cabin with the others. I concentrated on watching the suits float past in the silence of space, the close-ups spinning through the globe. One, two, three . . . A dozen men, lifeless and frozen, drifting in the spotted silence, forming a funnel-shaped path back to the ship for which they had once crewed. Then the suits were gone and there was only a glittering beach of stars with a small red smear in the center that grew steadily larger. When it came within the smallest hologram range, I spun the controls and it leaped to full view. I motioned to Coleman, who slanted over to the console and inspected the image in the globe as if it were a tissue slice under a microscope.

"Freighter class, Model A-18, two hundred years old— closer to two-thirty. Tell by the flare to the tubes."

"You're too sure," I said.

"Made models when I was a kid," he grunted. "Won a lot of prizes."

I stared at the ship in the globe. It was old, all right—the ancient dumbbell shape, with small circular ports and awkward radar antennae projecting out beyond the hull. And then I saw it—an exit hatch gaping open as if some celestial dentist had asked it to say "Ah." I got the same feeling I used to get on Earth looking at the people on the moving sidewalks from 200 stories up: a lurching sensation in my stomach and a loose feeling around my anus.

We drifted into a tight orbit around the derelict and waited. I started to sweat—a thin film of slime that oozed out all over my body—and I knew that I stank; algae-based meals have something in them that's worse than garlic. We kept inspecting the freighter in the viewing globe, hoping to get some clue, but there was nothing to be seen from a distance—only the ship itself silhouetted against the stars, one hatch open to space. There was no sign of any physical activity and no sudden burst of chatter from our radio receiver, which was running up and down the frequency spectrum like a squirrel on a tree, hoping to lock onto a signal. There was no sign of life on the infrared detectors and only residual pile activity showed on the Geigers.

"You going to board her?" Coleman asked hesitantly. I could sense the attention of the crew suddenly switch from the viewing globe to me.

"How many long-voyage ships fail to reach their destination?" I mused. "Thirty percent? Forty?"

Reluctantly. "About that."

"Anybody know why?" I asked quietly. "No. Anybody ever found a freighter that didn't make it? No again—in the deeps of space, there isn't even any sense looking. But somebody just found one. We did. And somebody can now hold an autopsy. Us."

Coleman's face was all lines and angles, his brows two greasy black thumbprints over his small brown eyes. "Look— we're freighter class, *long-voyage* freighter class. The only weapons on board are knives less than three inches in length."

"You think aliens are a possibility?" None had ever been found.

"Not likely."

"Then what's bothering you?"

"I—don't know." His usual growl faded to a mumble and he wouldn't meet my eyes; I was forcing him into a corner and I knew he hated me for it. "I don't think we ought to bother. It doesn't really concern us."

I stared at him for a moment and his face grew red. Then I glanced back at the viewing globe, at the lonely ship framed against the glitter of the galaxy, and made up my mind. I turned to the crew and said curtly, "Any volunteers for a boarding party?"

Nobody looked at me and nobody raised a hand. I let the silence grow and finally Jimenez said in his hoarse croak, "This isn't a military cruiser and you're not a real captain, Martin. You're elected—and we can elect another if we want."

I shrugged to myself. I had half expected it and it really didn't matter. If they wanted a new captain, that was jake with me. And then I thought about it a moment longer, about maybe Jimenez running the ship, and decided—much to my surprise—that it wasn't jake at all. Not really.

"Fine," I lied. "I didn't ask for the job. Anybody who wants the responsibility and the work that goes with it"—there wasn't much, but you'd have to be captain to know that—"can have it. Anybody want to nominate himself? Hulsman?" He looked alarmed and shook his head. "Ball?" He declined, too, which surprised me—I figured if anybody would have grabbed it, Ball would have. "Jimenez?" He hesitated. "Come on, Jimenez," I said, "the involvement will be good for you."

It worked, of course. He shook his head and rasped, "No thanks."

"Anybody else?" There were no takers. "Thank you all for the honor, gentlemen. Jimenez, Coleman, suit up." I turned to the others. "Ball is acting captain. If we fail to return within three time periods, resume voyage. Do not try rescue."

I unwrapped my legs from the console, motioned Ball over to it, then floated to the space-suit locker. We suited up in silence and all the while I felt vaguely unhappy. Nobody had wanted to get involved with my excursion over to the derelict, but nobody had really put a fight against it, either; and for some reason, that bothered me.

It was while drifting across to the derelict that I had my first really bad time of it. In space, you tend to react one of two ways. For some, the environment has no meaning—Outside is a room of black velvet with small lights for stars embedded in the black, and you, your shipmates and your ship comprise the immediate horizons. The psychological *Gestalt* is not one of vastness but one of an odd miniaturization. For others, particularly if they lose their referent points, reality floods their sensory apparatus and they panic. It was something that hadn't been foreseen by the early astronauts, who could position themselves in space by the huge bulk of the Earth nearby and their own space capsules. In deep space, a man can't conceive of the vastnesses, the immense stretches in any direction, the feeling of no horizon, no end to the uncharted silent reaches.

It hit me when I was halfway across. I had twisted slightly to get at my laser flashlight and for a split second I lost sight of the *Cassiopeia*, the derelict, and Coleman and Jimenez. I could suddenly *feel* the immensities, the intense quiet, the frozen loneliness, the indifference. It was like being cast adrift on a huge ocean at night, an ocean in which there was no spark of life in the black waters below and no familiar beating of wings in the dark skies above and the nearest land was so far away you could not even imagine the distance.

My muscles spasmed and my suddenly clenched hand automatically turned on the laser flash. My eyes followed the beam outward until it was lost in space—a beam of light that penciled out and vanished in the immensities, but which in my mind's eye kept running on and on and on. And then the sense of my own insignificance crushed me and there was only blackness and I closed my eyes and knew I was falling but there was no floor that I would ever hit.

It sounded at first like a baby crying and then I realized it was myself. I jerked my eyes open wide, started to cartwheel, then caught a glimpse of Coleman and Jimenez on my left, silently watching. Their size immediately told me their distance from myself and suddenly the whole scene collapsed and inverted itself, like a curious optical illusion. The vastness was actually a room with dimension, the *Cassiopeia* and the derelict marking the positions of the walls of black velvet studded with the tiny lights that looked like stars.

I caught my breath, swallowed, pushed the panic from my mind and set my suit rockets so I slowly circled the derelict. At the far end I spotted the name, almost pitted into illegibility: The *John B.*—I couldn't tell what the last name was. Then the hatch was yawning open below me and Jimenez and Coleman had already disappeared inside. I clung to the lip for a moment before ducking through and stared back at the black depths behind me, at the sandy sifting of stars and the *Cassiopeia* riding in silhouette half a mile away. The words came automatically: *ghostly galleons*. Nor did the feeling vanish once inside. The shadow screens, shutting out sight and sound, were on, apparently still operated by the residual activity of the pile, cutting the ship into cubicles and compartments and a main corridor. The cold light tubes were also on, bathing the empty corridor in brilliance after—how many time periods? I knew without looking further that the ship was deserted and I could imagine echoing footsteps and pale ghosts.

> *Oh pilot, 'tis a fearful night! There's*
> *danger on the deep.*

Jimenez and Coleman drifted up to me, looking like oddly articulated fish in their suits. "We won't split up until we can turn off the shadow screens," I said, trying very much to sound like a ship's captain. "Crew's quarters first, then communications, then the pile room." Even to myself, I sounded officious.

Jimenez' voice was an irritating squeak in my headphones. "What are we looking for?"

"Don't you think you'll know when you see it?" I asked. And then it occurred to me that he wasn't being sarcastic after all.

We hit the crew's quarters first—the one long compartment with individual ports, elasto-hammocks, and individual viewing screens hooked up to the central computer, the standard source of information and entertainment, the electronic tit on which we all suckle as soon as we're on board. There were switches for the read-out screens, plus additional switches so you could partition off your section with a shadow screen for Privacy. And that struck me as odd—*all* the screens were on, which was highly unlikely, though I had noted their increasing use aboard the *Cassiopeia*.

I ignored my own dictum about staying in sight and pushed through into one of the screened-off compartments. It was empty, of course, but there were telltale signs of human occupancy, like a fading whiff of perfume in the air. The archaeologist entering the burial tomb, I thought. And from an ax handle and a shard of pottery, I'll resurrect the man who lived here. But there was damn little in this tomb. A chessboard had been set up—it was forbidden to bring anything personal aboard, but Coleman had smuggled one aboard the *Cassiopeia* and I had no doubt but what it was a standard bit of contraband—and dates of games played and who had won and who had lost marked with a soft pen on the bulkhead. I knelt down and looked at the dates. At first a game had been played every time period, then it was every other, then every tenth time period, and finally—the 1267th time period out— two members of the crew had played their last game. The pieces were still on the board and by the looks of it, the game had only just begun. Then there had been an interruption and the players had left and the game had never been resumed.

I shoved through to the next screened compartment and just then Coleman located the central switch and all the shadow screens dissolved and we were in one large compartment. At the far end was the pile room and at the near one, the control console and communications. Crew's quarters were in between, spiraling like a gigantic helix around what had been the main corridor. I started to drift over to join Coleman, then suddenly hung back. A thin magnetic food tray was on the deck by one of the elasto-hammocks. I bent and ran a metal finger across the residue on the tray. The meal had been half eaten, the remains now effectively freeze-dried. Somebody had obviously set the tray down, magnetic fork carefully placed back in the indentation provided, and walked away. The tray hadn't been dumped in panic, the food particles in the standard gummy sauce that adhered to the metal tray hadn't been scattered—what looked like artificial rice, steak and peas were still within their shallow compartments.

There was a sound in my headphones and I looked up to see Jimenez waving at me from the power pile. I floated over. The dials and rheostats indicated that the pile was at neutral—a high enough level of activity to supply power for the cold light tubes and the shadow screens and perhaps a few other facilities, but hardly enough to provide any thrust.

Jimenez had the engineer's log open and I glanced down to where his finger was pointing. *Shut pile down, time period 1436. Signed, Dickinson, Physicist.* So it had happened 169 time periods after the last chess game had been started, I thought. If I guessed correctly, that was the time period the ship had been deserted. From then on, the *John B.* had drifted.

"Coleman . . ."

He floated over, the beard behind his faceplate making him look like a monkey in a glass cage.

"Granted the pattern in which we found them, do you have any idea within how much time of each other the crew members would had to have left the ship?"

His voice sounded metallic and puzzled. "Not the faintest, not over a drift pattern of two hundred years. The computer could figure it." He paused. "Probably within a few time periods of each other, maybe a few hours."

"Could they have all left together?"

"No, we would have found them all clumped together then. No, I think they left within hours of each other."

I shivered. So one by one they had suited up and walked out, I thought. Walked out to a certain death, indifferent to the ship, indifferent to their mission, indifferent to life itself. And no indication as to why. No struggle, no hurriedly scrawled notes, no indication of force.

We ended our search at the far end of the compartment, by the control console and the central computer. I had a sudden hunch and sat down at the console. There was enough pile activity to energize the computer. I tapped out a request for a Biblical passage as a test. There was a soft whine and clicking and then the passage appeared on the readout screen, the lines moving slowly up from the bottom to the top.

Lord, make me to know mine end, and the measure of my days, what it is; that I may know how frail I am.

I hesitated a moment, guessed at a date, ran my fingers over the keys and requested a list of read-outs for the 437th time period. Soft clicking. Biologist Scheer had requested information on chess, mathematician Bailey had requested current light fiction, Captain Shea had wanted a history of the Renaissance. I jumped to the 989th time period. No requests. I tried a few periods later. Still none. There were no further requests for another 31 time periods, then psychologist Hendrix had suddenly wanted to read everything about the problems of cities in the late 20th, early 21st Centuries. There were no requests after that until the 1436th time period, when physicist Dickinson had wanted technical information on the pile. From there on, the request files were completely blank.

I suddenly felt a hammering through the metal soles of my boots and looked up from the read-out screen to see Coleman tearing at a bulkhead safe with a spanner wrench. The safe abruptly gave way and Coleman did a slow flip, grabbing a brake ring to stop himself. He fumbled around in the safe, then drifted over to me with a half dozen log tapes. The inscription on one of the small cans read: *Log of the John B.*

McClellan. The name jogged my memory and I recalled it in a footnote in a textbook, one of the names in a long listing of lost ships.

I told Coleman to take them back with him, then turned to Jimenez: "We miss anything?"

. . He dutifully glanced around at the cabin behind him, but I got the feeling that he really wasn't seeing it. "You can't think of anything, I sure as hell can't."

I started for the hatch, then drifted back to the central computer and took the big reel of tape with its listing of read-out requests. Who knew . . .

On the way out, what had been in the back of my mind finally hit me. *I hadn't found anything wrong.* No signs of being boarded, no signs of violence—nothing wrong with the ship itself. Which left—what? The crew?

And then I didn't think of it anymore, because we had left the cave of the *John B.* behind and I was in the emptiness of space again, frantically trying to locate the *Cassiopeia* and get a bearing before the illusion reversed itself and I was once more an insignificant speck suspended in a black void without end.

We committed the unknown crewman to space once more with appropriate ceremony, made the necessary course corrections and resumed the long voyage. The *John B.* dwindled in the distance behind us and then was nothing more than a memory and a half dozen computer tapes.

I spent the next three or four time periods listening to the contents of the *John B.'s* log, almost all of which consisted of routine, technical entries. Those entries that weren't—most of these were at the beginning—mentioned winners in the daily chess tournament and what could be classified as mild gossip items about members of the crew. Toward the end, there were stretches of missing entries where the captain had failed to file his daily report.

The last entry was for the last time period. *Am going Outside.*

There was no explanation given, no reason, no mention of any threat. I could imagine the captain putting down his speakalong, suiting up and walking out. But I had no clue as to why.

I stored the log tapes in the computer locker, made a mental note to give them a more thorough run-through in the near future and spent the next few time periods speculating about them while stretched out in my compartment, the shadow screens on, staring quietly out the port at the sowing of stars in the unfathomable distance. The tapes gradually slipped from my mind and I started thinking about Earth and New Chicago and the green fields of the Midwest and the 500 time periods we had to go before we made planet-fall. And then one period I was lying there thinking of those 500 segments of time and wondering what it would be like to run down a sidewalk again or dive into a pool of water, when I suddenly reflected that there was a certain unreality to my thinking. Planet-fall, another world, blue skies . . . But there was no conviction to my thinking, no real belief that that kind of future was going to happen.

I really came awake then, and it was like waking up in a house in the middle of the night, when you catch yourself listening, and you're sweating and shaking and just lying there waiting. And then I had my finger on it and the thought didn't shift fast enough to get away. I really didn't believe we were going to make planet-fall. What I *did* believe, way down deep, was that one day we were going to suit up and casually walk out of the *Cassiopeia*.

I sat up on the edge of my hammock and cocked an ear and let my shadow screen fade and just listened to the ship for a moment. The silence was smothering, and yet I could remember laughter and curses and games in the corridor and times when you could see the whole undivided compartment for time period after time period.

My mind started to race and fall all over itself. The *John B.* hadn't been hulled by a meteorite or boarded by alien life forms. Mechanical failure? But long-voyage freighters had triple safeguards; it was impossible for something to go wrong with the pile or the computer or the electrical setup. The life-systems setup—something *could* go wrong there, but chances were vanishingly slim. Which left . . .

The crew, of course.

But there had been no signs of violence, no signs of mutiny. A saboteur on board? But there had to be an opposing political or military setup and there was none. Mass insanity? Hardly—not in the accepted sense.

I thought about what the *Cassiopeia* had been like right after blast-off and what it was like now, and shivered. It had been like watching a clock run down. The life had gradually seeped out of the crew while the shadow screens had grown like ivy. When was the last time Coleman had played a chess game? And when was the last time I had filed a log report?

I had to do something about it, I thought, lying back down on the elasto-hammock—the very next time period. And then I realized what I was doing and turned pale. Not the next time period, *now*! I tumbled off the hammock and shoved over to Jimenez's compartment and pushed through the shadow screen, not waiting to palm for permission.

He was sacked out on his hammock, his eyes closed, his heavy reddish body hair covering him like a soft auburn fuzz. When he had first come on board, he had been alert, alive, almost obnoxiously eager—constantly checking the pile, filling his calculating slate with row after row of figures, delighted that the central computer contained enough information on his specialty to keep him busy for three solid years.

He suddenly sensed I was there and opened his eyes to stare quietly at me, without expression. I said, "Hello, Specs."

"Privacy, Martin."

"I wanted to ask you what you thought about the *John B.*," I said.

He turned his back, his spine looking like a long, reddish caterpillar. "I don't think about it, Martin."

"Why not?"

"If you're playing twenty questions, I'm not interested."

"It's serious," I said.

"Sure." He was quiet for a moment and I began to think he had actually drifted off to sleep, when he suddenly said, "I don't think about it because there's nothing we can do about it and it's none of our business."

"I think——" I started.

"I don't give a damn *what* you think! I want Privacy—now get the hell out, will you?"

"What would you do," I said slowly, "if I told you that the pile was redlining?"

He sat up on one elbow and glared. "I'd call you a goddamned liar! Nothing's wrong with that pile—nothing ever has been and nothing ever will be! It doesn't need the attention of *men*, Martin! This ship doesn't *need* a physicist or a metalsmith or an astronomer—or a captain, for that matter. Something could happen to any one of us and it wouldn't matter a damn—we're passengers, Martin, passengers!" He sagged back down and stared quietly at the screened overhead. His voice was barely audible. "Get out of here, will you?"

I backed out and drifted over to Hulsman's compartment. The shadow screens were on there, too—all of the ship's screens were on, I noted—and I hesitated a moment before floating through. Hulsman was the youngest on board, our mascot when we had left Earth. He was the likable type—blond hair, freckles, a smile that was catching. You wanted to rub your knuckles on the back of his head and send him to the outfield to shag flies.

I pushed through and found him watching me. It was an older face now—much older—framed by long, dirty blond hair, and the bright-blue eyes were a dull and dirty slate.

"Hello, Martin." The voice was listless.

"I was thinking about the *John B.*," I said casually. "I was wondering what you thought."

A tired look flooded his face, as if talking and thinking were too much effort. "I guess I haven't thought much about it, Martin. I guess I don't much care."

"Don't you think the same thing could happen to us?"

A flicker of concern wandered uncertainly over his face and then fled. "That was a long time ago, wasn't it?"

"You're not curious?"

"I guess I ought to be, but I'm not." He lay there quietly for a moment, then suddenly closed his eyes and turned his back to me. "Look, Martin, would you—you know—leave me alone? I guess I can't help much."

I stood there and looked at him, helpless. "That's Ok, I understand, Hully."

I had started to drift out when he suddenly said in a low voice, "I got this funny feeling, Martin, this feeling that I ought to be doing something—only somehow I can't get started. I *ought* to be able to do something on board, Martin." Then he turned slightly and jammed his face into the hammock. "It scares me," he whispered in a muffled voice. "It scares the hell out of me."

The first real crisis came 20 time periods later, when life on board the *Cassiopeia* had unwound even further and we were all nonthinking slow-motion ghosts. I was in the life-systems compartment, along with Hulsman, Ball and Coleman, lining up for the "evening meal," though most of the crew now preferred to draw their meals when nobody else was around and they didn't run the risk of having to talk to any-

body. I was at one of the food dispensers working the selec-
tors above my tray when Potter pushed in to take a tray from
the rack and shove over to the next food slot a few feet
away. When he shoved away from the rack, his tray caught
in the food slot and he slid on past it.

It happened quickly enough. The thin tray, worn sharp
from hundreds of insertions into the metal mouth of the food
dispenser, caught in the slot, and when Potter slid past it, the
sharp edge of the tray slashed deep into his forearm.

None of us said a word, we just stared. Potter had grabbed
a brake ring and now floated in the middle of the compartment, a big frightened kid staring wide-eyed at his left arm
where the blood spurted, balled, then flattened slowly toward
the deck.

It seemed like a full minute went by and still nobody
moved. I stood glued by the side of the food dispenser, my
mind split. One part of it—a large part—wasn't reacting at
all. It was simply watching Potter, watching him bleed,
watching the blood pool on the deck, wondering curiously
what Potter was going to do next. It was like watching a fascinating stereocast. The hologram that was Potter was going
to die, right before my eyes, from a slashed main artery. It
was something I had never seen before.

And then it made connection. Maybe none of us were vital
to the *ship*, but Potter was the life-systems man and he was
vital to the *crew*. And Potter was going to *die*!

I dropped my tray and dove over to him. He stood there in
semishock, trembling and staring stupidly at his arm. I tore at
my loincloth and bound the rag tightly around his arm, then
whirled to Hulsman, watching blank-faced.

"Get Reynolds, on the double!"

He didn't move; his eyes were glazed.

I tightened the bandage, knotted it, then grabbed a handful
of food off my tray that had settled to the deck nearby and
threw it at Hulsman. The mess hit along the side of his neck
and slid slowly off toward his shoulder.

*"Move, you sonofabitch, or I'll push you face first into the
nearest dispenser and let you drown in that slop! Snap it!"*

"Privacy . . ." Hulsman started to chatter.

"MOVE, DAMNIT!"

He shot from his bench into the cold light corridor, frantically grabbing at brake rings to guide his progress. I could
hear him bawling for Reynolds even as he disappeared from
view.

Pain and shock were now washing through Potter. He clutched his arm and started to moan, then looked up at me, his face horror-stricken. "I could have died," he blubbered. "They would have let me die."

A dozen time periods after Potter had slashed his arm, the rest of the crew had faded even further into long-voyage apathy, remote to one another, remote even to themselves. The ship was now a jungle of shadow screens preserving Privacy. Crew members went out of their way to avoid one another, and when they did meet, it was with hostile noncuriosity.

I made friends with Potter because he saved my life.

There had come a time period when, psychologically speaking, I caved in and started to avoid the others. I spent more and more of my time floating in my compartment, staring out the port and thinking of home or maybe of absolutely nothing at all. I had been the only one to worry about the ship and the crew—all right, now, to hell with them. And shortly after that, when Potter shoved through my shadow screen without palming for permission. I caught myself saying automatically, "Privacy, Potter."

"You've got trouble, Captain."

I came out of it like a man waking up in the morning. "Whadd'ya mean?"

"Ball's suiting up to go Outside. You've got maybe three minutes to catch him."

I rolled off my hammock, shoved against a brake ring and shot up the corridor, grabbing rings as I passed to give myself a little additional thrust each time. I clipped through one shadow-screened compartment, taking a chance of colliding with its occupant, then rounded a corner and bore down on the space-suited figure quietly working the controls of the inner air lock. I sailed in between the figure and the lock, grabbing a ring and braking to a halt with a speed that almost tore my arms out of their sockets.

"Going someplace, Ball?"

He stared at me, then reached up and unclamped his helmet and took it off. He shook his head, sending his black beard and long hair flying, and smiled woodenly. He looked like one of the prophets out of the Old Testament, wild eyes and all.

"I'm going Outside, Captain," he said gravely.

"You never checked with me," I said.

"Sorry about that, I really meant to."

"Do your duties take you Outside?" I asked, stalling.

The wooden smile again. "Clear view of the stars. Unimpeded view and all that. Natural observations. It's provided for . . ." His voice changed slightly, losing its formal tone. He took a ragged breath. "Regs state that the captain is not to interfere with technicians in the normal pursuit of their duties."

"Regs also state that no man leaves the ship without a tether line, unless it's ship-to-ship transfer. Where's your line, Ball?"

He stared stupidly down at his equipment belt. "Did I forget that?"

"And what about your tanks? You've got one of those we used to go over to the *John B.* with. There's no more than twenty minutes in it, if that."

His eyes became shifty. "I hadn't left yet. I was going to change tanks."

I forced a nervous smile. "Look, Ball, we need you. And you'll be needed at destination planet."

Ball licked his lips. His face had a hunted look. "This ship doesn't need me," he mumbled. "Neither does anybody in it. And planet-fall's . . ." His voice trickled away. He cocked his head to one side and smiled faintly. "You're not going to let me out, are you, Martin?"

I saw it coming that vital fraction of a second before it actually happened. A slight hardening around the eyes, then all expression abruptly vanished, like fingerprints on a freshly baked cake, and Ball hit me like a docking tug, howling *"I'm going Outside, damnit, I'm going . . ."*

He was thin but with the deceptive hardness that thin mechanics sometimes have. He yanked me away from the air-lock hatch, then shoved me, hard, down the corridor.

I flew backward about 20 feet, the breath momentarily knocked out of me, then scrambled upright and shot back from a brake ring. Ball whirled, his suit small handicap in the near-weightless ship.

"You can't keep me cooped up with bloody strangers!"

I tried to brake and hit him all at the same time, but I overshot and Ball grabbed me around the waist as I shot by. I doubled up and tried to get my knees between me and his suit, but his metal-clad right arm shot out and caught my head between his forearm and biceps and he squeezed, gripping his wrist with his other hand. I kicked out with my feet, found no purchase and flailed wildly at the empty air. The pressure abruptly increased and I started to black out.

"Going Outside, goddamnit, going Outside."

"Grab him, Martin, grab him!"

The pressure suddenly let up and I squirmed free. I shook my head to clear it, then whirled to see what had happened. Potter was clinging to the collar of Ball's space suit with one hand, his slashed arm hanging uselessly at his side.

It couldn't last but a second longer, I thought, dazed. I dug my feet into a brake ring, crouched, then shot up at Ball. The timing was just right. I hit Ball at chest level and wrapped my legs around him as he toppled backward. Then I clasped both hands together and clubbed, once. His eyes dulled and I could feel him go limp.

I let go, brushed the sweat off my face and caught my breath in racking sobs. Then everything caught up with me and I bent double, suddenly afraid I was going to lose my dinner all over the corridor. Potter caught my arm and I mumbled "Thanks" and forced myself to swallow the bile. I felt dizzy and sick, and to cover, I said, "What made you help, Potter?"

"It was the logic of it," he said with an intense seriousness. "If I didn't care what happened to Ball, then I couldn't very well be sore at the guys who hadn't cared what happened to me when I was bleeding, could I? So I figured I had to care."

I didn't answer, still trying to control my stomach.

"Do you think the rest of the crew would have followed him out?"

I nodded. "Yeah—one by one, until this can of worms was empty—and we probably would have been among them." I stared down the empty corridor and shivered. There were people behind the shadow screens, but the *Cassiopeia* seemed deserted already.

Ball started to moan and I bent over and slapped him lightly in the face. His eyelids fluttered a little and then he was staring up at me, blank-faced.

"Get out of the suit," I growled. "Hang it up and go to your compartment. I'll be by later."

We watched him drift off down the corridor and Potter said, "What are you going to do when he tries to leave again?"

"Stop him, what else?"

"And the time after that?"

I shrugged and started to float back to my compartment,

then suddenly turned. "Look, we've got the tapes of read-out requests from the *John B.* If you want to help, we can take turns running them through the computer and briefing the material requested. Maybe we can come up with something."

Potter gave me a strange look. "You're the captain, Martin—you want me to do something, you just tell me to do something."

We fed the punched request tapes from the *John B.* into the *Cassiopeia's* own memory tanks and took turns scanning the material requested. We were hardly thorough—you couldn't read five years of read-out requests in ten or twenty time periods—and the requests themselves were something of an enigma, the third derivative of the personalities on board, their likes, their dislikes, their passing fancies. Was it significant, for example, that mathematician Bailey had gradually changed from a diet of light fiction to heavy treatises on mathematics during a thousand time periods? There was no way of knowing.

It was Potter who suggested a solution. "Look, we're not being objective, we're too close to the trees to see the forest."

"How so?"

"I think we ought to be working by analogy. We're assuming that we're the only ones worried about the future of the *Cassiopeia* and what has gone wrong—and we're right. But why? Why are you concerned, for example? Why did you stay on duty when the rest of the crew were crapping out? And why am I concerned?"

I felt that he had overstated it; myself, I knew that I had gradually been giving up; but I thought about it a long moment, then said, "A matter of responsibility—to the crew. Being designated captain, the mere act of designation, gave me a feeling of responsibility. The same, I guess, for you. Both of us have a responsibility to the crew as a whole; the others don't."

He looked at me quizzically. "Wouldn't somebody on board the *John B.* have been in a similar position?"

"Ok," I said slowly, "I see your point. Obviously, the captain. And they had a psychologist on board. I think that would have been about it."

"I think I ought to take the captain's requests, and you, the psychologist's," he said thoughtfully. "It'll probably make for greater objectivity."

It was good logical reasoning and it's what I should've

done, but I guess if a parent can learn from his child, a captain can learn from his crew—even if it's only a crew of one.

Two time periods later, I had a fairly good picture of Peter Hendrix, the psychologist on board the *John B.* A young man—maybe 25—and something of an athlete, at least enough of one to be vain about his physique and worry about getting out of shape (requested read-out on *Koptka's Isometric Exercises* the 29th time period out). Probably hadn't actually practiced in his profession (*Five Years of Case Histories:* Horney), was a pipe collector (*Vanderhof's Briars and Meerschaums*) and something of a dog fancier (Reisman: *Man's Animal Friend,* Fifth Edition, Rev.). About the 800th time period out, the requests started to fade. It was obvious that Hendrix was reading less and less, that he had gotten to the point where he stayed within his compartment, shadow screens on, floating in the dark and avoiding other crew members. Then, suddenly, the 1020th time period, he had requested Vandercook's *Problems of the Cities* and Walter's *Man by Himself,* two studies of the megapolis of the 20th Century. There was a flurry after that of similar volumes and then these requests, too, began to taper. From the 1045th time period on, Hendrix had made no more requests.

I pondered the list for a moment, then shrugged and started checking to see which ones were in the *Cassiopeia's* central computer. Both the Vandercook and the Walter were still available; some of the others had been deleted. I made myself comfortable at the read-out console, set the controls for SLOW SCAN and started to read.

I didn't get it all at once—parts of it didn't fall into place until I thought about it for a while—but after about three hours, I began to see the connections. A few time periods later, I was a sweaty mess, pretty sure of what the problem was but much less sure of a solution. I was surprised that any of the long-voyage freighters had made it at all. Part of the problem was built into the nature of the long-voyage, part of it undoubtedly depended on the random selection of crew. All of it gave me the chills. I slept on it for a period, then shoved over to Potter's compartment and violated Privacy with no regrets at all.

He was asleep, curled up in a fetal position on his hammock. I grabbed him by the shoulder. "Wake up, Potter—c'mon, snap it!"

"*Wha . . . what . . .*"

"What did you find out about the captain?"

He swung his hairless legs over the side of the hammock, yawned and scratched his naked belly. "Is that what you woke me up for? Jesus Aitch Christ. Look, I didn't find out a goddamned thing. He liked Italian cooking and he was fond of horses—I guess they weren't extinct then, he owned one or something." And then he snapped wide awake. "What's the story on Hendrix?"

I told him, talking for almost a full hour. When I had finished, he looked round-eyed and whistled. "So what happens now, sir? As a theory, it sounds good to me, but what do we do about it? It's one thing to know, another to——"

"I'm not sure what I'll do," I said slowly. "I guess I'll try talking. If that doesn't work, then I'll just have to think of something else."

I tried Coleman first. We had been friends once and I thought my chances of reaching him were better than any of the others.

I palmed permission to enter his compartment, got no response and shoved through the screen anyway. Coleman's arms were folded behind his head, his eyes closed.

"Joe."

No response. I drifted closer and slapped him lightly in the face. His eyes slowly opened; there was no sign of anger.

"Privacy, Martin." His eyelids started to sag shut again.

I slapped him once more, a little harder. His eyes stayed open this time. I drifted over to the port and turned my back. I was sweating now, beginning to stink with nervousness.

"You know, Joe, I was thinking about the other time period, when Potter got his arm slashed. I started thinking to myself—what would happen if Potter had died and then the algae tanks went out? And that kind of shook me up for a moment, because it occurred to me that even if we're not important to the ship, Joe, we're important to one another. And I hadn't really thought about that before."

I stole a quick glance at Coleman. Nothing.

"See, without Potter, Joe, we don't eat, we don't breathe. If I hadn't gotten a tourniquet on him, he would've bled to death and all the rest of us would have died if anything happened to the tanks. It was lucky I realized that, wasn't it, Joe?"

No response.

"It's pretty cold Outside, Joe, pretty dead. No life for mil-

lions and millions of miles. The only living things are right
here inside the *Cassiopeia*. You and I and Potter and Jimenez
and the rest of them. Ten little pulsing blobs of jelly against
all that nothingness out there. We need one another, Joe we
can't shut one another out anymore. If we do, then some
time period somebody's going to walk Outside and the rest of
us are going to pick up our marbles and follow. And none of
us will have sense enough to realize it's suicide."

I was both sweating and cold by the time I had finished. So
far as I could tell, Coleman didn't even know I was there.

Something snapped inside my head then and I started yell-
ing and swearing at him and calling him every name I could
think of. After a few minutes of that, my stream of curses
turned to a trickle and then I dried up completely. It was like
railing at a corpse. I turned to leave and then I spotted Coleman's chess set against the bulkhead, the little Dresden china
figurines standing guard over their tiny land of red and black
squares. They were lovely pieces, delicate, with soft, glowing
colors.

I picked up a queen, regal and aloof in her glazed, rose-
colored dress and little slippers of spidery fired china. Then I
took Coleman's big magnetic screwdriver from the bulkhead
where it had stuck, hefted it by the blade and whacked the
handle down on the queen in my other hand. It was like
cracking ice. The figurine shattered and fine china dust powdered out through my fingers. I opened my hand and the
crushed pink-and-blue queen started to disperse through space.

"It was against regs to bring these on board," I said icily. I
picked up a bishop in fine china miter and cloak and a second later he, too, was powder. I lifted up a rook next and
glanced up at Coleman. There was something in his eyes
now, something that, on other occasions, would have sent
shivers down my spine.

"You shouldn't have violated regs," I said. The rook was
dust. I bent to pick up a knight. Whatever was in Coleman's
eyes had to be coaxed out, even if it were murder. I casually
smashed the knight.

"You bastard!"

And Coleman was on me. He staggered for a moment, but
I had expected it and managed to step partly aside. He
grabbed my leg, then twisted and dove for my throat. I
dodged and clutched an arm as he shot by and got his head
with my other hand. The speed was already there and all it
needed was for me to guide him a little. He slammed into the

glassteel port and there was a soft *splurt* and the cubicle was shot through with a fine spray of blood. I grimaced—a shade too hard; Coleman had probably broken several teeth. I still had hold of his arm and suddenly whipped it back and wrapped my legs around him and squeezed. He bucked, arched for a second, then all his strength flowed out and he went limp. I hung on for a moment, wary, then let him go except for a hand on his arm to steady him.

He surprised me, then. He turned, buried his head in my shoulder and started to sob.

We held the council of war in Potter's compartment, with all the shadow screens on and our voices low, though the chances of being interrupted were just about zero.

"We can't go around to each member of the crew and try to convince him of anything by sweet reasonableness," Potter said thoughtfully.

"I wasn't going to," I said. "The only thing I think will work is shock—we'll have to force them to become involved."

"I don't know . . ." Potter began.

"It worked on me," Coleman said, faintly unfriendly. "But I don't know if it will work on anybody else."

I idly scratched the matted hair under my arm, squashing something that had so far evaded the ultraviolet tubes overhead, then turned to Potter. "Any ideas?"

He shook his head. "I'm no psychologist."

"Fake it," I said bluntly. "I'm no captain, either. So what would you do if you *were* a psychologist?"

Potter's smile was toothy. "You want me to think like a shrink—Ok, I'd play on their strongest emotions, love and hate and fear, try to shake them up. But the catch is, we don't *know* what they love and hate and fear. If this had been a military ship—you know, ankles to elbows all the time—there would have been constant involvement and we'd know one another a lot better." He shrugged. "As it is——"

"What about the personnel tapes in the computer," Coleman interrupted. "Wouldn't they help?"

The personnel tapes were a thought. They contained our psychological profiles, medical histories and short résumés about our home life—our guts and souls reduced to minor alignments of iron oxide on tissue-thin tape to aid the placement service at destination planet.

"Those tapes are under sealed circuits," I said dubiously. "There's no way we can get a read-out on them."

Coleman snorted, the sudden creases on his monkey face cracking open his beard so the hairs stuck out like the bristles on a brush. "Any idiot could break those seals."

"Could you?" I asked.

He shrugged. "I might blow the whole computer, but I doubt it."

"And then we go to work on the crew, that it?" Potter asked.

"That's right," I said. "Frighten them, irritate them, make them angry."

"You can adapt to irritation," Potter said, suddenly doubtful.

"It all depends," I said thoughtfully, "on the irritation."

We started with Jimenez, because he had an easy weakness we could play on and because we needed his strength, if we could arouse it. He was now a quiet, almost completely passive Jimenez who had given up any pretense whatsoever at routine. He either slept or stared out the ports, padding to the food dispenser at regular intervals, eating silently, not talking, not really aware of anybody else at all, except from time to time he seemed apprehensive when somebody else was around. He was a native of Tijuana, Mexico, the festival center of the North American continent, and according to the personnel tapes, he hated the area and not without reason—it was alive with rattlers and Jimenez had a phobia about snakes.

It took skill to turn a twisted piece of cloth into what we wanted. Skill, some coloring and some hardened grease to make ridges and scales. Then we waited until Jimenez was asleep. I was elected to creep cautiously through the shadow screen and drop the "snake" in the reddish fuzz that covered Jimenez' chest. Then I lightly dragged the tips of my fingers through his chest hair and made a rattling sound with my tongue against my teeth, and quickly ducked out of the compartment.

There was a moment's tense wait and then Jimenez bolted through the screen, his red beard flying and his eyes wild. I could imagine the scream he must have let out. He saw me, hung in space for a moment while he figured it out, his eyes rolling, then grabbed a brake ring and plunged feet first at me. Coleman and Potter grabbed his arms and hauled him back.

I said, "I'd like to talk to you, Jimenez."

He spat in my face and turned his back—but I talked to him anyway.

I think I could have figured out Hulsman without reading through his profile. We had to splice some of the medical "techniques and responses" tapes and cut back and forth with a "home movie" tape of Hulsman's family; and when we were through, I was pretty disgusted with myself. I let a time period go by and then dropped by Hulsman's compartment and told him the computer was out of whack and there might be involuntary screenings of some of the memory banks but there was no way of doing anything about it. I don't think he even heard me. I told him again and left and a few hours later we programmed his compartment and opened the circuits and waited.

He was part way out five seconds after the circuits were opened, his face ashen and showing signs of extreme shock. Then he hesitated and slipped back in. I followed a few minutes later. He was staring at the screen, fists balled, the muscles in his face little flat areas of concrete. I waited a moment until I was sure he knew I was there, then loudly cleared my throat.

"Your mother, Hulsman," I said acidly, "did she ever work on stage?"

He blacked an eye and almost broke my nose before Potter and Coleman could restrain him.

We kept it up for a dozen time periods. Various indignities broke Reynolds, who had a personal sense of cleanliness that bordered on the pathological. First I smashed the ultraviolet sanitary tubes in his compartment. He was only vaguely aware of it, a slight irritation that slowly started to feed on him. Then I made sure he kept finding little bits of dried food on his dispenser tray whenever he went to eat. And, of course, I laughed and joked about his tray whenever he was in earshot, and one period in the life-systems compartment I casually let slip that I was the one who kept fouling his food tray and what a great joke it was.

He came within an ace of decapitating me by skimming the sharp-edged tray across the compartment at me. I ducked and it hit the bulkhead with enough force to bend the lip of the tray back about an inch.

Ball's weakness was his physical vanity. He was a big man

and his code, of course, included not hitting any man smaller than himself—to have done so would have been to lose face. He didn't know what to do when Coleman kept stumbling into him and snarling that it was all Ball's fault. Coleman managed it cleverly enough—a push off a brake ring with only a slight miscalculation and Ball would be on the receiving end of an unexpected jostle or jab. After a while, Ball became very apprehensive about it—a transit-shuttle passenger not knowing what the abusive drunk across the aisle is going to do next. With growing awareness came a conscious effort to ignore Coleman, except that Coleman wouldn't be ignored. He spared neither Ball's family nor his personal proclivities nor his courage—which he implied was obvious more by its absence than its presence. Ball's frustration was like an itch and one time period he finally scratched it and bloodied Coleman's nose, more to his amazement than Coleman's. He stood there, vaguely upset and angry, and I promptly said the appropriate thing about their relative sizes and something to the effect that Ball should pick on a man his own size.

I had forgotten how much closer I came to being a match for him than Coleman was. *"You bloody bastard!"* he screamed, and almost four years of fear and frustration came pounding at me. This time it took four of us to calm him down—and he was really calm only after I hit him along the side of the head with a half dozen trays. Kentworthy, Adams and Herschel were next.

But all the time I was breaking the crew, I knew it really wasn't going to work. I hadn't changed the basic situation nor the basic surroundings. I could supply more irritation, but Potter was right—eventually I would become the small boy crying wolf and then I would lose them for good. What I had to do was manufacture an emergency, a genuine emergency in which there would be an honest element of chance that we might not make it, an emergency that could be coped with—but just barely.

I wanted to confide in Potter and Coleman but knew I couldn't take the risk, so I researched it myself with the aid of the computer. It was the cargo manifest that finally gave me the idea. There were dangers in it—there had to be—and in the end it would all depend on the ingenuity of the crew. And if I had guessed wrong—well, it would be no worse than bleeding their lives away staring out the ports, to finally get so fed up with themselves that they would walk out forever and spend the rest of eternity cartwheeling through the lonely reaches of space.

I waited until a time period when most of the shadow screens were on, found a crowbar and crept back to the life-systems compartment. Behind the food-dispenser fronts was a small compartment containing the automated algae tanks, the small farms of living organisms that were our life's blood. I wedged the bar into the lip of the dispenser and slowly bent it down, hooking my feet under a brake ring to gain leverage. The front gradually yielded and finally there was an opening wide enough for me to wiggle through. I squeezed past the driers and the formers and the flavorers and then started swinging the crowbar. Tanks erupted and the contents splattered against the bulkheads—streams of green slime geysering through the compartment, filling the air with a thick green mist and coating the bar with a viscous slime. I was so frightened I wanted to vomit, but I kept swinging. I *had* to be right.

I finally squeezed out, heaving and gagging and dripping slime, and made my way to the control console. I located the central bank of shadow-screen controls, opened the panel beneath and rammed the crowbar into the wiring at the same time I pressed the general alarm.

The brassy clangor of the alarm beat through the ship like heavy surf, and simultaneously the control board for the shadow screens arced and sputtered and one by one the screens went off, until I was looking at a single long compartment with nine alarmed and almost nude crew members scrambling off their elasto-hammocks.

A second later somebody hollered, men started to stumble into one another and then somebody spotted me standing by the console, covered with slime and still clutching the crowbar. And all the time the alarm was screaming throughout the ship like a hysterical air-raid siren.

They swarmed up to the console.

"Hey, what gives?"

"What, the hell?"

"Hey, Potter, the food dispenser!"

"What happened to the screens?"

"What the bloody hell is going on?"

"The food dispenser."

A shriek. *"THE FOOD DISPENSER!"* They swept to the other end of the compartment like a tide, then one by one they fluttered back to form a silent, watchful ring around me.

"You stupid bastard," Jimenez said in a freezing voice, "you've signed a death warrant for everybody here. For yourself, too."

I shook my head. "No, we can get through. There's grain in the cargo compartments and we can build hydroponics tubs. I think we can do it."

Everybody looked at Potter. Jimenez said, "Can we?"

Potter was squatting on the deck, holding his head in his hands and shaking and mumbling, "Holy Mother of Jesus, Martin, you shouldn't have done it, you should've warned me, you should've warned me." Jimenez' toe caught him in the ribs and he looked up, still pasty-faced and trembling. "I don't know, *I don't know*. It's a big maybe. We'll have to break into the cargo compartment and we'll have to—"

Reynolds squeaked, "We'll have to build a whole new ecology, that's what we'll have to do, a whole new ecology! You just don't make tubs, where'll we get the fertilizer?"

"I didn't think you'd ask anything so obvious," I interrupted. He turned green.

Coleman had turned his back to me when Jimenez asked him about the cargo compartments. "Yeah, maybe we can get through. It'll take a lot of work. We'll have to burn our way through and I don't even know if we have enough oxyacetylene to do it. One thing for sure, we'll be damned hungry by the time we get there."

It was Ball who said coldly, "Why'd you do it, Martin?"

They all stopped talking then and I could see the almost imperceptible movement to line up behind Ball. This was the big one, I thought, this was the final challenge. And I had no friends among them. "Because I had to, Ball," I said slowly. "Because that was the only way I could guarantee that we would get there at all."

He thought about it a minute, then said logically, "You may have guaranteed just the opposite."

I nodded. "I might have, but I don't think so. Be honest, Ball—would you bet that we would have made it anyway?" I turned to the rest. "Would any of you bet? Did any of you really give a good goddamn before right now? Oh, sure, you care now all right—you *have* to!"

Ball and I stared at each other, fencing, and after the longest moment in my life, he said quietly, "Maybe you're right. We'll see."

I glanced at the rest of them. Coleman was nodding slightly to himself, Reynolds looked a little uncertain. I even thought I detected a slight glimmer of approval in Jimenez's small myopic eyes.

Well, I had done it, I thought with absolutely no feeling of elation. They were valuable to one another now, they were involved now—they had to be, their lives depended on it.

Then Hulsman stepped out of the crowd clutching a spanner wrench and shaking his head slightly to clear away the dirty blond hair from in front of his blazing eyes. He was all tiger now, I thought; he would try something foolish if ticked just right. I had the feeling he was still furious about the other.

"I ought to kill you, Martin!"

I sized him up and said contemptuously, "No, you won't, Hulsman. Neither you nor anybody else would dream of it right now."

He showed his teeth and waved the wrench and said, "Why not? What makes you so sure?"

I was pretty tired and I was starting to shake with reaction. I wished to God that I could go to sleep and forget about it all, but I realized I couldn't do that now any more than they could.

"Because you need a captain," I said. "And I'm the only one who's qualified, I'm the only one who really wants it. Everybody else had his chance and nobody took it, nobody wanted the responsibility. So I'm it, Hulsman, don't bother looking any further." I shoved forward slightly and grabbed the wrench away from him. "Now get the torches and get to work—all of you. Snap it!"

The tenth day after touchdown, I sat in the portmaster's office going over the manifest receipt. I was uncomfortable—it would be a long time before I got used to shoes and shirts and trousers again, and taking a shower struck me as something that really wasn't necessary more than once or twice a month—but a good part of the discomfort was simply the fact that we were coming to the end of the manifest and there were certain items that were missing and unaccounted for.

Callahan, the portmaster, was a comfortable sort—genial and ruddy, with 20 extra pounds that somehow seemed to translate into an air of authority rather than merely coat his bones with fat. He was an important man of Xerxes—the portmaster on a colony planet always was—and I had no doubt his relaxed attitude would vanish in a hurry when we came to the subject of the missing items.

Much to my astonishment, he really didn't seem to notice and had started to write his name at the bottom when I interrupted him.

"I'm very sorry, sir," I said formally, "but there are some missing items."

He put down his pen, leaned back in his wicker chair and raised an eyebrow. "Oh?"

"The seed grains," I said stiffly. "I think there's something less than one tenth the allotment tonnage present. And certain flat metal items are not present—in the form listed."

He lit his pipe, puffed for a moment, then looked up at me with alert brown eyes that seemed a little out of place in his fleshy face. "You're referring to the flat metal sheets you converted into hydroponics tubs?"

"I didn't know——" I started, surprised.

He waved a hand. "Of course I know, I'm no idiot, Martin. I've been portmaster here for almost ten years, handling an average of an Earth ship a month. The first thing we do—after unloading, delousing the crew and fumigating the pigpen that the crew's quarters have been turned into—is to check the manifest against what actually arrives here. And then we check the ship's log. You missed a lot of entries, but you were still pretty explicit as to what happened."

I reddened. "I didn't mean——"

"As to missing items," he continued, "it doesn't matter. The virtue of bureaucracy is that it constantly seeks to minimize risk. Three out of the five ships carrying identical cargoes as yours made it on the long voyage. That's not to say the seed grains won't be missed—but they weren't really vital."

"You're trying to tell me that the ship and its cargo weren't very important," I said bitterly."

"I mean nothing of the sort," he said kindly. "Look, Martin, you did what you had to do for the good of the ship and the crew. On a larger scale, Earth does what it has to do for the good of the colony planets. And as important as the cargo is, don't forget that the crew is even more important— we need their technical skills badly. You got them all here safely; for that, you're to be congratulated." He suddenly looked grim. "You ought to see how some ships come in— murders, insanity, crews in mutiny, sometimes half the crew dead. You did pretty well, Martin, better than you realize."

I stared out the window behind him, not listening. Port tugs were hauling the *Cassiopeia* away, to be smelted down for scrap. There were few exports as yet from Xerxes and the extra incoming ships were melted down for badly needed metals. My mind started to drift, remembering the loneliness on board and the stink of the crew's quarters and Potter's slashed arm and what we had done to Hulsman and——

"I think I was right about what I wrote in the log," I said suddenly.

Callahan gave me a long look, then rolled a cigar at me across his desktop. "If you want to talk about it, I want to hear about it."

It was flattering and I lit the cigar and felt expansive. "You said that the triumph of bureaucracy was that it sought to minimize risk. I'll buy that—but that, and necessity, made the ship what it was. The reason why freighters are spartan is obvious. And since the crew is going to be green, a crew that makes only one trip, the ship has to be pretty much automatic. Which means there's nothing for the crew to really do—in one sense, it isn't needed. And it knows it."

"Is that necessarily bad?" Callahan asked, surprised.

"Any environment that doesn't require a man to do something is a hostile environment," I said slowly. "And the less it requires him to do, the more hostile it is."

Callahan looked blank. "I don't get it."

I frowned. "I didn't either. Not until I had read the same material that Hendrix, the psychologist on board the *John B.*, had read about the problems of cities in the 20th Century. Those early cities were a mess—they were overcrowded and they suffered from air pollution and traffic strangulation and crime and all of that, but there was another problem, a more serious one." I concentrated on the cigar for a minute. "Man's gregarious, he tends to clot in groups—first in hamlets, then villages, then towns, and finally in large cities. But nobody ever figured there would be a law of diminishing returns. The larger the city, the larger the population cluster, the less important the individual man within. He's a smaller and smaller cog in a larger and larger machine and finally he really doesn't matter at all. And those early cities *were* machines, tremendous machines made up of traffic flows and power grids and communication networks and huge water systems and disposal plants. Eventually, a man became aware of his own insignificance, and when he did, he started to withdraw. They had a word for it. They called it alienation—*anomie*."

Callahan didn't say anything, just puffed on his pipe and watched me with those alert brown eyes that could see two inches below the surface of my skin.

"There was something else," I continued. "The closer you *had* to live with your neighbors, the less close you felt to them. You didn't *want* to know the people who lived next door, or down the hall, or across the street. They were just part of the faceless mass. Besides, you *knew* they didn't give a crap about you, so why should you give a crap about them?" I shivered. "A man could be murdered in a transit shuttle and nobody would come to his defense. Nobody wanted to be involved. A woman could scream for help in the streets and people would plug their ears and close their windows. They accepted horror—and weren't even aware of it."

"Apathetic?" Callahan asked.

I nodded. "That's right. Not only toward one another, but toward themselves as well. Once, during a power black-out, people stranded in the transit shuttles didn't panic, didn't riot, didn't try to get out. They just sat there. The marvelous machine had stopped working and all the little cogs couldn't function on their own. They had forgotten how."

I fell silent, watching the activity of the port outside the window and remembering. "What's the connection?" Callahan prodded gently. "You're talking about a city with millions of people—there were only ten of you aboard the *Cassiopeia*."

I wondered for a moment if the man were stupid, then realized he only wanted me to confirm what he already thought. "It was a spacegoing slum," I said. "There were only ten of us, but on a numbers-per-square-foot basis, it would make the most overpopulated city look like a prairie. And like the people in those early cities, we had no control over our environment. We were helpless. We had routine jobs to perform—make-work—but none of them really mattered. *We* didn't matter. We had no say-so in what was happening to us. And there was the final factor." I could feel my armpits start to bleed sweat. "We didn't need one another—and the horrible thing was that it had all been planned that way. The Colonization Board was afraid we might kill one another during the long voyage, so they provided shadow screens, taught us to respect Privacy above all, and arranged routine so we could avoid one another. And no weapons, of course, of any kind. Which made us even more helpless in the face of the unknown. And like the city dwellers, the final result was loss of identity. We became remote from one another, from ourselves, from our own feelings. Like the people in the transit shuttles, we could watch Potter bleed to death and feel nothing. We weren't involved."

Callahan said, "Why did the crew of the *John B.* walk out?"

"The environment," I said slowly. "The horrifying, indifferent environment, and the loneliness. When you're alone in a crowd, you're *really* alone. And then you become afraid. Finally, all you want to do is get away from that crowd."

"But walking Outside was suicide."

I shrugged. "They didn't know it. They had lost touch with reality by then. As for Outside, it's not always world without end—sometimes it's more like a little black room with lights studding the walls. It's as real one way as the other." I sat there quietly for a moment, my cigar slowly turning to ash in the tray, unnoticed. "I can understand why the crew of the *John B.* walked out. The poor bastards wanted to get away from the ship, away from one another." I could feel myself start to break then. "The opposite of love isn't hate," I said slowly. "It's indifference. Ask any kid."

Callahan stood up and said, "I'll make recommendations and send them back to the Board. Probably urge that they make the ships less foolproof. They may lose some ships that way; but in the long run, I think it will be better." He stood up and handed me the manifest receipt. "We need leaders here, you know. That's one category we're always short of."

"It's a difficult one to train for and ship," I said.

"We've never asked them to ship us any," Callahan said quietly. "They sort of develop along the way." I had my hand on the doorknob when he suddenly said, "We need a good man at the port here. After you've looked around a bit, come on back."

I saluted and turned and walked out into the bright sunlight. Three blocks from the spaceport, the Rod and Pile nestled beneath some of Xerxes's tall, palmlike trees, set well back from the boulevard.

They had rounded up a dozen girls and everybody cheered when I walked in. Jimenez was the first to buy me a drink; his glasses were clean and his beard was trimmed and he had clothes on and I damn near didn't recognize him. He called me a dirty gringo, smiled when he said it, then bought another drink, downed it and did a magnificent fall off his stool. Hulsman was next, the all-American-boy grin having suffered a sea change into a happy, drunken smile, and then Ball was buying and slapping me on the back and even Reynolds, scrubbed and pink in a spotless uniform, broke down and bought a round. We drank and sang and made passes at the girls and dates for later and roared with laughter at anecdotes that had been anything but funny at the time. We made arrangements to have a reunion every year and I wondered to myself what lies we would be telling one another after we had spread across the continents of Xerxes and had wives and kids and the *Cassiopeia* was almost forgotten and the stars only something to look at at night and feel romantic about.

Then I found myself alone at a table with Coleman. I reached into my pocket and pulled out a small package I had treasured all afternoon and set it gently on the table in front of him. He stared at it, puzzled.

"Go ahead," I said. "Open it."

He fumbled at the wrappings and then spread the contents out on the table. A bishop, a queen, a knight and a rook. They were lovely, delicate figures, almost exact duplicates of the ones I had smashed.

"When it comes to porcelain," I said, "Xerxes has the best craftsmen this side of Earth." I stretched out in the chair and watched Coleman play delightedly with his chess pieces and listened to the overhead fan and stared at the pool of sunlight by the open door. Then I ordered a drink, relaxed and let myself remember just a little bit of what it had been like on board the *Cassiopeia*.

I tried to repeat with "East Wind, West Wind" but *Playboy* rejected it. They liked the idea but didn't care for the action-oriented plot. (A friend suggested the real reason for rejection may have been because the automobile was the symbolic villain of the piece and the magazine was trying to attract automobile advertising. If true, it was a valid reason for bouncing the story. The fact remains, I tried alternate approaches and none of them worked.)

Which leads to an important digression about stories that are rejected. "Rejection doesn't necessarily imply lack of merit . . ." is the way the classical rejection slip reads. This isn't just a sop for the writer's ego, sometimes it's quite true. There are those stories that are obviously amateurish and which the editor will bounce after the first paragraph. And a lot of stories are border-line; you'll buy them if you have to fill an issue. If you're overstocked, you'll send them back.

But if it's any satisfaction to the potential writers reading this, editors frequently have their regrets and second thoughts about the stories they've bounced. An editor may reject a story only to discover that he's still thinking about it a week later. When it's happened to me, I've sometimes asked the author to resubmit the story for further consideration. (Ray Russell, former editor of *Playboy*, has also admitted recalling several stories for another look. It can, however, be a dangerous practice. Authors who have been rejected twice for the same story have been known to come looking for the editor with blood in their eye. Bill Hamling once asked for a resubmission and rewrite, bounced the story yet again, and was confronted two days later with 300 pounds of angry author, ready, willing and more than able to commit mayhem.)

Most editors strive to be objective but there's no denying that a certain amount of picking and choosing is strictly by whim—just as you've always suspected. There are those Eternal Variables, such as how you're feeling when you get up in the morning or how vivid your memory of the hard time the author gave you when you dealt with him last.

(One Very Famous Writer for *Rolling Stone* got his start in *Rogue* but turned me off completely when he wrote a letter describing how he used to sit on the front porch of his cabin in Big Sur and take pot shots at the Gays sunbathing just down the hill.)

"East Wind, West Wind" eventually found a home in an anthology by Harry Harrison. The story was based heavily on fact: The killing smogs of Donora, Pennsylvania in 1948, and that of London in 1952, in which 4700 people are reported to have died. Plus my own experiences in Los Angeles. One afternoon, it was so bad in the City of the Angels that I hopscotched down Hollywood Boulevard, ducking into air-conditioned stores so I could—quite literally—take a breather. My eyes were burning and it felt like something very heavy was resting on my chest. In a nearby parking lot, the attendant was swearing a blue streak and threatening a departing motorist with physical violence. The driver of the car had gunned his engine on leaving the lot, this at a time when the attendant must have been slowly suffocating from the CO level.

A pox, incidentally, on the science fiction critic who accused me of exaggeration. He had obviously never been in L.A. on a bad day.

East Wind, West Wind

It wasn't going to be just another bad day, it was going to be a terrible one. The inversion layer had slipped over the city four days before and it had been like putting a lid on a kettle; the air was building up to a real Donora, turning into a chemical soup so foul I wouldn't have believed it if I hadn't been trying to breathe the stuff. Besides sticking in my throat, it made my eyes feel like they were being bathed in acid. You could hardly see the sun—it was a pale, sickly disc floating in a mustard-colored sky—but even so, the streets were an oven and the humidity was so high you could have wrung the water out of the air with your bare hands . . . dirty water, naturally.

On the bus a red-faced salesman with denture breath recognized my Air Central badge and got pushy. I growled that we didn't *make* the air—not yet, at any rate—and finally I took off the badge and put it in my pocket and tried to shut out the coughing and the complaints around me by concentrating on the faint, cherry sound of the "corn poppers" laundering the bus's exhaust. Five would have gotten you ten, of course, that their effect was strictly psychological, that they had seen more than twenty thousand miles of service and were now absolutely worthless. . . .

At work I hung up my plastic sportscoat, slipped off the white surgeon's mask (black where my nose and mouth had been) and filled my lungs with good machine-pure air that smelled only faintly of oil and electric motors; one of the advantages of working for Air Central was that our office air was the best in the city. I dropped a quarter in the coffee vendor, dialed it black, and inhaled the fumes for a second while I shook the sleep from my eyes and speculated about what Wanda would have for me at the Investigator's Desk. There were thirty-nine other Investigators besides myself but I was junior and my daily assignment card was usually just a listing of minor complaints and violations that had to be checked out.

Wanda was young and pretty and redhaired and easy to spot even in a secretarial pool full of pretty girls. I offered her some of my coffee and looked over her shoulder while she flipped through the assignment cards. "That stuff out there is easier to swim through than to breathe," I said. "What's the index?"

"Eighty-four point five," she said quietly. "And rising."

I just stared at her. I had thought it was bad, but hardly that bad, and for the first time that day I felt a sudden flash of panic. "And no alert? When it hits seventy-five this city's supposed to close up like a clam!"

She nodded down the hall to the Director's office. "Lawyers from Sanitary Pick-Up, Oberhausen Steel, and City Light and Power got an injunction—they were here to break the news to Monte at eight sharp. Impractical, unnecessary, money-wasting, and fifteen thousand employees would be thrown out of work if they had to shut down the furnaces and incinerators. They got an okay right from the top of Air Shed Number Three."

My jaw dropped. "How could they? Monte's supposed to have the last word!"

"So go argue with the politicians—if you can stand the hot air." She suddenly looked very fragile and I wanted to run out and slay a dragon or two for her. "The chicken-hearts took the easy way out, Jim. Independent Weather's predicting a cold front for early this evening and rising winds and rain for tomorrow."

The rain would clean up the air, I thought. But Independent Weather could be bought and as a result it had a habit of turning in cheery predictions that frequently didn't come true. Air Central had tried for years to get IW outlawed but money talks and their lobbyist in the capital was quite a talker. Unfortunately, if they were wrong this time, it would be as if they had pulled a plastic bag over the city's head.

I started to say something, then shut up. If you let it get to you, you wouldn't last long on the job. "Where's my list of small-fry?"

She gave me an assignment card. It was blank except for *See Me* written across its face. "Humor him, Jim, he's not feeling well."

This worried me a little because Monte was the father of us all—a really sweet old guy, which hardly covers it all because he could be hard as nails when he had to. There wasn't anyone who knew more about air control than he.

I took the card and started up the hall and then Wanda called after me. She had stretched out her long legs and hiked up her skirt. I looked startled and she grinned. "Something new—sulfur-proof nylons." Which meant they wouldn't dis-

solve on a day like today when a measurable fraction of the
air we were trying to breathe was actually dilute sulfuric
acid. . . .

When I walked into his office, old Monte was leaning out
the window, the fly ash clinging to his busy gray eyebrows
like cinnamon to toast, trying to taste the air and predict how
it would go today. We had eighty Sniffers scattered throughout the city, all computerized and delivering their data in
neat, graphlike form, but Monte still insisted on breaking internal air security and seeing for himself how his city was doing.

I closed the door. Monte pulled back inside, then suddenly
broke into one of his coughing fits.

"Sit down, Jim," he wheezed, his voice sounding as if it
were being wrung out of him, "be with you in a minute." I
pretended not to notice while his coughing shuddered to a
halt and he rummaged through his desk for his little bottle of
pills. It was a plain office, as executive offices went, except
for Monte's own paintings on the wall—the type I like to call
Twentieth Century Romantic. A mountain scene with a crystal clear lake in the foreground and anglers battling huge
trout, a city scene with palm trees lining the boulevards, and
finally, one of a man standing by an old automobile on a
winding mountain road while he looked off at a valley in the
distance.

Occasionally Monte would talk to me about his boyhood
around the Great Lakes and how he actually used to go
swimming in them. Once he tried to tell me that orange trees
used to grow within the city limits of Santalosdiego and that
the oranges were as big as tennis balls. It irritated me and I
think he knew it; I was the youngest Investigator for Air
Central but that didn't necessarily make me naive.

When Monte stopped coughing I said hopefully, "IW
claims a cold front is coming in."

He huddled in his chair and dabbed at his mouth with a
handkerchief, his thin chest working desperately trying to
pump his lungs full of air. "IW's a liar," he finally rasped.
"There's no cold front coming in, it's going to be a scorcher
for three more days."

I felt uneasy again. "Wanda told me what happened," I
said.

He fought a moment longer for his breath, caught it, then
gave a resigned shrug. "The bastards are right, to an extent.

Stop garbage pick-ups in a city this size and within hours the rats will be fighting us in the streets. Shut down the power plants and you knock out all the air conditioners and purifiers—right during the hottest spell of the year. Then try telling the yokels that the air on the outside will be a whole lot cleaner if only they let the air on the inside get a whole lot dirtier."

He hunched behind his desk and drummed his fingers on the top while his face slowly turned to concrete. "But if they don't let me announce an alert by tomorrow morning," he said quietly, "I'll call in the newspapers and. . . ." The coughing started again and he stood up, a gnomelike little man slightly less alive with every passing day. He leaned against the windowsill while he fought the spasm. "And we think this is bad," he choked, half to himself. "What happens when the air coming in is as dirty as the air already here? When the Chinese and the Indonesians and the Hottentots get toasters and ice-boxes and all the other goodies?"

"Asia's not that industralized yet," I said uncomfortably.

"Isn't it?" He turned and sagged back into his chair, hardly making a dent in the cushion. I was bleeding for the old man but I couldn't let him know it. I said in a low voice, "You wanted to see me," and handed him the assignment card.

He stared at it for a moment, his mind still on the Chinese, then came out of it and croaked, "That's right, give you something to chew on." He pressed a button on his desk and the wall opposite faded into a map of the city and the surrounding area, from the ocean on the west to the low-lying mountains on the east. He waved at the section of the city that straggled off into the canyons of the foothills. "Internal combustion engine—someplace back there." His voice was stronger now, his eyes more alert. "It isn't a donkey engine for a still or for electricity, it's a private automobile."

I could feel the hairs stiffen on the back of my neck. Usually I drew minor offenses, like trash burning or secret cigarette smoking, but owning or operating a gasoline-powered automobile was a felony, one that was sometimes worth your life.

"The Sniffer in the area confirms it," Monte continued in a tired voice, "but can't pinpoint it."

"Any other leads?"

"No, just this one report. But—we haven't had an internal combustion engine in more than three years." He paused. "Have fun with it, you'll probably have a new boss in the morning." *That* was something I didn't even want to think about. I had my hand on the doorknob when he said quietly, "The trouble with being boss is that you have to play Caesar and his Legions all the time."

It was as close as he came to saying good-bye and good luck. I didn't know what to say in return, or how to say it, and found myself staring at one of his canvases and babbling, "You sure used a helluva lot of blue."

"It was a fairly common color back then," he growled. "The sky was full of it."

And then he started coughing again and I closed the door in a hurry; in five minutes I had gotten so I couldn't stand the sound.

I had to stop in at the lab to pick up some gear from my locker and ran into Dave Ice, the researcher in charge of the Sniffers. He was a chubby, middle-aged little man with small, almost feminine hands; it was a pleasure to watch him work around delicate machinery. He was our top-rated man, after Monte, and I think if there was anybody whose shoes I wanted to step into someday, it would have been Dave Ice. He knew it, liked me for it, and usually went out of his way to help.

When I walked in he was changing a sheet of paper in one of the smoke shade detectors that hung just outside the lab windows. The sheet he was taking out looked as if it had been coated with lampblack.

"How long an exposure?"

He looked up, squinting over his bifocals. "Hi, Jim—a little more than four hours. It looks like it's getting pretty fierce out there."

"You haven't been out?"

"No, Monte and I stayed here all night. We were going to call an alert at nine this morning but I guess you know what happened."

I opened my locker and took out half a dozen new masks and a small canister of oxygen; if you were going to be out in traffic for any great length of time, you had to go prepared. Allowable vehicles were buses, trucks, delivery vans, police electrics and the like. Not all exhaust control devices worked very well and even the electrics gave off a few acid fumes. And if you were stalled in a tunnel, the carbon monoxide ratings really zoomed. I hesitated at the bottom of the locker and then took out my small Mark II gyrojet and shoulder holster. It was pretty deadly stuff: no recoil and the tiny rocket pellet had twice the punch of a .45.

Dave heard the clink of metal and without looking up asked quietly, "Trouble?"

"Maybe," I said. "Somebody's got a private automobile—gasoline—and I don't suppose they'll want to turn it in."

"You're right," he said, sounding concerned, "they won't." And then: "I heard something about it; if it's the same report, it's three days old."

"Monte's got his mind on other things," I said. I slipped the masks into my pocket and belted on the holster. "Did you know he's still on his marching Chinese kick?"

Dave was concentrating on one of the Sniffer drums slowly rolling beneath its scribing pens, logging a minute-by-minute record of the hydrocarbons and the oxides of nitrogen and sulfur that were sickening the atmosphere. "I don't blame him," he said, absently running a hand over his glistening scalp. "They've started tagging chimney exhausts in Shanghai, Djakarta and Mukden with radioactives—we should get the first results in another day or so."

The dragon's breath, I thought. When it finally circled the globe it would mean earth's air sink had lost the ability to cleanse itself and all of us would start strangling a little faster.

I got the rest of my gear and just before I hit the door, Dave said: "Jim?" I turned. He was wiping his hands on a paper towel and frowning at me over his glasses. "Look, take care of yourself, huh, kid?"

"Sure thing," I said. If Monte was my professional father, then Dave was my uncle. Sometimes it was embarrassing but right then it felt good. I nodded good-bye, adjusted my mask, and left.

Outside it seemed like dusk; trucks and buses had turned on their lights and almost all pedestrians were wearing masks. In a lot across the street some kids were playing tag and the thought suddenly struck me that nowadays most kids seemed small for their age; but I envied them . . . the air never seemed to bother kids. I watched for a moment, then started up the walk. A few doors down I passed an apartment building, half hidden in the growing darkness, that had received a "political influence" exemption a month before. Its incinerator was going full blast now, only instead of floating upward over the city the small charred bits of paper and garbage were falling straight down the front of the building like a kind of oily black snow.

I suddenly felt I was suffocating and stepped out into the street and hailed a passing electricab. Forest Hills, the part of the city that Monte had pointed out, was wealthy and the homes were large, though not so large that some of them couldn't be hidden away in the canyons and gullies of the foothills. If you lived on a side road or at the end of one of the canyons it might even be possible to hide a car out there and drive it only at night. And if any of your neighbors found out . . . well, the people who lived up in the relatively pure air of the highlands had a different view of things than those who lived down in the atmospheric sewage of the flats. *But where would a man get a gasoline automobile in the first place?*

And did it all really matter? I thought, looking out the window of the cab at the deepening dusk and feeling depressed. Then I shook my head and leaned forward to give the driver instructions. Some places could be checked out relatively easily.

The Carriage Museum was elegant—and crowded, considering that it was a weekday. The main hall was a vast cave of black marble housing a parade of ancient internal combustion vehicles shining under the subdued lights; most of them were painted a lustrous black though there was an occasional gray and burst of red and a few sparkles of old gold from polished brass head lamps and fittings.

I felt like I was in St. Peter's, walking on a vast sea of marble while all about me the crowds shuffled along in respectful silence. I kept my eyes to the floor, reading off the names on the small bronze plaques: *Rolls Royce Silver Ghost, Mercer Raceabout, Isotta-Fraschini, Packard Runabout, Hispano-Suiza, Model J Duesenberg, Flying Cloud Reo, Cadillac Imperial V 16, Pierce Arrow,* the first of the *Ford V8s, Lincoln Zephyr, Chrysler Windsor Club Coup.* . . . And in small halls off to the side, the lesser breeds: *Hudson Terraplane, Henry J., Willys Knight,* something called a *Jeepster,* the *Mustang, Knudsen,* the 1986 *Volkswagen,* the last *Chevrolet.* . . .

The other visitors to the museum were all middle-aged or older; the look on their faces was something I had never seen before—something that was not quite love and not quite lust. It flowed across their features like ripples of water whenever they brushed a fender or stopped at a hood that had been opened so they could stare at the engine, all neatly chromed or painted. They were like my father, I thought. They had owned cars when they were young, before Turn-In Day and the same date a year later when even most private steam and electrics were banned because of congestion. For a moment I wondered what it had been like to own one, then canceled the thought. The old man had tried to tell me often enough, before I had stormed out of the house for good, shouting how could he love the damned things so much when he was coughing his lungs out. . . .

The main hall was nothing but bad memories. I left it and looked up the office of the curator. His secretary was on a coffee break so I rapped sharply and entered without waiting for an answer. On the door it had said "C. Pearson," who turned out to be a thin, over-dressed type, all regal nose and pencil moustache, in his mid-forties. "Air Central," I said politely, flashing my wallet ID at him.

He wasn't impressed. "May I?" I gave it to him and he reached for the phone. When he hung up he didn't bother apologizing for the double check, which I figured made us even. "I have nothing to do with the heating system or the air-conditioning," he said easily, "but if you'll wait a minute I'll—"

"I only want information," I said.

He made a small tent of his hands and stared at me over his fingertips. He looked bored. "Oh?"

I sat down and he leaned toward me briefly, then thought better of it and settled back in his chair. "How easy would it be," I asked casually, "to steal one of your displays?"

His moustache quivered slightly. "It wouldn't be easy at all—they're bolted down, there's no gasoline in their tanks, and the batteries are dummies."

"Then none ever have been?"

A flicker of annoyance. "No, of course not."

I flashed my best hat-in-hand smile and stood up. "Well, I guess that's it, then, I won't trouble you any further." But before I turned away I said, "I'm really not much on automobiles but I'm curious. How did the museum get started?"

He warmed up a little. "On Turn-In Day a number of museums like this one were started up all over the country. Some by former dealers, some just by automobile lovers. A number of models were donated for public display and. . . ."

When he had finished I said casually, "Donating a vehicle to a museum must have been a great ploy for hiding private ownership."

"Certainly the people in your bureau would be aware of how strict the government was," he said sharply.

"A lot of people must have tried to hide their vehicles," I persisted.

Dryly. "It would have been difficult . . . like trying to hide an elephant in a playpen."

But still, a number would have tried, I thought. They might even have stockpiled drums of fuel and some spare parts. In the city, of course, it would have been next to impossible. But in remote sections of the country, in the mountain regions out west or in the hills of the Ozarks or in the forests of northern Michigan or Minnesota or in the badlands of the Dakotas. . . . A few would have succeeded, certainly, and perhaps late at night a few weed-grown stretches of highway would have been briefly lit by the headlights of automobiles flashing past with muffled exhausts, tires singing against the pavement. . . .

I sat back down. "Are there many automobile fans around?"

"I suppose so, if attendance records here are any indication."

"Then a smart man with a place in the country and a few automobiles could make quite a bit of money renting them out, couldn't he?"

He permitted himself a slight smile. "It would be risky. I really don't think anybody would try it. And from everything I've read, I rather think the passion was for actual ownership—I doubt that rental would satisfy that."

I thought about it for a moment while Pearson fidgeted with a letter opener and then, of course, I had it. "All those people who were fond of automobiles, there used to be clubs of them, right?"

His eyes lidded over and it grew very quiet in his office. But it was too late and he knew it. "I believe so," he said after a long pause, his voice tight, "but. . . ."

"But the government ordered them disbanded," I said coldly. "Air Control regulations thirty-nine and forty, sections three through seven, 'concerning the dissolution of all organizations which in whole or in part, intentionally or unintentionally, oppose clean air.' " I knew the regulations by heart. "But there still are clubs, aren't there? Unregistered clubs?

Clubs with secret membership files?" A light sheen of perspiration had started to gather on his forehead. "You would probably make a very good membership secretary, Pearson. You're in the perfect spot for recruiting new members—"

He made a motion behind his desk and I dove over it and pinned his arms behind his back. A small address book had fallen to the floor and I scooped it up. Pearson looked as if he might faint. I ran my hands over his chest and under his arms and then let him go. He leaned against the desk, gasping for air.

"I'll have to take you in," I said.

A little color was returning to his cheeks and he nervously smoothed down his damp black hair. His voice was on the squeaky side. "What for? You have some interesting theories but. . . ."

"My theories will keep for court," I said shortly. "You're under arrest for smoking—section eleven thirty point five of the health and safety code." I grabbed his right hand and spread the fingers so the telltale stains showed. "You almost offered me a cigarette when I came in, then caught yourself. I would guess that ordinarily you're pretty relaxed and sociable, you probably smoke a lot—and you're generous with your tobacco. Bottom right hand drawer for the stash, right?" I jerked it open and they were there, all right. "One cigarette's a misdemeanor, a carton's a felony, Pearson. We can accuse you of dealing and make it stick." I smiled grimly. "But we're perfectly willing to trade, of course."

I put in calls to the police and Air Central and sat down to wait for the cops to show. They'd sweat Pearson for all the information he had but I couldn't wait around a couple of hours. The word would spread that Pearson was being held, and Pearson himself would probably start remembering various lawyers and civil rights that he had momentarily forgotten. My only real windfall had been the address book. . . .

I thumbed through it curiously, wondering exactly how I could use it. The names were scattered all over the city, and there were a lot of them. I could weed it down to those in the area where the Sniffer had picked up the automobile, but that would take time and nobody was going to admit that he had a contraband vehicle hidden away anyway. The idea of paying a visit to the club I was certain must exist kept recurring to me and finally I decided to pick a name, twist Pearson's arm for anything he might know about him, then arrange to meet at the club and work out from there.

Later, when I was leaving the museum, I stopped for a moment just inside the door to readjust my mask. While I was doing it the janitor showed up with a roll of weather-stripping and started attaching it to the edge of the doorway where what looked like thin black smoke was seeping in from the outside. I was suddenly afraid to go back out there. . . .

The wind was whistling past my ears and a curve was coming up. I feathered the throttle, downshifted, and the needle on the tach started to drop. The wheel seemed to have a life of its own and twitched slightly to the right. I rode high on the outside of the track, the leafy limbs of trees that lined the asphalt dancing just outside my field of vision. The rear started to come around in a skid and I touched the throttle again and then the wheel twitched back to center and I was away. My eyes were riveted on Number Nine, just in front of me. It was the last lap and if I could catch him there would be nothing between me and the checkered flag. . . .

I felt relaxed and supremely confident, one with the throbbing power of the car. I redlined it and through my dirt-streaked goggles I could see I was crawling up on the red splash that was Number Nine and next I was breathing the fumes from his twin exhausts. I took him on the final curve and suddenly I was alone in the world of the straightaway with the countryside peeling away on both sides of me, placid cows and ancient barns flowing past and then the rails lined with people. I couldn't hear their shouting above the scream of my car. Then I was flashing under banners stretched across the track and thundering toward the finish. There was the smell of burning rubber and spent oil and my own perspiration, the heat from the sun, the shimmering asphalt, and out of the corner of my eye a blur of grandstands and cars and a flag swooping down. . . .

And then it was over and the house lights had come up and I was hunched over a toy wheel in front of me, gripping it with both hands, the sweat pouring down my face and my stomach burning because I could still smell exhaust fumes and I wanted desperately to put on my face mask. It had been far more real than I had thought it would be—the curved screen gave the illusion of depth and each chair had been set up like a driver's seat. They had even pumped in odors. . . .

The others in the small theater were stretching and getting ready to leave and I gradually unwound and got to my feet, still feeling shaky. "Lucky you could make it, Jim," a voice graveled in my ear. "You missed Joe Moore and the lecture but the documentary was just great, really great. Next week we've got *Meadowdale '73* which has its moments but you don't feel like you're really there and getting an eyeful of cinders, if you know what I mean."

"Who's Joe Moore?" I mumbled.

"Old time race track manager—full of anecdotes, knew all the great drivers. Hey! You okay?"

I was finding it difficult to come out of it. The noise and the action and the smell, but especially the feeling of actually driving. . . . It was more than just a visceral response. You had to be raised down in the flats where you struggled for your breath every day to get the same feeling of revulsion, the same feeling of having done something dirty. . . .

"Yeah, I'm okay," I said. "I'm feeling fine."

"Where'd you say you were from, anyway?"

"Bosnywash," I lied. He nodded and I took a breath and time out to size him up. Jack Ellis was bigger and heavier than Pearson and not nearly as smooth or as polished—Pearson perspired, my bulky friend sweated. He was in his early fifties, thinning brown hair carefully waved, the beginning of a small paunch well hidden by a lot of expensive tailoring, and a hulking set of shoulders that were much more than just padding. A business bird, I thought. The hairy-chested genial backslapper. . . .

"You seen the clubrooms yet?"

"I just got in," I said. "First time here."

"Hey, great! I'll show you around!" He talked like he was programmed. "A little fuel and a couple of stiff belts first, though—dining room's out of this world. . . ."

And it almost was. We were on the eighty-seventh floor of the new Trans-America building and Ellis had secured a window seat. Above, the sky was almost as bright a blue as Monte had used in his paintings. I couldn't see the street below.

"Have a card," Ellis said, shoving the pasteboard at me. It read *Warshawsky & Warshawsky, Automotive Antiques,* with an address in the Avenues. He waved a hand at the room. "We decorated all of this—pretty classy, huh?"

I had to give him that. The walls were covered with murals of old road races, while from some hidden sound system came a faint, subdued purring—the roaring of cars drifting through the esses of some long-ago race. In the center of the room was a pedestal holding a highly-chromed engine block that slowly revolved under a baby spot. While I was admiring the setting a waitress came up and set down a lazy Susan; it took a minute to recognize it as an old-fashioned wooden steering wheel, fitted with sterling silver hors d'oeuvre dishes between the spokes.

Ellis ran a thick thumb down the menu. "Try a Barney Oldfield," he suggested. "Roast beef and American cheese on pumpernickel."

While I was eating I got the uncomfortable feeling that he was looking me over and that somehow I didn't measure up. "You're pretty young," he said at last. "We don't get many young members—or visitors, for that matter."

"Grandfather was a dealer," I said easily. "Had a Ford agency in Milwaukee—I guess it rubbed off."

He nodded around a mouthful of sandwich and looked mournful for a moment. "It used to be a young man's game, kids worked on engines in their backyards all the time. Just about everybody owned a car. . . ."

"You, too?"

"Oh sure—hell, the old man ran a gas station until Turn-In Day." He was lost in his memories for a moment, then said, "You got a club in Bosnywash?"

"A few, nothing like this," I said cautiously. "And the law's pretty stiff." I nodded at the window. "They get pretty uptight about the air back east . . ." I let my voice trail off.

He frowned. "You don't *believe* all that guff, do you? Biggest goddamn pack of lies there ever was, but I guess you got to be older to know it. Power plants and incinerators, they're the ones to blame, always have been. Hell, people, too—every time you exhale you're polluting the atmosphere, ever think of that? And Christ, man, think of every time you work up a sweat. . . ."

"Sure," I nodded, "sure, it's always been blown up." I made a mental note that someday I'd throw the book at Ellis.

He finished his sandwich and started wiping his fat face like he was erasing a blackboard. "What's your interest? Mine's family sedans, the old family workhorse. Fords, Chevys, Plymouths—got a case of all the models from '50 on up, one-eighteenth scale. How about you?"

I didn't answer him, just stared out the window and worked with a toothpick for a long time until he began to get a little nervous. Then I let it drop. "I'm out here to buy a car," I said.

His face went blank, as if somebody had just pulled down a shade. "Damned expensive hobby," he said, ignoring it. "Should've taken up photography instead."

"It's for a friend of mine," I said. "Money's no object."

The waitress came around with the check and Ellis initialed it. "Damned expensive," he repeated vaguely.

"I couldn't make a connection back home," I said. "Friends suggested I try out here."

He was watching me now. "How would you get it back east?"

"Break it down," I said. "Ship it east as crates of machine parts."

"What makes you think there's anything for sale out here?"

I shrugged. "Lots of mountains, lots of forests, lots of empty space, lots of hiding places. Cars were big out here, there must have been a number that were never turned in."

"You're a stalking horse for somebody big, aren't you!"

"What do you think?" I said. "And what difference does it make anyway? Money's money."

If it's true that the pupil of the eye expands when it sees something that it likes, it's also true that it contracts when it doesn't—and right then his were in the cold buckshot stage.

"All right," he finally said. "Cash on the barrelhead and remember, when you have that much money changing hands, it can get dangerous." He deliberately leaned across the table so that his coat flapped open slightly. The small gun and holster were almost lost against the big man's girth. He sat back and spun the lazy Susan with a fat forefinger, spearing an olive as it slid past. "You guys run true to form," he continued quietly. "Most guys from back east come out to buy—I guess we've got a reputation." He hesitated. "We also try and take all the danger out of it."

He stood up and slapped me on the back as I pushed to my feet. It was the old Jack Ellis again, he of the instant smile and the sparkling teeth.

"That is, we try and take the danger out of it for *us*," he added pleasantly.

It was late afternoon and the rush hour had started. It wasn't as heavy as usual—businesses had been letting out all day—but it was bad enough. I slipped on a mask and started walking toward the warehouse section of town, just outside the business district. The buses were too crowded and it would be impossible to get an electricab that time of day.

Besides, traffic was practically standing still in the steamy murk. Headlights were vague yellow dots in the gathering darkness and occasionally I had to shine my pocket flash on a street sign to determine my location.

I had checked in with Monte who said the hospitals were filling up fast with bronchitis victims; I didn't ask about the city morgue. The venal bastards at Air Shed Number Three were even getting worried; they had promised Monte that if it didn't clear by morning, he could issue his alert and close down the city. I told him I had uncovered what looked like a car ring but he sounded only faintly interested. He had bigger things on his mind; the ball was in my court and what I was going to do with it was strictly up to me.

A few more blocks and the crowds thinned. Then I was alone on the street with the warehouses hulking up in the gloom around me, ancient monsters of discolored brick and concrete layered with years of soot and grime. I found the address I wanted, leaned against the buzzer by the loading dock door, and waited. There was a long pause, then faint steps echoed inside and the door slid open. Ellis stood in the yellow dock light, the smile stretching across his thick face like a rubber band. "Right on time," he whispered. "Come on in, Jim, meet the boys."

I followed him down a short passageway, trying not to brush up against the filthy whitewashed walls. Then we were up against a steel door with a peephole. Ellis knocked three times, the peephole opened, and he said, "Joe sent me." I started to panic. *For God's sake, why the act?* Then the door opened and it was as if somebody had kicked me in the stomach. What lay beyond was a huge garage with at least a half dozen ancient cars on the tool-strewn floor. Three mechanics in coveralls were working under the overhead lights; two more were waiting inside the door. They were bigger than Ellis and I was suddenly very glad I had brought along the Mark II.

"Jeff, Ray, meet Mr. Morrison." I held out my hand. They nodded at me, no smiles. "C'mon," Ellis said, "I'll show you the set-up." I tagged after him and he started pointing out the wonders of his domain. "Completely equipped garage—my old man would've been proud of me. Overhead hoist for pulling motors, complete lathe set-up . . . a lot of parts we have to machine ourselves, can't get the originals anymore and of course the last of the junkers was melted down a long time ago." He stopped by a workbench with a large rack full of tools gleaming behind it. "One of the great things about being in the antique business—you hit all the country auctions and you'd be surprised at what you can pick up. Complete sets of torque wrenches, metric socket sets, spanner wrenches, feeler gauges, you name it."

I looked over the bench—he was obviously proud of the assortment of tools—then suddenly felt the small of my back grow cold. It was phony, I thought, the whole thing was phony. But I couldn't put my finger on just why.

Ellis walked over to one of the automobiles on the' floor and patted a fender affectionately. Then he unbuttoned his coat so that the pistol showed, hooked his thumbs in his vest, leaned against the car behind him and smiled. Someplace he had even found a broom straw to chew on.

"So what can we do for you, Jim? Limited stock, sky-high prices, but never a dissatisfied customer!" He poked an elbow against the car behind him. "Take a look at this '73 Chevy Biscayne, probably the only one of its kind in this condition in the whole damned country. Ten thou and you can have it—and that's only because I like you." He sauntered over to a monster in blue and silver with grillwork that looked like a set of kitchen knives. "Or maybe you'd like a '76 Caddy convertible, all genuine simulated-leather upholstery, one of the last of the breed." He didn't add why but I already knew—in heavy traffic the high levels of monoxide could be fatal to a driver in an open car.

"Yours," Ellis was saying about another model, "for a flat fifteen"—he paused and shot me a friendly glance—"oh hell, for you, Jim, make it twelve and a half and take it from me, it's a bargain. Comes with the original upholstery and tires and there's less than ten thousand miles on it—the former owner was a little old lady in Pasadena who only drove it to weddings."

He chuckled at that, looking at me expectantly. I didn't get it. "Maybe you'd just like to look around. Be my guest, go right ahead." His eyes were bright and he looked very pleased with himself; it bothered me.

"Yeah," I said absently, "I think that's what I'd like to do." There was a wall phone by an older model and I drifted over to it.

"That's an early Knudsen two-seater," Ellis said. "Popular make for the psychedelic set, that paint job is the way they really came. . . ."

I ran my hand lightly down the windshield, then turned to

face the cheerful Ellis. "You're under arrest," I said. "You and everybody else here."

His face suddenly looked like shrimp in molded gelatin. One of the mechanics behind him moved and I had the Mark II out winging a rocket past his shoulder. No noise, no recoil, just a sudden shower of sparks by the barrel and in the far end of the garage a fifty-gallon oil drum went *karrump* and there was a hole in it you could have stuck your head through.

The mechanic went white. "*Jesus Christ, Jack, you brought in some kind of nut!*" Ellis himself was pale and shaking, which surprised me; I thought he'd be tougher than that.

"Against the bench," I said coldly, waving the pistol. "Hands in front of your crotch and don't move them." The mechanics were obviously scared stiff and Ellis was having difficulty keeping control. I took down the phone and called in.

After I hung up, Ellis mumbled, "What's the charge?"

"Charges," I corrected. "Sections three, four and five of the Air Control laws. Maintenance, sale and use of internal combustion engines."

Ellis stared at me blankly. "You don't know?" he asked faintly.

"Know what?"

"I don't handle internal combustion engines." He licked his lips. "I really don't, it's too risky, it's . . . it's against the law."

The workbench, I suddenly thought. The goddamned workbench. I knew something was wrong then. I should have cooled it.

"You can check me," Ellis offered weakly. "Lift a hood, look for yourself."

He talked like his face was made of panes of glass sliding against one another. I waved him forward. "*You* check it, Ellis, you open one up." Ellis nodded like a dipping duck, waddled over to one of the cars, jiggled something inside, then raised the hood and stepped back.

I took one glance and my stomach slowly started to knot up. I was no motor buff but I damned well knew the difference between a gasoline engine and water boiler. Which explained the workbench—the tools had been window dressing. Most of them were brand new because most of them had obviously never been used. There had been nothing to use them on.

"The engines are steam," Ellis said, almost apologetically. "I've got a license to do restoration work and drop in steam engines. They don't allow them in cities but it's different on farms and country estates and in some small towns." He looked at me. "The license cost me a goddamned fortune."

It was a real handicap being a city boy, I thought. "Then why the act? Why the gun?"

"This?" he asked stupidly. He reached inside his coat and dropped the pistol on the floor; it made a light thudding sound and bounced, a pot metal toy. "The danger, it's the sense of danger, it's part of the sales pitch." He wanted to be angry now but he had been frightened too badly and couldn't quite make it. "The customers pay a lot of dough, they want a little drama. That's why—you know—the peephole and everything." He took a deep breath and when he exhaled it came out as a giggle, an incongruous sound from the big man. I found myself hoping he didn't have a heart condition. "I'm well known," he said defensively. "I take ads. . . ."

"The club," I said. "It's illegal."

Even if it was weak, his smile was genuine and then the score became crystal clear. The club was like a speakeasy during the Depression, with half the judges and politicians in town belonging to it. Why not? Somebody older wouldn't have my bias. . . . Pearson's address book had been all last names and initials but I had never connected any of them to anybody prominent; I hadn't been around enough to know what connection to make.

I waved Ellis back to the workbench and stared glumly at the group. The mechanic I had frightened with the Mark II had a spreading stain across the front of his pants and I felt sorry for him momentarily.

Then I started to feel sorry for myself. Monte should have given me a longer briefing, or maybe assigned another Investigator to go with me, but he had been too sick and too wrapped up with the politics of it all. So I had gone off half-cocked and come up with nothing but a potential lawsuit for Air Central that would probably amount to a million dollars by the time Ellis got through with me.

It was a black day inside as well as out.

I holed up in a bar during the middle part of the evening, which was probably the smartest thing I could have done. Despite their masks, people on the street had started to retch and vomit and I could feel my own nausea grow with every

step. I saw one man try and strike a match to read a street
sign; it wouldn't stay lit, there simply wasn't enough oxygen
in the air. The ambulance sirens were a steady wail now and
I knew it was going to be a tough night for heart cases.
They'd be going like flies before morning, I thought. ...

Another customer slammed through the door, wheezing
and coughing and taking huge gulps of the machine-pure air
of the bar. I ordered another drink and tried to shut out the
sound; it was too reminiscent of Monte hacking and coughing
behind his desk at work.

And come morning, Monte might be out of a job, I
thought. I for certain would be; I had loused up in a way
that would cost the department money—the unforgivable sin
in the eyes of the politicians.

I downed half my drink and started mentally reviewing the
events of the day, giving myself a passing score only on figur-
ing out that Pearson had had a stash. I hadn't known about
Ellis's operation, which in one sense wasn't surprising. Nobody was going to drive something that looked like an old
gasoline-burner around a city—the flatlanders would stone
him to death.

But somebody still had a car, I thought. Somebody who
was rich and immune from prosecution and a real nut about
cars in the first place. . . . But it kept sliding away from me.
Really rich men were too much in the public eye, ditto politicians. They'd be washed up politically if anybody ever found
out. If nothing else, some poor bastard like the one at the end
of the bar trying to flush out his lungs would assassinate him.

Somebody with money, but not too much. Somebody who
was a car nut—they'd have to be to take the risks. And somebody for whom those risks were absolutely minimal. . . .

And then the lightbulb flashed on above my head, just like
in the old cartoons. I wasn't dead certain I was right but I
was willing to stake my life on it—and it was possible I
might end up doing just that.

I slipped on a mask and almost ran out of the bar. Once
outside, I sympathized with the guy who had just come in
and who had given me a horrified look as I plunged out into
the darkness.

It was smothering now, though the temperature had
dropped a little so my shirt didn't cling to me in dirty, damp
folds. Buses were being led through the streets; headlights
died out completely within a few feet. The worst thing was
that they left tracks in what looked like a damp, grayish ash

that covered the street. Most of the people I bumped into—
mere shadows in the night—had soaked their masks in water,
trying to make them more effective. There were lights still on
in the lower floors of most of the office buildings and I figured some people hadn't tried to make it home at all; air was
probably purer among the filing cabinets than in their own
apartments. Two floors up, the buildings were completely hidden in the smoky darkness.

It took a good hour of walking before the sidewalks started
to slant up and I knew I was getting out toward the foothills
. . . I thanked God the business district was closer to the
mountains than the ocean. My legs ached and my chest hurt
and I was tired and depressed but at least I wasn't coughing
anymore.

The buildings started to thin out and the streets finally became completely deserted. Usually the cops would pick you
up if they caught you walking on the streets of Forest Hills
late at night, but that night I doubted they were even around.
They were probably too busy ferrying cases of cardiac arrest
to St. Francis. . . .

The Sniffer was located on the top of a small, ancient
building off on a side street. When I saw it I suddenly found
my breath hard to catch again—a block down, the street
abruptly turned into a canyon and wound up and out of
sight. I glanced back at the building, just faintly visible
through the grayed-down moonlight. The windows were
boarded up and there was a For Rent sign on them. I walked
over and flashed my light on the sign. It was old and peeling
and had obviously been there for years; apparently nobody
had ever wanted to rent the first floor. Ever? Maybe somebody had, I thought, but had decided to leave it boarded up.
I ran my hands down the boards and suddenly paused at a
knothole; I could feel heavy plate glass through it. I knelt and
flashed my light at the hole and looked at a dim reflection of
myself staring back. The glass had been painted black on the
inside so it acted like a black marble mirror.

I stepped back and something about the building struck
me. The boarded-up windows, I thought, the huge, oversized
windows. . . . And the oversized, boarded-up doors. I flashed
the light again at the concrete facing just above the doors.
The words were there all right, blackened by time but still
readable, cut into the concrete itself by order of the proud
owner a handful of decades before. But you could still noodle
them out: *RICHARD SIEBEN LINCOLN-MERCURY.*

Jackpot, I thought triumphantly. I glanced around—there was nobody else on the street—and listened. Not a sound, except for the faint murmur of traffic still moving in the city far away. A hot muggy night in the core city, I thought, but this night the parks and the fire escapes would be empty and five mililon people would be tossing and turning in their cramped little bedrooms; it'd be suicide to try and sleep outdoors.

In Forest Hills it was cooler—and quieter. I glued my ear to the boards over the window and thought I could hear the faint shuffle of somebody walking around and, once, the faint clink of metal against metal. I waited a moment, then slipped down to the side door that had "Air Central" on it in neat black letters. All Investigators had master keys and I went inside. Nobody was upstairs; the lights were out and the only sound was the soft swish of the Sniffer's scribing pens against the paper roll. There was a stairway in the back and I walked silently down it. The door at the bottom was open and I stepped through it into a short hallway. Something, maybe the smell of the air, told me it had been used recently. I closed the door after me and stood for a second in the darkness. There was no sound from the door beyond. I tried the knob and it moved silently in my grasp.

I cracked the door open and peered through the slit—nothing—then eased it open all the way and stepped out onto the showroom floor. There was a green-shaded lightbulb hanging from the ceiling, swaying slightly in some minor breeze so the shadows chased each other around the far corners of the room. Walled off at the end were two small offices where salesmen had probably wheeled and dealed long ago. There wasn't much else, other than a few tools scattered around the floor in the circle of light.

And directly in the center, of course, the car.

I caught my breath. There was no connection between it and Jack Ellis's renovated family sedans. It crouched there on the floor, a mechanical beast that was almost alive. Sleek curving fenders that blended into a louvered hood with a chromed steel bumper curving flat around the front to give it an oddly sharklike appearance. The headlamps were set deep into the fenders, the lamp wells outlined with chrome. The hood flowed into a windshield and that into a top which sloped smoothly down in back and tucked in neatly just after the rear wheels. The wheels themselves had wire spokes that gleamed wickedly in the light, and through a side window I could make out a neat array of meters and rocker switches, and finally bucket seats covered with what I instinctively knew was genuine black leather.

Sleek beast, powerful beast, I thought. I was unaware of walking up to it and running my hand lightly over a fender until a voice behind me said, "It's beautiful, isn't it?"

I turned like an actor in a slow-motion film. "Yeah, Dave," I said, "it's beautiful." Dave Ice of Air Central. In charge of all the Sniffers.

He must have been standing in one of the salesman's offices; it was the only way I could have missed him. He walked up and stood on the other side of the car and ran his left hand over the hood with the same affectionate motion a woman might use in stroking her cat. In his right hand he held a small Mark II pointed directly at my chest.

"How'd you figure it was me?" he asked casually.

"I thought at first it might be Monte," I said. "Then I figured you were the real nut about machinery."

His eyes were bright, too bright. "Tell me," he asked curiously, "would you have turned in Monte?"

"Of course," I said simply. I didn't add that it would have been damned difficult; that I hadn't even been able to think about that part of it.

"So might've I, so might've I," he murmured. "When I was your age."

"For a while the money angle threw me," I said.

He smiled faintly. "It's a family heirloom. My father bought it when he was young, he couldn't bring himself to turn it in." He cocked his head. "Could you?" I looked at him uneasily and didn't answer and he said casually, "Go ahead, Jimmy, you were telling me how you cracked the case."

I flushed. "It had to be somebody who knew—who was absolutely sure—that he wasn't going to get caught. The Sniffers are pretty efficient, it would have been impossible to prevent their detecting the car—the best thing would be to censor the data from them. And Monte and you were the only ones who could have done that."

Another faint smile. "You're right."

"You slipped up a few nights ago," I said.

He shrugged. "Anybody could've. I was sick, I didn't get to the office in time to doctor the record."

"It gave the game away," I said. "Why only once? The

Sniffer should have detected it far more often than just once."

He didn't say anything and for a long moment both of us were lost in admiration of the car.

Then finally, proudly: "It's the real McCoy, Jim. Six cylinder in-line engine, 4.2 liters displacement, nine-to-one compression ratio, twin overhead cams and twin Zenith-Stromberg carbs. . . ." He broke off. "You don't know what I'm talking about, do you?"

"No," I confessed, "I'm afraid not."

"Want to see the motor?"

I nodded and he stepped forward, waved me back with the Mark II, and opened the hood. To really appreciate it, of course, you had to have a thing for machinery. It was clean and polished and squatted there under the hood like a beautiful mechanical pet—so huge I wondered how the hood could close at all.

And then I realized with a shock that I hadn't been reacting like I should have, that I hadn't reacted like I should have ever since the movie at the club. . . .

"You can sit in it if you want to," Dave said softly. "Just don't touch anything." His voice was soft. "Everything works on it, Jim, everything works just dandy. It's oiled and greased and the tank is full and the battery is charged and if you wanted to, you could drive it right off the showroom floor."

I hesitated. "People in the neighborhood—"

"—mind their own business," he said. "They have a different attitude, and besides, it's usually late at night and I'm out in the hills in seconds. Go ahead, get in." Then his voice hardened into command: "Get in!"

I stalled a second longer, then opened the door and slid into the seat. The movie was real now, I was holding the wheel and could sense the gearshift at my right and in my mind's eye I could feel the wind and hear the scream of the motor. . . .

There was something hard pressing against the side of my head. I froze. Dave was holding the pistol just behind my ear and in the side mirror I could see his finger tense on the trigger and pull back a millimeter. *Dear God. . . .*

He relaxed. "You'll have to get out," he said apologetically. "It would be appropriate, but a mess just the same."

I got out. My legs were shaking and I had to lean against the car. "It's a risky thing to own a car," I chattered. "Feeling runs pretty high against cars. . . ."

He nodded. "It's too bad."

"You worked for Air Central for years," I said. "How could you do it, and own this, too?"

"You're thinking about the air," he said carefully. "But Jim"—his voice was patient—"machines don't foul the air, men do. They foul the air, the lakes, and the land itself. And there's no way to stop it." I started to protest and he held up a hand. "Oh sure, there's always a time when you care—like you do now. But time . . . you know, time wears you down, it really does, no matter how eager you are. You devote your life to a cause and then you find yourself suddenly growing fat and bald and you discover nobody gives a damn about your cause. They're paying you your cushy salary to buy off their own consciences. So long as there's a buck to be made, things won't change much. It's enough to drive you—" He broke off. "You don't *really* think that anybody gives a damn about anybody else, do you?" He stood there looking faintly amused, a pudgy little man whom I should've been able to take with one arm tied behind my back. But he was ten times as dangerous as Ellis had ever imagined himself to be. "Only suckers care, Jim. I . . ."

I dropped to the floor then, rolling fast to hit the shadows beyond the circle of light. His Mark II sprayed sparks and something burned past my shirt collar and squealed along the concrete floor. I sprawled flat and jerked my own pistol out. The first shot went low and there was the sharp sound of scored metal and I cursed briefly to myself—I must have brushed the car. Then there was silence and I scrabbled further back into the darkness. I wanted to pot the light but the bulb was still swaying back and forth and chances were I'd miss and waste the shot. Then there was the sound of running and I jumped to my feet and saw Dave heading for the door I had come in by. He seemed oddly defenseless—he was chubby and slow and knock-kneed and ran like a woman.

"Dave!" I screamed. "Dave! STOP!"

It was an accident, there was no way to help it. I aimed low and to the side, to knock him off his feet, and at the same time he decided to do what I had done and sprawl flat in the shadows. If he had stayed on his feet, the small rocket would have brushed him at knee level. As it was, it smashed his chest.

He crumpled and I ran up and caught him before he could hit the floor. He twisted slightly in my arms so he was staring at the car as he died. I broke into tears. I couldn't help that, either. I would remember the things Dave had done for me long after I had forgotten that one night he had tried to kill me. A threat to kill is unreal—actual blood and shredded flesh has its own reality.

I let him down gently and walked slowly over to the phone in the corner. Monte should still be in his office, I thought. I dialed and said, "The Director, please," and waited for the voice-actuated relay to connect me. "Monte, Jim Morrison here. I'm over at—" I paused. "I'm sorry, I thought it was Monte—" And then I shut up and let the voice at the other end of the line tell me that Monte had died with the window open and the night air filling his lungs with urban vomit. "I'm sorry," I said faintly, "I'm sorry, I'm very sorry," but the voice went on and I suddenly realized that I was listening to a recording and that there was nobody in the office at all. Then, as the voice continued, I knew why.

I let the receiver fall to the floor and the record started in again, as if expecting condolences from the concrete.

I should call the cops, I thought. I should—

But I didn't. Instead, I called Wanda. It would take an hour or more for her to collect the foodstuffs in the apartment and to catch an electricab but we could be out of the city before morning came.

And that was pretty funny because morning was never coming. The recording had said dryly that the tagged radioactive chimney exhausts had arrived, that the dragon's breath had circled the globe and the winds blowing in were as dirty as the air already over the city. Oh, it wouldn't happen right away, but it wouldn't be very long, either. . . .

Nobody had given a damn, I thought; not here nor any other place. Dave had been right, dead right. They had finally turned it all into a sewer and the last of those who cared had coughed his lungs out trying for a breath of fresh air that had never come, too weak to close a window.

I walked back to the car sitting in the circle of light and ran a finger down the scored fender where the small rocket had scraped the paint. Dave would never have forgiven me, I thought. Then I opened the door and got in and settled slowly back into the seat. I fondled the shift and ran my eyes over the instrument panel, the speedometer and the tach and the fuel and the oil gauges and the small clock. . . . The keys dangled from the button at the end of the hand brake. It was a beautiful piece of machinery, I thought again. I had never really loved a piece of machinery . . . until now.

I ran my hands around the wheel, then located the starter switch on the steering column. I jabbed in the key and closed my eyes and listened to the scream of the motor and felt its power shake the car and wash over me and thunder through the room. The movie at the club had been my only lesson but in its own way it had been thorough and it would be enough. I switched off the motor and waited.

When Wanda got there we would take off for the high ground. For the mountains and the pines and that last clear lake and that final glimpse of blue sky before it all turned brown and we gave up in final surrender to this climate of which we're so obviously proud. . . .

It was two years before I hit *Playboy* again and during the interregnum, I left Los Angeles. In L.A., I had been working with Bob Shea on *Cavalier* and we had commissioned an article on the Diggers, a hippie charitable group operating in San Francisco. When the article came in, I was fascinated. I was old enough to be skeptical but young enough to be actively curious about "hippies."

I promptly paid a visit to San Francisco. (I was anxious to leave L.A. anyway; *Cavalier* had been sold and there was no sense staying. I didn't drive and for people who don't, the city can be a prison.) A friend of mine gave me a quick tour of the town, including a visit to "Hippie Hill" just inside Golden Gate Park. I was wandering along the path at the foot of it when somebody called my name. It was a former staffer of *Rogue*, sitting halfway up the hill, mildly stoned, watching the tourists below. I joined him and he waved to another friend a few feet away, a Chicago photographer who used to do assignments for us. I soaked up the sun for a few minutes and when he offered me a toke, I accepted. (I once threatened to fire an assistant editor in Chicago if he ever smoked dope—I still believed in the myth of the Killer Weed then. So much for my former value system.)

For a month I lived in Berkeley behind Max Scherr, former editor/publisher of the *Berkeley Barb*, and did some reporting for him under the pseudonym of "Thomas Benji." Then I moved into San Francisco close by Golden Gate Park, where the Avenues sidle up to the Haight-Ashbury. I became casually friendly with Mouse and Kelly, who did most of the posters for the Fillmore and the Avalon, and briefly met some of the characters who were to become legend later: The Grateful Dead, Janis Joplin, Emmett Grogan and rock impressario Bill Graham among others. (I and a friend, Rick Nanas, once interviewed Graham. It ran in the *Haight-Ashbury Tribune* and was quoted at length in Nicholas von Hoffman's book, *We Are the People Our Parents Warned Us Against*. It was the first interview I'd ever written and I was oddly proud of it.)

It was the Summer of Love and I had never seen anything like it nor am I ever likely to again. The newcomers to the Haight were beats and San Francisco State students and rock musicians trying to get a start. (A lot of them worked for the Post Office. Those who had a regular income shared with those who didn't—the concept of the saintlike Diggers was already well-ingrained in the area). The original inhabitants of the Haight—retirees, blue collar workers, and Blacks who spilled over from the Fillmore—hung on, living in uneasy jutaxposition with long-haired musicians and kids who had read all about the scene in their hometown newspapers and migrated to San Francisco looking for free love and free dope. (They found out soon enough that nothing was really free . . .)

Poet (and future novelist) Richard Brautigan hung out at the I/Thou Coffee Shop and science fiction writer Chester Anderson ran the Communications Company, which published news bulletins and manifestos regarding what was happening in the hippie community of the Haight. The kids on the street gave away cookies and stale French fries, smiled a lot, panhandled money, sold dope and chanted, "Hey, man, you're beautiful!" like it was a litany. Nobody read books, unless it was the I Ching or Stranger in a Strange Land. (Bob Heinlein writing an underground bestseller . . . !)

It was a social revolution that had started with the Free Speech Movement in Berkeley circa 1964 and had been gathering momentum ever since, fueled primarily by the universal reluctance to fight in the jungles of Vietnam. So those of draft age flocked to the Haight and nobody gave their right name and most of them worked for peanuts because they didn't dare list their Social Security number—they could be traced that way. (Shopkeepers and restaurant owners knew it and young hippies suddenly became a bigger employment bargain than wetbacks.) A lot of people were loving and friendly and shared what they had—the VD clinic did a land office business—and for a few months maybe Look was right, maybe the hippies really were the new Christians. . . . For a while the scene fascinated me. There was enough of the journalist in me to want to be on the cutting edge of society, to be in the right place at the right time, to be a part of what the historians call "an era of social ferment." And then . . .

And then.

LSD ("acid") hadn't been illegal at the start. Marijuana was, but not acid. So people bought it and traded it and finally it became a medium of exchange and dealing in it became a vocation instead of a hobby. So did dealing in pot. Then the Gentle People split and the "righteous" dealers were squeezed out by the Big Dealers. Chocolate George was murdered and methedrine became the most popular drug on the street and suddenly the Haight held the murder record for the city: One per square block. And one night the local Police Community Relations Officer showed me a photograph of a young girl and asked if I had seen her around. I hadn't but something about the picture struck me as peculiar. She was a runaway, he said (it was a national scandal—all the runaways in the country headed for the Haight). She was also dead and the first inkling I had that people didn't die with their eyes closed.

I knew then that I wasn't long for the Haight, but before I left I wrote a lengthy article about what life there was really like. It differed radically from the "early Christians" approach that *Look* had taken. Unfortunately, Joan Didion beat me to it with an expose in *The Saturday Evening Post* ("Slouching Toward Bethlehem"). Herb Gold was still painting a rosy picture for *Playboy* but Quadrangle had brought out Nicholas von Hoffman's book (the first serious reporting on the scene), and *Esquire*, which first rejected my own piece as too downbeat, later published a frightening portrait of the Haight . . .

"A Life in the Day Of" is based on some parties I went to in Berkeley and San Francisco, as well as on a friend of mine in Chicago who had become a hippie with more enthusiasm than thought (at least in my—by that time—jaded opinion).

I wanted to say something in the story, to do something more than just tell a story. In style and intent and life itself, I had put on a lot of years in a rather short span of time.

My agent was somewhat dubious about the story but as it turned out, *Playboy* liked it.

A Life in the Day Of . . .

It was going to be a great party, Jeff thought, inspecting himself in the bathroom mirror, even if it had been a pain in the ass to get ready for. He'd had his sideburns professionally trimmed, but the mustache and beard he'd had to do himself, shaping the beard carefully so it curled under just *so* and working on the mustache literally hair by hair, to get it to lie right. But the effect was worth it—far *out*, but not too far.

He smiled at the mirror and his image smiled back: long brown hair falling to his shoulders, with the bangs over his forehead curling away just above the eyebrows, blue eyes shining, teeth even and white, skin a smooth healthy tan—say what you wanted to about WASPs, man, but they weren't hard to look at. He smiled again and the smile caught him and he tried a few other expressions. The Sincere look, which could move mountains or, at least, a chick from the living room into the bedroom; the youthful Anything Is Possible If You Only Believe look; the Help Me! look, for the older creeps; and, finally, the turn-off one of Irritated Uninterest. Not bad, not bad at all.

One last smile and he shook his head in pleased amazement. *Damn*, he was a good-looking bastard! God bless genetics or whatever.

He stepped back from the mirror and smoothed his togalike garment, carefully draped over his left shoulder and caught just above the ankle. *Great, just great!* He'd picked it up from the Hare Krishna people, but in another month or so it'd be the "in" thing, *his* thing. He splashed a little lime lotion on his face, flashed a congratulatory look at the mirror, then padded into the living room for a final check.

The stereo had been programed for early Glenn Miller at the start—good for mood music as well as a laugh—then an old Beatles tape, plus some country rock around midnight, when everybody was stoned out of his gourd on grass or wine, and to finish up with some harpsichord tracks when people wanted to make out.

Chips and dip, salami and cheese on the coffee table under the Saran Wrap (risky, but a great ploy—"It's just to remind us, man"—and *he* could get away with it). The new *Barb*, an

old copy of *Crawdaddy* and especially Tuesday's issue of the
Times. The one with the photograph showing him clutching
his STUDENTS FOR FREEDOM sign just before the pigs waded
in. The photographer had caught him just right—nobody
could look at it without feeling for him—but he liked the
caption even better. *"Youth in anguish."* Youthful innocence,
the hope of tomorrow (all summed up in himself) being
crushed by the fascist state. What was the name of the kid
who had really been hit? The ugly kid with glasses? He
couldn't remember, but it really didn't matter.

And then the front-door buzzer was blasting away and he
straightened up, smoothed the wrinkles from his toga and let
The Smile flood his face like light from the morning sun.

By ten o'clock, the party was going full blast, the stereo
blaring, couples sprawling out on the rugs and couches,
people rapping in little groups, a few huddling in corners,
turning on—only God knew who had brought what, but there
were a lot of glazed looks floating around. Politically, it was
pretty well balanced. A few old-line activists, but mostly second echelon, all of whom had seen the *Times* and really fell
out when he flashed on them. Some over-30s, but that only
made for contrast, so what the hell.

And then a chick was plastered up against him and it took
him a second to place her. How long had it been since he
had done a number with Sue? Jesus, she had been forgettable.
He wondered who she had come with; he sure as hell hadn't
invited her.

"It's a great party, Jeff, really great," she breathed, and he
felt like telling her to go brush her teeth. There was a brief
lull in the music and for a moment, the background noises
came crashing through—cubes tinkling in glasses, a chick gig-
gling, some kid coughing, who hadn't been able to hold in the
smoke, the overloud talking of people not yet adjusted to the
sudden silence.

There had been a sticky moment earlier in the evening,
when an older type had shown up, with a guitar yet; there
was nothing for it but to accompany the square on a battered
12-string Jeff kept hidden in the closet, then do a solo number before flashing a smile and saying, "This is a party, not a
performance," and turning the stereo back on. Mr. Guitar
Man was pretty well out of it by then and was now sitting on
the big beat-up couch by the window, staring moodily out at
the night.

". . . Been so long," Sue was saying, trying to sock it in.

He was only half aware of her; all he wanted to do was get away, get a drink and rap with the little blonde in the living room who had been so awed by him earlier.

Accusingly: "You're not listening!"

Oh, God. . . . He peeled her hand off his shoulder and felt her stiffen. The light from the kitchen was pale, but he could make out the faint veins pulsing in her neck and the fine network of lines starting to firm up around her eyes. "I'm sorry, Sue, you were saying something?" Messy bit, but if he didn't let her know the score, somebody else would—you get to be 25, man, you're a stone drag. Then he had pulled loose, mumbling a bland " 'Scuse, Sue, gotta fill my cup," and she fled past him into the living room, to fold up on the couch next to Mr. Guitar Man. Maybe they deserved each other, he thought. *American Gothic,* up to date.

And then he had refilled his paper cup from the jug of rosé on the coffee table and the party was picking up again and it was great, just great.

"Gee, Mr. Beall, I saw your picture in the *Times* with the pig clubbing you."

A freshman, the warm wine sweat glistening on his smooth cheeks—Jeff had seen him hanging around the edges of the sit-in at the Poly Sci lecture hall. "It didn't hurt—the pigs are all queer, they don't hit too hard."

"It must've been a really inside trip," the kid said sympathetically, then drifted off, while Jeff frowned after him and wondered uneasily just what the hell the kid had meant to say, and reflected, but only for a moment, how great it would be to be 17 again. Then he started sipping at the wine and let the conversation in the room close over him like soapy water over dishes in a sink.

" . . . *The synthetics are really a bummer.* . . ."

" . . . *Trustees are out to kill the third world.* . . ."

" . . . *Sure, but Dylan copped out, man.* . . ."

" . . . *Soul food, that's an issue.* . . ."

"Fuck the establishment," Jeff said amiably to nobody in particular, then ducked into the kitchen for a refill on the salami. The blonde was in a corner with a short-haired squeaky-clean wearing a Nehru jacket and beads—the poor slob had been stuck with hand-me-downs. He was also very stoned and the chick looked like she badly needed rescuing.

He picked up a couple of plates of lunch meat and said, "Hey, chickie, how about a hand?" and she slipped away and flashed him a grateful smile. She was maybe 17, with waist-long hair and green eyes—she *definitely* made the other chicks at the party look like old hags.

"Look, man, she came with me, she's mine!"

The Level, Reserved look, eyes slightly narrowed. "You some sort of reactionary, man? You don't own *anybody!*" And then he had shoved the chick into the living room and he was dumping the plates onto the table. Somebody offered him a joint and he took a toke and passed the roach on to the girl. Always take a puff for social standing, but never get stoned; too easy to let down the old guard.

The girl was looking up at him big-eyed and he nodded to himself; she was *the* one, all right. "Thanks," she said. There was just the right amount of quiver in her voice and he gave her the Sincere look and said, "The means of production belong to the state," which wasn't a bad line at all.

She sucked on the joint, coughed, then held her breath for a long moment. After she let it out, she nodded toward the stereo and said, "The All for One are really boss."

"Womb to Tomb," he couldn't help correcting. "On *Walkin'*. WSAN played it this morning; tomorrow it'll be all over the country."

She shook her head and looked serious. "Sounds like but isn't—the lead cimbalom's a friend of mine," and just for a second the world slipped sideways, because he suddenly wasn't sure.

Then he was off again, flashing her The Smile and squeezing her hand, saying, "Don't go home early—in fact, don't go home," and he knew she wouldn't.

There was an angry murmur rising above the background mumble, like smoke over burning brush. A little knot of Maoists had lined up against the Progressive Leftists, and somebody shouted over to him. "What do you think, Jeff?" and they were respectfully silent and that was more like it.

"You work with the pigs," he said automatically, "you're just playing into the hands of the establishment." A buzz of approval and the confrontation splintered a dozen different ways, then a rock number came up on the stereo and the heavy beat rolled over the room like a tide.

"Sharp," a voice said.

Old, middle-30s, balding. Maybe a professor crashing the party to score on a chick. "It's the all-purpose answer," Jeff said easily.

"I'm Jenkins, Asian Studies. Saw the picture of you in the *Times.*"

A nod. Wait him out, see what he wants.

Jenkins studied him thoughtfully for a second, then cleared his throat and said, "After class, I run the Free Tutorial Studies. We need tutors for the ghetto freshmen—I saw you at the F.T.S. rally last week and thought you might like to help out."

There was no end to the freaky things people wanted you to do. "Sorry, man, that's not my bag," he said coldly and started to move away. The blonde was back in a corner with the Nehru jacket and it was time to break it up.

Jenkins smiled faintly down at his drink. "Not much press coverage, no guarantee you'll get your picture in the paper."

Why, the condescending old fart; you'd think he had never run into that one before! Jeff whirled.

"Heavy, old man! Look, *you* sit in, *you* carry the signs, *you* get clubbed! Think anybody's going to cry for *you*? Get laid, will you! I do my thing, you do yours!" Holier than thou, bull*shit*.

The mumble of the party again, somebody being sick in the john, the click of the lock on the bedroom door, a chick crying in the kitchen and somebody laughing hysterically in the living room, the sour smell of smoke and wine and too many people. Christ, he hadn't invited half that number—a few more cigarette burns on the window sill and spreading puddles on the faded rug slowly seeping into the wool, the sweet smell of pot and he was getting a contact high and. . . .

Somebody was clutching at him and doing the heavy-breathing bit. "Want to . . . see you alone, Jeff."

Old women, dogs and Ann Polanski loved him. Yesterday's radical, the professional student, working for a Ph.D. in sociology and she'd get it about the time of the Second Coming. Drunk out of her mind and probably feeling very sorry for herself because, at 30, she was the last of the vestal virgins; love me, love my guilt complex, and who wanted that kind of package deal?

"Damsel in distress in the kitchen and all that rot," he said, trying to edge past. "Be right back."

She hung onto him and licked her lips and tried to get the words out without slurring them, and when they finally came, they were like pearls strung on a string. "Just want to say . . . magnificent party." She closed her eyes and for a panicky moment he was afraid she was going to vomit down his toga. Then she was fishing a damp strand of hair out of her eyes and trying hard to focus on him. "Don't know . . . how you do it, Jeff," she said, closing her eyes again. "Goddamn generations . . . two years apart now . . . can't figure out the right attitudes from one day to nex'—next . . . changes, everything changes so fast . . . got to be a real phony to keep up with them."

He could feel the heat at the back of his neck. Overage and 20 pounds overweight and she wouldn't get her Ph.D., not in a million years, and *she* was putting *him* down. "Ever think about it?" she asked, suddenly wistful.

"I don't think," he said lightly. And then she was holding onto him again and it wasn't for support and he could feel his skin crawl—hot and sweaty and the monthly smell. He forced himself to hold her gently for a moment and nuzzle her neck, and when she was blinking with sudden hope, he murmured, "I would like to help you, Ann, I really would, but it would be like balling my own mother."

"You're a stinking son of a bitch," she said calmly.

Then he was back in the living room again and Ann was fading into the background, like roses on old wallpaper, and the noises and the heat in the room were smothering him and he could feel himself start to drown in his own party.

Out of the corner of his eye, he caught a glimpse of the huge old couch by the window. Mr. Guitar Man, toying with a drink in which the ice had long since melted; Sue, sitting next to him, looking 35 instead of 25, starting to shrivel right before his eyes: Jenkins beside her, his face a remote mask; and Ann at the far end, eyes closed, probably passed out. All of them with that odd, frightening, glazed look about them, like wax dummies in a museum.

He shivered, then was caught up in the party once more. He was the guy who made it tick, who made it go, the one who was with it. He was the mirror for people who wanted to check how the mustache lay, how the toga fit, whether the smile was right and the attitude was "in." He was the hero, the star, the winner, to be chaired through the market place.

He could feel his ego expanding and filling the room like Styrofoam, and he knew he was getting *very* stoned, but it felt good, good, good—the music was as sharp as diamonds and the food was ambrosia and everybody . . . everybody loved him.

It was two in the morning when, suddenly, above the roar of the party, he heard the door buzzer and instinctively knew it wasn't the police and, just as instinctively, that whoever it was shouldn't be let in. Then there was laughter and shouting in the hallway and a pounding on the door and the party around him froze—it was like watching a film where they end up on a single frame and hold it. Dancing, laughing, shouting and then sudden silence and the living room was filled with plaster statues.

Somebody stepped to the door and he wanted to shout *Don't let them in!* and then the door was open and the laughing crowd outside tumbled in like a bushel of leaves driven by the wind. They pulled at his party like so many human magnets and the movement in the room started to quicken and, within seconds, the party was roaring again.

Jeff didn't know any of them.

He was standing in a corner all alone, with the party swirling about him but never touching him, like waves breaking around a rock, and then somebody was standing in front of him. "So you're Jeffrey." He hated the full name and he hated the tone of condescension.

The stranger was dressed in black and had a drooping black mustache, like an old-time cowboy villain, and something within Jeff whispered *That's sharp,* and he was wearing a FREE LEONARD button and who the hell was Leonard, anyway?

"Name's Lee," the stranger said in a deep bass voice, and Jeff guessed that he had really worked at it to pitch it that low, and then he was fingering Jeff's toga and the people around them were suddenly silent and tense and the stranger said, "Too bad it spots so easily," and somebody laughed and Jeff couldn't think of anything to say, and then a chick he didn't know came up and said, "I saw your picture in the *Times*—you looked cute," and a lot more people laughed and then they all drifted away and Jeff caught himself staring down at the wine in his paper cup and noting that the cube he had dropped in to cool it had almost melted.

He fled into the kitchen and bumped into the blonde and she dropped a plate of sandwiches on the floor and he almost skidded on them, then blurted, "You're going to stay over, aren't you?" and she looked at him as if she wasn't quite sure who he was and said, "Did you ask?" and ducked under his arm into the living room.

He turned back to the party, trying to quiet his panic, and ran into the kid who had been at the Poly Sci sit-in. *The goddamned toga,* he was thinking furiously, *goddamned asshole toga.* He tried to start a conversation, but the kid snickered and said, "Later, man," and wandered over to the group that had gathered around the cowboy in black.

"*You can't trust the dogs,*" the cowboy was saying, "*they'll gut the proles every time. On the other hand, the police are predictable.*" There was a chorus of agreement; the crowd grew. Jeff didn't have the faintest idea what they were talking about.

He reeled over to the open window and tried to suck in some fresh air and stop the room from spinning. There was singing and shouting in the street below and he leaned out to see what was happening. Some stoned students were lurching down the street, singing a pop song—but he couldn't place the tune, *he couldn't place the tune,* he couldn't remember ever having heard it. Farther down the street, beneath a street lamp, a small army of workmen were painting over storefronts and changing signs. He squinted his eyes, but he couldn't find the familiar Me and Thee coffeeshop; the sign that swung out over the sidewalk was gone and in its place was something called THE ROOKERY. He didn't know the street anymore, he realized suddenly; all the "in" spots, *his* spots, were gone, and he had never heard the songs, and he couldn't keep his groups straight, and he didn't know the people, and . . . *who was Leonard, anyway*?

Every two years, Ann had said. And faster all the time. But you never noticed the buds until the day they blossomed.

And then he was sinking down into the sofa by the window, still clutching his paper cup, to sit next to Mr. Guitar Man and Sue and Jenkins and Ann. He could sense the glaze creeping over his face and felt something very light and feathery on his neck and shoulders.

It was, he imagined, the dust settling gently down.

In 1969, they were reading *Slaughterhouse Five* by Kurt Vonnegut, *The Love Machine* by Jacqueline Susann and *The Godfather* by Mario Puzo. In films, it was *The Lion in Winter, Rosemary's Baby, Funny Girl* and *Charly* (the latter was adapted from "Flowers for Algernon," a story that ran in *Fantasy and Science Fiction*). General Motors recalled five million cars, the old *Saturday Evening Post* published its last issue and for the first time U.S. combat deaths in Vietnam exceeded those in Korea. Harvard students took over the main administration building, black students staged a sit-in at Cornell, and the National Guard evicted the "squatters" from People's Park in Berkeley. . . .

Four hundred thousand rock fans showed up at Woodstock, New York, for a rock festival; the fading hero of the Beats, Jack Kerouac, died at 47; a U.S. Infantry battalion was accused of slaughtering 450 men, women, and children at a town in Vietnam called My Lai; and the hippie movement—if it was a movement—went down to a bloody death in the living room of a house in Beverly Hills, knifed by Charles Manson and a small band of followers. . . .

But the big news in 1969 was that the first men had landed on the moon, years ahead of anybody's prediction. Sixty-six years after Konstantin Tsiolkovsky published his first technical paper on rockets, forty-three years after Robert H. Goddard launched his first rocket using liquid propellants, Neil Armstrong stepped down on the dusty lunar surface. Like everybody else, I was glued to the television set. It was a three-ring circus for most of the public.

But it was vindication for science fiction writers.

A few days later, *Playboy* called and asked if I wanted to interview Robert Heinlein. I hastily accepted. The interview went well (though it was never to be printed in *Playboy*): Bob Heinlein was generous with his time and hospitable to a fault. By prearrangement, my questions revolved primarily around the moon landing and his reactions to it. I have never heard any man say "I told you so" with such feeling. . . .

There were minor glitches: He would not talk about his

own work, nor would he discuss the work of his con-
temporaries. It was, as much as anything else, part of his
Code of Honor and he would not violate it. It was to make
for difficulties later.

Late that August, I took the finished—so I thought—interview to Chicago. Murray Fisher, who edited the interviews
for *Playboy* at the time, liked it but wanted more work
done on it (I did not pass "GO," I did not collect my
$2,000. . . .) While there, Nat Lehrman (now Associate
Publisher) poured me a Dixie cup of Scotch and offered
me a job. They wanted somebody to be their in-house
stereo expert and, most importantly, function as the "Playboy Advisor." I was an unlikely choice but the inducement
to become Mr. Lonelyhearts was more money than I had
ever made before. And by now I had become disenchanted
with being poor. . . .

I said I would think it over and went back to San Francisco. When I got there, I discovered I had been ripped off,
even down to the posters on the walls. I packed everything
I had and a day later, I was on a return flight to Chicago.
The Summer of Love had lasted three months and I had
stayed almost three years. Acid to aches, dreams to dust. . . .
I was ready to go home.

Professionally, *Playboy* had always fascinated me. I had
seen dozens of competitors fall by the wayside, I had tried
to compete with it myself, and finding out the reasons for
its success had become an obsession. I soon discovered the
reasons were absurdly simple: A strategy of reinvesting
profits in the magazine, of hiring the best talent available,
and having enough money so they could afford to bury
their mistakes. At *Rogue,* we had had to run with ours. . . .

The "Advisor" department had a staff of five women who
answered the approximately one thousand letters the department received per month. (For the curious, the answers
to the most often asked questions are: 1. No, it won't. 2.
There's no known way. 3. An augmentation mammaplasty is
the best method. 4. Because she doesn't like you. And 5.
Break it to her gently in a crowded restaurant.*) I did not,

---

* For the even more curious, the questions are: 1. Will masturba-
tion grow hair on my palms? 2. Is there any sure fire way to increase the size of the penis? 3. How can I increase the size of my
bust? 4. Why won't this absolutely gorgeous girl go out with me?
5. How can I break off a relationship with my girl so she won't
cause a scene?

as I thought I might, become so involved with the letter writers that I turned into a real-life version of Nathaniel West's hero.

Shortly after arriving at *Playboy*, I had my first failure, a failure that was to gall me for three years. Neil Armstrong had landed on the moon on July 20th. The "Manson murders" took place on August 9th. Later, when Manson was apprehended, a West Coast newspaper interviewed Manson and dutifully reported that he had taken Valentine Michael Smith (the protagonist in *Stranger in a Strange Land*) as a role model. There was an immediate flurry at *Playboy*. What did Heinlein think of this? The interview had been announced in the magazine and the issue was ready to go to press.

I wired Bob asking for a paragraph or two on the subject and got a firm refusal. He never discussed his own works; that hadn't been part of the deal. A. C. Spectorsky, the associate publisher at the time, went over to the Playboy mansion late one night to argue with Hugh Hefner for the inclusion of the interview. He lost. Manson had grabbed the headlines and Hefner thought it imperative that Heinlein make some comment on the subject. The interview was killed, though a 5,000 word version of the original 12,000 word interview appeared later in the first issue of *OUI* magazine.

It was no fault of mine, nor was it Murray's nor Spectorsky's. In one sense, I couldn't even fault Hefner. Nevertheless, I felt that in some way I had let Heinlein down. He had granted the interview because he wanted to encourage some of the youngsters who read *Playboy* to go into the sciences. It was a passion of his, one that I had understood only too well.

Playboy, as anticipated, turned out to be a fascinating magazine—and an unusually idealistic one. Despite the "sexist" nature of the magazine, it contributed heavily to feminist causes and lobbied for the consensual sex laws eventually passed by a number of states. Through the Playboy Foundation, it sponsored sex research, paid for the telephone network that linked America's major colleges after the Kent State shootings, and defended in the courts those who felt they had a right to sexual freedom in the privacy of their own bedroom. *Playboy*'s involvement was above and beyond any requirements of "promotion." In many instances, one of the stipulations to gain the magazine's help was that *Playboy* not be mentioned.

Another minor digression: *Playboy*'s story rates were the equal—if they didn't exceed—the story rates of the other major slicks. A short story could earn its author as much as $4,000. They should have been swamped with submissions. But they never were. The bane of A. C. Spectorsky's life was to read in *Fantasy and Science Fiction* a story he would gladly have published if only it had been submitted to *Playboy* first.

Every editor has a dream assignment and mine came about because Spectorsky assumed that, as a science fiction enthusiast, I was also something of an expert on Eastern religions, specifically Zen. The idea was to hold a dialogue between Alan Watts, America's leading interpreter of Zen Buddhism, and Arthur C. Clarke. I would fly to New York, along with Alan, and we would all put up at the Hotel Chelsea where Clarke was staying.

I had met Clarke only casually at a few early conventions; I had met Watts not at all nor did I know a damned thing about Zen. The three-day session in New York was more than engrossing, partly because the two men were the exact opposite of what I had expected. It was Clarke who ate at the Automat, who knew all the booksellers along Eighth Avenue, who had the common touch. It was Watts who took us to the Hotel Sutton Oyster Bar and, remembering that we were on the *Playboy* expense account, immediately started my education in fine wines. And it was Watts who chummed with the millionaires along Sutton Place . . .

The first day they politely chipped at each other, almost as a sort of intellectual one-upmanship. Clarke certainly didn't believe in any of the fantasies he thought Watts was touting. And Watts was inclined to look down his nose at what he considered was Clarke's scientific materialism. The second day, however, they had a great time, argued amiably about a variety of subjects, and wandered down to the local Automat (it still existed then) tastefully attired in Zen and Burmese robes respectively. (I walked five paces behind, hoping nobody would notice. Nobody did.) And finally up to a penthouse apartment on the roof of the Chelsea to experiment with a small laser, shining it on the sidewalk and on nearby buildings. One drunk spotted the small reddish dish on the sidewalk and danced with it. . . .

It was great fun. Perhaps one of the reasons why was that I knew I would never have an assignment like this again. . . .

A few months later John Campbell came to town to visit relatives and I had dinner with him at Leon Stover's. I had lost none of my awe for Campbell and mumbled—as I usually did on meeting him—that I would have to get back to writing someday. He would have none of that. He looked at me over the end of his cigarette holder and said without malice: "If you wanted to be a writer, you'd be writing." He was, of course, right.

The comment rankled. Then the opportunity came to do something about it. Jim Spurlock, a young editor at *Playboy*, had left the magazine and was looking around for work. He was offered the editorship of a new magazine, to be titled *Gallery* (it had been offered to a number of *Playboy* staffers and they all had turned it down). I urged Jim to take the job. What the hell, it would be income and *Gallery* was never going to get off the ground anyway . . .

Much to everybody's surprise, it did. It looked remarkably like *Playboy* but the shock was that it had come out at all. Jim needed copy and his former friends at *Playboy* quickly unloaded their trunks. I sold a couple of minor articles under pen names and then once again tried a piece of fiction, this time under my own name. It was a return to the Haight, in effect a reminiscence of an actual event, using an italicized lead-in commenting on how the Haight looked a few years later. (It looks different today; Andy's piroshki shop is gone and a number of little boutiques have sprung up. There is an Improvement Association and the street has lost its bombed-out look. It's become an attractive, young, middle-class neighborhood with baby carriages on the street and couples gathering for morning coffee at the Tassajara Bakery at Cole and Carl.)

Writing it was more than a nostalgic trip. It was the final exorcism of something that had, at one time, been strongly attractive to me. It's now quaintly dated and safely relegated to the wide screen. The hippies I knew have vanished, back to college to get their degrees or back to the arms of their parents and into the family business. A few decamped to The Farm in Tennessee or the wilds of Mendocino County. I'd be a liar if I didn't admit that I miss them.

Downhill All the Way

I once knew a writer for a New York literary magazine who spent a weekend in San Francisco's Haight-Ashbury getting drunk and getting blown and who went back East with enough material for a bad novel. I also knew a stringer for Newsweek—or so he claimed—who said any time he wanted to know what was happening, all he had to do was throw a party and pass around the Js and sit there and listen. And I knew a liberal columnist who lived on a houseboat in Sausalito and did an exposé of the dealers in the Haight and was the first to report that Look magazine was full of crap and Emmett Grogan and the Diggers didn't represent the Second Coming after all.

That was six years ago. The Free Medical Clinic is still there and so is Andy's piroshki shop, but the ghost of Janis Joplin now pushes her baby carriage with the bottle of Southern Comfort in it past a collection of middle-class boutiques and struggling handicraft shops. The I/Thou coffee shop is gone and so are the Insomnia Bookstore and the God's Eye Ice Cream Parlor and the Psychedelic Shop and Love's hamburger stand. Sgt. Pepper no longer blasts from behind peace-signed windows, Clover no longer gives free concerts at the Straight theater, the Grateful Dead and the Airplane sold out for the best that money could buy, and Jim Morrison is a memory that died in a bathtub in France. Huckleberrys for Runaways has moved to the Avenues and the kids who live on pills and old movies no longer come to San Francisco to wear flowers in their hair and search for love and free dope and a crash pad.

I had gone to San Francisco to write about the Love Generation, probably since I had come from no generation myself. I stayed too long and left when I found myself loving what I didn't understand and hating what I did; I lived there for three years—I was a slow study and a long time growing up.

A lot of garbage has been written about the Haight and almost all of it is a lie. A hundred thousand kids lived there at one time or another and there were a hundred thousand Haights. . . .

We called him Mike but that wasn't his real name. It was Mikhail Pasitoru, and he was a Rumanian refugee I had met in the I/Thou coffee shop. He never told me why he had fled Rumania and I never asked him; I was dumb enough to assume that he left because he loved democracy. He was thin and not too tall, about 25 years old, with a friendly face and big, expressive eyes set as wide apart in his face as the headlights on a car. His hair was black, his accent atrocious, and his pants baggy. He liked to laugh and his attitudes towards the mores of the U.S. ran the gamut from mild amusement to unbelieving hilarity.

He didn't understand English very well and once asked if he could move in with me; I could teach him English and he would pay me. I turned him down for no good reason except that while I didn't like living alone, I disliked living with someone even more. I was a decade older than most of the kids in the Haight and relatively set in my ways, though like many of them I suffered from a severe case of innocence and trusted anybody who said "You're beautiful, man" and shared his stash. I was naive but it was America in the late Sixties and I had had enough of it; like the kids, I had moved to the Haight to search for Salvation.

Some weeks after I met Mike I couldn't stand being poor anymore and blew 100 dollars for a fancy FM radio. I was broke but still had a credit card and hoped that by the time the payments came due, I'd have the money. Apart from my typewriter, it was the only thing of value that I owned. And the day it was delivered, I knew it was going to be stolen.

Two weeks later, it was. It was on a Thursday afternoon and I figured that the thief waited until after I left, then picked the lock on the front door and walked in. Some books had been thrown around and a few letters opened in a search for money but of course there wasn't any. Whoever had broken in hadn't bothered to take the typewriter but then it was an old office standard and weighed a ton.

That same day I drove nails in the sides of the window frames so the windows could be opened just so far and I bought a chain lock for the front door. I told the Chinese landlord who lived upstairs about the theft and between us we decided that it was the newsboy who had stolen the radio. I lived in a oneroom basement apartment and the last time I had paid him he had stood at the top of the stairs and cased the place while I was fishing around in my pockets for

change, his eyes searching the corners until they flashed on
the radio. I had been surly with him because I thought he
was double-billing me but when I saw his eyes lid over, I
knew what was going on and became almost apologetic—in a
subtle way, I was asking him please don't take my radio.

After it was stolen I called the cops and went through the
serial-number bit, but didn't bother reporting the kid—it was
pretty circumstantial—and then went down to the I/Thou
coffee shop and told everybody the story of my stolen radio.
A few of them asked what I had against spade kids and then
Wendy, a young girl who was crashing at the Baron's, told
me that a fellow crasher had disappeared with the Baron's
small tape recorder that same afternoon. Maybe he had paid
me a visit, too. He had been over for dinner once with the
Baron and Wendy shortly after I got the radio, and I had to
admit that it was a good possibility, but I hated to add another suspect because once you start, where do you stop?
And I desperately didn't want to believe that somebody I had
befriended had ripped me off.

A few days later, I walked down to Haight Street late at
night and ran into Mike at Bob's Drive-In. I asked him to
buy me a cup of coffee and he said if I needed money, he
would lend me a couple of bucks and I said no, I was going
to the bank in the morning anyway. We had coffee at the
Drive-In and then drifted up to the doughnut shop at Stanyan
and Frederick for another cup, the atmosphere of the Drive-
In being too straight and stifling. The stools were all full and
Mike started to gag around, standing behind one of the customers and bugging his eyes and just staring and I thought
Christ, he's a real nut. I told him to cut it out and we had
coffee and then started walking home. Mike lived on Fourth
near Hugo, and I lived on Sixth so his place was right on the
way.

It was around midnight and we were walking past Kezar
Stadium when suddenly he asked, "Did you find who take
your radio?"

I yawned and said no, I hadn't, but that it probably was
the newsboy or maybe the kid who had crashed with the
Baron. After I finished, he said, "I took it."

Suddenly I was wide awake and the night was like crystal
and every detail was etching itself on my memory—the stars
overhead, the shadowy trees, the bulk of the stadium on my
right, the darkened houses slowly vanishing behind me on my
left as we walked along, and Mike telling me he had stolen

my radio as nonchalantly as if he were telling me it was going to rain tomorrow.

"You what?"

"I took it—I took your radio."

He had to be putting me on, I thought. He didn't know the
language very well and he wouldn't know a bad joke from a
good one.

"How'd you get in?" I asked, thinking I would trap him.

"Not difficult," he said cheerfully. "I get in my door all the
time and not use a key. We get there, I show you."

I began to feel like I sometimes did on pot, when the
whole world would tighten up around me.

"What'd you do with it?"

"I pawned it. You can see it at the end of the month in a
little shop on Third street near bank. We get home, I show
you pawn ticket—" He snapped his fingers. "No, I threw it
away."

There were a lot of pawn shops on Third street all right
and Mike had been in town long enough to know about
them. My stomach felt funny and I didn't think I wanted to
play along with the gag anymore.

"What'd you get for it?"

"Twenty dollars."

I snapped then—twenty would be just about right for a
100-dollar radio. "Jesus Christ, what the hell did you steal it
for?"

His eyes were innocent and enormous. "I needed money,
why else?"

We walked along in silence; I didn't know what to say. I
had been sure he was kidding me, but he had all the details
down pat, he sounded too convincing. And then he was sprint-
ing up the steps to his apartment and calling, "Hey, I show
you how to open a door without a key!"

I walked the few remaining steps to the corner, then
turned, really angry and bitter. "Shit, no," I said, "I'm going
home. It's a lousy joke, Mike, a really lousy joke." He cocked
his head and looked at me, apparently not understanding, and
I turned away and walked home and went to bed and lay
awake for most of the night.

The next morning, I figured I was really getting paranoid—
that Mike had been kidding and if I thought it was a bad
joke, well, what the hell, he hadn't been over here very long

and didn't realize there were more petty thieves in and around the Haight than in all of Rumania. Later that afternoon I stopped in at the I/Thou and ran into the Baron. He was a fat and phlegmatic rock in a community of quicksand, an overage student who was taking a couple of courses at San Francisco State and working nights in a new hotel downtown as a janitor. I told him about the radio and Mike and asked him what he thought.

"I think you ought to go down to Third street and make the rounds of the pawn shops," he said. "He was probably telling you the truth."

"The cops have the serial number," I said. "If it's down there, they'll find it."

"You want to believe that, baby, go right ahead." He shoveled more sugar into his coffee and I wondered if Laura knew it was impossible to make a profit on the Baron even at 20 cents a cup. "You know," the Baron went on, "when I was in the army I was stationed in Berlin and we had to process refugees fleeing East Germany. Damned few of them were political refugees—you started digging and you quickly found out that most of them were thieves or pickpockets or murderers or had deserted their wives or were in some other kind of trouble. We're egocentric over here—we like to think they split for political reasons, but that's usually not the story at all. Mike ever tell you why he left?"

In all my conversations with Mike, he had never explained why he had fled the country. He had said his father was a machinist and he himself had been a student; he had never mentioned his mother, or possible brothers and sisters. Nor had he ever mentioned politics.

"Mike's real success-oriented," the Baron added. "He thinks you and I are failures."

"Why the hell does he think that?" I was angry.

"Because we have no money, baby—his words." The Baron nibbled on a cookie and glanced around to see if there was anybody who might buy him another cup of coffee; he already knew I was broke. "When I first met him, he said he was living with an old man and wanted to move out because the old man talked Russian all the time, and Mike wanted to learn English. He asked if he could rent a room at my place and I said no—I just didn't trust him."

It jarred me because once I had dropped in on Mike and there was only one room and one bed and what you knew instinctively was the litter of only one person. I had no idea why he had lied to the Baron, or even if he had lied; after all, it might have been two apartments ago.

I finished my coffee and went home and sat at the typewriter trying to write and after a couple of hours gave it up. It was six o'clock when the doorbell rang. Mike was standing at the top of the landing, his hands deep in the pockets of his raincoat, Balkan version of Humphrey Bogart. It had been drizzling out and little trickles of water were running off his coat onto the linoleum. "If you are busy, I go home," he said with a big smile.

I wasn't getting anything done anyway so I said, "Come on in, just let me finish this one paragraph." I sat down at the typewriter again, facing the stairs. Mike came in and closed the door behind him. He stood at the top of the stairs and suddenly asked, "Did you go to the bank?"

I remembered the night before when I had been broke and he had offered to lend me a couple of bucks. "Yeah, I went there earlier in the day."

"Give it to me."

The right hand pocket of his overcoat had suddenly grown an erection and was pointing straight at me. There was a faint smile on his face and the hand that was buried deep in his pocket moved slightly. "Come on," he said impatiently. "Give it to me."

I couldn't believe it. I sat there thinking he had to be putting me on, that it had to be a joke, that he was playing games. But I also knew that in real life such things sometimes happen and right then they were happening to me. After all, I really didn't know Mike very well . . . and with that came a sudden wash of self-pity because I had been one of the few to befriend him. But mostly I felt that I was watching a B movie with myself as one of the actors.

Mike came down a few steps, and I searched his face for the clues that would tell me he was kidding. His big eyes told me nothing.

I shoved the chair back and walked over to the kitchen counter where I had left my wallet; there were only a few bucks in it—I had been too broke to withdraw more. I picked it up and brushed past the stove where a pan of water was boiling for coffee and wondered if I could get him with it. The situation was unreal enough that the possibility of getting shot if I threw the water at him was also unreal.

I tossed the wallet to him and he caught it and then came

down the steps the rest of the way, his hand still in his pocket. He stood by the table and looked at me. I was sitting on the nearby couch, my heart making giant thumps.

"What percent?" he asked after a minute.

"Look," I said, "why don't you just take the goddamned money and leave me alone?"

He dropped the wallet on the table and took off his raincoat and draped it over a chair. "What percent?" he repeated thoughtfully.

I stared at him. "What do you mean?"

"What percent did you believe me?" he asked, looking a little sad. "I think maybe a hundred percent. I think maybe I scared you very much."

"What the hell did you expect me to believe?" I asked. "The other night you said you took the radio and tonight you come in—"

"You never played?" he asked slowly. "When you were young—you know, stick your hand in pocket and pretend to have a gun, you never did this?"

I started to protest and Mike just shook his head. "You have no friends? You think a friend would steal from you? Take your money? Your life, maybe? You think a friend would do this?"

He had pulled a lousy joke, I thought frantically, a really crummy joke and how the hell long did you have to be in this country to know it was a crummy joke? But I knew that he was right and he was peeling me like an onion and if he kept it up he'd get down to the meat and discover what a poor, loveless, paranoid bastard I really was.

"I do not think that I will forget tonight," Mike said and turned to go.

"Look," I pleaded, "so I'm tired and I believed you. What the hell did you expect me to do? Let's forget it."

He shook his head. "You do not believe me now. Maybe on stairs you thought I was serious, maybe now I am fooling and you are not sure if I took your radio or not."

He had me again and it hurt. "It's a bad night," I said at last. "Why don't we go down to the I/Thou for coffee?"

But all the way there we had nothing to say to each other, and when we hit his place, he begged off and turned in.

The next afternoon I sat with Wendy in the I/Thou and told her about it and said I thought I had it figured out. "Look," I said, "to me Mike is just a casual acquaintance"—which was a lie, I really liked Mike. "I drink coffee with 100 people in here and I'm friends with all of them, up to a point. But from Mike's point of view, I was one of the few people who talked to him, who'd come over to sit and help him with his English. To him, I was probably one of his best friends."

"It was a stinking joke," Wendy said simply.

"Not if he thought I was a really good friend," I said. And then I started to wonder if I were trying to convince myself of something. How does anybody know if somebody is really their friend? Especially, how did anybody in the Haight know?

Somebody at the next table over was talking about a man who had been killed by a train in a news story he was reading and something about the description caught my ear and I bummed the paper when he was through. An immigrant in his early twenties had walked in front of a Southern Pacific train at the Millbrae crossing and been scattered over 300 feet of track. The name was being withheld pending positive identification . . . I read it and felt the guilt gather like rainwater around my ankles. It was ridiculous and maudlin but it had been building all morning. Mike had been on his own in a strange country where he didn't understand the language or the mores very well and where he had had few friends. I had been one of the better ones and I had neither completely understood nor completely forgiven him the night before and he had gone home feeling pretty bad. Alone in a strange country, I thought, projecting like mad. No friends, a job he hated, not much of a future . . .

I walked through the rain over to his apartment and waited in the doorway, hoping it was all my imagination and he would show up any minute on his way home from work. I waited until 6:30 and no Mike. Then I remembered a cop I knew in Community Relations who could check the identification for me . . . I turned up my collar and walked back to Stanyan street, letting the rain drive against my face and soak my coat and not really feeling it. I spotted the Baron inside the doughnut shop and ducked in.

"I think I lost a friend," I said hollowly. His eyebrows arched and I shoved the paper at him. He read it, then looked up, puzzled. "The Millbrae crossing," he said. "That's down the peninsula, by Palo Alto. You know somebody down there?"

I felt like a fool and at the same time relieved as hell. When I ran into Mike later that evening. I almost felt like kissing him. He was glad to see me, too.

"You help me," he said, grabbing my arm. "You are a writer. I need a letter written."

"Sure, what kind of letter?"

He had the newspaper rolled up under his arm and gave it to me." A letter for employment—you know, answer ad?"

So we went over to my place and I sat down at the mill and said, "What kind of a job?"

He hunched forward in his chair and flattened out the paper and pointed to an ad. The boldface type said "Live-In Houseboy." It was strictly for a 17-year-old wetback. Live in, be a valet, mix drinks, shine shoes, and, this being San Francisco, take it up the ass occasionally.

"Why the hell do you want to apply for this, Mike?" I asked, disgusted. Once I had suggested, since he knew Russian, that he try to get a job at the Army's foreign-language center in Monterey or maybe even teach at Berlitz but he had never been enthusiastic about the idea. "It's mixing drinks for some rich slob," I said. "It'll pay peanuts."

He shrugged. "I do not mind that type of work. And I like a nice house." The smile suddenly flashed across his face like somebody had turned on a light. "And Piedmont is a very wealthy town, no? *Very* wealthy? You know how to say it, you write me a letter."

I stared at the typewriter for a moment and then started to hit the keys one by one. Under my breath I cursed whatever chain of improbable circumstances had made me what I was but most of all I cursed Mike for showing me the end of my own particular kind of innocence, for teaching me that my friends would always stand condemned not so much by what they had done, that their own lack of virtue would always reflect my own lack of faith.

I had to make up my mind about Mike then and I did. "Make sure you get your own room and the weekend off," I said, rattling along the keys. "And if they want anything more than a friendly smile and a handshake, tell them to go fuck themselves." I knew then that I would always befriend Mike, and always suspect him, and that I would never know, never really know, if he had ripped me off or not. But neither did it matter. It wasn't so much that Mike had cured my disease as he had taught me to live with it.

I never saw Mike again though eventually even the Baron became positive that it was his crasher who had taken the radio. But the incident with Mike had ended all my dreams of finding love and laughter in the Haight and I left a year later.

Believe me, that last year was downhill all the way.

It was Winter and I was sitting at my desk at *Playboy* when the fire sirens sounded. Along with everybody else, I drifted over to the windows to see what was happening. The fire was across the street and a block up, right on the corner. One glance and you knew there was no way the small, three-story building was going to be saved. It was an odd jutaxposition of fire and ice and you could empathize for the firemen, freezing on one side and blistering on the other. . . .

It was a spectacular blaze.

That same week, Tom Scortia called up from California. He had a great idea for a novel but needed help to get it out as soon as possible (ideas are perishable). It was about a fire in a high-rise and the people trapped at the top.

I can recognize the clink of gold when I hear it. And Campbell's comment still burned: If I wanted to be a writer, I'd be writing. . . .

I took a year's leave of absence and headed for the coast. Tom moved up from the peninsula and both of us settled in San Francisco in the same housing development so we'd have easy access to one another. It was a lot of research, numerous story conferences and winging of ideas— and sheer shock and disappointment when we found out that somebody else had had the same idea and was going to beat us into print. . . . Later, there was even greater disappointment when we heard that Warner Brothers had purchased the other book for a movie. Both of us were working on the ragged edge of poverty and had at least hoped a movie sale was possible. . . .

Then our agent advised us to add a few more sympathetic characters and some "visuals." He took the novel out in outline form. A week later, Twentieth Century Fox bought *The Glass Inferno* for producer Irwin Allen. Allen had the entire novel story-boarded (full-color renderings made of the dramatic scenes) and then had the paintings hung on the walls of his empty office. The next move was to invite the officials of Warner Brothers in for a conference. They took one look, assumed they couldn't possjbly beat Allen into the theaters, and went along with the suggestion that they combine both books into a single movie. *The Glass Inferno* and Richard Martin Stern's book, *The Tower*, eventually became the movie, *The Towering Inferno.*

The third time around had been the charm. I was now a free-lance writer for good and forever and gave up any thought of returning to *Playboy.* One of my few regrets was that John Campbell had died; I would never be able to tell him that he had been right.

In retrospect, I would hardly claim to be a child of the century. But I was certainly a child of science fiction. I had been a fan, I had been a collector, I had started a writing career by writing science fiction, and I had progressed (or retrogressed, depending on your point of view) to "mainstream" fiction. I had written about men on the moon and been thoroughly amazed to watch the actual event happen on television. None of us had predicted that it would happen this soon; none of us had predicted that it would happen quite this way. And few of us had foreseen that someday we would sit in our living rooms and watch Jupiter and its moons from a vantage point of a relative few thousand miles away.

There is, I sometimes think, a certain lineliness about science fiction readers. At least there used to be. You were one of those people who believed in that "Buck Rogers' junk" and you spent too many days indoors reading when you should've been outdoors playing.

But there was a flip side to that coin, and there still is. We believed passionately in The Future. We lived for it, we speculated about it, some of us wrote about it.

And maybe that's the real contribution of science fiction, over and above offering a few hours of enjoyable reading.

We believe in the future.

We really think there's going to be one.

ABOUT THE AUTHOR

FRANK M. ROBINSON, a former editor at PLAY-
BOY, has established himself as an accomplished
writer of short fiction, mostly in the genre of science
fiction. He is the author of THE POWER, which
was made into a major motion picture. He has also
co-authored such bestselling novels as THE GLASS
TOWER, THE PROMETHEUS CRISIS and THE
NIGHTMARE FACTOR.

Meet a hard-boiled private eye battling in the back alleys of tomorrow

MATHEW SWAIN
by
Mike McQuay

He's a tough-guy detective living in a seedy 21st century America. He smokes hard and drinks hard and is certainly no soft touch when it comes to the ladies. More often than not, he's smack in the middle of danger —but he thinks on his feet and has a great nose for snooping. Catch Mathew Swain in his first three futuristic adventures:

HOT TIME IN OLD TOWN
   When someone ices one of Swain's friends, Swain sets out to nail the killer. His relentless thirst for justice takes him to Old Town, a radiation-soaked mutant enclave where Swain uncovers a secret so deadly it's been paid for with a thousand lives. (#14811-7 • $2.25)

WHEN TROUBLE BECKONS (*on sale October 15, 1981*)
   When Swain's rich friend Ginny Teal asks Swain to visit her on the moon, he's awfully reluctant. But Ginny sounds desperate and Swain gives in. But when he gets to the Moon, Swain finds Ginny out cold on the floor next to a dead body. (#20041-0 • $2.25)

THE DEADLIEST SHOW IN TOWN (*on sale February 15, 1981*)
   Swain is hired for more money than he's worth to find a missing #1 newswoman and plunges deep into the dazzling world of a big video network, a ratings war and the misty borderline between reality and illusion that makes up the video of tomorrow. (#20186-7 • $2.25)

Read all three of these exciting Mathew Swain novels, available wherever Bantam paperbacks are sold.

"LITTLE, BIG is indescribable:
a splendid madness, or a delightful sanity,
or both. Persons who enter this book
are advised that they will leave it a different
size than when they came in."

"LITTLE, BIG is a book that all by itself
calls for a redefinition of fantasy."
—Ursula K. LeGuin

Little, Big

An enchanting new novel by

John Crowley

It's about Smoky Barnable, who falls
in love with Daily Alice of the Drinkwater
family—and all the things that keep
happening... or seem to.

On sale August 15, 1981.
#01266-5 • $8.95 • A large format paperback